Praise for *USA TODAY* bestselling author

LORI
FOSTER

"Lori Foster pens a sizzler this month as she threads
hot sensual tension into a suspenseful tale."
—*Romantic Times BOOKreviews* on *Wanton*

"You can pick up any Lori Foster book
and you know you're in for a good time."
—*New York Times* bestselling author Linda Howard

"A master at creating likeable characters
and placing them in situations that tug at the heart
and set your pulse racing."
—*Romance Reviews Today*

"The best thing about Lori Foster is her characters.
She gives them hopes, dreams, problems and love.
Her series are so much fun to read because
she makes you feel like you're visiting family
with each and every book."
—*Romantic Times BOOKreviews*

Dear Reader,

I have a tendency to link books here, there and everywhere. It's not entirely my fault, though. You often make requests for secondary characters when I least expect it, and I hate to disappoint you!

So when Harlequin Books decided to reissue two of my most popular, hard-to-find books, *Beguiled* and *Wanton*, along with a new novella, I jumped at the chance to give you Harris Black's story.

Harris made appearances in *Men of Courage,* a Harlequin anthology, and *Riley* (Harlequin Temptation #930). Many of you immediately wrote me to ask when he'd have his own story. Well, here it is—one of the funniest novellas I've ever written! At least, I think it's funny, and I'm hoping you do, too.

To tie in with the two reissues, Harris's ladylove works for the popular P.I.'s from *Beguiled* and *Wanton*, Dane Carter and Alex Sharpe.

I hope you enjoy this special packaging. If you like, you can e-mail me your thoughts at lorifoster1@juno.com or send a SASE to Lori Foster, P.O. Box 854, Ross, Ohio 45061. I always have bookmarks to share.

Happy reading!

Lori Foster

LORI FOSTER

FALLEN ANGELS

HQN™

To Ashley Carter.
What a wonderful, sweet and very beautiful young lady you are.
I'm so glad you're a part of our lives!
Love ya,
Lori

ISBN-13: 978-0-373-77306-0
ISBN-10:   0-373-77306-4

FALLEN ANGELS

Copyright © 2004 by Harlequin Books S.A.

The publisher acknowledges the copyright holder of the individual works as follows:

BEGUILED
Copyright © 1999 by Lori Foster

WANTON
Copyright © 1999 by Lori Foster

UNCOVERED
Copyright © 2004 by Lori Foster

This edition published by arrangement with Harlequin Books S.A.

® and TM are trademarks of the publisher. Trademarks indicated with ® are registered in the United States Patent and Trademark Office, the Canadian Trade Marks Office and in other countries.

www.HQNBooks.com

Printed in U.S.A.

CONTENTS

BEGUILED

PROLOGUE

HARSH WIND THREW icy crystals of snow down the back of his neck, causing him to shiver. He raised his collar, then shoved his hands deep into the pockets of his coat, resisting the urge to touch the gravestone. The grave was all but covered in white, making everything look clean, but Dane Carter didn't buy it. Not for a minute.

He'd missed the burial by almost four months. His family was outraged, of course, but they'd never really forgiven him for past transgressions, so he figured one more didn't matter. Except to himself.

His face felt tight, more from restrained emotion than from the biting cold. The death of his twin was a harsh reality to accept, like losing the better part of himself even though he and Derek hadn't been in contact much lately. Dane had been away from the family, disconnected from the business, for quite a few years now. He deliberately took the cases from his P.I. firm that kept him out of town as much as possible. Though his office was only an hour away, he'd been out of reach when his brother had needed him most.

Though everyone seemed to accept Derek's death as an accident, concerned only with keeping the news out of the media to avoid a panic with the shareholders, Dane couldn't let it rest. He wouldn't let it rest. He had a nose for intrigue, and things had begun to smell really foul. It wasn't anything he could put his finger on, just a gut feeling, but his instincts had held him in good stead as a private detective for several years now—ever since he'd left the family business in his brother's capable hands.

He hunkered down suddenly and stuck one hand through the snow to the frozen ground. "What the hell happened, Derek? This was a lousy trick to play on me. I never wanted this, not the company, hell, not even the family most of the time. You left too damn many loose ends, brother."

The wind howled a hollow answer, and disgusted with himself, Dane drew his hand back and cupped it close to his face, warming his fingers with his breath. "And what about this Angel Morris woman? I got a letter from her, you know, only she assumed you'd get it. Seems she doesn't know you're gone and she wants to pick up where the two of you left off. I believe I'm going to oblige her."

His mind skittered about with ramifications of deceit, but he had to cover all the bases. According to the records he'd uncovered, Angel Morris had been seeing Derek on a regular basis until the takeover of her company. Derek had used information Angel gave him to make the takeover easier, and Angel had gotten fired because of it. She had plenty of reasons to despise Derek, and he certainly deserved her enmity. Yet now she wanted to see him again. After so long, he had to wonder if Angel had assumed Derek was dead, but with Dane's return, she felt she had unfinished business. After all, no pronouncements had been made.

As far as the outside world was concerned, Derek

Carter was still running the business. Only a select few knew of his demise. The family had thought it best if Dane filled in for a while. If he pretended to be Derek no one would start rumors about a company without a leader, or a family with a scandal. All in all, Dane wasn't sure which possibility worried his mother more. The company was her life, and the Carter name was sacred in her mind. She wouldn't want either one damaged. And if Derek had been murdered, if the accident wasn't an accident at all as Dane feared, it would certainly hit the news.

But that wasn't why Dane had agreed to come back, why he was filling in for his brother. No, he wanted the truth, no matter what. And he'd damn well get it.

If Angel knew anything, if she was involved with Derek's death in any way, even peripherally, Dane would find out. He may have disassociated himself from the family, but he could be every bit as ruthless as the best of them.

Dane shook his head. "I'll be seeing her first thing tomorrow, alone, away from the family as she insisted. I'll let you know how it goes." With that banal farewell, he turned and trod back through the snow to the road where his car sat idling, offering warmth, but no peace of mind.

What a laugh. Dane Carter hadn't had peace of mind since he'd walked out on his family, regardless of what he told them, what he insisted to himself. Maybe Angel, if she wasn't an enemy, could prove to be a nice distraction from his present worries. His brother had always had excellent taste in women.

CHAPTER ONE

ANGEL TRIED TO METER her breathing, to look calm, but her heart felt lodged in her throat and wouldn't budge. She hated doing this, had sworn she'd never so much as speak to the man again after his last, most devastating rejection. But she'd been left with little choice.

With her shoe box tucked beneath her arm and one hand on the wall, offering support, she made her way down the hall to Derek's office. She still felt awkward without her crutches, but she knew better than to show him any weaknesses at all. When she reached the open door, she straightened her shoulders, forced a smile, and tried to make her steps as smooth as possible.

Derek sat behind his desk, his chair half turned so that he could look out the window at the Saturday morning traffic. The rest of the building, except for the security guards, was empty, just as she'd planned.

He was still as gorgeous, as physically compelling as ever, only now he looked a little disheveled, a little rumpled. She liked this look better than the urbane businessman he usually portrayed. The only other time she'd seen him relaxed like this was right after he'd made love to her.

That thought licked a path of heat from her heart to

her stomach and back again, and she had to clear her throat.

His chair jerked around and his gaze pierced her, freezing her on the spot. Even her heartbeat seemed to shudder and die. Only his eyes moved as he looked her over, slowly and in excruciating detail, as if he'd never seen her before and needed to commit her to memory, then their eyes met—and locked. For painstaking moments they stayed that way, and the heat, the intensity of his gaze, thawed her clear down to her toes. Her chest heaved as she tried to deal with the unexpected punch of reacting to him again. It shouldn't have happened; she didn't care anymore, wasn't awed by him now. Her infatuation had long since faded away, but seeing him with his straight brown hair hanging over his brow, his shirtsleeves rolled up, made him more human than ever. His gaze seemed brighter, golden like a fox, and she tightened her hold on the shoe box, using it to remind herself of her purpose.

She saw some indiscernible emotion cross his face, and then he stood. "Angel."

His voice was low and deep. As he rounded the desk his eyes never left hers, and she felt almost ensnared. She retreated a step, which effectively halted his approach. He lifted one dark eyebrow in a look of confusion.

Idiot. She didn't want to put him off, to show him her nervousness. That would gain her nothing. She tried a smile, but he didn't react to it. Moving more slowly now, he stepped closer, watching her, waiting.

"Can I take your coat?"

She closed her eyes, trying to dispel the fog of emotions that swamped her. When she opened them again, she found him even closer, studying her, scrutinizing her every feature. He lifted a hand and she held her breath, but his fingers only coasted, very gently, over her cheek.

"You're cold," he said softly. Then he stepped back. "Can I pour you a cup of coffee?"

Angel nodded, relieved at the mundane offer. "Thank you. Coffee sounds wonderful." Walking forward, she set her shoe box on the edge of the desk and slipped out of her coat, aware of his continued glances as he collected two mugs from a tray. She didn't mean to, but she said, "You seem different."

He paused, then deliberately went back to his task. "Oh? In what way?"

With one hand resting on the shoe box, she used the other to indicate his clothes. "I've never seen you dressed so casually before. And offering to pour me coffee. Usually you—"

He interrupted, handing her a steaming mug. "Usually I leave domestic tasks to women, I know." He shrugged, gifting her with that beautiful smile of his that could melt ice even on a day like today. "But you insisted no one else be here today, so I was left to my own devices. It was either make the coffee, or do without."

Angel fidgeted. "You know why I didn't want anyone else here. Your family would have asked questions if they'd seen us together."

He nodded slowly. "True." Then he asked in a low curious tone, "Why are you here, Angel?"

Flirting had never come easy to her, but especially not these days. She smiled. "I've missed you, of course. Didn't you miss me just a little?"

He stared a moment longer, then carefully set his mug aside. "Most definitely," he said. He took her coffee as well, placing it beside his, then cupped her face. Strangely enough, his fingers felt rough rather than smooth, and very hot. He searched her every feature, lingering on her mouth while his thumb wreaked havoc on her bottom lip, smoothing, stroking. "Show me how much you missed me, Angel."

Now this was the Derek she understood, the man who always put his own pleasures first, the man who had always physically wanted her. That hadn't changed. Without hesitation, surprised at how acceptable the prospect of kissing him seemed when all day she'd been dreading it, she leaned upward. He was much taller than her, and her leg was too weak for tiptoes, so she caught him around the neck and pulled him down.

When her mouth touched his, tentative and shy, she felt his smile. She kept her eyes tightly closed, mostly because she knew he was watching her and she felt exposed, as if he'd guess her game at any moment. It had been so long since she'd done this, since she'd kissed a man, and she was woefully out of practice and nervous to boot. If necessity hadn't driven her to it, she'd have gone many more months, maybe even years, without touching a man. Especially this man.

But now she was touching him, and shamefully, to her mind, it was rather enjoyable.

Tilting her head, she parted her lips just a bit and kissed him again, more enthusiastically this time, nibbling his bottom lip between her teeth. His humor fled and he drew a deep breath through his nose. "Angel?"

"Kiss me, Derek. It's been so long."

The errant truth of her words could be heard in the hunger of her tone, something she couldn't quite hide. His answering groan sounded of surprise, almost anger, but kiss her he did. *Wow.* Angel held on, stunned at the reaction in her body to the dampness, the heat of his mouth as he parted her lips more and thrust his tongue inside. His body, hard and tall and strong, pressed against hers. It had never felt this way, like a storm on the senses. Her heart rapped against her breastbone, her stomach heated, her nipples tightened, and he seemed to be aware of it all, offering soft encouragement every time she made a sound, every time she squirmed against him. She wasn't being kissed, she was being devoured.

"Damn, Angel."

"I know," she said, because everything was different, somehow volatile. "I didn't plan on…this."

He paused, his lips touching her throat, then raised his face to look at her. He said nothing, but his hand lifted and closed over her breast, causing her to suck in her breath on a soft, startled moan. Oh no. She was so sensitive, and she hadn't realized. "Derek…"

He kissed her again, hard, cutting off her automatic protest, then backed her to the desk. His groin pressed against her, making her aware of his solid erection, of the length and heat of it. Her plans fled; there was no room in her brain for premeditated thought, not when her body suddenly felt so alive again, reacting on pure instinct. His hand smoothed over her bottom, pulling her even closer, rocking her against him. Her leg protested, but she ignored it, an easy thing to do when his scent, his strength, filled her.

"How long has it been, Angel?"

She clutched his shoulders, her head back, her eyes

closed, as he kneaded her breast with one hand, and kept her pelvis close with the other. Surely he knew as well as she did, so she merely said, "A long time."

"And you've missed me?" He nibbled her earlobe, then dipped his tongue inside. "Why didn't you call?"

Even in the sensual fog, she saw the trap. "After the way you acted last time?" She was astounded he would even ask such a thing!

He hesitated, then asked, "How exactly did you expect me to act?"

She stiffened as she pulled back. "Not like you couldn't have cared less! And after the way you'd betrayed my trust! You got me fired, you—"

"Shhh." He kissed her again, lingering, and his hand started a leisurely path down her body, measuring her waist, which thankfully was slim again, then roving over her hip. Her thoughts, her anger, turned to mush. She caught her breath with each inch he advanced. His fingers curled on her thigh, bunching her skirt, then moved upward again, this time underneath, touching against her leggings. He cupped her, startling her, shocking her actually. But she didn't move and neither did he. She tried to remind herself that this was what she'd hoped for, but it wasn't true. She'd stupidly hoped for so much more.

His fingers felt hot even through her clothes, but he was still, just holding her, watching her again. "Why now, Angel? Why this secret arrangement?"

She decided a partial truth would serve. "There's been no one but you."

"And you needed a man, so it had to be me?"

"*Yes.*" That was true, too. She didn't know who to trust, who to fear, so for what she needed, no one else would serve. But she hadn't planned on her own honest participation. Her body reacted independently of her mind; she felt shamed by her response to a man she should have loathed, but overriding that was some inescapable need, swamping her, causing her whole body to tremble. Maybe the pregnancy had altered her hormones or something, but she'd never in her life felt like this, and it was wonderful.

She pressed her lips together and squeezed her eyes shut. Her body felt tightly strung, waiting, anticipating. She dredged up thoughts of the past, of all the reasons she had to despise him, why his touch could never matter…

He seemed a bit stunned as she moaned softly and her fingers dug into his upper arms. He held her close, his own breathing harsh while his mouth moved gently on her temple. In all her imaginings, she had never envisioned this scenario, allowing him to touch her there, with her half-leaning on his damn desk, her face tucked into his throat. His heartbeat drummed madly against her own, and she grabbed his wrist to pull his hand away. "Derek, no."

Her voice shook with mortification, freezing him for an instant.

"Shhh." He dropped her skirt back into place and softly rocked her, soothing her. She bit her lip to keep her tears from falling, but even now she was painfully aware of his scent, his warmth. And the delicious, unexpected feelings didn't leave now that his touch was removed, they only quieted a bit.

She put one hand on his chest and lifted her face. He didn't smile, didn't ask questions. She couldn't quite look him in the eyes. "I'm sorry. I...I don't know what came over me."

"Am I complaining?"

She shook her head. No, he looked pleased, but not really smug. Not as she'd expected. "That's never happened before. I don't understand."

"What's never happened?"

"Between you and me. Usually everything was just so...controlled. And uncomfortable. I've never felt..."

His face darkened, and she hastened to explain. "I don't mean to insult you, but Derek, you know yourself that sex between us was...well, *you* seemed to like it okay, but I was a little disappointed. Not...not that it was all your fault. It's just that I didn't...it wasn't..."

He smoothed her hair, his jaw tight. He seemed undecided about something, and then suddenly he clasped her waist and lifted her off her feet. He sat her on the edge of the desk, roughly spreading her thighs and stepping between them in the same movement. Pain shot through her and she gasped, curling forward, her hand reaching for her leg, wanting to rub away the sharp pounding ache. Her breath had left her and her free hand curled into his biceps, gripping him painfully. Derek froze, then growled, "What the hell?"

Her teeth sank into her bottom lip, but God, it hurt, and with more gentleness than she knew he possessed, Derek lifted her into his arms and headed for the leather couch.

Nothing was going right. "Derek, put me down."

"You're as white as a sheet." He looked down on her as he lowered her to the sofa cushions, and she flinched at the anger in his eyes. "I noticed you were limping a little when you came in, but I didn't realize you were hurt."

"I'm not," she protested, the issue of her leg meant for another day. "Really, I'll just…"

"You'll just keep your butt put and tell me what's wrong. Is it your hip? Your leg?"

Before she could answer he reached beneath her long skirt and caught at her leggings, hooking his fingers in the waistband and tugging downward. "Derek!"

With his hands still under her skirt, his eyes locked on her hers, he said, "After what we just came close to doing, you're shocked?"

Flustered was more apt, and appalled and embarrassed and… "Derek, please." But already he had her tights pulled down to her knees. She felt horribly exposed and vulnerable. He explored her thighs, being very thorough, and it was more than she could bear. "It's my lower leg," she snapped. "I broke it some time back and it's still a little sore on occasion. That's all."

He stared at her, and she had the feeling he didn't believe a single word she'd said. "Let me get your shoes off."

She sat up and pushed at his hands. "I don't want my shoes off, dammit!"

"At the moment, I don't care what you want." And her laced-up, ankle-high shoes came off in rapid order, then her tights. As he looked at her leg, at the angry scars still there, his jaw tightened. "Damn."

Angel bristled, her only defense at being so exposed. "It's ugly, I know. If it bothers you, don't look at it."

One large hand wrapped around her ankle, keeping her still, and the other carefully touched the vivid marks left behind by the break and the subsequent surgery. "A compound fracture?"

"So you're a doctor now?"

He ignored her provocation. "This is where the break was, and this is where they inserted a rod." His gaze swung back up to her face, accusing.

Disgruntled, but seeing no way out of her present predicament, she said, "I'm fine, really. It's just that when you sat me on the desk, you jarred my leg and it…well, it hurt. It's still a little tender. I only recently got off crutches."

His gaze was hot with anger. "And you're running around downtown in the ice and snow today?"

"I wasn't running around! I came to see you."

"Because you needed a man," he sneered, and her temper shot off the scales.

"Damn you!" Struggling upward, pulling herself away from his touch, she pointed to the shoe box still sitting on his desk. "I came to bring you that." Then she added, "Whether you wanted it or not."

He turned his head in the direction she indicated, but continued to kneel beside the couch. "What the hell is it?"

Angel came awkwardly to her feet and limped barefoot across the plush carpeted floor. She picked up the box, but then hesitated. She hadn't planned to raise hell with him, to anger him and alienate him. She had to move carefully or she'd blow everything. She closed her eyes as she gathered her thoughts and calmed herself. She hadn't heard him move, but suddenly Derek's hands were on her shoulders and he turned her toward him.

"What is it, Angel?"

He sounded suspicious, an edge of danger in his tone. She'd always known Derek could be formidable, his will like iron, his strength unquestionable. But she'd never sensed this edge of ruthlessness in him before. She shuddered.

"I don't mean to shock you, Derek. And I realize you weren't all that interested when I told you, but I was hoping you'd feel different now."

His arms crossed over his chest and he narrowed his eyes. "Interested in what?"

She drew a deep breath, but it didn't help. "Our baby."

Not so much as an eyelash moved on his face. He even seemed to be holding his breath.

"Derek?"

"A baby?"

She nodded, curling her toes into the thick carpet and shivering slightly, waiting.

"How do you know it's mine?"

She reeled back, his words hitting her like a cold slap. After all she'd been through, everything that had happened, not once had she suspected he might deny the child. That was low, even for him. She had to struggle to draw a breath, and once she had it, she shouted, "You bastard!" She swung at him, but he caught her fist and the box fell to the floor, papers and pictures scattering.

"Miserable, rotten…" Her struggles seemed puny in comparison to his strength, but he had destroyed her last hope, delivered the ultimate blow. She wanted to hurt him as badly as she'd been hurt, but he was simply too strong for her and finally she quit. He hadn't said a word. Panting, shaking from the inside out, she whispered, "Let me go."

Immediately, he did. Keeping her head high, refusing to cry, to contemplate the hopelessness of the situation in the face of his doubt, she went to the couch and sat, snatching up her tights and trying to untangle them so she could get them on.

Even though she refused to look at him, she was aware of him still standing there in the middle of the floor, fixed and silent. When he squatted down to pick up the contents of the box, Angel glanced at him. His face was set, dark color high on his cheekbones. He lifted one small photo and stared at it.

All Angel wanted to do was get out. She jerked on her shoes, pulling the laces tight, fighting the tears that seemed to gather in her throat, choking her. She'd humiliated herself for no reason. She'd allowed him to touch her for no reason. He wasn't going to acknowledge the baby.

"I'm sorry."

She glanced up as she shrugged on her coat. Derek still crouched in the middle of the floor, a single photo in his hand, his head hanging forward.

Angel frowned. "What did you say?"

He slowly gathered up the rest of the things and came to his feet. "I said I'm sorry. The baby looks like me."

"Oh, I see. Otherwise, you wouldn't have believed me. In all the time you've known me, I've proven to be such an execrable liar, such an adept manipulator, it's of course natural that you would have doubts. Well, it's a good thing he doesn't have my coloring then, isn't it? You'd never know for sure."

"Angel…" He reached a hand out toward her, and there was something in the gesture, a raw vulnerability she'd never witnessed. In fact, too many things about him seemed different, some softer, many harder edged. Had something happened to him in the months since she'd last seen him?

She shook her head. She would never be drawn in by him again. "Those things are yours to keep. They're duplicates. Records, photos, a birth certificate, which if you notice, has the father's name blank."

"Why?"

He sounded tortured now and she frowned, tilting her head to study him. "You weren't interested, Derek, though I admit I was hoping you'd changed your mind by now."

"I'm interested," he growled.

She thought of the last time she'd called him, the hell he'd put her through. "When we spoke on the phone, you rudely informed me you didn't want any attachments to a baby. You told me I was completely on my own, not to bother you."

He actually flinched, then closed his eyes and remained silent. But she had no pity for him, not after all that had happened. "That's not why the name is blank, though. Remember what you told me about your family? Well, I love my son, and I won't lose him to anyone, not to you, not to your damn relatives."

He looked blank and her irritation grew. "Your mother is a damn dragon, determined that everyone live according to her rules. You said that's why your brother left, why he became so hard. Your family frightens me, if you want the truth. Especially your brother."

His golden eyes darkened to amber. "That's ridiculous."

"You said he was the only one strong enough, independent enough to leave the company without a backward glance, to go his own way and tell the rest to go to hell. You said he was the only one who could make your mother nervous or your sister cry. You said he could do anything he set his mind to."

"No one makes my mother nervous, and my sister is a younger replica of her. Nothing touches them."

Angel buttoned her coat. "You've changed your mind then, but I won't. I won't take a chance that they'll try to take him away from me. I don't want them to know about my baby."

"Our..." He stopped and she saw his Adam's apple bob as he swallowed. "Our baby."

This was a point too important to skimp on. She went to him, holding his gaze no matter that he tried to stare her down. She pointed at his chest and forced the words out through stiff lips. "I don't know what new paternal mode you're in, but don't try to take him from me, Derek. I swear I'll disappear so quick you'll never find me or him again. I can do it. I've made plans."

"No."

She was incredulous. "You can't dictate to me! Not anymore. Whatever power you held over me, you gave up months ago when you rejected my pregnancy."

He didn't shout, but his near whisper was more effective than any raised voice could be. "Is that right? Then why are you here?"

She had to leave, now, before she tripped herself up. She turned toward the door. "There's an address in with the papers and photos. A post office box." She slanted her gaze his way. "I'm sure you remember it. You can get in touch with me there."

"Give me your phone number."

"I don't think so. But I'll call you soon."

"You're playing some game, Angel, and I don't like it."

She had her hand on the doorknob and slowly turned. "It's not a game." As she stepped through the door, she said over her shoulder, "And I don't like it either. Think about the baby, Derek, what you'd like to do, and I'll call you tonight. We can talk then, after you've gotten used to the idea."

He took two quick steps toward her. "What I'd like to do?" He frowned. "You want me to marry you?"

"Ha!" That was almost too funny for words. As she pulled the door shut, she said, "I wouldn't marry you if you were the last man on earth."

And she knew he'd heard her ill-advised words, because his fist thudded against the door.

Well, that hadn't gone off quite as planned. Actually, nothing like she'd planned. She'd hoped to seduce him, to regain his interest. She needed his help, his protection, and that was the only way she could think to get it. Sex had been the only thing he'd been interested in before, so it was what she'd planned to offer him now.

Only it felt as if she was the one seduced. Damn, why did he have to have this effect on her? Her body was still warm and tingling in places she'd all but forgotten about, and all because of a man she thought she'd grown to hate.

A man who had never affected her so intensely before.

Damn fickle fate, and whatever magic had made Derek Carter into a man her body desired.

CHAPTER TWO

DANE HIT THE DOOR once more for good measure, vexed with himself and the turn of events. Dammit, he hadn't meant to touch her. He had intended to get close to her, but not that close. He'd wanted to learn about her, to discover any involvement on her part, whether or not she could provide a clue to his brother's death. But he'd also planned to keep his hands to himself.

She'd made that impossible.

He'd wanted her the minute he'd seen her. She was lush and feminine and seemed to exude both determination and vulnerability. He'd also been stunned because Angel Morris looked nothing like the usual polished, poised businesswoman his brother tended to gravitate toward.

And then she'd demanded he kiss her.

Without knowing the exact nature of her relationship with Derek, he couldn't take the chance of turning her away without raising suspicions. And at the moment, given everything that had just transpired, he needed to keep her close, not drive her away.

He'd suspected she was there for a purpose, but God, he'd never considered a child.

Stalking across the office, he picked up the phone and punched in a quick series of numbers. His hand shook as he did so, and he cursed again. He could still feel the tingling heat of her on his hand, still pick up the faint hint of her scent lingering in the office. Angel might have been sexually aroused—her first time with him, to hear her tell it—but he felt ready to burst, not only with lust, but with a tumultuous mix of emotions that nearly choked him.

If not for her injured leg, he had a feeling they'd have both found incredible satisfaction. He'd have taken her and she would have let him. He grunted to himself, disgusted. Making love in his brother's office, on a damn desk, with a woman he barely knew and whose motives were more than suspicious. His own motives didn't bear close scrutiny.

"Sharpe here."

"Be ready," Dane barked, frustrated beyond all measure. "She should be leaving the building any second now." After receiving Angel's note, Dane had gone through her file, learning what he could about her, which wasn't much. When he'd first decided on the tail, he'd been reacting on instinct, his life as a P.I. making decisions almost automatic. Now he was driven by sheer male curiosity, and the possessive need to keep what was his. She had his nephew, and that formed an iron link between them that he wouldn't allow to be severed.

"Description?"

All his agents were very good, but Alec Sharpe, a brooding, almost secretive man of very few words, was the best. Dane trusted him completely.

"Blond, petite, probably limping a little. Wearing a long wool skirt and a dark coat."

"Got it."

The line went dead and Dane sighed, putting the

phone down. Alec would contact him again using the cell phone once he was sure of his lead. He figured it would take Angel at least a few minutes to maneuver out of the building. If she was parked in the lot, that would take even more time. If she hailed a cab, no telling how long he'd be left waiting.

Alec knew he was still checking out the circumstances of his brother's death, but no one else did. So far he'd found only enough to raise his concerns, but not enough to form any conclusions.

His brother's home had been discreetly searched, his papers rifled through. And Derek had some unaccounted time logged in his otherwise very orderly date book that made Dane think he'd had meetings best left unnoted.

Dane settled himself back behind his brother's desk and began going through the papers and pictures Angel had given him. The first picture of the baby had shaken him and he stared at it again for long moments. It was a photo taken at the hospital of a tiny red-faced newborn that looked almost identical to the twin photos his mother still displayed on her desk. The shape of the head was the same, the soft thatch of dark hair, the nose. He traced the lines of the scrunched-up face and a tiny fist, then smiled, feeling a fullness in his chest.

The next picture was more recent, and the changes were amazing. As plump as a Thanksgiving turkey, the baby had round rosy cheeks, large dark blue eyes, and an intent expression of disgruntlement that reminded him of Derek. Dane wanted to hold the baby, to touch him, make sure he was real. He was a part of his brother, left behind, and Dane knew without a doubt he'd protect him with his life. He hadn't even met the baby yet, but already the little fellow had found a permanent place in his heart just by existing.

Dane turned the picture over and found the words, *Grayson Adam Morris.* A very recent picture, only a week old. And the name, it was respectable, solid, except that it should have read *Carter,* not *Morris.* Dane intended to see to that problem as soon as possible.

There were also copies of the birth records, and the baby's footprints, not much bigger than Dane's nose. He made note of the hospital Angel had gone to, the name of the doctor who'd attended her, and considered his next move. He shook his head, then looked impatiently at the phone. As if he'd willed it, the phone rang and he jerked it up.

"Yeah?"

Without preamble, Alec said, "She's getting on a bus and she has a baby and some tall guy with her."

Dane went still, then shot to his feet. The baby had been here with her? "Are you sure it's a baby?"

"Bundled up in a blue blanket, cradled in the guy's arms. I don't think it's her groceries."

"Who's the guy? Are you certain he's with her?"

"Tall, dark hair, sunglasses. Wearing a leather bomber jacket and worn, ragged jeans. He's holding her arm, they're chatting like old friends. You want me to find out?"

"No." His hand clenched iron-hard on the phone, and Dane decided he'd figure that one out on his own. "Just concentrate on the woman. You can see if he goes home with her, but other than that, ignore him."

"I'm on it. I'll get in touch when we reach a destination."

Again Dane hung up the phone, only this time he

used a little more force than necessary. Damn her, had she been lying all along? Why would she bring the baby and a boyfriend with her when she claimed to have missed him—*Derek?* Didn't she think that was a bit risky, considering he could have followed her out?

He seethed for almost a half hour before Alec called him back with an address. The guy with Angel had in fact gone into the same building, and the building was located in one of the less auspicious areas of town. Dane pulled on his coat and put everything back into the shoe box, tucking it beneath his arm. He couldn't risk leaving anything behind where his family might find it. He locked the office on his way out.

Angel Morris thought she knew how to deal with him, but she was judging her moves on how Derek would react. Dane wasn't a game player, never had been and never would be. His family had figured that out too late; the sooner Miss Morris figured it out, the quicker they could get things settled. He intended to explain it all to her this very day.

WITH THANKSGIVING not too far off, many of the houses had Christmas decorations already up. All the shops he passed had their front windows filled with displays. But as he neared the address given to him by Alec, the spirit of Christmas melted away. Bright lights were replaced with boarded-up windows. Graffiti rather than green wreaths decorated the doors. None of it made any sense. Dane knew Angel had lived in a very upscale apartment complex while working for the Aeric Corporation. He knew from her file that she'd lost her job there after Derek had taken information from her to assure the success of a hostile takeover. But surely she wasn't destitute. She'd made a good yearly wage.

Wary of the denizens in the area, Dane parked his car in a garage and walked the last block to Angel's home. The bitter November wind cut through his clothes and made him shiver, but filled with purpose, he easily ignored the cold. When he reached the brick three-family home that matched the address Alec had given him, he gave a sigh of relief. Calling the house nice would be too generous, but it was secure and well-tended, located on a quiet dead-end street of older homes. Angel and his nephew should be relatively safe here.

At least until he moved them.

The front door wasn't barred. He entered a foyer of sorts and looked at the mailboxes. There was no listing for an Angel Morris, and he frowned. Then he saw an A. Morton and his instincts buzzed. Going on a hunch, he figured that had to be Angel. Why would she hide behind an alias, unless she had a reason to hide? He recalled his purpose in first starting this ruse. Though it was obvious she knew nothing of Derek's death, he couldn't discount the possibility that she might have helped set him up for the fall, even innocently. She certainly had plenty of reason to hate him and want him out of her life, and she professed to fear his family, so why then had she approached him today? Because she was surprised he *wasn't* dead? Did she have contact with an insider who had informed her of his resurrection? Very few people were privy to the fact of his and Derek's relationship.

The apartment number listed was on ground level and he went to the door, then knocked, bracing himself for the sight of her again. She'd really thrown him for a loop with her sensual response to him. And he knew in his gut her reaction hadn't been feigned. Just remembering it made his every muscle tense.

"Come on in, Mick."

Dane tightened his jaw and his temper slipped. So the guy who'd been with her, Mick, was welcome in any time? Did she respond as hotly with Mick as she did with him? Dane turned the doorknob and stepped inside.

Angel was lying on a sofa, her injured leg propped up on pillows. She wore only a flannel shirt and loose shorts cut down from a pair of old gray sweats. Thick socks covered her feet. She shoved herself half upright and stared at him in undiluted horror.

Dane looked at her from head to toe, and as a man he appreciated the earthy picture she presented. But he'd use caution from here on out. Angel seemed to vacillate between fear and awareness. Dane decided that either way he'd use her emotions against her to find out for sure what her purpose might be.

Her fair hair was tousled and spread out over the arm of the sofa. Her breasts beneath the worn flannel looked soft and full, without the casing of a bra. Her legs were very long and pale. He saw the vicious scars on her left leg, still angry and red, and his simmering temper jumped in a new direction.

He closed the door quietly and her incredible green eyes went wide and wary. "Derek."

He indicated her cushioned leg. "You're hurt worse than you let on."

Color washed over her face as she started to rise from the sofa. Dane was beside her in an instant. He caught her shoulders, pressing her back down, feeling

the narrow bones beneath his hands, aware of her small-
ness, her softness. "Be still. It's obvious you overdid it
today. You shouldn't have been up and around."

He perched on the sofa cushion next to her, feeling
her apprehension while he examined her leg, trailing his
fingers gently over her smooth skin. Just seeing the
scars left behind made him wince in sympathy.

She seemed to gather herself all at once. "Just what
are you doing here?"

"Checking up on you."

"How? How did you find me?"

"I had you followed." His gaze swung from her leg
to her outraged face. "Why use an alias?"

Angel paled a little. "What are you talking about?"

"Your mailbox."

Rather than answer, she tried bluffing her way with
anger. "That's none of your business. And why do you
care anyway?"

He was good at lying when it suited him. "Because
I have the feeling you'd never have let me get this close.
But I second-guessed you, didn't I?" He waggled a
finger in her face, bringing back her healthy surge of
angry color. "I think I'll keep close tabs on you from
now on."

She gasped and he added a not-too-subtle warning.
"You can keep your secret, Angel—for now. But when
I'm ready, I will know what's going on."

Her lips firmed and her look became obstinate. But
beneath it all, he saw a measure of pain. "You're not
completely mended yet, are you? Were you hurt
anywhere else?"

She gave him another stubborn frown and his attention dropped to her body. Holding her gaze, he

asked quietly, "Would you like me to find out for myself?"

She jerked and her arms crossed protectively over her breasts. "All right! I also had some bruised ribs and a few cuts and scrapes—all of which are now healed."

He continued to look at her, and she turned her head away. "My shoulder was dislocated, too."

"Good God. What the hell happened to you?"

Even before she spoke, he knew no truths would cross her beautiful lips. Amazing that he could read her so easily after only knowing her such a short time, but he could.

Her chin lifted and she said, "I fell."

"Down a mountainside?"

"Down a long flight of stairs, actually."

Keeping his hands to himself became impossible. He cupped her cheeks in both hands. Whatever had happened, it had been serious, and talking about it obviously agitated her. "You could have been killed."

She started, and her eyes met his. For the briefest moment she looked so lost, he wanted to fold her close and swear to protect her. *Idiot.* Then she shook her head and that stubbornness was back tenfold, forcing an emotional distance between them. "My leg is the only thing scarred. Nasty-looking, isn't it?"

Without missing a beat, he said, "You have beautiful legs. A little scarring won't change that." And it was true. Her legs were long, smooth, shapely. He imagined those long legs wrapped around him while he touched her again, only this time she would climax, holding him inside her so he could feel every small tremor, every straining muscle. He nearly groaned.

He let his hand rest lightly on her knee and moved

his thoughts to safer ground. "You've no reason to be embarrassed, Angel. The scars will fade."

"You think a few scars matter to me?"

He did, but he wasn't dumb enough to tell her that, not when she was practically spitting with ire. She hadn't forgiven him yet for Derek's past sins, and for his own, in questioning the baby's parentage. But she would. He'd see to it.

He put his hand to her cheek and noticed again the way her pulse raced, how she held her breath. "I'm sorry you were hurt." Then he kissed her. As angry as he was, he needed a taste of her again. She may have decided her little sampling of lust in the office was enough, but he'd found only frustration. He'd barely touched her, barely begun to excite her, and she'd heated up like a grand fireworks display, perilously close to exploding. He was still semi-hard because of it and caught between wanting to bury himself inside her, to see her go all the way, climaxing with him, and wanting to shake her into telling him what her ridiculous game was.

At first she froze, but seconds later her body pressed into his. One small hand lifted to his neck and that simple touch made him shudder. He pulled back, not wanting to test himself. Angel stared at him, wide-eyed.

"Nice place," he said, hoping to distract her and himself. His gaze wandered around the sparse room, taking in the worn wallpaper and faded carpet. He didn't really mean to be facetious, but she took it that way.

"You don't have to like it, Derek, since you don't live here."

He dropped his gaze back to her flushed face. With one arm above her, his body beside her, he effectively caged her in. He could tell she didn't like it; he liked it a little too much. "I want to know why you're living here. What happened to your apartment?"

Her eyes narrowed. "I lost it."

"Why?"

"Because I hadn't paid the rent."

He sighed. This was like pulling teeth, but she obviously wasn't going to make it easy for him. "Okay, we'll play twenty questions. Why didn't you pay the rent?"

Angel stared at him, then put one arm over her eyes and laughed. "God, you're incredible. Everything is so simple for you."

Wrapping long fingers around her wrist, he carried her arm to her stomach and held it there. He felt her muscles clench. "Why didn't you pay your rent?"

In a burst of temper, she slapped his hand away and half raised herself to glare at him. "Because I had no money, you ass! I lost my job, thanks to you, and no one else would hire me for what I was good at. After you finished, I was considered a *bad risk*. I tried everywhere, and in the process, ran through a lot of my savings. For a short time, I had a job as a waitress, but then I had the accident and was laid up for a while. People won't hire women on crutches, you know. My savings weren't so deep that I could afford to stay in an expensive place, keep up my medical insurance, and pay additional medical bills besides, so I moved here. Satisfied?"

Her shout had awakened the baby, and Dane looked toward the sound of disgruntled infant rage. Angel groaned. "Now look what you've done. Well, don't just sit there, get out of my way."

Her mood shifts were almost amusing, and fascinating to watch—when she wasn't ripping his guts out with regret for the way his brother had treated her. She started to sit up, and again he pressed her back. "I'll get him."

"No!"

He caught her chin and turned her face up to his. "Now or later, Angel, what difference does it make? I want to meet him. I promise, I'll bring him to you."

She bit her lip and her eyes were dark with wariness, but she apparently realized there would be no contest if they tried to match strength or wills. At least, not at the moment. He had the feeling, on a better day, her strength would amaze him.

Dane stared a second more, wishing there was a simpler way to reassure her, then went to fetch the baby. He followed the sounds of the cries to where Grayson was making his discontent known. When Dane entered the room he was assailed by the scent of powder and baby lotion, soft soothing scents. Grayson's pudgy arms and legs churned ferociously, and with incredible care, Dane lifted him to his shoulder. The baby was soaking wet.

Cloth diapers and plastic pants were on top of a dresser, along with a few folded gowns. Dane scooped up what he thought he might need and went back to the main room and the worried mother. Angel immediately reached her arms out.

"No, he's soaked, which means I'm soaked. No reason for both of us to become soggy. I think if you talk me through it, I can get him changed."

Angel's mouth fell open and she stared at him as if he'd grown an extra nose. He smiled at her reaction.

She looked dumbfounded and utterly speechless.

"I know," he said, grinning, "changing diapers isn't part of my established repertoire, either. But I'm efficient at adapting."

In the short time he'd known her, she'd thrown him off balance more times than he cared to think about; it was only fair that he get a little retaliation when and where he could.

He didn't know a hell of a lot about babies, but he figured now was as good a time as any to learn. "Where should I put him to clean him up?"

Finally managing to close her mouth, Angel fretted, then pointed to a table. "There's a plastic changing pad there. You can put him on that and change him."

"Good enough." Dane shook out the padded plastic sheet with one hand, spread it out on the table, and carefully laid Grayson down. The baby wasn't pleased with delayed gratification, so Dane hurried. With Angel's instructions, he got the baby diapered and dried and redressed, all in under five minutes which he considered a major accomplishment. Grayson had stopped squalling, but he still fussed, one fist flailing the air, occasionally getting caught in his mouth for a slurpy suck or two.

This time when Angel held out her arms, Dane handed the baby to her. The entire right side of his shirt was wet and clinging to his chest.

She looked away, pressing her face against the baby. "He's hungry."

"Do you want me to get him a bottle?"

"No." Angel cleared her throat, then said, "He's… breast- fed. I just…need a little privacy."

"Oh. *Oh.*" Dane looked at her breasts, imagined the process, and didn't want to take so much as a single step from the room. He also couldn't bear to hear the baby whimpering. "I'll, uh, just go in the kitchen and try to rinse out my shirt."

"You do that. And stay in there while it dries."

He leaned down and caught her chin. Her eyes opened wide on his and she drew in a deep startled breath. "All right. But don't always expect me to follow orders, honey. You're going to have to get used to me being here." Knowing he shouldn't, but unable to stop himself, he leaned down and pressed a firm kiss to her mouth. It felt damn good. He walked out while she sputtered.

He wanted to kiss her again, as a starting point, knowing where they'd finish. He wanted to show her he was no sloth in bed, contrary to her damn misconception. He wanted to find out the truth about his brother's death and her involvement with him, and he wanted to protect her and take care of her and Grayson. There were a lot of *wants* piling up on him too quickly and contradicting each other.

Christ, what had his brother gotten into?

He pulled off his shirt and rinsed the damp spot under running water, then wrung it out and hung it over a chair to dry. The apartment, thankfully, wasn't cold. He scratched his bare chest and looked around.

Her tiny kitchen was all but empty. The cabinets held the essentials, but not much else. With further inspection, he found the refrigerator was in similar shape. Dane frowned, then began snooping. Hell, maybe he should call her Mother Hubbard.

The conclusion he came to was not a happy one. Damn the little idiot, she should have contacted him sooner, before she got in such miserable shape. He immediately snatched that thought back because if she'd tried, she would have encountered his family, and the mere thought made him queasy. She was right to fear them.

He had wondered what she was after, why she'd come to him if indeed marriage wasn't her goal. Now he assumed sheer desperation had been her motive. She needed financial help, and as the baby's father, he could give it. She was proud, and she claimed to have already suffered several rejections from Derek, a possibility that made Dane so angry he wanted to howl. But pride was no replacement for desperation, especially with a baby to think about. But if that's all it had been, then why hadn't she simply said so? Why come on to him, pretend she still cared?

He sat in a kitchen chair, stewing, listening to her murmur to the baby, hearing the sweet huskiness of her voice. Goose bumps rose on the back of his neck. He called out, "Angel, why don't you use disposable diapers? Aren't they easier?"

There was a hesitation before she said, "I don't like them."

Which he translated to mean they cost too much. His fingertips tapped on the tabletop, followed by his fist. "Where did you take therapy for your leg?" He hoped it was someplace close, so she hadn't had to travel too far.

There was mumbling that he couldn't decipher, then she said, "I didn't take therapy. And what do you know about it anyway?"

He stiffened. No therapy? With a lot of effort, he curbed his temper. "I've seen similar breaks. I recognize the incisions on your ankle and knee where they inserted the titanium rod. It was a hell of a break, so I know damn well therapy was suggested."

Silence. He almost growled. He did stand to pace. "How long ago were you hurt, Angel, and don't you dare tell me it isn't any of my damn business!"

Another pause, and a very small voice. "A couple of months ago."

It took him a second, and then he was out of the kitchen, stalking back to the couch to loom over her. She took one fascinated look at his naked chest, squeaked, and pulled her flannel shirt over her exposed breast as much as possible. Grayson's small fist pushed the shirt aside again. But Dane was keeping his gaze resolutely on Angel's face anyway. In a soft, menacing tone, he asked, "A couple of months ago, as in when the baby was born?"

She gave a small nod. "Grayson was early, by a little more than six weeks. The accident started my labor."

His insides twisted and he could barely force the words out. "Who took care of you?" He drew a breath and felt his nostrils flare. "Who helped you when you were in the hospital? When you first came home?"

Her gaze shifted away and she smoothed her hand over the baby's head, ruffling his few glossy curls. The sound of the baby's sucking was loud and voracious. "There was no one, Derek, you know that. No family, no close friends. Grayson and I helped each other."

Without meaning to, without even wanting to, he looked at the baby. Grayson's small mouth eagerly drew on her nipple while a tiny fist pressed to her pale breast. His eyes were closed, his small body cradled comfortably to Angel's. Dane felt a lump in his throat the size of a grapefruit and had to turn away.

So he'd seen her breast? So what. He'd seen plenty in his day, just never any with a baby attached. He didn't feel what he should have felt at the sight of her pale flesh, which was undiluted lust. Lust he understood, but this other thing, whatever the hell it was, he didn't like.

He snatched up his still-damp shirt and shrugged it on, then grabbed his coat. There were a lot of things he had to do today. "I'll be back in a couple of hours." He looked at her, his expression severe. "Make sure you're here when I get back, Angel. Do you understand?"

She hugged the baby tighter, then waved a negligent hand without looking at him. "Go on. Just go."

"I'll be back."

She nodded, more or less pretending he was already gone. Dane didn't know what to say to her, what to think or feel. He was reaching for the doorknob when a soft knock sounded, and a second later it opened.

It was a toss-up who was more surprised, Dane, or the young man standing in front of him, his arms laden with a large pizza and a wide grin on his face.

That grin disappeared real quick, replaced by a ferocious look of menace. "Who the hell are you?"

Dane, at his most autocratic and not in the least threatened by the rangy youth, lifted his eyebrow and turned to Angel. "I think that may be my question."

CHAPTER THREE

"No," ANGEL SAID, keeping her voice low and managing to cover herself as Grayson fell asleep and released her breast. He was such a good baby, so sweet. She loved him so much she'd gladly do anything necessary to protect him. "It's not your question because it's none of your business."

She quickly buttoned up her shirt. Mick automatically put the pizza on the coffee table and took the baby from her while Derek stood there, that damn imperious eyebrow raised high, and watched. Slowly, because her leg really was aching, she lifted herself into something closer to a sitting position, resting against the arm of the couch with her leg still outstretched.

"Well." Derek smiled, but it wasn't a particularly nice smile, more a baring of teeth which Mick responded to with a scowl. "I'm not leaving until I know who he is." He sat down and stretched out his own long, strong legs, at his leisure, and waited.

Angel sighed. God, she really didn't need this. First the trip downtown, which had tired her leg terribly. Then the kiss and his naked chest… Her mind was turning to mush.

Mick bristled. "Just who the hell do you think you are, coming in here and demanding answers?"

"The baby's father."

"Oh." Mick straightened, blinked, then glanced at Angel. Derek had said that with so much relish, so much ridiculous pride, she was temporarily stunned herself. His complete acceptance was such a swift turnaround, she was having trouble accepting it.

It took her a moment before she nodded, giving Mick permission. She knew he wouldn't say another word without it and yet Derek wasn't likely to leave unless he got his answer. She knew how incredibly stubborn he could be. And even though he wasn't acting like himself, he could pull out his ruthlessness at any moment. She didn't want Mick caught in the cross fire.

"I'm Mick Dawson, a neighbor." Mick jutted his chin. "And a friend."

"A very good friend," Angel added, thinking of how much help Mick had been to her since she'd first moved here. She surveyed Derek, lounging at his leisure, his shirt tight across his broad shoulders and his hands laced over his flat stomach. She wanted to kick him for looking so damn good. "You asked who helped me. Well, once I moved here, Mick did. He picks up my groceries for me, gets my mail and paper." She waved at her leg. "Until recently I've been pretty much out of commission. Mick lives upstairs, his mother owns the building, and he's been an enormous help."

Mick started to hand her the baby back, still keeping one eye on Derek, and that seemed to galvanize Derek into action. "I can take him," he said, reaching for Grayson. "You should go ahead and eat."

Mick again looked at her for guidance. Derek's willingness to take part wasn't something she'd counted on. It was an awkward situation, but it shouldn't have been—not if he would just act like himself. But he didn't seem to be in an accommodating mood today, which she supposed was like him after all.

Exasperation made her tone extra sharp. "Really, Derek, weren't you just about to leave?"

He smiled. "I can stay a little longer. Besides, I like holding the baby." He pressed his cheek to the top of Grayson's head, and his expression caused a silly sick reaction in Angel's stomach. "He smells good."

Mick folded his arms and stared. "So you're just now showing up? You waltz in today and pretend to be the happy father? To my mind, you're about two months too late."

Oh no. Angel tensed her muscles in dread of Derek's response. "Mick…"

Derek nodded, cutting off Angel's warning. "I agree. Actually, I'm close to a year late by my calculations. But I'm going to be near at hand from now on." Then without missing a beat, he asked, "How old did you say you were?"

Mick grinned his sinister street-tough grin. "I didn't." Before Derek could react, he added, "But I'm sixteen. And before Miss Morris makes it sound like I've done her any big favors, she's helped me out a lot, too. Without her, I doubt I'd make it out of high school."

Angel couldn't stand it when Mick did that, put himself down, especially since he was such a remarkable young man. Unfortunately, he still didn't believe her about that. "That's not true, Mick, and you know it. You're very bright and you'd have figured out that math with or without my help." She turned to Derek, for some reason anxious for him to understand. "Mick works two jobs, plus school, plus he pretty much runs this place. His mother is often…sick."

Mick gave Derek a solemn, measuring look. "My mother is an alcoholic."

Angel closed her eyes on a wave of pain. Mick had such a chip on his shoulder with everyone but her. He asked for disdain, as if he felt it was his due, then would fight tooth and nail to prove a point. She still wasn't certain what that point might be, though.

With no visible sign of reaction, Derek looked at Mick. Angel knew Mick looked much older, much wiser than any sixteen-year-old boy should look. She also knew, deep down, he was still a kid, a little afraid at times, a lot needy given that his life had been nothing but empty turmoil. Her praise always embarrassed him, but he thrived on it. And she loved him like a little brother. If Derek said anything at all that would upset Mick, she'd manage to get her sorry butt off the couch and kick him out.

But he surprised her by cradling the baby in one arm and offering Mick his hand, which Mick warily accepted. "I appreciate what you've done for her. Did she move here when she was first hurt?"

"Yeah, not long after." Mick narrowed his eyes again, very nice dark brown eyes that she knew all the high school girls swooned over. But Mick didn't spare time for serious girlfriends. He was too busy surviving. "If I hadn't been here, I don't know if she'd have made it. She was pretty banged up, and Grayson was just a tiny squirt. Even getting herself something to eat was difficult, but she did it, because she had to stay healthy for Grayson. Truth is, I don't know how the hell she managed."

"Don't be so melodramatic, Mick." Angel didn't want them talking about her and she didn't want Derek to view her as a helpless, pitiful victim. He seemed to be hanging on Mick's every word, analyzing them and drawing his own conclusions. She didn't like the way his intense interest made her feel.

Later, after she figured out what he was up to, then she'd confide her biggest worry and hopefully he'd be able to take care of it. She cleared her throat. "Derek, you can put Grayson in his crib if you'd like. I don't want to hold you up."

He surprised her again by agreeing. After he settled Grayson, he came back in and walked over to her, giving her a gentle kiss on the forehead that made her skin tingle and her breath catch. She frowned at him, but held her tongue. When they were alone, safe from Mick's protective nature, she'd set him straight about his familiarity.

Derek looked at Mick. "Could you walk me out?"

The bottom dropped out of her stomach. "What for? I think you can find your way out the door. It's straight ahead."

Derek grinned at her. "Man talk, honey. Mick understands."

"It's all right," Mick said to her, then followed Derek out despite her protests.

For all of two minutes, she fretted, imagining every kind of hostile confrontation. But when Mick came back in he was shaking his head and almost laughing.

"What? What did he want?"

"A list."

She searched his face, stymied. "A list of what?"

"Everything you might need." Her mouth fell open.

"He also wanted to know if there was anyplace safe around here for him to park his car since he plans to be hanging around a lot. I told him he could use the garage."

"But you don't let anyone use the garage!"

"Yeah, but he has a *really* nice car. I wouldn't want it to get stripped."

She could imagine what kind of car he had: expensive. What was it about males of all ages that made them car crazy?

Mick picked up a huge slice of pizza and took a healthy bite, then went into the kitchen for plates. "You want juice to drink?"

Absently, her thoughts on Derek, she said, "Please." She made it a habit to drink juice, since it was healthier for the baby. Real juice was her one small luxury.

They ate in near silence, and Angel was aware of the passing minutes. When she caught Mick watching her watch the clock, he grinned. "I'm not about to leave until he comes back. He raised hell with me because the door was unlocked when he got here."

Indignation rose, hot and fierce, crowding out her other, more conflicting emotions. "He yelled at you?"

"No, he just told me I should be more careful. I, um, gave him your key. He's having a couple made, so I can have one, and he can have one. That way, he said, you can keep your door locked, and you won't have to get up to let us in if you're resting your leg or feeding the baby or something."

"Didn't you tell him you already had a key and that he didn't need one?"

"It didn't seem like a smart thing to do."

He was still grinning at her. She shook her head.

Never before had she seen Mick take to another person this easily. "Well, I'll tell him. If he actually does come back."

"Oh, he'll be back, all right." Mick tilted his head at her. "Are you going to tell him what's been happening?"

"Not right away. I have to find out first if he's going to get involved with Grayson, if I can count on him to help without having to worry that he'll sue me for custody. I can't risk having Grayson around that family. It's my bet the threats start with them. His mother, according to him, is as far removed from the grandmotherly type as a woman can get, and the stories he shared about his brother don't even bear repeating they're so dreadful. And," she said, when Mick's mouth twitched, "before you start grinning again, I don't need his help with anything but protection and you know it."

He handed her another piece of pizza. "For a little bitty single lady you've done okay. But you know as well as I do that things are getting worse for you. First the job, then your old apartment, then the accident. That bit with your car still makes me sick when I think of it. You can't keep up. You never get enough rest and your leg hurts all the time from overdoing it. You need to let it heal. Hell, you need therapy."

Angel had long ago quit trying to curb Mick's colorful vocabulary. Now she just rolled her eyes. "I'm getting more papers to type up every day. Pretty soon, everything will even out."

He only shook his head. He didn't really approve of the late hours she spent transcribing papers for local businessmen and college students, but he helped her anyway by picking up the papers and dropping them off. Like her, Mick knew she had few options.

They both looked up when they heard the doorknob turn. It was locked as per Derek's instruction. He looked supremely satisfied as he used the key to get in. "Much better."

Angel glared at him. "You're not keeping a key to my apartment, Derek, so forget it."

He didn't look daunted. "Mick, you want to help me carry a few things in?"

"Sure." Mick was already on his feet, setting the half-eaten slice of pizza aside. He looked anxious, and Angel imagined he was every bit as curious as she was.

Then she remembered herself. "Now wait a minute! I don't want or need anything from you! I already told you that."

Derek went out the door whistling. Mick followed him, trying to hide his smile. Angel hadn't seen him grin this often in one day since she'd met him. They returned with several boxes and various brands of disposable diapers. Angel could have wept. Using cloth had been so tiring and so much added work, but the expense of disposables was out of the question.

As they carried them in, Derek explained. "The woman at the store told me some kids are allergic to some kinds. You can tell me which works best and I'll pick up more of them. But this ought to hold you for now."

He set the boxes in the living room, a huge wall of them, then tiptoed into Grayson's room where she couldn't see him. The apartment was tiny, only the two small bedrooms, a closet-sized bath, then the open area of the living room and kitchen, separated by half a wall which cornered the refrigerator. Angel seethed, even more so when he came back out carrying the almost filled diaper pail. "Where are you taking that?"

"To the dumpster." He made a face, turning his nose away. "I left the clean ones in there in case you wanted to use them for dust rags or something."

She started to get up, but he was already out the door again and she slumped back in frustration.

By the time he and Mick finished carrying things in, she had full cupboards, a stuffed refrigerator and freezer, a bathroom that practically overflowed with feminine products, and a sore throat from all her complaining, which Derek blithely ignored.

Not only did she now have the basics, but she had luxuries she hadn't recently been able to afford. Had Mick told Derek that she missed conditioning her hair and giving herself facials? That she missed creamy lotions and scented bath oils? Or had he figured it out on his own? She wouldn't ask. He'd simply have to take it all back; she wouldn't be bought. Material things weren't what she wanted or needed from him.

Mick dropped the last large sack behind the couch and straightened. "I've got to get going. I have to be at work in fifteen minutes."

Derek came in and handed him a newly purchased ice-cold soda, holding his own in his other hand. Another luxury she'd avoided. She had milk, water, tea and for health reasons, juice. The soda looked so good, her mouth watered.

Derek propped his hip on the back of the couch, close to her head, and Angel forgot about the soda to scoot away. Derek winked at her, knowing damn good and well she didn't want him that close, before turning to Mick. "Where do you work?"

"Part of the week at the garage on the corner. The weekends at the Fancy Lady. It's a neighborhood bar. I wash dishes there."

Mick had his chin jutted out, his obstinate expression that dared Derek to make a wisecrack. Instead, Derek appeared thoughtful. "Aren't you too young to work in a place like that?"

"I look old enough. No one ever questions it."

"I suppose not." Again, he stuck out his hand. "I appreciate your help today, Mick."

"No problem."

"You know, if you ever wanted to work just one job, for decent pay, I have a friend who's looking for someone."

Mick narrowed his eyes, skeptical. Few things had ever been given to him, and when something good came along, he generally doubted it, and with good reason. "Doing what?"

"Various things. Cleanup, phone duty, running errands. The hours are flexible, but the pay's good."

Silence dragged out while Mick considered the suggestion. Finally he shrugged. "I'll think about it."

"Take your time. The job's not going anywhere." Derek locked the door behind Mick after he left, then turned to Angel. He stared at her until her pulse picked up and her blood raced. "Now."

Startled, she stiffened her shoulders and frowned. "Now what, you…you…? How dare you come barging in here rearranging my life?" She'd been so enthralled, listening to the male bonding taking place before her eyes, and then he'd looked at her with such warmth in his gaze she'd practically jumped when he spoke. Now all her grievances came swamping back. "You can take all this right back out to your car, and you can hand me back my key." She thrust her hand, palm up, toward him. "Right now."

Derek leaned against the door, studying her for a moment, seemingly gathering his thoughts. After a moment, he said, "I like Mick. He's a good kid."

That threw her off guard. Again. Slowly, her hand fell back to the couch. "Yes, he is. I don't know what you were up to with that job offer, but if it isn't legitimate, I'll...."

He grinned. "You'll what? No, don't answer that. The possibilities are too frightening to contemplate." He walked to her and sat down beside her on the couch, then took her hand before she could try to get up. "It's a real job, certainly a better one than what he'll find around here. I thought you'd like to know he was working someplace safer. Hell, I could even get my friend to throw in a car with the job, to make sure he's protected when driving."

Angel was struck speechless. Between his touch and his words, she couldn't seem to draw enough breath. Such generosity had never been a part of Derek, at least not a part she'd seen. "I don't understand you."

His thumb rubbed over her knuckles. She tried to tug her hand away, but he held firm. "I know you don't, and I'm sorry about that. Sorry about a lot of things." He gave her a sideways look, then sighed, the sound tinged with real regret. "I hesitate to make you angry, but—"

"Then don't."

"Here's how it's going to be, honey." His tone was stern, his expression determined. "You're going to keep everything I've just given you. And you're going to use it, too. And enjoy it, I hope, but I suppose that's up to you. I know you don't like me or trust me right now, and that's okay. I understand it. But I'm not just going to disappear or come visit once a month for fifteen minutes.

And I'm not going to sit back and ignore you when I know you need things. I can help you, and you're going to accept my help. God knows, you should have had it all along."

Angel shook her hand free, then kept it held protectively away from him. A glint of amusement brightened his eyes. She felt swamped in confusion, uncertain what to do or say next. She'd never dealt with Derek in this mood, firm but concerned and caring. It was sort of…sweet. *No, whoa on that thought.* She would not be suckered in by him. Never again.

Glaring at him, she said, "Why don't you just tell me now what you're up to and save us both some time?"

"What I'm up to? Well, all right. Let's see. I want to help you. I want you to trust me again—"

"Ha!"

"—and I want to be with you." He said that last part with a small smile, and his fingertips grazed her chin. She ducked her face away. "I want to be a part of Grayson's life and be a father to him. I want to show you that I can be responsible and honorable and that I'm not a total jerk. I want…a lot of things."

She stared at him hard, unnerved. "You're an alien, right? Derek was zapped into space and you were sent to replace him? That's the only thing I'll believe."

He laughed, but his eyes looked sad. "Would you like that, if the real Derek was gone for good?"

None of this, most especially his somber tone, made any sense. Angel dropped her head against the back of the couch and sighed. "I never wished you any harm, Derek. Not even when I thought I hated you, when you suggested we'd both be better off without the baby. I just didn't want to ever see you again."

"But you invited me back into your life. I may be trying to take up more of that life than you're comfortable with, but I won't hurt you again. I promise."

Without lifting her head from the couch, she turned her face toward him. In a soft whisper, she said, "Do you actually believe I'd ever trust you again?"

"Yes." He said it without hesitation. His eyes were dark and sincere and intense, probing into her mind, trying to read her thoughts. "I can get you to trust me again."

The mere possibility scared her half to death. She could never leave herself that vulnerable again; her baby's well-being depended on her strength. "And then what? You'll steal my baby away from me?" Her chest squeezed tight with the thought and she knew her voice shook. She couldn't help it. She'd known the risks involved when she contacted him, but Mick was right. She couldn't handle things on her own anymore. The threat was there and it was real and she was afraid, not so much for herself, but for Grayson. He relied on her, and she had to protect him. That's what mattered most.

If it was Derek's family behind the awful threats, as she suspected, he might well be the only person who could protect her.

Derek stood, giving her his back. His fists rested on his hips and he looked angry and frustrated and somehow heartsick. "I would never take him from you," he said, the words low and raspy. "I'd swear it to you, but I realize my promises mean nothing—yet. All I want to do is help."

"But you never wanted to help me before. You made it clear you wanted no part of me or the baby."

She heard him swallow, then he turned to face her.

He looked angry, and almost confused, a bit desperate. "I was an ass. An idiot and a bastard. *I'm here now, Angel.* Don't shut me out."

She really had little choice in the matter. It was difficult to say the words, but he seemed so different, not at all like the man she'd known. Her reactions, her feelings toward him, were different, too. He touched something inside her that the old Derek hadn't gotten close to. She supposed anyone could change, and she knew how Grayson had affected her life, the impact he'd made on her.

As if reading her mind, he whispered, "Grayson hit me like a punch in the heart. A tiny little person, part of my blood." His eyes narrowed. "You said it yourself. How holding him made you feel."

"But I carried him and went through all the changes the pregnancy caused. I got sick in the mornings, stayed awake at night as he kicked, stayed tired *all* the time. I felt him grow and I saw him born. I saw him take his first breath, give his first cry."

"You think I don't regret missing all that?"

He sounded so sincere, but she just didn't know. Unless he planned to take the baby from her, she could see no reason for an emotional deception. She searched his face, but it was a futile effort; whatever he felt was well hidden. Damn, she had so few choices in this. "All right."

He let out a gust of air, ran a hand through his hair, rubbed his chin, then smiled. "Okay. Shew, I'm glad that's settled." He looked much relieved, his shoulders no longer so tense, his eyes no longer worried. "Okay. On to the next battle. I want to move you someplace else."

Angel could only stare at him in disbelief. "You're nuts. I give ground on one little thing and you want to take over!"

"Come on, honey, you can't *like* living here."

She wanted to shove his condescension back into his face until he choked on it. "I most certainly do like it," she lied, knowing Mick to be the only redeeming factor of her present residence. "I'm close to the downtown businesses and I do transcription at home for a lot of the offices and the students. I make enough money to keep the rent paid and my health insurance active. It's convenient and I enjoy the people and I'm not moving."

He pursed his mouth and studied her, then must have decided not to push his luck. "I'll let that go for now."

"You'll let it go forever!"

"Now, about therapy." Angel rolled her eyes, which didn't even slow him down. "I've known people with compound fractures. It can take months to heal with proper treatment, and you've not had that."

"I have a very good doctor."

"Who no doubt told you that you needed therapy."

That was true, but it had been out of the question. Not only did she not have anyone to watch Grayson, but she had no way of getting back and forth each day to the therapist and her insurance would have only covered a small percentage of the bill. She shook her head at Derek, hopeless. "It's been almost two months. It's too late for therapy."

"Nonsense. I know the perfect person. I'll have her come here. What would be convenient for you?"

Angel rubbed her eyes. He was coming too fast and too hard, and suddenly she was tired. He'd invaded her life, her emotions. She'd had such a simple plan, and she'd thought for a while it might work. Then he'd held Grayson, and he'd kissed her and taken off his shirt and bought her disposable diapers and lotion and she just couldn't take it all in. She didn't have it in her to continue fighting him, at least, not right now. "Derek, please. Let off a little. You're here. You've met your son. My apartment is stuffed with new purchases. Isn't that enough for now?"

"I have a lot to make up for."

She certainly wouldn't argue that point with him. "Well, let's save it for another time, okay? Right now, I'm exhausted. I worked really late last night finishing up some papers that were due this morning and Grayson still wakes up during the night to be fed. If you'll take yourself out of here, I'd like a nap."

"What papers?"

With barely veiled impatience, she explained once again. "I transcribe files or notes for the local offices when one of the secretaries is ill, and I do term papers and such for students at the college. I'm sure you remember I have top-of-the-line office equipment, even if my computer *is* getting a little dated."

"You don't have to continue working. I can give you money."

Just like that, he expected her to become totally dependent on him. She wanted to get up and smack him, and she wanted to cry. Neither would have brought about the results she needed. "I'll pretend you didn't say that."

He stood there, obviously undecided, and she waited. But he only smiled, his look rueful. "Come on, I'll help you into bed."

Panic edged into her weariness. She didn't want him touching her again, getting so close. He'd kissed her, and that brief touch had unnerved her, had made her belly tingle. When he'd taken off his shirt, she'd almost groaned. He'd been her first lover, her only lover. And she'd never found fault with his physique. Though their single night together hadn't been great, she knew a lot of the blame was due to her own uncertainty. And now, she missed so much the closeness of being with a man, not necessarily sexually, but with gentleness and concern, a special friendship between two people who know they're destined to be lovers. Or who have been lovers in the past. The intimacy was there for her, whether she despised him or not.

But despising him was no longer an issue. He was too damn different.

"No thank you," she muttered, shaken by her own revelations, afraid of her own weaknesses. But true to form, he wasn't listening and had her pulled up close to his side before she could move away. With one hard muscled arm around her waist, the other holding her elbow, he practically carried her into her room. She could feel his heat, his strength, and it felt too good to be coddled, to have some of the burden lifted, even if in a superficial way.

Closing her eyes didn't help, only made her more aware of the shifting of muscle, the hardness of his body, his incredible heat and enticing scent. The man even *smelled* different, more welcoming, more comforting. More exciting.

Her bedroom door had been shut until now and when Derek stepped inside he paused to look around. She pulled away from him, her hands shaking, and he took her elbow to assist her to the bed. Her hobbling gait embarrassed her.

"Really, Derek. How do you think I ever managed when you weren't around?"

Her sarcasm was wasted, judging by his frown. "I've been wondering about that myself." He lifted her legs onto the bed and pulled the sheet and blankets over her. "Are you comfortable?"

With him looming over her while she rested in a bed? His shoulders looked hard, his chest broad. When she'd glimpsed him with his shirt off earlier, she'd noticed the remains of a tan. He'd been in warm weather recently, sunning himself.

His hair hung over his forehead, soft and silky dark and a tracing of beard shadow was showing on his face. No, she was far from comfortable. "I'm fine."

"This is a pretty room. It…suits you."

The things he said seemed so strange, as if another man had taken over his body. Derek had never before commented on furniture or even noticed it as far as she could tell. Her belongings were nice, but they weren't picked by an interior decorator as his had been.

Still, they were hers, and she loved them. She'd hated to spend so much of her dwindled savings on movers when she'd left her old place, but she'd been unable to do the work herself, had no friends to call on, and she refused to live on someone else's furniture.

Besides, the familiar objects gave her comfort, as if her entire life hadn't been reorganized by the vengeful hand of fate.

Unable to help herself, she said, "The bed is new."

"Oh?" He looked it over, but she could tell he hadn't realized it.

"I thought about burning the other one, sort of as an exorcism given the hideous memories attached to it, but that seemed wasteful in my financial predicament, regardless of the sentiments attached." She propped a pillow behind her head and smiled at him, enjoying his scowl and the two spots of hot color high on his lean cheekbones. "I sold it instead. Cheap."

Like an animal of prey moving in, Derek slowly approached the bed and leaned over her, his eyes never leaving hers. He braced an arm on either side of her head and lowered his face until only inches separated them. Angel pressed back into her pillow and held her breath.

His voice was low and rough, compelling. "You keep pushing me, honey, practically daring me with those big green eyes of yours."

He looked away from her eyes to her mouth, and she bit her lip. "Derek…"

"Shh." His lips brushed hers, light, teasing. "I told you I'd never hurt you again. You can believe it. Besides, it's too soon for much, but not for this."

That was all the warning she got before his mouth settled warmly over her own, devouring. Angel gasped, clasping the soft blanket next to her hips, tightening her fists to keep from kissing him back. But it was impossible. Nothing like this had ever happened to her. Surely it hadn't been like this before or she'd have remembered.

Heat exploded, radiating out to her arms and legs in tingling waves; behind her closed eyes, tiny sparks ignited. She squirmed—then felt his tongue at the same time he groaned, giving her the sound, letting her feel it deep inside herself. Wet, warm, he shifted for a better angle and she leaned up to him, anxious for more.

It seemed an eternity before the kiss ended, before

Derek was slowly pulling away, taking small, nibbling, apologetic kisses along the way. He breathed hard, but when he lifted his head, there was a gentle smile on his mouth.

Angel didn't trust herself to speak.

"Don't look like that," he chided.

"Like…like what?"

"Like you're afraid, and sorry." His thumb rubbed the corner of her mouth. "One way or another, everything really is going to be okay."

Reality intruded. "Derek, swear to me you won't tell anyone about Grayson."

"You'll believe me?"

Tears filled her eyes. "Do I have a choice? I don't want to run again. I don't—"

"Again?"

He had her rattled, that was the only reason she'd made such a slipup. Shaking her head, she said, "If you tell your family about Grayson, I'll go."

His large warm hand cupped her cheek. "I won't let them bother you, and I won't let you go."

She was afraid they were already bothering her, because she couldn't think of another single enemy she could have. Why they would want to hurt her, she couldn't guess. Unless they knew of Grayson and were afraid she'd come to Derek for marriage. She just didn't know what lengths they might go to in order to protect their son from a woman they'd consider beneath him.

Her hands shook, as did her voice. "How could you stop them if they knew? Especially your brother." She shivered, knowing her fear of the brother was out of proportion, based on Derek's dramatized bragging and her own wild imagination. But in her mind, he'd become her nightmare, and she was very afraid. "Out of all of them, I fear him the most."

He leaned back, watching her carefully. "Angel…"

"No! They can't know. Ever. If that seems selfish of me, I don't care." Her hands trembled, despite her tight grip, because she knew if he decided to take her baby away, he could. And she was already proving how weak she was against him. "I'm a good mother, Derek, I swear it."

He sighed. "I never doubted it, honey." He shoved himself reluctantly from the bed and pulled a pen from his pocket. Using a notepad on the bedside table, he scribbled down some numbers. "I'm going to give you my number."

"I already have it."

He stalled, looking harassed for a moment, then shook his head. "It's hard to reach me at home these days. Here are the numbers to my cellular and my pager. You can always reach me with them. If you ever need me, for anything, call either one of these numbers."

Angel nodded, feeling foolish for her outburst. She was just so weary, so tired of being afraid. He cupped her cheek again.

"I'll be back tomorrow." His gaze probed hers, demanding. "You'll be here?"

"Yes."

"Good." He leaned down and kissed her once more, a light kiss that still made her shiver. "Pretty soon, you'll stop looking so afraid, Angel. And you'll start to trust me. I promise."

As he walked out of the room, Angel looked at the paper with his numbers. Somehow, just having someone to call made her feel safer.

She heard the front door close, the lock turn, and she dropped her head back on the pillow, closing her eyes. As she drifted off to sleep, the paper was still in her hand.

CHAPTER FOUR

"I WAS TAILED last night," Dane said the minute Alec had taken his seat. He looked at his closest friend, waiting for his reaction.

"From the woman's place?"

"No, thank God. Later, from my house. It was dark, and I have no idea who it was, but I don't like it. I want you to set up a watch at her apartment. Something is definitely going on and I don't want her hurt."

"The man who was with her yesterday?"

Dane shook his head, again remembering how protective Mick had been. "No, he's a kid and a blessing as far as I can tell. If it hadn't been for him, she'd probably never have made it."

Alec said nothing. It was one of the things Dane liked most about him. He didn't pry. In fact, he was one of the most closemouthed bastards he'd ever met.

"Something about her just doesn't add up. It's like she wants Derek around, but she's forced to it." Then he shook his head again. "No, that's not entirely true. There's something there—but it sure as hell isn't trust or friendship. She initiated things, but now that I'm, or rather Derek's, interested, she's trying to back off. I think she got more than she bargained for."

"You want me to check into her background, the time

she spent with your brother?" Alec's eyes were almost black, the same as his hair, and piercingly direct. Dane knew he could find out anything he wanted. *How* he found things out sometimes left him curious.

"No." He didn't want anyone snooping into Angel's past but himself. He had no idea what clues he might uncover, but they were his business and no one else's. He didn't question his protective attitude. He'd find out what happened to his brother, but he'd find it out his way, and isolate Angel's involvement as much as possible. After all, she was his nephew's mother; for now, that was all the excuse he needed. "I'll take care of it. In fact, I have Raymond coming in today."

Alec snorted, shifting his big body uneasily in the chair. He was in his usual jeans and a flannel shirt, his hair pulled back in a ponytail. He looked like a mugger, or the typical bad guy. Dane grinned.

"You don't like him either? Why?"

Alec shrugged, indifferent. "I don't really know him."

"Dammit Alec…"

"Something about him just doesn't sit right. You know it yourself."

"Yes. I know you're also suspicious of just about everyone." Dane assumed his own dislike of Raymond was personal. He was engaged to Dane's sister, Celia, and Raymond reminded him too much of his own family—ruthless, business-oriented. He probably suited Celia to a tee.

"I do have some info for you."

Dane straightened, his thoughts once again in perspective. "Let's have it."

"Where your brother's car went off the road, there's

an extra set of skid marks. Two cars were going fast that day, and two cars braked. Unfortunately, your brother's was the one that went off the berm." Alec handed him a file folder. "I checked with the police on duty that day. They say that's a dangerous curve and people are always squealing their tires there, that the extra marks don't mean anything and could have been from long ago. I don't think so."

Dane took the folder, his temper heating as he pondered his brother trying to escape another car. He would find out what had happened.

"There's another thing."

Dane looked up.

"Your brother had been in a local bar, not the classiest of joints, which is what drew my attention, and he'd been drinking it up right before the accident. The bartender said he'd met someone there, but that nothing seemed unusual about it. He didn't have a description, only that it was a male."

"Dammit!" Dane exploded from his seat and paced around his desk. Playing the role of his brother was wearing on his nerves. Using Derek's office, his name, made him edgy. He'd left this life behind long ago and though he hadn't moved far away, he'd still managed to keep an emotional distance from it all; now he was back under the worst possible circumstances. "Why are the cops blowing this off?"

"You know as well as I do, everyone claims your brother was acting goofy for a month. They just summed this up to stress."

"Bullshit. My brother could run two companies and not be stressed. He was primed for it, raised to do it. And he thrived on it." Unlike Dane, who hated every minute of the corporate business agenda. He wondered why his mother didn't know any of this, why she hadn't pursued the truth.

"I'm not arguing with you."

Pressing a fist against his forehead, Dane muttered, "So what does Angel have to do with all this? I don't believe she was directly connected to Derek's death, but it is possible she helped pave the way for the killer, maybe unknowingly. She could be our only lead to what really happened since she was the last person to be close with him. But why would Derek have treated her so poorly?"

Alec shrugged, not forthcoming with a verbal response.

A knock on the door had both men swinging their heads around. "Come in."

Raymond Stern sauntered in, his three-piece suit immaculate, his hair styled. Dane winced at the sight of him. The man, though pleasant enough, represented everything Dane disliked about the corporate world and his family. "Thank you for stopping by, Raymond."

Raymond looked at Alec, a suspicious frown in place. "No problem. You said you wanted to talk?"

Dane nodded and reseated himself behind his desk. Alec stood. "I'll be going now, unless you need something else?"

Dane shoved the file folder into a drawer before answering. "No. I'll be in touch with you later."

As Alec left, his eyes briefly skimming over everything and everyone in the room, Raymond asked, "A crony of yours?"

"One of my top men."

A look of disbelief, or maybe scorn, passed over

Raymond's features. "Is he working on something right now?" Before Dane could answer, Raymond continued. "I think this P.I. business is fascinating, regardless of how your sister feels about it."

"Oh?" Dane cocked one eyebrow, wishing he could plant a fist in Raymond's face. "And how does Celia feel?"

He chuckled. "That you'll outgrow it. She seems to think now that you're enmeshed back in the office, you'll want to stay."

There was an unasked question in his tone. Dane started to reassure the man that once he married Celia, the business would be his, with Dane's blessing. In truth Dane wanted no part of it. He was already bored with the endless paperwork and the tedium of board meetings. But he decided against it. Let Raymond stew. Let him wonder if the company was part of the marriage bargain.

"Celia has never liked it that I stepped out of the family's affairs."

"I think it's incredible that you've always been located so close, yet I never met you."

"My own offices aren't that far away, true, but I've traveled a lot, especially in recent years. Some cases require constant surveillance, and that means you follow all leads, regardless of where they take you." He didn't add that he deliberately hadn't kept in touch with his family, hadn't clued them in to where he would be or for how long.

And now his brother was dead and he hadn't even made it to the funeral.

Quickly closing that particular subject in his mind, Dane went on to another. "I asked you here because I know you transferred over from the Aeric Corporation."

Raymond straightened with pride. "That's right. Derek was there often once his intent was known, and he and I met. I agreed it was a natural acquisition, combining your family's interests in health products manufacturing with Aeric's research capabilities. When Derek finalized everything, he asked me to join him here."

"You were at the funeral?"

Shaking his head, his eyes downcast in a regretful way, Raymond said, "No, unfortunately I missed it, also." He looked back up, his expression resigned. "I hadn't realized what happened until I reported here a week later. Derek had given me time to tie up my own loose ends and I spent two final weeks at Aeric, then took a break to sell my house and move closer. When I reported to work here is when I was told. That's also the day I really got to know your sister." A small smile now curved his mouth.

"I see."

"When I asked to see Derek, I was referred to Celia. Things were still in an uproar, your mother most upset and Celia constantly on the verge of tears. They couldn't locate you and they needed everything to be kept quiet, contained. Derek's death hit them all very hard..." Raymond stuttered to a halt. "I'm sorry. I wasn't making accusations. I realize it was very difficult for you as well."

"Yes." Dane knew that Raymond had shown up when the company needed him most, his past experience and lack of emotional involvement, along with Derek's written blessing, making him the ideal man to take temporary control. Every effort was made to keep the stockholders from panicking. If nothing else, he owed Raymond his gratitude for that.

But Dane deliberately kept his own dialogue brief in the hopes Raymond would say more. Trying to get information from his sister or mother had proved most provoking. Anytime he mentioned Derek's name, they would turn solemn, overwhelmed with the loss. The entire episode of the takeover of Aeric seemed very hush-hush.

"Anyway, I guess you could say your sister and I hit it right off. I care deeply for her."

And deeply for the Company, but Dane kept those thoughts to himself. His sister was old enough, and certainly wise enough, to choose her own husband.

"Did Derek associate on a regular basis with anyone else at Aeric?"

Raymond shrugged. "Most everyone on the board, the managers, the—"

"No, I mean in a social way."

"Well, there was the woman, secretary to the R&D department."

Research and Development. Dane already knew what Angel's position had been. Somehow, Derek had gotten information from her that had enabled him to take over the company.

And then he'd dropped Angel cold.

"Were they close?"

Raymond shrugged, looking thoughtful. "Everyone thought so. She'd never dated much, and then suddenly she had a steady date. At that time, no one realized Derek was after the company. But I suppose it should have been more obvious that he was using her. She was a mousy sort of person, not real talkative, withdrawn, but apparently good at her job. Good enough that the head of R&D often sent her top-secret information through a P.O. box to work on at home."

"A post office box? That's unusual." Derek remembered the address Angel had given him, not a home address, but the anonymity of a post office.

Raymond shrugged. "Her supervisor was from the old school and didn't trust the company computers, swearing too many secrets had been stolen. But he trusted the wrong person. Angel got the last of the information, a huge breakthrough worth top dollar that would have offset the takeover attempt, and she gave it to Derek. Of course, we found all this out after Derek dropped her." He laughed. "She got fired real quick. Most everyone else was able to keep their jobs."

"I see."

"Why do you ask?" Raymond straightened. "She's not here asking for a job, is she?"

Raymond looked appalled by the possibility. "No, of course not. I just wondered if I could get in touch with her, to talk to her about Derek."

"Why?" Raymond's eyes narrowed and he shifted forward. "What's going on?"

Keeping his tone smooth and nearly bored, Dane said, "Not a thing. It's just that I hadn't seen my brother for some time. I'd like to talk to the people who knew him." Raymond relaxed and Dane asked, "What happened to her, do you know?"

Dane had to keep his hands beneath the desk. His fingers had curled into fists as Raymond spoke and he imagined Angel's humiliation, her hurt. He didn't like feeling so much anger toward a dead man, especially when that man was his twin. The conflicting emotions ate away at his control.

"I have no idea. I haven't seen her since I left Aeric. And Derek broke things off with her during a board meeting, for everyone to see. He asked her to sit in on the meeting, then deliberately told everyone where he'd gotten his information. That pretty much proved she couldn't be trusted in the company."

"Good God." Sick dread churned in the bottom of his stomach.

Raymond laughed. "Yeah, she was stunned to say the least. But maybe it taught her a lesson about keeping business dealings private. As I'm sure you already know, even though you haven't been involved in some time, there's no room for deceit in the corporate world. You absolutely have to be able to trust your employees. Especially when they're in the position she was in."

Dane could barely see, he was so angry. The rage ran through him, red-hot, and he wanted only to get to Angel, to apologize, to… He stood abruptly, coming around his desk with stalking steps. He went to the coat tree and grabbed up his coat. Raymond quickly stood to face him.

It took two deep breaths before Dane could trust himself to speak without breaking Raymond's nose. This was exactly why he hated the business, why he had to separate himself from his family. Ruthless barracudas, all of them, with no thought for humanity or dignity. It sickened him.

Raymond looked at him warily. "Is that all you wanted?"

"Yes, thank you." He couldn't bear to shake the man's hand. He turned toward the door instead and opened it. "I appreciate your help, Raymond. Unfortunately, I have an appointment at my own offices shortly, so I'll need to ask you to go."

"Yes, of course." He hesitated. "You know, Derek

and I were somewhat better than associates before he died. If you'd ever like to talk about him, to know about him, I'd be glad to tell you what I can."

Dane's smile actually hurt, but he managed it. "Thank you. I'll keep it in mind."

"Will you be at dinner tonight?"

Damn, he'd forgotten his mother planned a family gathering. He had hoped to eat with Angel, to get to know her better. "Probably," he conceded, knowing his mother would demand a valid reason for missing the meal. It was to be a formal dinner in preparation for his sister's marriage, where the duties of the company would be discussed.

"I know it's difficult for you, stepping in here and keeping your own business afloat. If I can help in any way…"

"I'll keep that in mind. Thank you."

Raymond finally left with a lagging step, looking as if he had more to say but was reluctant to press. Dane knew he sensed where the present power lay, but that was just a fabrication of his mother's fancy. He didn't want the damn company. In fact, he would only stay in charge as long as was necessary to find out what had happened to Derek, to uncover the truth.

And to get things settled with Angel.

ANGEL SLOWLY HUNG UP the phone, her fingers tight on the receiver to keep her hand from shaking. Why wouldn't it stop? She'd never hurt anyone, she held no power. There was absolutely no reason for someone to harass her.

For one insane moment, she wanted to call Derek, but she quickly quelled that absurd thought. She wouldn't rely on him, ever again. For all she knew, he could be behind all this. That thought made her stomach queasy.

Moving slowly, she made her way to the bathroom and splashed water on her hot face, then leaned against the counter and took deep breaths.

When the knock sounded on her front door only seconds later, she jumped, her hand going to her throat. The apartment was quiet, Grayson sleeping soundly in his crib. It couldn't be Mick because he had left for school hours before after dropping off more papers to be typed, and no one ever called on her other than him. Derek would surely be at work and—

The knock sounded again, this time a little harder and she feared Grayson would wake. She hurried to the door, hesitated just a moment, then called out, "Who is it?"

"Ah," she heard in deep, satisfied tones, "much better than just letting anyone in. I see you're learning."

"Derek?" She turned the dead bolt and unlocked the door, swinging it open. "I always lock my door, except when I'm expecting Mick." She looked him over, the casual way he leaned against the doorjamb, his open-neck shirt, so unusual for him. "What are you doing here this time of day?"

His gaze went over her from head to toe. She wore a long caftan of muted gray-and-blue plaid. It was old and worn and the material draped her body softly. It unzipped down the front, making it easy for her to feed Grayson. Right now, the zipper was just low enough to show her cleavage and assure Derek that her breasts were unrestrained by a bra. Typically of late, her feet were bare; since injuring her leg, she seldom bothered with shoes at home.

A long low whistle filled the air between them and Angel felt herself blushing. Self-consciously, she tried to smooth her hair which hung loose, but when she realized what she was doing she dropped her hand and scowled. "Aren't you supposed to be at work?"

"Yeah, but I missed you so I'm here instead."

Before she could move, or even guess what he would do, he leaned forward and kissed her. The touch of his mouth was warm and soft and fleeting, leaving her stunned. Then Derek pushed in past her, taking his welcome for granted. The door closed with a snap.

"Don't do things like that."

"Why not? You like it, and I can guarantee I love it."

She felt her temper rise and he quickly held up both hands. "Okay, okay. You don't like it. You're entirely repulsed."

"Derek…"

"What?" He smiled at her, a beautiful smile and she looked away. "I really do enjoy it, sweetheart. And I honestly did miss you." He stepped closer to her once again, his gaze bright and probing. "You didn't mind yesterday in my office. You asked me to kiss you then."

Angel drew a blank. He was right, she had pushed the issue. But that was when she'd thought he might not be interested, when she'd thought he'd need motivation.

For a single moment she wondered if he was toying with her, but his expression was enigmatic, impossible to read. "This is a bad time," she said, suspicious and determined to resist his classic charm. "I have tons of things to do."

"I can help."

"Derek…"

He came close to laughing, but swallowed it down.

"Okay, I'm sorry. I'm pushing again. But damn, I have so much to make up for and I'm anxious to get started."

Nonplussed, she moved past him, removed a large basket of laundry still needing to be folded, and sat on the couch. "The past is the past, Derek. You can't erase it, and since you haven't contacted me in all this time, I have to assume it didn't matter much to you until now."

"You're surprised at my easy acceptance of things?"

More than surprised. She was amazed.

His hands were deep in his trouser pockets, his coat pushed back, and he rocked on his heels as if in thought. Finally, his head down, he sat beside her. Silence hung heavy in the air. He turned to her. "I'm sorry." He shrugged his wide shoulders, his expression earnest. "I have no excuse, nothing, to explain why I was such a bastard. I wish I did, I wish I could pull up some believable tale to help smooth things over, to take away some of the hurt. But what I did to you was unforgivable. I know that. Still, I want you to forgive me." Dumbfounded by this outpouring of emotion, she allowed him to take her hand, holding it when she would have pulled away. "Do you think you can?"

When she merely frowned, he added, "For Grayson's sake?"

Angel stared at him, so many things he'd said clogging in her brain. He wanted forgiveness, even though he admitted there was no excuse for his behavior? And to use the baby's welfare against her...but that was her biggest concern, her reason for contacting him in the first place.

Only he didn't act the way she'd expected, as she'd planned for. She'd expected grudging help in calling off his family—if indeed they were behind the threats. She didn't even want to contemplate the possibility of another enemy.

She wanted only to live in peace, to be able to take care of herself and her son without fear of danger.

His hand was large and warm and again she noticed the roughness, which had never been there before. To buy herself some time, she said, "What have you been doing?" She turned his palm over and looked at it. "You have calluses."

He blinked at her, then looked down at his hand. With a twisted grin, he said, "Chopping wood, if you can believe that."

"It might be difficult."

"I know. I'm not normally the physical type."

She shook her head. "No, you're in shape, always have been. But from a gym, not from physical labor."

She continued to look at his hand and he raised it to her cheek, curling his fingers around her jaw and lifting so that her gaze met his. His eyes were bright, intent. "I'm glad you noticed, but it doesn't matter. Will you try to forgive me?"

His voice had been so soft, so cajoling. She hated herself for wanting to believe in him again, for wanting so many ridiculous things. But she'd been so alone for so long now. Her mind scurried for some response, some way of making him back off.

"We could start over," he said. "I'm different now, everything will be different. If I start to backslide and I disappoint you or Grayson, then you can toss me out."

At her skeptical look, he made a cross on his chest. "I promise. The decision is yours. You're right about my family, they wouldn't make good relatives at this point for Grayson and they'd likely make your life a living hell."

If Angel was right, they were already making her life hell—and determined that it get much worse. But she kept the words unsaid for now.

Derek smiled. "And since I plan to be involved, that means they'd make me miserable as well. They don't need to know anything about Grayson, or about you for that matter. At least, not until you're ready."

As she opened her mouth, he interjected, "*If* you're ever ready."

She had no defense against his optimism, his good humor. It was beyond her to remain disgruntled when he was being all she'd ever hoped for—for Grayson's sake. "All right."

His grin was wide and sexy and suggestive. "Thank you. Damn, but you know how to keep a man on pins and needles. I hope this is the last time you test me, because my heart can't take it."

She snorted, not ready to believe his heart was involved. Then to her disbelieving eyes, he set the laundry basket between them and began folding baby blankets. Angel stared.

"Shocked you, have I? Well, good. God knows you've done me in enough times lately." He lifted a small gown, struggled with it for a moment, then handed it to her. "I think I'll leave the more complicated garments to you, and stick to the blankets and—" His voice trailed off as he lifted a pair of panties from the basket. They were pink and satiny and her blush was so hot, she knew her face had to be bright red. She snatched them from his hand.

"Not a single word out of you or you can go."

"I'm mum." He continued to fold, now in silence, but she could see his devilish smile.

He was so very different, so unlike the Derek she knew, the man she couldn't forgive or ever care about, not with the way he'd turned on her. This Derek was considerate and warm and somehow, more of a man because of it. In the past, she'd been drawn to his confidence, his good looks and his sophistication. She'd been overwhelmed by his attention, so flattered she hadn't been able to think straight. Then he'd abruptly discredited her in every way possible.

They worked in near silence, other than Derek humming, until all the laundry was done and put away. After Angel had placed her unmentionables in her dresser, leaving Derek to put up the baby's things, she found him standing over Grayson's crib, just watching the baby sleep. When she crept in to stand beside him, it somehow felt right to be there together, sharing the sheer joy of seeing the baby, hearing his soft breathing. When Grayson made a grumbling squeak in his sleep, Derek smiled, a small, proud smile that touched Angel's heart and made her feel too warm and full inside. She turned around and walked out.

She'd barely reached the kitchen before she felt Derek's hand heavy on her shoulder. Her pulse raced, her breathing quickened. Slowly he turned her, and he whispered, "Angel," his tone low and husky and affected by some emotion she couldn't name but understood. Even before she met his gaze, she knew he was going to kiss her. She tried to tell herself it was necessary, that she had to keep him interested to have his help, but she knew she was lying. She wanted his kiss.

And he didn't disappoint her. This was no casual

peck as he'd given her when he first arrived. No, this time his mouth devoured hers, without hesitation, hot and hungry, his tongue immediately sliding inside while his hands held her face and kept her close.

Just that, nothing more. He didn't touch her anywhere else, didn't put his arms around her or pull her body into full contact with his. She could feel his heat, crossing the inches that separated them, and she wanted to be closer. But lovemaking was new to her and she wasn't sure how to initiate anything, or if she even wanted to.

Derek slanted his head, his breathing harsh in her ear, and a low groan came from deep in his throat. In the next instant, he pulled his mouth away and pushed her head to his shoulder. "This is crazy. I can't believe how you affect me."

Angel didn't know what to say to that. Crazy? It surely felt odd, but in a wonderful, miraculous way. Her hands were caught between them and she could feel his heartbeat, fierce and fast. "Why is it different this time?" she asked aloud, and all the confusion she felt could be heard in her tone.

Derek laughed, then groaned and squeezed her tight, finally pulling their bodies close together. "Because it just is, because I'm different."

He pushed her back so he could see her face and smiled at her. "I'd like to take you to lunch."

The topic had changed so suddenly Angel was caught off guard. "I…I can't go anywhere. Grayson…"

"We'll take him with us."

She shook her head, not even considering the possibility of them being seen in public together with the baby. "No, I already ate." She pondered all that had happened, all he'd done so far, then suggested, "Why don't you come here for dinner instead." She felt ridiculous, making such an offer, extending the verbal olive branch. But they did need to get reacquainted; she needed to decide if and how much she could trust him. She drew a deep breath and plunged onward. "I can cook us something."

He searched her face, and his continued silence made her wish she could withdraw her offer. Then he shook his head. "Damn, I'd like that. I swear I would. I can't imagine a better way to spend my evening."

"But?"

He released her and turned away. "My mother has this damn dinner planned." He waved a hand, essaying his feelings on the affair. "My sister is getting married soon and it's a sort of celebration dinner. All family is expected to attend."

"I see."

He ran a distracted hand over his face, then laughed. "I doubt you do. But at any rate, I appreciate the offer. Will you give me a rain check?"

"Yes, of course."

He looked at her, *into* her, and she shivered. His hand came up to cup her cheek. "Aw, Angel, you do know how to drive a man crazy."

She didn't know what he meant by that, so she ignored it. "If you're hungry now, I could make you a sandwich."

Like a starving man, he grabbed up her offer. "Thank you. Anything is fine. And while I eat, will you tell me more about Grayson, about yourself?"

That seemed like an odd request. As she pulled lunch meat out of the refrigerator, she glanced at him curiously and said, "You know everything there is to know about me."

"Not true. Tell me about the pregnancy, when you found out—"

Slowly, feeling as if she'd been doused in ice water, Angel turned back to him. She dropped a package of cheese onto the table with a thunk. It was cheese he had bought, so she knew he must like it. "About the pregnancy. Now why would you want details on that?"

Wary now, he shrugged and said, "I'm just curious."

"I see. Are you trying to verify that Grayson really is yours? Is that why you were so awful when I first called to tell you I was pregnant? You thought I was lying about you being the father?"

"Of course not!"

"You doubted me in your office. You had the nerve to ask me if I was certain."

His face tightened, his mouth grim. "It was a legitimate question, Angel." He faltered, looking tormented. "I just wasn't expecting you to…"

"Legitimate? When you were the only man I'd ever been with?"

There was a heartbeat of silence. "Ever?" His eyebrows rose in incredulous disbelief.

She slapped down a knife on the table. "So you thought once you humiliated me, once you'd *used* me, I would just willingly jump in bed with another man? You thought I found my one experience with sex so tit-illating I had to race out for more, and since you weren't available, I'd take any man who was?"

As she spoke, her voice rose almost to a shout, but it all came back on her, all the pain and mortification. She laughed, but it wasn't a happy sound. Derek sat staring at her, his expression almost comically blank.

Well, he wasn't used to hearing her yell. She'd always been meek and agreeable with him, so much so she'd made his objective pathetically easy. He'd overwhelmed her with his bigger-than-life persona, but not anymore. Now she'd changed, thanks to the way he'd screwed up her life. And he had changed as well.

"Believe me, Derek, you were the only one. And once with you was more than enough."

It was her sneering tone, meant to show him her loathing, only it didn't work.

She'd started to tremble and Derek was suddenly there, his arms around her, his lips against her temple. "Shh, baby, I'm sorry. So sorry."

"Just go back to work, Derek. Leave me alone."

"I can't do that." He leaned back, keeping her pelvis pressed to his, but putting space between their upper bodies. "You don't want me to do that. For whatever reason, Angel, you contacted me."

She opened her mouth, but she couldn't think of a single thing to say.

"Shh. It's all right. You don't have to tell me now. I'll wait until you're ready."

That he suspected her of having ulterior motives should have alarmed her, but she was just too tired to fight with him. And since she desperately needed his concession, she nodded, relief making her slump against him.

"I was an idiot in the office yesterday. Of course I know you haven't been with anyone else. Sometimes men just say…stupid things." He seemed to be floundering for the right words as his hands coasted up and down her back, soothing. "We won't mention that again, okay?"

Reluctantly, she nodded.

"Good." He stepped back, but rather than sit at the table again, he began compiling his own sandwich. "I do want to hear everything—no matter how insignificant—that's happened to you since we've been apart." He gave her a sharp, assessing glance. "I have a lot of catching up to do. All right?"

"Yes." The distraction of simple conversation would help her regain her balance. She didn't want to confide in him yet, not until she knew she could trust him with Grayson's safety. "Yes, I'll tell you…everything."

He stayed longer than she would have guessed, and he asked more questions than she could answer. When Grayson awoke, Derek changed the baby, cuddled him for long moments, and when Grayson demanded to be fed, he finally took his leave. But he promised to come back the next day.

And though she was annoyed with herself, Angel already looked forward to his next visit.

CHAPTER FIVE

DINNER SEEMED TO LAST forever. All Dane wanted to do was go home and ponder Angel's revelation. *She'd been a virgin.* God, he still felt stunned. And entirely too aroused.

From what she'd told him, she'd only been with Derek once, and that had been a disappointment.

Possessive heat filled him. She hadn't really belonged to Derek, not the way a woman should, not the way she would belong to him. Guilt plagued him as he considered making her his own while knowing Derek had been her first and only. But with every minute that passed, he felt more determined to tie himself to her. There were numerous reasons, none of them overly honest, but still, they served his purpose.

He adored Grayson, already loving him as if he were his own. Dane had never thought to fit the bill of *father*—his chance had been lost to him so long ago. But it was precisely because his chance had been lost, and why, that he wanted to protect Grayson. Angel was right to fear his family; they would take over without giving her a single chance if he let them. But her fear also seemed exaggerated and somewhat pointless. Sooner or later they'd find out about the baby. It was inevitable.

He planned to be there when they did, to soothe her fears.

Angel also deserved his protection, and the luxury the Carter name could supply. Whatever else Derek had become, he'd still been a wealthy man. Grayson had a birthright that would pave much of his way in the world. Derek should have seen that Grayson received his due; for reasons of his own, he hadn't, and Dane was determined to correct the oversight.

He also still believed Angel to be the most likely link in discovering what had happened to his brother. So far, nothing seemed to fit. Derek was capable of some pretty ruthless behavior, but the way he'd treated Angel seemed out of character even for him. Much of the cruelty had been deliberate and unnecessary. Why had Derek done it? And what was the real reason Angel had contacted him again, despite the damn past they shared? There were secrets there, things he had to discover, and that too, was a good reason to stay in touch with Miss Angel Morris.

The biggest reason of all, of course, was the chemistry between them. When he touched Angel, all his senses exploded like never before. And not even the memory of her and Derek's past experiences could dampen her responses; it was driving him insane.

Damn his brother for complicating things so, for hurting her. And most of all for letting himself get killed. What had Derek been up to?

"Dane?"

Startled out of his ruminations, Dane looked up to see his mother frowning fiercely across the table at him. She did it well, he thought as he speared a bite of asparagus and chewed slowly. Her look was so forbidding that most people immediately apologized even before they knew what they'd done wrong. At sixty, she was still a slim, attractive woman with her light-brown hair stylishly twisted behind her head, and her brown eyes sharp with intelligence. She kept herself in top physical shape; her pride would tolerate no less.

Dane stifled a bored yawn. He'd quit playing his mother's games long ago. "Did you want something, Mother?"

She pinched her mouth together at his lack of manners and deference due her. "Where in the world is your attention? You haven't been following the conversation at all."

Celia smiled toward him. "Do you have a big investigation that's got you stumped, brother?"

He sent her a chiding glance. Celia had been teasing him about being a P.I. since he'd walked in the door. She'd had the gall to ask him if he carried a spy kit. His sister seemed different than he remembered, more lighthearted, more playful. He liked the changes.

To his surprise, Raymond blurted, "You aren't still wondering about the Morris woman, are you?"

His mother straightened to attention, jumping on the topic like a dog on a meaty bone. She had plans for Dane, he knew. She'd sat him at the head of the table— a major concession for her, and an indication of what she expected from him in the future. She wouldn't want any threats to her plans, and his interest in anyone or anything other than the company would certainly be considered a threat.

He hadn't yet told her of his intentions, or rather lack thereof, toward the family and the company. He wanted everything settled first before he dropped his news on her.

"What's this, Dane?" Her face was alarmingly pale, her eyes flashing. "What's Raymond talking about?"

"Nothing of any import, Mother. I merely asked Raymond a few questions about Angel Morris. I was curious since Derek had been seeing the woman for a while."

Celia turned quiet and gave her attention to her food. His mother wasn't so reserved. Her hands fisted on the table, yet she managed to keep her tone calm. "He wasn't *seeing* her, for heaven's sake. He merely associated with her to ease the effort of the takeover. She was a secretary of sorts, no one important. Certainly no one important to Derek."

Forcefully keeping his emotions in check, feigning a certain lack of interest, Dane asked, "Do you know what happened to her?"

His mother carefully laid aside her fork, then looked down her nose at him. She sat to his right, Celia and Raymond to his left.

"After she was terminated, you mean? Why would I care?" She made a rude sound of condescension. "You certainly didn't expect us to employ the woman, did you, not after she gave away company secrets."

Celia spoke up for the first time, her voice clipped, her expression stern. "I already told you, Mother, Derek stole that information from her."

Dane felt as though he'd taken a punch on the chin. His mother made an outraged sound and Raymond sat watching them both, his expression somewhat satisfied. He stared at his sister and saw that two spots of bright color had bloomed on her cheeks. "What did you say?"

Celia gave her mother a lingering frown, then turned to face Dane. "Mother persists in making this woman out as a villain, even though I've told her repeatedly that it isn't so. If anything, she was a victim, and we certainly should have employed her in an effort to make amends. Derek explained to me himself that Angel hadn't volunteered the information to him. He rifled through her personal belongings until he found what he wanted."

Raymond held his fork aloft, using it to emphasize his point. "Ah. But she should have seen to it that the material was well secured. That was her responsibility. The heads at Aeric trusted her, and she let them down."

"I suppose part of the blame is hers," Celia agreed, her tone snide, "in trusting Derek too much, in thinking him honorable toward her—"

Dane's mother gasped, coming to her feet in furious indignation. Her hands slapped down on the cloth-covered tabletop while her voice rose to a near shriek. "How dare you suggest otherwise, Celia Carter? He was your brother!"

Looking belligerent and stubborn, Celia forced a shrug and met her mother's gaze. "Mother, he *stole* that information from her. He led her on, made her believe he cared for her, and then took shameful advantage. Would you rather I call that honorable?"

Raymond patted Celia's hand. "Sweetheart, he only did what was best for the company. That was always his first priority." His eyes slid over to Dane. "As is true of any CEO."

Dane waited, watching while his mother visibly struggled to regain her control. Such an outburst from her surprised him and piqued his curiosity. When she had grudgingly reseated herself, pretending to be appeased by Raymond's words, and Raymond had taken a healthy bite of his braised pork, Dane asked, "Are you saying, Raymond, that you wouldn't have a problem with using a woman that way?"

Raymond promptly choked, covering his mouth with his napkin.

"Really, Dane, enough of this nonsense!" his mother protested. "Raymond has been an enormous help to us and deserves better from you."

Celia looked at Dane, a wicked smile of appreciation curving her lips, then proceeded to pound her fiancé on the back until he'd managed to catch his breath. Dane leaned back in his chair, enjoying the dinner for the first time that evening.

Damn, so much to think about. So Angel was innocent all the way around. That fact twisted his guts, making him feel guilty as hell, as if he were the one who'd betrayed her. He determined to make it up to her somehow. Whether she wanted him to or not.

An hour later as they all gathered in the salon for drinks and conversation, Dane cornered his sister. Raymond was busy schmoozing their mother, and Celia was blessedly alone, staring out a window at the dark night. As he approached, she looked down at his hand and the drink he held.

"I thought you abstained."

He lifted the glass in a salute. "Pure cola and ice. Nothing more."

"It irritates Mother, you know. That you won't have a social drink."

Dane thought of Mick, so defiant as he explained his mother was an alcoholic. "In my line of work, I see too many drink-related cases. Men and women who abandon their families in favor of a bottle. They all started out as social drinkers." Shaking off his sudden tension, he smiled at Celia. "Besides, I enjoy irritating Mother."

To his surprise, his teasing wasn't returned. Celia turned fully to face him. "How do you do it, Dane? How do you just turn your back on everything, on all of us?"

A frontal attack. He hadn't expected it of his sister, but he relished a moment to clear the air. He'd missed her in the time he'd been away. Though she was a lot like his mother, her strength and determination not to be underestimated, she was also a woman who thought for herself, who didn't blindly accept his mother's dictates. He'd found that out tonight. In the years he'd stayed away, his sister had evidently come into her own.

Too long, too damn long. "There's nothing for me to stay here for, Celia. You know that. Mother made certain she drove me away—"

"She's sorry for that, Dane." Celia touched his arm. Her eyes, the same hazel shade as his, were dark with concern. "She realizes now that you really did love Anna, that she shouldn't have interfered."

He snorted. "Is that what you call it, interference? She deliberately destroyed my life, accused my fiancée of all kinds of reprehensible things, and just because she didn't approve of Anna's family."

Celia bit her lip, then forged on. "You were both so young. Besides, she did take the money, Dane. Mother didn't force it on her."

"She made Anna feel as if that were the only option, as if she couldn't possibly be my wife. Mother made sure she knew she'd never fit in." Even as he said the words, he accepted that he wasn't being a hundred percent truthful with her or himself. "Anna was pregnant, you know. After she ran off, she lost the baby. My baby."

Celia covered her mouth with a hand. "Oh no, I didn't know. I'm so sorry."

"I told Mother. I was angry and hurt and I wanted her to understand exactly what her manipulation had cost me. Do you know what she said?"

Numbly, Celia shook her head.

"She said it was for the best."

Celia lowered her forehead to Dane's shoulder and her voice was quiet, almost a whisper. "Mother's set in her ways, Dane. She means well, and she really does love you. It's just that sometimes she doesn't think."

He had nothing to say to that. It amazed him that his sister would always try to defend their mother, no matter what she did.

"Will you stay on at the company this time? We need you here."

Lifting a hand to his sister's fair hair, giving one silky lock a teasing tug, he said, "You already know the answer to that."

She sighed. "I suppose I do. But I was hopeful."

"It's not for me, sis. I don't feel comfortable there and besides, I love playing detective too much to give it up."

She smiled at his teasing, then turned to face the window again. "I miss him so much."

"Me, too. Even though we hadn't been in contact much lately, I always knew he was here. There were only miles separating us, and I knew we could get in touch if we chose to." Dane wanted to tell her that he suspected Derek had been murdered, but he held back. His sister had enough on her plate for the moment. "I'm proud of how you stood up to Mother."

She made a disgusted sound. "She's hurting. And it angers her if anyone even suggests Derek might not have been perfect. But I can't sit by and watch her persecute an innocent woman."

Dane thought his sister was pretty damn special at that moment, and more than ever, he regretted the amount of time he'd let pass without seeing his family.

"How long are you willing to help out?"

Until I see things settled, he thought, but he only shrugged. "I don't know. We'll see. Right now, I have every agent in my own business maxed out, working on two or more cases at a time. And running between offices isn't getting any easier." Especially while trying to uncover a murderer.

He looked up at that moment to see Raymond watching him while his mother chatted in Raymond's ear, no doubt regaling him with stories of old acquaintances, money and power. It was all his mother knew, all she cared about, and Raymond, with his desire to ingratiate himself, provided the perfect audience. Dane nodded then looked away. "Do you love him?"

Celia laughed. "You say that as if such a thing is unimaginable."

"I just want you to be happy."

"I'd be happy if you stayed on." She quickly raised her hands. "But I understand why you can't. Dane, why were you asking questions about Angel Morris?"

She effectively sidetracked him and he rubbed his chin, wondering what to tell her. Finally he said, "I suppose it just surprises me what Derek did. I don't like to think him capable of such things. Can you even begin to imagine what Angel Morris must have felt like?"

Celia leaned into him, their shoulders touching. "If it's any consolation, I think he regretted it. He was very distracted those last few weeks. And unhappy. He told me once that Angel would never forgive him, and that he didn't blame her. It was almost like he'd *had* to hurt her, though I never understood why. I planned to ask him, to understand, but then he died."

Dane didn't understand either, but he felt better for having talked with his sister. His mother he simply hoped to avoid so she couldn't try to nail him down on his intentions. He didn't want anyone to know his plans until he'd figured everything out. At this point, he wasn't certain who to trust, so he trusted no one.

Not even Angel. The more he learned, the more reason he had to wonder why she'd ever contacted Derek again in the first place. She had to hate him for all he'd done to her. But, his thinking continued, Derek had also given her Grayson, and the baby appeared to be the most important thing in her life. Maybe for that reason alone, she'd been able to give up on some of her anger and resentment. Maybe she'd come to the very reasonable conclusion that Grayson deserved a father and all that Derek could provide. It could be only misplaced pride that still made her insist she wanted nothing from him. Heaven knew, he'd had a hard enough time making her accept the essentials: food and diapers and damn shampoo. She also had plenty of reason to hang on to that pride, given the way she'd been treated.

As Raymond and Mrs. Carter joined them, Raymond smoothly slipped his arm around Celia and gave her an affectionate peck on the cheek. Watching them, Dane pondered the idea of starting over. Ever since Anna had abandoned him, allowing his mother to buy her off, he'd avoided relationships. He hadn't met a woman he'd wanted to see more than twice.

Anna hadn't trusted him, had believed his mother's tales over the truths he'd given her. He'd never admit it to anyone, but Anna's actions had proved his mother right; she wasn't the woman for him. He expected, needed, a woman to give him everything, not merely her trust, but her unwavering loyalty. Her soul. Anna hadn't been able to do that, and while he still regretted the loss, it was more the manipulation that he resented. He'd long since gotten over his first love. It had been a lesson to be learned, and he'd learned it well.

This time, he could think more clearly. He'd make certain the same didn't happen with Angel. He'd reason with his brains, not his heart, and sooner or later, he'd win her over. His ruthlessness was an inherent part of his nature. After all, much as he might dislike it on occasion, he was still a Carter.

Angel didn't stand a chance.

"I DON'T LIKE IT. I think you should tell Derek."

Angel was so sick of hearing Mick's refrain. He and Derek got along wonderfully, but then who wouldn't get along with him? Derek was generous and thoughtful and attentive and protective. He'd shown up every day for the past week, helping with everything from bathing the baby to shopping and housework. Twice he had brought over dinner, then cleaned up the mess so Angel could get caught up on her typing. He'd tried to give her money, but after she'd told him exactly what she thought of that idea, he hadn't mentioned it again.

Instead, he asked questions, hundreds and hundreds of questions. Sometimes it made her nervous, though she couldn't say why. He just seemed so…different.

"The job he got me is awesome."

She smiled at Mick's enthusiasm. He'd been with her since six o'clock while they went over his homework. Now it was nine and he'd done little else but talk about Derek in between lessons in calculus and conjugating Spanish verbs. "So you like it?"

"Are you kidding? What's not to like? It's a private investigations office and the people there are so laid-back and friendly. It's like a big family."

Angel's heart twisted. Mick had never had much family to brag about. His mother was more absent than not, and even when she was around, she didn't demonstrate any maternal instincts. Mick had pretty much raised himself, and Angel knew what a lonely existence that could be.

"They've been telling me some of the cases they've dealt with. Incredible stuff, like shoot-outs and drug busts and all kinds of stuff. This one guy, Alec Sharpe, he's actually sort of scary, but don't tell Derek I said so."

Angel smiled in amazement. If the man spooked Mick, who wasn't afraid of anyone as far as she could tell, he must be one frightening character. She pretended to lock her lips with an imaginary key. "Not a word, I promise."

"The guy has the darkest eyes and he's real quiet and when he talks, even if it's just to ask for coffee, everyone around him shuts up and listens. I think he's sort of a boss or something."

Angel gathered up pencils and pens and put the calculator away. "What do you do there?"

Mick made a face. "All kinds of stuff, from cleaning and running out for doughnuts to making coffee and putting files away. But they're all real nice about it. They don't act like I'm getting paid, but more like I'm doing them a huge favor and they really appreciate it. And Alec gave me this really cool car to drive. It has the best stereo."

Angel knew Mick would be paid more working there than he had made doing both jobs before. And it had been agreed he wouldn't work past six o'clock on school days, and only until the afternoon on the weekends. She was so incredibly grateful to Derek, seeing the change in Mick. He was more like the average kid now, happy and proud. And he adored Derek.

Of course, Mick didn't know everything that had happened between Angel and Derek in the past. And she'd never tell. Derek was doing his best to prove the past really was over; not for the world would she take away Mick's present happiness.

"Why do you still dislike him so much, Angel?"

"Mick..."

"He could help," Mick said, anxious to convince her. "The phone calls were bad enough, but now the letter—"

She rubbed her head. "I know. The letter proves whoever it is knows where to find me. I've been thinking about this a lot." She hesitated, almost afraid to voice her suspicions out loud. "It's possible Derek is the one behind all this."

He stared at her hard, then got to his feet and paced away. "You don't really believe that."

She didn't want to believe it. But the letter proved her

alias hadn't worked—an alias Derek had noticed his first time to her apartment. She didn't want to think he could be so vindictive, but he might have slipped up and told his family, and they were using the information to drive her away. That she could believe only too well.

"I don't know what all's going on between you two, but I do know you're in trouble. You're being stalked, and whoever's been making the calls could have gotten your number from anywhere, maybe even from the ads you ran for typing. But now he knows where you live. The letter proves that. If you keep putting off telling Derek, you could end up hurt."

"Well, I can't do anything about it tonight. Derek had business and couldn't come over. And it isn't something to discuss on the phone."

Mick nodded slowly as he slipped his jacket on. "I'll try to watch out for you, Angel. I wouldn't let anyone hurt you if I could help it, but I can't always be here."

Her blood ran cold with his words. "Mick, if you ever, *ever* hear anything suspicious, or see anyone around the mailboxes, you call the police. Don't you dare try confronting anyone on your own."

He didn't reply to that, merely made his way to the door. "I'll lock this behind me."

"Mick?"

"Call him, Angel. Tell him what's going on. He cares about you and Grayson. I know he does."

It would have been nice if Mick didn't act like the typical domineering, overprotective male. Why were men, of all ages, so blasted stubborn? She sighed. "I'll think about it."

Mick looked at her a moment longer, then nodded. "All right. I'll see you tomorrow?"

She smiled at him. She was very lucky she'd met him when she had. Knowing him, having his friendship, had made her life much easier. "Yes. Get some sleep so you're well rested for that test."

"Yes, ma'am."

After checking that the door was securely locked, Angel peeked in on Grayson. He was sleeping soundly, which would give her a chance to take a quick shower. With all of Derek's help of late, her leg had more time to rest. It didn't hurt as often anymore, but tonight it was sore. She'd sat too long typing at her desk earlier and the muscles felt cramped. A hot shower usually helped.

Leaving the bathroom door open so she could hear Grayson if he cried, she stripped off her clothes and reached into the tub to adjust the temperature of the water. Once the steam started billowing out, she slipped in under the spray.

It felt wonderful to once again wash her hair with scented shampoo, to use all the toiletries she'd given up on due to lack of funds. At first she'd tried returning the things to Derek, but he'd been so sincere in wanting her to keep them, so anxious to *relieve the guilt of his past sins*—his words for his execrable behavior of the past— that she couldn't deny him.

She lingered for a long time, relaxing in the hypnotic warmth of the steam and stinging spray, until she became sleepy and knew she needed to put herself to bed. Grayson still woke during the night for a feeding, and he was usually up with the birds in the morning.

She was just stepping over the side of the tub when the phone rang.

Her first thought was that it might be Derek, and ridiculously enough, her heart leaped. He'd taken to calling her several times a day, whereas before her phone had seldom rung at all. Many times now he'd called to tell her good morning, or good-night, even if he'd spent hours at her apartment.

Wrapping a thick white towel around herself, she hurried out of the bathroom and into the kitchen to snatch up the phone. She was smiling as she said, "Hello?"

A rough, rasping breath answered her, then turned into a growl. Her smile died a quick death.

Shaken, Angel started to slam the phone back down, and then she heard, "Bitch. Give me what I want."

The rasping tones didn't sound human and her blood rushed from her head, leaving her dizzy. "I don't know what you want," she said, her voice shaking despite her efforts to sound unaffected.

"Yes, you do." There was a laugh, taunting and high-pitched. "You're not as innocent as you like to pretend, Angel *Morton*. But your time is up. Do you hear me?"

"I'm hanging up now," she said, determined not to let the caller get the upper hand.

"Did you get my letter? I know where you are now. You better watch your back…"

Angel slammed the phone into the cradle. Her heart was beating so hard, it rocked her body and she quickly wrapped her arms around herself. She was only marginally aware of the water dripping from her hair down her back, leaving a puddle on the floor. Goose bumps rose on her skin, but she was frozen, unable to move.

When the knock sounded on the door, she let out a startled, short scream, jumping back two steps and bumping into the kitchen table. A chair tipped over and crashed to the floor. Grayson woke, his disgruntled wail piercing in the otherwise leaden silence.

She heard Derek call out, "Angel!" at the same time a key sounded in the lock. The door immediately swung open. She couldn't help herself, she gaped at him. How had he known to show up just when she needed him most?

In the next instant, doubt surfaced, and she had to wonder if it was a coincidence, or part of a plan. Was it possible he was working with his family to drive her away? Had she inadvertently stepped into the lion's den?

Derek stormed in like an avenging angel, took one look at her standing there with nothing more than the towel covering her, then crossed the room with long, angry strides. He grabbed her shoulders. "What's the matter? What's happened?"

Angel managed to shake herself out of her stupor. She clutched at her towel with a fist. "What are you doing here?"

He looked nonplussed by her calm question and tightened his hands on her. "I wanted to see you." His head turned in the direction of Grayson's wails and a fierce frown formed. "You're both okay?"

"Yes, of course."

"But you screamed." He turned back to her, raised one hand when she started to speak, then shook his head. "First things first. Go get dried off. I'll get the baby."

She was shaking all over, but he thankfully didn't comment on it. "Thank you. I think the phone disturbed him, and then your knock…"

Derek started her toward her bedroom with a gentle

push. "I understand, babe. Go. We'll talk about it in a minute."

Regardless of what he'd said, Angel followed Derek into the baby's room and made certain everything was all right. She never let Grayson cry, and even now, when she was so rattled, she couldn't stand to hear him upset. Derek cradled him close to his chest, rocking him, murmuring to him, and Grayson immediately began to quiet, his yells turning into hiccups as he recognized his father's scent and voice. Derek held his face close to the baby's, nuzzling, kissing his tiny ear, his cheek, smoothing his large hand up and down Grayson's back. Angel's throat felt tight and her chest restricted.

He turned suddenly when he realized Angel had followed him. Slowly, his gaze ran the length of her, lingering, she knew, on the still harsh scars of her left leg. His attention returned to the baby. "Go get something on, Angel, before you catch cold."

She wondered if her leg repulsed him; his voice had sounded unusually gruff and low. It really was ugly and overall she looked like a drowned rat at the moment. "All right. I'll…I'll be right back."

In the bathroom again, she quickly dried off, dragged a comb through her tangled hair, then shrugged into her housecoat. It was long and thick and covered her from head to toe. She hurried back in to Grayson. The baby now had his entire fist stuffed in his mouth, sucking loudly. She knew from experience that would only suffice for so long.

"Let me have him. After I nurse him, he should fall back to sleep."

Derek gave her a long look before nodding. "Let me change him first."

He disappeared into the other room and Angel paced. The letter this afternoon, then the phone call…. It was the first time she'd heard a voice. Usually the calls consisted of heavy breathing and ominous silences. Again, chills ran up her arms and she ducked her head, her brain working furiously. Mick was right; she had to trust Derek, had to tell him of her suspicions. But she wouldn't tell him everything. She'd only confide about the most recent events. After she saw how he reacted to that, then she'd consider telling him the rest.

When he touched her shoulder, she again jumped, whirling about to face him, her hand pressed to her throat. His expression was dark, his eyes narrowed, and she tried a nervous laugh.

"I'm sorry. You startled me."

"Obviously. But we'll talk about that in a minute."

She took the baby, quickly settled herself on the couch and then looked at Derek. He always left the room when she nursed Grayson, giving her the privacy she needed, but this time he stared right back. Slowly, his gaze never leaving her face, he took the chair opposite her. Heat bloomed inside her. "Derek…"

"No more secrets, Angel."

Grayson rooted against her, anxious for his meal, and she knew, judging by Derek's expression, arguing would gain her nothing. She pulled her gaze away from him, deliberately ignoring his very attentive audience, and went about feeding her baby. She felt stiff, unable to relax, so many things racing through her mind.

After a moment, Derek rose from his chair and reseated himself beside her. The soft, worn cushions of the couch slumped with his weight and her hip rolled next to his, bumping into him. He felt warm and hard, his presence overwhelming. Angel was acutely aware of his undivided concentration on her breast. She kept her visual attention firmly placed on Grayson.

Casually, Derek slipped his arm around her shoulders. She had trouble breathing. She moved Grayson to her other breast, closer to Derek, and as he nursed he began to fall back to sleep. He looked precious, and she couldn't hold back a smile.

"He's beautiful, Angel." Derek's warm breath fanned her temple and she shivered. "You're beautiful."

His voice sounded with awe, and as he scooted even closer, seeming to surround her with his heat and scent and power, she felt herself relaxing. This felt right. Derek was doing nothing untoward, only taking part in what was rightfully his. His left arm moved across her abdomen in an embrace, just below the baby, circling both mother and son. He kissed her temple, a light, loving kiss. Slowly, Grayson released her nipple and a drop of milk slid down his chin. With his fingertip, Derek wiped it away.

They neither one moved. She knew Derek was looking at her, studying her, but there was nothing lurid about his scrutiny. He dipped his head and kissed Grayson on his silky crown. In a low, husky whisper, he asked, "Would you like me to burp him and put him back to bed?"

Angel nodded.

As he was lifted, Grayson stretched and groaned and gave a loud belch, making any further efforts unnecessary. Derek grinned as he hefted the small weight to his shoulder and got to his feet. He looked down at Angel. "I'll be right back," he whispered. "Don't move."

Other than covering her breast and nervously shifting, she obeyed.

It was late, now close to eleven o'clock, but she was far from sleepy. So many emotions were pulling at her—fear and anxiety and anticipation, but also a deep contentment. Derek was everything a father should be, and she couldn't quite work up the energy to distrust him anymore. It took all she had as she fought herself to keep from falling in love with him. Despising him was out of the question.

Derek stepped out of the baby's room, softly closing the door behind him. For long moments, he merely stared at Angel across the room. The time of reckoning, she thought.

For the life of her, she couldn't seem to move. Her heart began racing, her palms grew damp. She saw Derek lock his jaw, saw his shoulders tighten and flex, and she knew, without him saying a single word, he was caught in the same inexplicable flow of emotions as she.

What would happen next, she couldn't guess, but she was anxious to find out.

And then the phone rang.

Angel gasped. Both wary and disgusted by the interruption, she stared toward the kitchen where the phone was located.

Derek frowned at her. "Do you want me to get that for you?"

"No, I'll…" She shook her head, wiped her palms across her thighs. And still she sat there, staring at the phone.

Sparing her a curious glance, Derek stalked to the phone and snatched it up on the fifth ring. "Hello?" He kept his gaze on Angel as he spoke and she tried to clear her expression, but she could see he'd already read too much there.

"Hello?" he said a little more forcefully. He looked at the receiver, then gently placed it in the cradle. As he walked back to loom over Angel, she could see the questions in his eyes. "What's going on, honey?" His tone was soft, menacing.

She shook her head. "I don't know."

He waited, not moving away, not saying another word. She recognized his stubborn expression, only now there was more of a threat there, more determination than ever.

"Sometimes I get strange calls."

She hadn't meant to make such a bald confession, but it just slipped out. After a deep breath while he raised one eyebrow, encouraging her, she continued. "Sometimes, eight or ten times now, someone has called and just…breathed in the phone. Today I finally heard a voice. He…said things to me." She lifted her gaze and got caught in his. "He called right before you got here."

Derek's eyes darkened, his eyebrows lowered, and suddenly he was crouching there in front of her, his hands holding hers, hard but not really hurting her. It did give her the feeling she couldn't get away, even if she tried.

His gaze was so intense, so probing, she squirmed. "You thought it might be me," he accused.

He didn't sound angry precisely, though she couldn't pinpoint the dominant emotion in his tone. She straightened her shoulders and frowned right back. "I wondered. I have no enemies that I know of, no reason for threats. You're the only person who ever seemed to despise me, and I've never really understood why."

There, let him deal with that, she thought and jerked away to walk carefully into the kitchen. She needed something to drink, some warm tea. And she needed to escape his close scrutiny.

Out of the corner of her eye, she watched Derek stand, then pace around her tiny living room. He had his hands back in his pockets and his head down in deep thought. She was familiar with that look now, that show of serious introspection. She'd seen it a lot lately, though in the past she couldn't recall Derek ever doubting himself, ever giving so much thought to anything pertaining to her.

She put water on to boil, then asked, "Would you like some tea?"

"Thank you."

After righting the fallen chair, she sat at her small kitchen table, waiting for the water to get hot. Moments later she felt Derek's hands on her shoulders, heavy and warm.

"The problem is," he whispered, "I'm not making the calls. And I don't despise you." His hands slipped up to her throat, caressing, then smoothing her damp hair back behind her ears. "On the contrary, Angel, I want to take care of you."

Anger caused her eyes to narrow. She wanted to believe him, to understand and accept his help. She twisted to face him. "Why? Why now, when you made it plain months ago how you felt? You deliberately humiliated me in front of my supervisors. You didn't just break things off, you tried to break me. *Why?*"

His eyes closed and he turned his head away. "You're right, of course. I can't undo the past. I can only have regrets, which don't amount to a hill of beans. But I'm here now and I'd like to help."

Since that was what she'd wanted all along, what her entire plan had been, she should have been relieved. But somehow everything was different than she'd expected. He wasn't the same man, easy to be detached from now. The Derek who'd first hurt her had been more of an illusion to her, an image of strength and power that had seduced her by sheer impression. She hadn't really known the man, other than in the most superficial ways; she'd merely been attracted to his image. But now she genuinely liked and respected him. When she could set the past aside, he was fun, and when he held Grayson, the affection in his eyes filled her with an insidious warmth that expanded her heart. More often than not, she didn't understand what she was feeling.

Only one thing was certain: Grayson could be at risk if she didn't find some sort of protection.

She got up to serve the tea, collecting her thoughts. After she set his cup near him on the table, she said, "I've gotten several anonymous calls lately, more than ever before. Usually, it's just breathing and such. They started before I'd moved, when I lived in my old apartment. After I moved here, they stopped for a while and I thought I'd lost whoever it was. But just recently they started up again. It's possible my phone number was taken from one of the posted ads around the colleges. The ads are generic, offering typing, but since I've been transcribing for colleges ever since the accident, it could be my number was relocated that way."

Derek nodded. "Very possible, I suppose. But the person making the calls would have to be damn determined."

Angel shivered. "He spoke for the first time today. He said, very clearly, that I couldn't hide. He called me a few…choice names and told me to give him what he wanted."

She saw Derek's jaw go hard and knew he was clenching his teeth. He stared at her and she shrugged helplessly. "I don't know what he wants. I wish I did."

"Go on."

"I also got a letter in my mailbox."

"Where is it?"

She pulled an envelope from the basket on top of her refrigerator and handed it to Derek. The letter was now wrinkled from her many hours of examining it, but Derek had no trouble making out the typed message. *"I've found you,"* he read aloud. He was silent for a long time, his face dark, his expression tight. He threw the letter on the table and turned on her.

"You thought I was behind this?" he asked, his teeth clenched, color high on his face. "You thought I would resort to sneaking around and stuffing threatening letters in a woman's mailbox, in *your* mailbox?"

His reaction was genuine and for the first time she felt absolutely positive that he played no part in the harassment.

A little truth now certainly wouldn't hurt. Problem was, as she tried to give it, tears gathered in her eyes, and she couldn't quite work up the nerve to accuse his family, the most likely of suspects. Not yet.

She shook her head. "No," she said, trying to sound sure of herself. "I don't really think you're behind it. But the letter came after I contacted you. Before that, all I'd gotten was phone calls. And you noticed the fake name on my mailbox that day. Now tonight, you showed up right after the call, and it was the first time he'd ever spoken to me. That's a lot of coincidences." She searched his face, hoping he'd understand. "I had to consider you, Derek. I couldn't take any chances with Grayson's safety."

Seconds ticked by, then he reluctantly nodded.

She drew a deep breath of relief. "The whole reason I contacted you again, the only reason I introduced Grayson to you is because deep down, for some incredibly insane reason, I guess I still trust you. Even after everything that happened, I thought… I thought you would help. I *hoped* you would help."

She swallowed, the sound audible, almost choked. "Derek…I've been so scared, and I don't have anyone else to go to."

A stunned moment of silence fell between them. She could feel the waves of emotion emanating from him, anger and regret and need. Then she was in his arms and it felt so good, so right, she curled closer and snuggled tighter, trying to fit herself completely against his long, hard length. His arms wrapped around her, urgently, almost violently, while his mouth nuzzled down her face, giving her small anxious biting kisses until finally he reached her lips and then he was devouring her and she was glad, so very, very glad.

CHAPTER SIX

DANE KNEW HE SHOULD pull back, that he was making a terrible tactical error. He wasn't completely in control, and he should be. But he couldn't put so much as an inch between them. He wanted, needed her, right now. Even two seconds more would be too long to wait. And Angel was so soft and anxious against him, her breasts pressed to his chest, her pelvis cradling his own. She wanted him, too, and that was all that mattered. The deceptions, the worries, could be taken care of in the morning. He'd make it all okay, one way or another, but for now, tonight, he wouldn't say a single thing that would put a halt to her greed.

Growling low, he slid his hands down to her backside and cuddled her even closer. She felt so damn good.

"Angel."

She pressed her face into his throat and shuddered. "I don't understand this, Derek," she said on a near wail. "I've never felt like this before."

How could he possibly explain it to her, when he didn't understand it himself? He knew she would compare him to Derek, and as much as he'd loved his brother, as dedicated as he was to finding out the truth, right now claiming her took precedence over everything else.

He shushed her with more kisses. "I've never felt this way either, honey. Don't worry about it now. Just let me love you."

She opened her mouth against him and took a soft, greedy love bite of his throat. Gasping, he quickly picked her up, mindful of her injured leg, and hurried to her bedroom, nudging the door shut behind them until it closed with a secure click. He didn't want to take the chance of waking Grayson. He wanted no interruptions at all.

He didn't put her on the bed, choosing to stand her beside it instead. He wanted her naked, and he wanted to look his fill. It felt as if he'd been waiting forever.

As he grasped the cloth belt to her robe, ready to pull it free, she caught his wrists. His gaze darted to her face and he was amazed to see how heavy and sensual her eyes had become, her thick lashes lowered, the green eyes bright and hot. Her high cheekbones were colored, but with need, not embarrassment. She took soft, panting breaths as she looked up at him.

She licked her lips, and even that innocently seductive sight had him trembling.

"I don't want to disappoint you, Derek."

He'd never before minded being mistaken for his twin. Through his entire life people had often done it, sometimes even his parents. Before their father had died, he and Derek had often played tricks on him, deliberately confusing him.

But now, he hated it. He had to struggle for breath. He gave her a hard quick kiss, which turned tender and hungry and lingered sweetly. When he pulled away, it seemed to take a great effort on her part for her to get her eyes open. He smiled. "There's no way you could disappoint me, honey."

"My body's changed. The baby…"

Still holding her gaze he tugged the knot out of the belt and pushed the robe off her shoulders. She dropped her arms and the robe fell free all the way to the floor. Angel lowered her head and turned slightly away.

For nearly a minute he was speechless. She was more beautiful than any woman had a right to be, and there was absolutely nothing motherly about her heavy, firm breasts, the stiff dark nipples. Her rib cage expanded and fluttered with her uneven breaths and her belly looked soft and slightly rounded, very pale. He spread one large, hot palm over her stomach and heard her small gasp.

"Derek…?"

"Shhh. I've never wanted a woman the way I want you, Angel. Trust me when I tell you there's not a single thing about you that could disappoint me." Her legs were long and so sexy, even with the harsh scars on her left shin. He immediately pictured those long legs wrapped around him, her heels digging into the small of his back, urging him on, and he groaned as his erection pulsed, demanding release.

Slowly, so he wouldn't startle her, he slid his palm downward until he was cupping her, his fingers tangling in the dark blond curls over her mound. They felt damp and soft under his fingertips, her flesh swollen, and he breathed deeply through his nose, trying to ease the constriction in his lungs. He held still, just holding her like that, letting her feel the heat of his palm, letting the anticipation build.

Angel moaned and stepped up against him. Her hands gripped his biceps, her forehead pressed to his shoulder.

Dane swallowed and smiled grimly. "Do you remember when I touched you in my office?" he asked against her temple.

She nodded her head.

He licked her ear and gently nipped the lobe. "You were so close then, Angel, and I'd barely done anything to you. Little more than kissing." He nearly groaned with the memory.

Her hips jerked, encouraging him. Anticipating her response, he inched his fingers lower, gliding over her warm flesh, opening her soft, plump folds, learning her, exploring. She was already so hot, so silky wet, and it amazed him the way she reacted to his touch. It also made him nearly crazy with a frenzied mix of lust and overwhelming tenderness.

Her body felt frozen against his, very still, waiting. Even her breathing became suspended, as if she was afraid to move for fear of missing something. Determination swelled within him. He had no intention of leaving her with complaints; her views on the joys of sex were about to be altered.

"Open your legs a little more for me, Angel." He could tell that she responded to his words, and he wasn't about to disappoint her. "Let me feel you. All of you."

With a shudder, her face well hidden against his chest, she carefully widened her stance. Immediately he pressed one finger deep inside her, at the same time he braced his free arm around her waist.

She needed his support.

Her body went alternately stiff and completely yielding. Holding her against him, acutely aware of her broken breaths, her soft moans, the way her fingers dug into his chest, he stroked her. He could feel her tightening, feel the small shudders moving up and down her body. He eased her a little away from him and she allowed the small separation, her head falling back on her shoulders, her still-damp hair trailing down to tickle against his arm. He saw her breasts heaving and dipped his head down to take one plump nipple into his mouth.

"Ohhh…"

He lapped with his tongue, nibbled with his teeth, drew deeply on her. Her hands raised from his chest to his head and her fingers tangled in his hair, tugging, trying to draw him even closer.

"I have to sit down," she moaned.

"No." He blew on her damp nipple, watching it go painfully tight. The pregnancy had no doubt made her breasts extra sensitive, and he intended to take advantage of that fact. "Right here, Angel. We'll get to the bed in a minute."

He switched to her other breast and heard her give a soft sob of compliance. Voluntarily, she parted her legs even more and then thrust against him. He slid his finger all the way out, teasing, then worked it heavily back into her again. "You're so wet for me, honey," he said on a groan, amazed and thrilled and so hot himself he wanted to die.

Forcefully, making him wince, she brought his mouth back up to her own and this time she kissed him, awkwardly but with so much hunger he thought he might burst. He rubbed his heavy erection against her soft hip while he carefully forced a second finger inside her. He found a rhythm that pleased her and went about seeing to her satisfaction. He was playing it safe, not about to remove his clothes or lie with her on the bed, knowing his control was thin at the moment and any little thing could send him over the edge. He wouldn't risk taking his own completion before he'd seen to hers.

Within minutes she was crying, her body tight and trembling, her hands frenzied on his back and shoulders. Slowly, he eased her down to the side of the bed so that her legs hung over the edge, then knelt between them. She dropped back, her hands fisting in the bedclothes, her hips twisting. Dane lifted her legs to his shoulders and before she could object—if indeed she would have given how close she was—he cupped her hips in his hands and brought her to his mouth.

She tasted sweet and incredibly hot and he was beyond teasing her, so close to exploding himself. His heart thundered and her scent filled him as he nuzzled into her, driving himself ever closer. As his tongue stroked over her sensitive flesh, as he found the small engorged bud and drew on it, teasing with his tongue, tormenting with his teeth, she gave a stifled scream and climaxed.

Quickly, wanting to feel every bit of her, he pushed his fingers back inside her. Her feminine muscles gripped him, the spasms strong as she pressed herself even higher, moving against his open mouth and continuing to cry and moan and excite him unbearably. It went on and on and he almost lost control. He was shaking all over when she finally quieted, her eyes closed, her lashes damp on her cheeks, her mouth slightly open as she gulped air.

She never so much as blinked when he lifted her legs gently to the bed and stood to look down at her. Slowly, drinking in the sight of her limp, sated body, he pulled his shirt free from his pants and began unbuttoning it. He forced himself to go slow, to savor the moment of his claiming. Even to his own mind, his thoughts, his responses, seemed primitive, maybe even ruthless. But he wanted her to be his and his alone—a feeling he'd never encountered before, not even with Anna. He wanted to take her so thoroughly, possess her so completely, she'd be willing to forgive him anything, willing to trust him in all matters.

She gave a shuddering sigh, lifted one languid hand to her forehead and pushed her hair away from her face. Dane watched her, so suffused with heat the edges of his vision blurred.

While he tugged his belt loose from the clasp with one hand, he dropped his other lightly to her soft thigh. Her skin felt like warm silk to him, and tempted him more than it should have.

Her lashes fluttered as his fingers trailed higher, and finally her eyes opened. She looked dazed and relaxed, on the verge of sleep. He smiled and carefully worked his zipper down past his throbbing erection. "You scream very well, Angel. I liked it."

"Oh." Her cheeks filled with color and she swallowed. When her gaze dropped to the open vee in his slacks, her eyes opened wide. *"Oh."*

Dane sat on the bed beside her, his hand still on her thigh. "No, don't get up. I like seeing you sprawled there." She relaxed back again and he used the toes of his left foot to work off his right shoe, while at the same time surveying her body. He traced a nipple with his fingertip, around and around until she made a protesting sound. Then he dragged his fingers over her ribs and to her belly. She shifted abruptly.

"Ticklish?"

"Derek…"

Leaning over, he pressed a lingering kiss to her navel. "I love the way you taste, honey."

She made a groaning sound of renewed interest, then tried to turn away from him. He caught her hips, stopping her.

"Derek, you can't expect me to…"

"Yes I do." Once again his fingers slid between her legs, anchoring her in place while he kissed his way up her abdomen to her breasts. "I expect you to let me pleasure you, and I expect you to continue enjoying my efforts."

He raised his head for just a moment, pinning her with a look. "You came, Angel. A nice long, hard climax. And if I didn't miss my guess, it was your first. So don't try to deny it."

She gasped. "I wasn't going to!"

"Good." When he drew her nipple into the heat of his mouth she writhed against him, then fisted her hands in his hair.

"No, Derek."

He jerked upward and pinned her hands next to her head. "Yes."

She said quickly, before he could kiss her, "I want you to take your shirt off. I want to see you, too. It's not fair for me to lie here…exposed, while you're completely dressed."

His grin was slow and wicked. He knew it, but didn't care. She wasn't denying him at all as he'd first thought. She only insisted on her fair share. "All right."

He pushed himself off the bed. "Don't move, Angel. You inspire me, lying there like that."

He shrugged his shirt off and grabbed the waistband of his pants. He stepped between her legs as he pushed them down, removing his boxers at the same time. When he straightened, he was naked.

Angel's gaze roamed over him and her face heated again. He stifled a laugh, delighted with her. Her particular brand of innocence and hot sexuality was driving him crazy. He loved it. He loved... No, his thoughts refused to budge any further in that direction. He firmed his resolve.

Using a knee, he spread her legs even more and lowered himself over her. Propped on his elbows, he smiled down at her. "Hi."

Rather than smiling back, she traced his face, over his eyebrows, the bridge of his nose, the dip in his chin. "You took me by surprise, Derek. Everything is so different..."

"So you keep saying." He didn't want to talk about that right now. Thinking of his brother with her like this was enough to make him howl at the moon.

"What happened was...unexpected."

"But nice?" He again caught her hands and trapped them over her head, leaving her submissive to his desires.

She looked thoughtful as she continued her study of his face. "Very nice. Incredible really. But ever since I saw you again, it's been that way. You look at me, and I get all hot inside. You touch me and I can't think straight. I try to despise you; I have good reason to despise you, but I can't. It doesn't make any sense. Unless having the baby changed me somehow."

"Angel." She was killing him with her words, but he didn't know how to tell her that.

"After everything that happened between us, I thought I'd always hate you."

He groaned. "Don't, babe." He kissed her, hard and long, his tongue thrusting deep, stroking in a parody of the sex act. He rubbed his hairy chest against her sensitive nipples and felt her legs bend, coming up to hug his hips. The open juncture of her legs was a sweet torture, her damp heat against his belly, her soft thighs cradling him. He rubbed against her, his muscles bound so tight he felt ready to break.

She shifted, and then his erection was smoothly pushing against her wet sex. Angel began moving with him, their mouths still fused together, both of them breathing rapidly, roughly.

She jerked and pulled her mouth away, crying out.

Dane was stunned as she quickly climaxed again, shuddering beneath him, her head arched back, her heels digging into his thighs.

His control snapped. Shaking, he grabbed up his slacks and fumbled like a drunk for his wallet. He found a condom and viciously ripped the packet open with his teeth. Angel was still gasping breathlessly and when he turned, catching her legs in the crook of his elbows, spreading her wide and driving into her with one hard thrust, she cried out again.

He couldn't think. His brain throbbed and his vision went blank and all he could do was feel and smell and taste her. She'd invaded his heart, his soul. He was the one who felt possessed and he rebelled against it even as he felt himself spiraling away. He squeezed his eyes shut and growled and pumped and when he heard Angel groan he knew she was with him yet again. It was too much. It felt like he exploded, his entire body gripped in painful pleasure, but it was so damn wonderful he never wanted it to end.

It took him a long time to come back to reality, to hear Angel's soft sniffling, to feel the shudders in her body. Slowly, feeling drugged, he struggled up to his elbows again. Tears dampened her eyelashes and her lips looked swollen. His heart twisted.

Damn, her leg. His arms were still tangled with her legs and he knew she had to be in pain. He'd taken her roughly, almost brutally. That he'd hurt her made him wince in self-loathing. Carefully, he straightened, letting her legs down easy. She groaned and pressed her face to the side, away from him.

He cupped her chin and turned her back. "Angel, honey, I'm sorry."

She shook her head.

"Babe, look at me."

Her eyelashes lifted and she stared up at him. The tears in her eyes twisted his guts. He pressed his forehead to hers and kissed her gently. "I'm so sorry, sweetheart. I didn't mean to hurt you."

She frowned.

"I got a little carried away." He tried a smile but it felt more like a grimace. "You moaned, and all rational thought fled my mind. I'm sorry." He sounded like a parrot, apologizing over and over again.

"Derek…"

Goddammit, he hated having her call him that. "Shh. It's all right." Her hair, dry now and tangled impossibly, lay wild around her head. He tried to smooth it. "Can I get you anything? Some aspirin or something?" He felt like an idiot, having sex with a woman then offering her medicine for the pain.

She shook her head again and her voice, when she spoke, was tentative and as soft as a whisper. "I'm fine, just a little…stunned. Is it always like that?"

Now he felt confused. Buying himself some time, he sat up and carefully moved to the side of her. Her body had been damp and warm from their exertions and combined heat, and she shivered in the cool evening air. He pulled the corner of the spread up to cover her, but left her leg bare. Gently, he massaged her calf and saw her wince.

"Dammit, I'm an unthinking bastard. I—"

She laughed, catching his hand and twining her fingers with his. "No, you're not. I'm fine, Derek."

He forcefully ignored the continued use of his brother's name. "Then why were you crying?"

She sat up and put her arms around him, burrowing close. "Because it was so wonderful."

His heart pounding, Dane hugged her back. "I didn't hurt you?"

She laughed. "Maybe a little, but I didn't notice… until after."

He pressed her back down on the bed and stood. "I'll be right back." With those words, and one last glance at her naked body, he left the bedroom. He wanted to make sure the apartment was secure for the night. There were three windows, one in the kitchen over the sink, but it was too small for an intruder, and one in the living room on that same wall. He checked to make sure it was locked, then realized the window was so old and warped, opening it would be a true effort. He'd be in the bedroom, so he wasn't worried about that window. He'd already locked the front door when he'd first come in. He glanced at the phone, scowled, but put that particular worry from his mind. Right now, he wanted to concentrate on Angel.

He peeked in on Grayson to see the baby sleeping

soundly. He'd been afraid their commotion might have disturbed the infant, but Grayson was snuggled warm and comfy in his crib. He lay on his side, and one chubby cheek was smooshed, his rosebud mouth slightly open.

Damn, Dane felt good. He hadn't felt this good in... He'd never felt this good. Angel was the perfect bed partner, wild and abandoned and responsive. She burned him up. She was also sweet and caring and strong.

And she had Grayson, his nephew, the strongest bond he had left to his brother. In his heart, Grayson was his own.

As soon as he set things right with Angel, they'd be able to work together to find out what had happened to Derek. Likely, the threats to her and Derek's death were related. He hated the unknown, hated how ineffectual he felt when dealing with the whole problem. Somehow he had to uncover a mystery and protect Angel at the same time. Thank God the threats to her were so far only abstract, not physical. Long before they got too serious, he intended to have everything resolved. From here on out, he'd double his efforts.

Dane returned to the bedroom moments later with a damp washcloth. He'd disposed of the used condom, and set two more on the nightstand. The night was still young, and he was still hungry.

Angel looked almost asleep and the fact she hadn't been concerned with him roaming her apartment assured him that she was starting to trust him, at least a little. It also proved, to some degree, that she had nothing at all to hide.

She opened her eyes and blinked sleepily up at him when he sat on the edge of the mattress. "What are you doing?"

"I was just going to make you more comfortable." So saying, he swiped the warm, damp cloth over her face, her neck, then down her body. She smiled and arched into his hand with a sigh of pleasure.

"You wore a…a…"

Dane cocked one eyebrow. "A what?"

Pointing down to his lap, she said, "You know. Before you made love to me."

"A rubber? I didn't want to take any chances. Much as I adore Grayson, the last thing you need right now is another pregnancy, what with your leg and—"

"And my financial situation and the threats."

Dane leaned down and kissed her. "I'll take care of the threats. Don't worry about that. And as far as I'm concerned, you don't have any financial worries. I can take care of everything." As quickly as he said it, he raised a placating hand. "I didn't mean that quite the way it sounded."

But Angel was already scowling fiercely. "I've told you enough times now, Derek, I don't need anything from you."

Dane eyed her heaving breasts, her flushed cheeks, and tossed the washcloth away. "I wouldn't say that's precisely true." In the next instant they were sprawled on the bed again. Angel moaned his brother's name.

As he shoved the spread out of his way so nothing would be between their bodies, he whispered, "I'm spending the night, honey, and in the morning we'll figure everything out. But for now, I want you again."

"Derek."

He'd have to settle things soon. Being called another man's name while making love to a woman who was quickly obsessing his mind couldn't be borne.

In the morning, he thought. He'd clear it all up in the morning. Then Angel could begin accepting things. She could begin dealing with Dane Carter. And he'd be sure to remind her how much more she liked him than Derek.

CHAPTER SEVEN

ANGEL WOKE WITH A GROAN. She felt sore in places she'd never thought about before, her muscles protesting as she stretched, her mind foggy from too little sleep.

She and Derek had made love several times during the night. The man seemed insatiable, yet she wouldn't complain. Everything he'd done to her had been wonderful, if a bit shocking. She smiled as she looked toward the window and saw that the sun was coming up in a blaze of orange light. She loved dawn in the winter, the promise of sunshine when the weather was so bleak and cold.

Turning back to the center of the bed, she reached for Derek, only he wasn't there. Angel frowned, and then her gaze fell on the clock on the nightstand. Eight-thirty. Good grief, she hadn't lain abed so late in ages. She wondered if Derek was in another part of the apartment, but it was then she noticed the note on his pillow. She straightened in the bed and unfolded the slip of paper.

Sorry I had to run off, but I had to be at the office early today. I didn't want to disturb you—any more than I already had through the night.

Angel smiled. She could almost hear the boasting tone of his voice in the teasing words.

A lot to do. I'll call you later. Stay in the apartment and don't worry. I'll take care of things.

D.

Don't worry, indeed. How did he presume to magically "take care of things"? she wondered. She dropped the note as she yawned and stretched once more. Time to get up and check on Grayson. At least Derek had had the foresight to leave the bedroom door open. He'd closed it during the night, against her protests, but true to his word, he'd heard Grayson when the baby awoke, and had even fetched him to her so she hadn't been forced to leave the warmth of the bed. After she'd nursed him, Derek had taken him back to his crib, then since they were both awake, he'd made love to her once more. Even that last time it had turned fast and furious and she'd bitten his shoulder to keep from screaming like a wild woman.

Her face heated with the memory of Derek's satisfied smile. He'd looked at the small teeth marks on his shoulder and grinned with pride.

Unaccountable man. Angel smiled.

It was as she was slipping on her housecoat that the crash sounded. Breaking glass and a loud thunking sound, followed by a low hissing. Her heart leaped into her throat and it took her a moment to unglue her feet, to get herself in motion. She raced out of the bedroom, and was immediately assailed by the smell of smoke. Billows of it poured out of the kitchen into the rest of the tiny apartment.

"Oh my God." Angel stared, then ran for Grayson. The baby had just been jarred awake, and his face was blank for only a second before he began to squall. She jerked him up into her arms, wrapped a blanket tightly around him and then raced to the front door. It took her too much time to manipulate the lock and she was cursing as she finally got the door to open. Once in the hallway she froze, wondering what to do, if maybe the fire had been deliberately set for just that reason, to get her out of the apartment, vulnerable. Shaking, her heart beating too fast, she tried to soothe Grayson even as she ran the length of the hall to Mick's apartment.

She pounded on the door, trying to look around herself, to be aware of any danger. The door opened and Mick's mother stood there, her face ravaged from a long night, her clothes rumpled as if she'd slept in them. She looked unsteady and very put out. Before Angel could say anything, Mick came around his mother.

"What's happened?" He jerked Angel into the apartment and looked her over. She knew her housecoat was only hastily closed and she tried to adjust Grayson to better cover herself.

"A fire. In my apartment. Someone broke a window I think."

Mick stared at her, then started to thrust her aside, determined, she knew, to investigate. Angel grabbed his arm. "No! Just call the fire department, for God's sake."

He shook her off and spared a glance for his mother. "Make the call. I'll be right back."

Mrs. Dawson made no effort to stop her son, frustrating Angel beyond measure. She watched the woman pick up the phone and try to make a coherent call, but it was obvious she was hungover.

Gently, Angel took the receiver from her and gave the details as best she could. The man on the other end told them all to vacate the building and that someone would be there right away. Angel prayed Mick would hurry back. She'd never felt so afraid in her life.

Mick stormed back just as Angel was trying to bundle Grayson up. "It's okay. It was only a small fire and it's out now, but to be safe, let's wait for the firemen outside." He went into his own room and fetched two blankets to bundle Angel in, and then slipped on his own coat.

His mother made grumbling noises and held her head. "I think I'll just go over to Jerry's. You can handle this, can't you, Mick?"

Mick gave a quick, abrupt nod. "Yes." Mrs. Dawson picked up her coat and walked out, one hand holding her head. Mick's face looked set in stone.

He took Angel's arm and started her outside. Already they could hear the sirens. He put his arms around Angel and the baby, trying to lend his warmth and comfort.

Angel wished with all her heart that he was her son. "Thank you, Mick."

He ignored that. "First thing once the place is declared safe, you're calling Derek."

She swallowed. "All right."

"You have to tell him everything now, Angel. No more playing around."

"I know."

She could feel how tense he was, his anger tangible. "Damn, I wish I'd seen whoever it was."

Angel was eternally grateful he hadn't.

It only took the firemen minutes to confirm what Mick had told her. Someone had broken her small kitchen window with a rock, then tossed in a bundle of gas-soaked rags. The result had been more smoke than anything else. Mick had smothered the flickering flames with a blanket, much to the firemen's dismay. They lectured him on safety matters, on the importance of walking away from a fire rather than trying to handle it himself. Mick, she could tell, only halfheartedly listened to their speeches.

Endless questions followed, but finally it was all put down to a prank. It was obvious to the firemen that while the fire could have become serious, that hadn't been the intent. More of a lark, they said, their tones edged with anger. Angel didn't tell them about the other threats—the phone calls and the letter. She wanted to talk to Derek first. She had a feeling he'd want to be with her when she spoke to the police.

Mick skipped school that day, opting to stay with Angel instead. He'd already missed his morning classes arguing with his mother, who'd come home drunk once again. Angel felt for him, even as she gladly accepted his company.

The apartment was a mess, the smell of smoke lingering on everything. All of her clothes stank. She could do nothing about her jeans, but Mick loaned her a fresh sweatshirt to wear. They were in the apartment for mere moments, only long enough for her to gather the necessities for Grayson and a few of her own things. She didn't have apartment insurance, and the thought of the expense of replacing several things overwhelmed her. The firemen had suggested she call a professional cleaner to tackle the smoke damage and the singed areas of her kitchen, but she knew she couldn't afford it. She would have to do the cleaning herself.

Mick hovered over her as she settled herself on the couch in his mother's apartment. He handed her the phone. "Call Derek now. You've put it off long enough."

She sighed, knowing he was right, but not sure how to tell him. He was going to be angry, no doubt about that. And her thoughts still felt so jumbled.

Buying herself a little time, she thumbed through the personal phone book she'd retrieved from her desk. Her eyes closed as she thought of all the papers still to be typed, all of them gray with ash dust. How such a small fire had done so much damage she couldn't imagine. Her world was quickly unraveling around her, her choices falling away one by one until now she had no choices at all—she needed Derek. The idea didn't panic her nearly so much as it had only a week ago.

Deciding not to dawdle anymore, she found Derek's work number and punched it in. A secretary answered.

Angel cleared her throat. "I'd like to talk to Derek Carter please."

A very polite voice regretfully turned down her request. "I'm sorry, ma'am. Mr. Carter can't take your call right now."

Angel drew a calming breath and tried to pull herself together. Yelling at a secretary wouldn't gain her a thing. "You don't understand. I *have* to speak with him. It's an…an emergency."

There was a slight hesitation before the secretary said, "Just a minute please."

But it wasn't Derek who came on the line. Angel didn't recognize the impatient male voice, but at his inquiry, she repeated her request.

Suspicion crept into his tone when he asked, "Who is this?"

Because she was rattled, Angel answered without thinking. "Angel Morris."

Stunned silence followed, then a rough laugh that was quickly squelched. "Well, well. I'm sorry to be the one to break it to you, sweetheart. But Derek Carter is dead." There was another moment of silence where Angel could hear her own heartbeat, and then he added, "Maybe I can help you. What do you need?"

Angel dropped the phone as her heart kicked violently in panic. She couldn't draw a deep enough breath. Mick frowned at her and picked up the receiver. "Angel?"

She shook her head, slowly coming to her feet. She knew her face was white, her breathing too fast. It couldn't be true; it was likely part of the threat, some vicious game to taunt her, confuse her.

A cleansing rush of anger ran through her. First the damage to her apartment, and now this contemptible prank. She absolutely refused to believe it was any more than that.

Mick started to speak into the receiver but Angel snatched it away from him and slammed it down in the cradle. "No. Don't say anything else to him."

"Him? What's going on, Angel?"

She paced in front of Mick, her stride stiff and angry. "He said Derek's dead, but I know it can't be true! It can't be."

Mick frowned. His face turned pale with confusion and concern. "Of course it's not." He looked undecided for only a second, then determination replaced every other emotion on his face. "Come on." He hauled Angel along behind him with a firm grip on her arm.

"Where are we going?"

"To his company. You'll see for yourself that Derek is just fine, and then you're going to tell him everything. This is starting to get too damn weird."

"Yes." Angel nodded, not at all concerned with her mismatched clothing, her tangled hair, or her ash-smudged face. She only cared about seeing Derek, alive and well.

Her reaction was telling, she thought, but she refused to dwell on it. He was okay. She was certain he was okay. Her hands shook with anger and her heart ached as she bundled Grayson into a blanket and followed Mick out the door. Once she knew for certain it was all part of the threats, that Derek was indeed fine, she intended to tell him everything.

She'd never doubt him again.

DANE STARED AROUND at the solemn faces watching him. He knew his mother wanted to protest this little meeting he'd called, but so far she'd held herself silent. That alone confused him, because his mother had never been one for circumspection. She had a tendency to go after what she wanted with the force of a battering ram.

Which made her acceptance of Derek's *accident* all the more suspect. He pushed that aside for the moment.

The meeting wasn't officially with the board; it was a family matter and Dane intended to treat it as such. His two uncles, both older and naturally calm, held positions on the board, but it was their positions as heads of differing departments, as well as the fact they were family, that had guaranteed their presence here now. His mother was again seated to his right. His cousin, an amicable sort in charge of the sales department, was at the end of the table. They were waiting for Raymond and his sister, who had each been attending to previous meetings of their own.

His sister walked in first, looking chic in a stylish business suit, her fair hair loose, her face pale. She knows, Dane thought. His sister was well aware of how he felt about playing corporate head; it wouldn't take much deduction on her part to realize he was ready to make his exodus from the company. He hoped his mother would consider giving the position to Celia instead of Raymond. It would be his recommendation, with the promise he'd visit more often if his wishes were met. It was blackmail of a sort, something his mother could understand and appreciate.

Raymond hurried in right behind Celia, straightening his tie and tucking his shirt in more firmly. His hair was mussed, his face flushed. Very unusual for Raymond, who made a great effort to always look immaculate and composed. Dane had the disquieting thought that the two of them had been together, possibly playing around rather than attending to business. What in the world his sister saw in the man, he didn't know. Dane watched Celia give Raymond an inquiring glance, saw him quickly smile and pull out her seat, then take his own beside her. Maybe they hadn't been together, he thought, seeing his sister's dark frown, but at that moment his mother cleared her throat, impatient.

Dane stood. He wanted to get this over with quickly. He'd been at the office for hours now, anxious to get back to Angel. He pictured her lying soft and warm and exhausted in her bed and his groin tightened. He should have been well sated, but he was beginning to believe no amount of time with her would be enough.

He had to tell her everything, to remove all secrets

between them. In truth, he should have done so before making love to her, but he hadn't wanted to risk being turned away. Now, he needed her help, both to find the truth behind Derek's death, and the source of the threats against her. In his gut, he knew the two were undeniably tied together, and they needed to share information in order to get to the truth.

Dane now had two agendas, avenging his brother and protecting Angel. He couldn't do either one while playing the role of his twin, with Angel or at the office.

He glanced around the table at the curious expressions of his family. "I have a few announcements to make, then you can all get back to your plans."

His mother stared ahead stonily, her mouth pinched, her eyes hard. For the first time, Dane noticed the signs of her age, the tiredness, the brittleness that suddenly seemed a part of her. He turned to his sister and saw that she was staring down at her hands.

Only Raymond seemed attentive, almost anxious, and Dane wished there was some way to exclude the bastard, to kick him out on his ear. But as Celia's fiancé and his mother's first pick, the man had a right to sit in on any and all business.

"To say I was pleased to step in for my brother would be a lie. You all know I have my own business to run and cases are piling up with me absent so much."

His mother shifted, crossing and recrossing her legs.

"I never wanted to be a part of this company, at least, not for many years now. Everything is now in order. I think it's past time I—"

A wild commotion in the outer office drew everyone's attention. Dane frowned, staring at the closed door and the raised voices coming through it. His mother came to her feet. "What in the world?"

Raymond also stood, his eyebrows lowered, his eyes flickering back and forth. "Would you like me to see what's going on?"

The uncles gave a disinterested glance over their shoulders, and everyone started murmuring at once.

The door was thrown open and Angel, looking ragged and harassed and determined, pushed her way in, despite Dane's secretary's hold on her arm. Dane felt his mouth fall open, his heart lurch. Behind Angel, Mick hovered, Grayson in his arms.

Angel ignored everyone but him, her gaze zeroing in on him, and then her face crumbled and she cried out. She'd obviously strained her leg again, given the awkward way she rushed toward him.

Dane skirted the end of the table and met her halfway, gathering her up in his arms, filled with confusion. "Angel?" He stared over her head toward Mick, who looked too grim by half.

She pushed back in his arms, her fingers clutching at his dress shirt. "They said you were dead!" She yelled the words at him, and now she seemed more angry than anything else. Her face was smudged, her hair wild, and she began to babble. "I wanted to talk to you because of the fire, but I was told you were busy and then they came right out and told me you were dead! I had to see for myself. I had to know you were all right. When I got here, they told me Mr. Carter was in a meeting and couldn't be disturbed, but don't you see, I had to have proof." Her hands went busily over his face, reassuring herself, confirming his safety.

Dane glanced around at the stunned faces watching them, aware of the mounting tension, the delicacy of the situation. Everyone was now standing, expectant.

Angel's babbling barely made sense and he hesitated to upset her further. Few people knew Derek was dead, so who the hell had told her? But first things first. "What fire?" he demanded, concentrating on the one thing that wasn't guaranteed to get him in any deeper.

Angel drew a shuddering breath. "Oh, Derek. Someone threw a mess of burning rags through my kitchen window! Everything in the apartment stinks of smoke."

His mother gasped and went two shades paler, grabbing the conference table for support. "Dane, what's going on here? Who is this person?"

The muscles in his face felt like iron. "Give me a minute, Mother."

"Oh my God! It's Angel Morris, isn't it?" Celia stepped forward, trying to get a better look at Angel. "What in the world happened to her, and why is she calling you Derek?"

Dane closed his eyes. He heard the conference room door slam and looked up to see Mick standing against it, Grayson held in his arms, his expression so hard he looked more like a man than ever.

Raymond barked out, "I'm calling security!" and reached for the phone. His movements were jerky and frantic.

"No." Dane stopped him with a word, and everyone seemed to turn to stone, frozen and shocked and confused.

"This is insane," Raymond argued. "She's upsetting the women!" And again he reached for the receiver.

Dane released Angel as she slowly backed away from him. "No, Raymond, everything is fine."

"Fine?" Raymond argued, filled with outraged indignation. "The woman is mad, coming in here calling you by your dead brother's name. For God's sake, man, your mother and sister have been through too much already."

His mother did look shaken, pale and drawn and confused, but Celia looked titillated. Her eyes were bright and wide and didn't budge from Angel's face. "You are Angel Morris, aren't you?"

Angel looked around the room at all the avid expressions and she swayed. Dane grabbed her, but she jerked back from him and her expression was so dark, so accusing, he felt it like a blow. Her bloodless lips moved twice before the words finally whispered out. "You're not Derek?"

Again Dane reached for her, firmly taking hold of her shoulders while she tried to shake him off. "Dammit, Angel, sit down before you fall down." Then he looked around the room and ordered, *"Everyone out."*

His mother started to protest and he said, *"Now."*

Grayson chose that inauspicious moment to give one short, protesting cry. Dane thought it might have been Mick's tight hold on the baby that prompted the objection.

Again, everyone froze.

Drawing on lost reserve, Dane again tried to take control of the situation. "Mick, I want you to stay. Please sit down so everyone else can leave."

Obligingly, looking as if he wouldn't have left anyway, Mick went to the leather couch and sat. He whispered nonsense words to Grayson and glared at anyone who tried to get closer to the baby.

Dane took Angel to the same couch, trying to support her weight when he saw how badly she was limping, but she sidled away from his touch as if she found him re-

pulsive. Once she was seated, Dane strode over to the
door and held it open. "All of you, wait outside. I'll
explain everything in a minute."

One of his uncles shook his head. "Can't wait to hear
it."

The other agreed. "Always did say that boy knew
how to shake things up." They left together. His cousin
gave him an uncertain, wide-eyed look and hurried out.

Raymond stopped, holding Mrs. Carter's arm. "Are
you sure you don't require security?" he asked. "I could
get them up here, just in case. Or I could stay with you,
as a precaution. You can't be too careful with crazy
people."

Dane ground his teeth together, sparing only a very
brief glance at his mother's angry, drawn face. "Out,
Raymond."

Mrs. Carter stared up at her son. "Don't trust anything that woman tells you about Derek."

"Mother…"

"I'm giving you the benefit of the doubt, son. Do
what's right, for us and yourself." With that caustic
warning, she walked out, Raymond hanging on her arm.

Celia paused in front of Dane. Her lips were trembling, her eyes wet with unshed tears. But she brazenly
tried to act in control, unwilling to contribute to the
chaos. "I hope you know I'm not budging from this
outer office until you give me a full report."

Dane nodded, appreciating her reserve.

Celia licked her lips nervously, then ventured, "I
could hold the baby while you two talk."

"No!" Angel sat forward on her seat, but Dane
ignored her, his attention on his sister.

"Thanks, sweetheart, but Mick can handle things and

the baby's already used to him." Celia looked so crushed, Dane touched her cheek and added softly, "Get Mother something to drink. She looks ready to faint. And be patient, please."

Celia nodded at him, offering up a shaky smile. "Good luck."

As he closed the door, Dane muttered, "I'm going to need more than luck now." He drew a long, calming breath before turning to Angel. His mother's warning rang in his ears. Would Derek have seen his actions as a betrayal? Had he felt justified in his treatment of Angel? Things had seemed so simple when he'd first started this. Now he felt mired in conflicting emotions. But one thing was certain, he couldn't lie to her anymore.

Angel's entire posture showed how wounded she felt, both physically and emotionally. She stared at Dane, her expression fixed, her arms crossed belligerently over her chest. As she'd been doing since Grayson's birth, she held herself together by sheer force of will.

Something inside Dane felt like it was breaking apart. Despite his mother's warning, despite his loyalty to his twin, Dane knew he couldn't ever hurt her again. And that meant he had to give her the full truth. "Derek's dead. He died months ago."

For about ten seconds she looked shocked, then she jerked to her feet. Comprehension dawned in her face and her eyes widened on him, appalled. "Oh my God."

Dane nodded slowly. "Yes, I'm the dreaded evil twin, of course." He took a measured step toward her. "I can explain everything, honey."

Her eyes went wild. "Don't you come near me. I don't want to hear anything you have to say."

"Well, you're going to hear it," he said, tightening himself against her disdain. He was well aware of how she felt about him, and the damn reputation Derek had amplified. But it still hurt as he felt her emotional withdrawal, the separation between them growing. He bit off a curse, knowing if he didn't push now, he'd lose her for good, along with the opportunity to discover what had really happened to Derek.

"Angel…"

All signs of fear were replaced by anger. Her face was flushed, her body practically vibrating with her temper, her scorn. "You miserable lying bastard."

Dane closed his eyes and tipped his head back. He heard Angel's furious whispering, heard Mick grumble a reply, and quickly faced her again. "You're not going anywhere, babe."

"The hell I'm not!" She tried to take the baby from Mick, but he resisted her efforts. She turned her cannon on Dane again. "You can't dictate to me, and I'm certainly not going to listen to any more of your lies. There is absolutely no excuse for what you've done!"

Mick glared at Dane, but spoke to Angel. "Nothing's changed. There's still someone trying to hurt you, and your apartment is still a mess. Think of Grayson. At least hear…" He looked at Dane, then shrugged in his direction. "At least hear him out. Whoever the hell he is."

Dane tightened his jaw. "Dane Carter." The formality of an introduction was ludicrous.

Angel sneered. "Derek told me all about you. You're the worst of the lot!"

"I was going to explain everything to you today, Angel. In fact, I was just telling my family that I won't work for the company—"

"I don't care what you were telling them."

"Angel." He felt hollow inside. "Honey, you have to hear me out. The only reason I came back to the company in the first place is because I think Derek was murdered."

He shouldn't have blurted it out like that, but he knew he had to make her listen. Angel wrapped her arms around her middle and sank back onto the couch, slowly rocking. "No, no, this can't be happening."

Dane knelt down in front of her. "I'm so sorry, honey. At first, when you contacted me, I was suspicious of you, thinking you had more reason than most to hate Derek, to want him dead. I thought you might have had something to do with setting him up and then when I came home, you thought you hadn't succeeded. There's been no official announcement of Derek's death and my family has done everything they could to keep the news quiet." He spoke quickly, hoping to get his explanations out while she was still listening.

She laughed, a harsh, broken sound and rocked that much harder.

"It took me only a short time of knowing you to realize how ridiculous that theory was."

"No, not at all," she said, her grin twisted and mean. Provoking. "I did despise him. Almost as much as I despise you."

"Angel," he chided. "You don't mean that. Not after last night."

He caught her right fist just inches from his face and stared at her in incredulous disbelief. "Dammit, Angel, that wouldn't have been a little ladylike tap! Are you trying to—"

A split second later, her left fist connected with his

temple, almost knocking him off balance and making his brain ring. "Goddammit!" Dane caught both her hands and pulled her to her feet, struggling to subdue her. "If you can refrain from inflicting your vicious temper on my head, I think we can get this all straightened out!"

Angel tugged her hands, obviously accepted that he had no intention of releasing her, and went still. "Let me go."

"Not on your life. We have a hell of a lot of talking to do and I think we'll accomplish it more easily if my brain is left intact." He lowered his voice to a mild scold, somewhat amused by her despite his still ringing ears. "I had no idea you were such a fury. Why don't you just settle down and behave yourself."

She growled, anger flushing her face crimson. "Behave myself? *Behave myself!* Do you mean I should try conniving and manipulating and lying!" She jerked against him again, but he held tight. "You and your brother are two of a kind."

Dane grew somber. "No, actually we're not." He let her go and paced two steps away, out of harm's reach. "Angel, this is the first I've seen my family in years. We hadn't been on the best of terms, precisely because I'm not like them. I don't approve of what Derek did to you—"

"What you did was worse," she growled, then grudgingly dropped back into her seat.

She looked defeated and he hated it. "I suppose it was, regardless of what my excuses are. But I want to make things right. That's what I've been trying to do this morning. I want to take care of you and Grayson, and don't shake your beautiful head at me! The threat to you is very real, dammit. Derek is dead, and somehow you're tied to it!"

She gave him a look of contempt. "You think I don't know how serious it is? Someone tried to run me off the road. That's the accident, you know, that started my labor and injured my leg. I almost died. Obviously whoever did that isn't very happy that I survived."

Every muscle in his body jerked at the ramification of her words. His heart pounded, his knees locked. *She could have been killed.* And he'd been thinking the threats against her weren't physical? "Goddammit, why didn't you tell me this sooner?"

Her brow lifted. "Trust goes both ways."

He let loose with a string of curses that had Mick chuckling and Angel frowning.

"At first I thought the accident was just that—an accident. I was disoriented for a long time and in a lot of pain after the wreck, not to mention I had a brand-new baby to take care of. There wasn't a lot of room in my thoughts for suspicions. But then, the phone calls started and I got spooked. Then I had to wonder."

"And finally," he said, his voice low and barely controlled, "you realized you had to have some help. That's when you came back to Derek. Not because you wanted to, but because you truly had nowhere else to turn."

She nodded. "I thought if nothing else, he might be willing to check into things for me."

They stared at each other, and Dane read her thoughts. She'd been willing to try seducing Derek to gain the help she needed, to get protection for her baby.

She had truly despised Derek, and now she felt the same about him. Angel was still very pale, but more collected. Her eyes glinted with raw determination and he knew it was only her concern for Grayson that was keeping her in the same room with him. He had his work cut out for him. "Derek was run off the road. Unlike you, luck wasn't on his side that day."

Angel closed her eyes on a sigh. "You should probably know, someone followed us here today. From the time we rushed out of the apartment until we pulled in the lot, we were followed."

Dane hesitated only a second, then stalked to his desk phone and quickly punched out a series of numbers. He waited, but then the office door opened and Alec strolled in, holding up his blinking cell phone. "No need to call me. I'm right here." Raymond tried to follow him in, but Alec slammed the door in his face.

Angel sank back against her seat with his entrance, but Mick perked up. "It's Alec!"

The dark visage merely nodded in their direction. "I got there too late to find out what was going on until they'd already left the building." His look was reproachful when he added to Dane, "You left earlier than I thought you would."

Again Angel surged to her feet. "What is he talking about, Der…Dane?"

Satisfaction settled into his bones. Finally, finally she was calling him by his rightful name. "Alec works for me, honey. I'm the one who hired Mick, not a friend. And I've had Alec watching you for several reasons. At first, because I thought you might take off before I could figure out what's going on, whether or not you could give any insight into Derek's death. But then for your safety when I couldn't be there."

Her eyes narrowed. "So you told him you were spending the night with me last night?"

Mick made a choking sound and got up to stroll to the other end of the room, pretending to keep all his attention on Grayson.

Feeling as if a trap were closing around him, Dane tried for a show of bravado. "I didn't have to tell him. Alec's good at what he does or I wouldn't have him working with me. He knew I had gone in your apartment, and he was able to figure things out quickly enough, given I didn't leave right away."

Alec nodded. "That's about it. Only I didn't figure on you rushing off so early today or I'd have been there to cover her."

"That's my fault. I made up my mind on what I wanted to do and saw no reason to wait. I should have contacted you."

Angel threw up her hands. "*Someone* should have contacted me!"

The conference room door crept open and Celia tried peeking in. Her eyes were huge and went immediately to Alec. "Why is he allowed in and I'm not?"

Dane groaned. The last thing he needed added to the mix was his sister's curiosity. Alec merely turned away and headed for the door, while Celia quickly started backing out. "Dane?" she called, but Alec kept going until they were both on the other side of the closed door. Dane could hear his sister's loud and nervous protests.

"I can always count on Alec to know what needs to be done." Dane's smile had no seeming effect on Angel. She glared at him.

"Honey, there's a lot we have to settle." He sat close to her on the couch and pretended not to notice her efforts to move away. "First off, I want you to know that last night was genuine."

"Spare me your diatribe on last night, Der—Dane. I won't believe anything you have to say about that."

Dane had to trust she'd eventually change her mind, but now wasn't a good time to push her. Instead, he concentrated on what had to be done. "Tell me about the fire."

She did, in totally detached tones that made Dane want to shake her. Didn't she care about last night? Hadn't it affected her at all? The way she was behaving now, last night might as well have not happened. The timing was unfortunate, but he'd been counting on it to soften her some when presented with his truths.

Mick filled in some of the details on the fire, apparently more concerned with it than Angel was at the moment.

Dane decided he'd make a quick trip by there to check out the apartment himself. Maybe there was a clue that the others had missed. "I'll pay for the damages and the cleaning, Mick, so that the apartment will be as good as new."

"You don't need to do that. It's my mother's building. We'll handle it."

Dane's respect for the youth doubled. "It's the least I can do, given all you've done to keep her safe." Seeing that Mick's pride would force him to argue further, he added, "Angel, you and Grayson can come to stay with me."

She snorted. "Not on your life."

Inconspicuously drawing a fortifying breath, Dane took his last shot, and prayed she wouldn't fight him too hard. He knew things were happening too fast, for him as well as her. Without hesitation, he'd gladly taken over his brother's life, his role in the company. He'd consoled himself with the fact he was trying to find his brother's killer. Even as he'd walked through his brother's office and gone through his desk and personal notes, he'd been empowered by the fact that he had a mission, a purpose. But now he was taking Derek's woman and son, too, for no other reason than he wanted them. Despite all the very real motives he had justifying his actions, he knew the truth, and it was tough to swallow.

Regret that he hadn't taken the time to make his peace with Derek squeezed his heart. Still, he had to think Derek would approve of what he was about to do. Regardless of how he'd treated Angel, Dane refused to believe he'd want Angel terrorized, or his son abandoned. Grayson deserved the family name, and the power and protection that came with it.

With renewed resolution, Dane said, "It seems like the best solution, honey."

"How do you figure that?"

"Because as soon as I can manage it, we'll be married."

CHAPTER EIGHT

ANGEL STARED AT DEREK...no, *Dane*. She had to
remember that. This man—a man she'd slept with—was
a total stranger. He'd betrayed her, used her, and as far
as she could tell, despite all his assurances to the contrary, he was no different from his family. *But everything
about him had seemed different*.

No, she didn't trust him, and she'd been right to fear
him all along.

"We could make it a Thanksgiving wedding," he said,
sounding absurdly enthusiastic. "Not very romantic, I
know, but there you have it. I really do think the sooner
the better."

Angel could only shake her head. "I'm not marrying
you."

"Have you forgotten my family, honey?"

What a joke. As if she could ever forget such a thing.
"It's not likely, not when I've suspected them most from
the start."

"Suspected them?" Dane sounded confused, his
eyebrows slowly drawing down.

"They, more than anyone, have reason to want me
gone. After all, I know firsthand just how unscrupulous
Derek could be, when they're bound and determined to
make him out a saint. If I chose to go to the papers..."

"Being snide isn't going to help anything."

"It's making me feel a damn sight better!"

"Angel, my family wouldn't try to physically harm you."

"Ha!"

He sighed. "Okay, look at it this way. It's obvious whoever tried to run you off the road, succeeded with Derek. Now surely you're not going to suggest my family could be responsible for that? The two incidents are too closely related to not be done by the same person or people."

He was right, and that made the peril even worse. When she'd thought she knew who was after her, it was bad enough. But not knowing...

"I just found out about Derek today. Before now, my reasoning seemed sound."

"Possibly. I had my own suspicions about why my mother has been so accepting of Derek's death. Normally, she'd be looking for a person to blame, and you could have been a target. But I think you may have hit the nail on the head. She knew he was unscrupulous, knew the way he'd treated you lacked any sense of professional honor. Could be she just didn't want any reporters getting wind of the story and embellishing on it."

Angel's brain felt stuffed to overflowing with problems, and she needed to get away from him so she could think. She looked toward Mick, but Dane quickly regained her attention.

"You still need my protection from the family, honey, just not in the way you thought. Look at yourself. You haven't made the best first impression on any of them, and believe me, they'll use your little show today to their advantage. They'll call you a crazy woman running in here all mussed and smelling of smoke. Just the fact of the danger involved is enough to give them an edge. They'll gladly use anything they can to cow you. My mother would love to claim you unfit, taking into consideration your financial predicament, your insecure life, compared to everything their money and influence can provide—"

"All right!" Angel stood and began pacing. It seemed her options were sorely limited, and by her own design, she'd put herself in his family's righteous path. She couldn't, wouldn't lose Grayson, not to anyone, not for any reason.

Dane slipped up behind her, not touching her, but his warmth did and her stomach gave an excited little flip. *Fool,* she thought, disgusted with herself and her feminine responses to him.

Well, she'd wondered many times why things were different now, why she would be more attracted to Derek now after the way he'd used her. She had her answer of sorts, the mere fact that it wasn't Derek, but his brother instead. Again, she shuddered with the humiliation of it. Everything Derek had told her of Dane had scared her spitless. He'd been like a dark, silent enemy, someone she'd wanted to avoid at all costs. But now, she didn't really fear him at all. On the contrary, she was madder than hell.

"As my wife, they couldn't touch you, Angel. Grayson would be safe, and you would be safe, from them and the threats."

"Why?" Angel whirled around to face him, his motivations very suspect given everything she now knew. It had seemed strange enough that Derek would be interested in her, but then she'd found out he only wanted to use her. What could possibly be driving Dane? "Why would you want to marry me, damn you?"

Dane's eyes lifted briefly to where Mick hovered in the corner. Then he leaned down until their foreheads nearly touched. He didn't look at her face, choosing instead to stare at her mouth. "Grayson is my nephew, but I care about him as if he were my own. I'd gladly kill, or die, for him. And we're good together, babe. Last night proved that." His fingers touched gently on her cheek, then dropped away. "I think we could make a go of things. It's the only logical solution."

Weary defeat dragged her down and she rubbed her forehead. He hadn't said anything about caring for her. His reasoning was so far from love as to be laughable. But then, she didn't love him either. *She didn't.* How could she possibly love a man she didn't even really know? She felt boxed in and almost desperate, as much by the circumstances as her own emotional needs. "I'd want a marriage of convenience."

Dane straightened with a short, curt laugh. "Hell no."

"Dane—"

"I love how you say that, Angel. You have no idea how damn difficult it was being called by another man's name."

He was impossible and she couldn't deal with him. She felt caught between a good cry and a hysterical laugh.

Dane took her shoulders and gently shook her. "Let me take you home. To my house. You look exhausted and we need to talk without the threat of my family bursting in any minute. You need to tell me everything this time; no more secrets. And Grayson needs to get settled down. We have a lot to take care of today."

Since she didn't know what else to do, she finally nodded. Dane let out a long breath of relief and smiled at her. "Don't look so glum. Marrying me won't be nearly the hardship you're imagining. I promise."

Her look of intense dislike was rudely ignored.

The outer door opened then and Dane's sister marched in, looking militant for all of three steps— until Alec's long arm appeared, grabbed her by the shoulder, and tugged her back out again. The door closed quietly on her outraged complaints.

Dane chuckled. "I think my sister is anxious to meet the baby."

It was almost impossible to beat down her panic. "Dane…"

"Shh. I won't let anything happen to him, honey. You're going to have to trust me on this."

Before she could tell him she had no intention of trusting him ever again, he continued. "Let me do the talking, okay? I don't want my family to know everything yet. My mother might want to start her own campaign to find Derek's killer, and that could put you at risk."

"Then what will you tell them?"

He shrugged. "As little as possible."

He went to the door and opened it. Angel could see Dane's sister standing on her tiptoes, one manicured finger poking at Alec. Angel marveled at how the woman stood up to him, as scary as he appeared, so cold and hard. But Alec seemed to ignore her, arms crossed over his chest, his black gaze pinning Raymond across the room. Dane's mother sat quietly beside Raymond, her hands clasped in her lap.

"Celia, would you like to meet your nephew?"

Halting in midcomplaint, Celia squealed, loudly, which caused Alec to wince. "Then he really is Derek's son? I wasn't wrong in that?"

She looked so anxious, so excited, Angel felt her heart twist. Dane laughed. "Yes, he really is."

Casting only a quick triumphant glare at Alec, Celia rushed in. Alec shook his head and chuckled behind her.

As Celia cooed over the baby, Mick willingly giving him up to her. Seeing her baby in Celia's arms made Angel begin to shake. This was exactly what she hadn't wanted to happen, what she had always feared the most.

There was more chaos as Dane's family started their interrogation. He gave an edited version of how they'd met and when. He managed to make it sound romantic while excluding any suggestion of suspicions, and explained about Grayson in the process. He told them of the fire and why Angel had appeared looking so harried. They waited to hear why she'd called him Derek, but Dane ignored that and Angel realized he had no intention of explaining. It seemed he didn't care what his family thought, and given his closed expression, they were just as reluctant to question him.

"How do you know the baby is Derek's?"

Silence fell as every face turned to Mrs. Carter. Feeling stiff from the roots of her hair all the way to her toes, Angel met the older woman's glare and refused to look away or give any sign of defense. Mrs. Carter could think whatever she wanted; Angel had no reason to be ashamed.

But Dane laughed. "Excellent, Mother. If you don't believe the baby is his, then I don't have to concern myself with your interference."

Raymond looked at Grayson over Celia's shoulder. "I don't remember Ms. Morris ever dating anyone else. In fact, it caused a buzz in the company that she was dating at all, especially that Derek had shown an interest. But the baby is…what? A couple months old? That's cutting it close."

Dane narrowed his eyes, and he suddenly looked near violence. "He was born six weeks early."

"Ah. Then the timing fits, doesn't it?"

Celia beamed. "Of course it does. He looks just like Derek and Dane. Mother, I don't have a single doubt."

Angel had always heard what a formidable dragon lady Mrs. Carter was, but now, she looked so vulnerable it pained even Angel. As she approached the baby, she breathed hard, her nostrils quivering as she tried, and failed, to find some measure of control. Her hand came up to touch the baby's head. "He does have a family re-semblance."

Celia smiled and rocked the baby.

Dane's tone was very gentle, but firm, and only Angel seemed to notice the way he watched his mother. "I don't mean to rush off, but we have a lot to do today and we'd better get to it."

Stepping forward, Raymond looked at each family member in turn. He wasn't a scary-looking man, like Alec, but he did appear rather cold and calculating.

"I'd be glad to help you out around here, Dane. It does seem you have your hands full at the moment, and as you'd been saying before the…ah, interruption, you have your own business to run."

Angel wanted to deny her familiarity to Dane, but the truth was, she could already read him, and what she saw in his complacent gaze was a sort of evil anticipation. He didn't smile, but she could see the satisfaction in his gaze as he faced the other man. "Thank you, Raymond, but I was going to suggest Celia take over. The board will, of course, have to approve her, but with my mother's backing—" he glanced toward his mother, who gave an imperial nod of her head, but withheld any verbal comment "—and of course my own, I don't think it should be a problem. Anyone who wants to fight it, would have to fight me. And I assure you that's not a pleasant prospect."

Angel noticed that Dane had just made his sister a very happy woman. Like her mother, she kept still, but as she kissed the baby again, Angel could see a small exuberant smile on her face.

With that apparently settled to his satisfaction, Dane glanced at his watch. "We have to get going. I need to get Angel and Grayson settled down in my house."

"In your house?"

"Yes, Mother. I've asked Angel to marry me as soon as I can arrange it, and she's agreed."

Dane's announcement started a new flurry of comments and Angel wished there was some way to remove herself and Grayson. They all deserved to fight among themselves; she just didn't want to take part in it. Mick sidled up beside her, and she had the feeling he was as disoriented by the Carter family as she.

"I can keep the baby while you go on a honeymoon."

Angel's heart skipped a beat at Celia's anxious offer, but Dane easily covered her reaction. His arm slipped around her shoulders and gently squeezed, offering her reassurance, she knew. But with him so close, she felt far from comforted.

"Thanks, but we're not going to even think about anything like that for a while. And Grayson is too young to be left. If you want to visit him, you can come to the house and sit with Angel sometime." His arm squeezed again, and he added, "Call first, though, and clear it with Angel. I know you wouldn't want to wake Grayson from a nap or interrupt his feeding."

Celia looked at Angel, and there didn't appear to be any animosity in her expression. "You'll join us for Thanksgiving? Please? I realize it's short notice, but then all of this is, and we're very anxious to get to know the baby better." Tears welled in her eyes and she snuggled Grayson closer. "He's all that's left to us of Derek, now."

Angel licked her lips, feeling cornered. Celia's sincerity smote her, made her feel petty and mean. But she was still afraid, and she refused to trust any of them. "I... Dane and I will discuss it."

Dane gave her an admiring glance for her tact. "Yes, we'll let you know, sis. It may be we'll have our wedding by then, if I can get a wedding together in two days. I really have no idea how these things are done."

"I can help."

"No thanks. Angel and I can handle it, I'm sure, once we have a chance to sit down and put our heads together."

Regaining her aplomb, Mrs. Carter said, "This is absurd! I've just discovered my grandson, but you're refusing us any rights. You can't simply cut us out this way. I won't have it."

Dane smiled at his mother. "Watch me."

"You've always been deliberately difficult, but this time I insist you be reasonable! We're talking about Derek's son, his heir, and you want to whisk him away?"

"No one is stopping you from visiting, Mother, as long as you check with Angel first."

Her face flushed darkly. It was apparent to Angel that Mrs. Carter wasn't used to asking permission for anything. "Check with her? Don't be outrageous! We have as much right as anyone to be with the child. In fact, more." Her eyes narrowed. "And frankly, I think it's unconscionable that she's dared to keep this a secret."

Dane stared at his mother, his eyes narrowed. "I'm sure you can understand her reasons."

"Dammit, he's my grandson!"

Having heard enough, Angel stepped forward, away from Dane's side. She lifted her chin and spoke firmly. "But I'm his mother."

The two women stared at each other, and Angel had the feeling they were coming to an understanding. It wasn't easy to face the older woman down, but she couldn't allow Dane to continue shielding her. Now that they knew about Grayson, they were bound to have regular contact.

Mrs. Carter looked undecided on how to react, but Celia interceded and smoothed the waters. "The important thing is that you're going to be family, Angel. I hope you'll let me know if there's anything I can do to help you get settled."

Angel didn't want to be a part of this family; the very thought appalled her. But Celia was so sincere, Angel didn't have the heart or the energy to tell her that. "Thank you."

Raymond took Mrs. Carter's arm and consoled her, as if she'd been horribly victimized. Dane rolled his eyes, then began making plans.

"Alec, could you take Mick with you to the apartment and pick up whatever Angel or Grayson might need?"

Alec nodded and Angel noticed a look passing between them. She started to question Dane, but Mick looked thrilled for the excuse to be with Alec and Angel couldn't disappoint him by countermanding Dane's order.

Then Dane handed Alec a credit card. "And stop at the store to buy whatever needs to be replaced."

Angel glared at him. It was time she stood up to Dane, too. She went on tiptoe to look him in the eye, then whispered low, "Don't press your luck."

He grinned, but quickly removed the sign of humor. "Uh, did you have a better suggestion to make?"

"No. But you've been steamrolling me and I don't like it. Stop treating me like I can't make my own decisions."

"Is that what I've been doing?" His words were soft, intimate. He totally ignored the rapt faces of his family.

"Yes, and I don't like it." She tried to sound firm, rather than affected by the tender way he watched her.

"I'll try to reform." His sincerity seemed doubtful, but then, right in front of his whole family, he kissed her. "It won't be easy though, honey. I like taking care of you."

Bemused, Angel wondered if this was part of his plan to convince his family they were marrying by choice, rather than need. Before she could completely sort her thoughts, Dane took control, settling things to his satisfaction.

WITHIN AN HOUR they were ensconced in his house, a
spacious ranch out in the middle of nowhere with a
wraparound porch and too many windows to count. It
sat about a quarter of a mile from the road and was surrounded by gently rolling hills and huge, mature trees.

Angel had shivered at the isolation of it; her life
would be irrevocably changed now, but then, that had
been true of so many recent events: meeting Derek,
being dismissed from her job, the car accident.
Grayson's birth. Because of the baby, she couldn't truly
regret her ill-fated relationship with Derek.

*And if she hadn't met Derek, she'd never have met
Dane.*

That thought shook her, and made her face her own
feelings. Lately, she'd been so busy surviving, getting
through one day at a time, she'd almost underestimated
how precious life could be. Not once had she ever considered that Derek might be gone. What if it had been
Dane? What if the murderer had finally reached her?

Life was too short to carry grudges or pass up
chances. The awful fact of Derek's death was just
starting to sink in, making her tremble all over again. If
she put her emotional hurt aside, she could understand
Dane's behavior toward her. It hadn't been unconscionable as Derek's had been, but rather motivated by
the strong need to find a killer.

Angel intended to help him in his efforts.

She glanced around the house without much interest.
It was open and airy, the colors bright and clean. It had
been professionally decorated and seemed impersonal
to Angel, not at all suited to Dane.

She fed Grayson while Dane grilled her on a dozen
questions and she did her best to answer them to his sat-

isfaction. Dane was antsy, pacing around her as he tried to find out exactly when her accident had occurred, when the phone calls had begun. Angel had contacted Derek for the last time when she was five and a half months pregnant. He'd turned her away. Shortly after that, he'd died. Two months later, her own car was run off the road, starting her labor. The timing made Dane even more agitated.

Angel put Grayson down for his nap in an empty guest room. Dane lit a fire in the family room then called Alec at her apartment. Unfortunately, though Alec was very thorough, there were no additional clues to be found there.

Angel was tired, but she had no idea what the sleeping arrangements would be. She assumed they would share a certain amount of intimacy. Dane had certainly been insistent, and with her new revelations, she wasn't averse to the idea. She wanted him; in the middle of all the crises they'd managed to find something very special. Dane made her feel things she'd never felt before, things she hadn't even known existed. She had no idea how much time they might have together so she didn't intend to waste any of it.

Which meant she needed to clear the air first. "Dane?"

He had just hung up the phone and now he lifted his head to stare at her.

"I never wished Derek any physical harm. I'm so sorry for what happened to him."

Just that quick, the distance between them was narrowed. Dane strode to her, stopping a mere inch in front of her. "I don't know if it means anything honey, but Derek regretted what happened." His gaze was searching, warm and direct. "Celia claimed he was almost sick with remorse, and that he knew you'd never forgive him. She said he seemed preoccupied by it all in the time before his death."

Angel nodded, thinking that was at least something, though she wasn't certain she believed it.

Dane laid his large warm hands on her shoulders and gently squeezed. "When I think of all the time we could have saved if either of us would have simply been honest, it sickens me." He drew a deep breath and let it out slowly. "You've been at risk all this time, and I didn't know it. If anything had happened to you—"

Angel gently laid her fingers against his mouth. He was trying his best, even willing to sacrifice himself to marriage to keep her safe. The least she could do was be totally honest with him. He was right about that.

She tipped her face up to him and had to catch her breath at the tender look in his eyes. Somehow, despite the fact he was the mirror image of Derek, her heart had always known he was different. She still didn't appreciate the underhanded way he had manipulated her, but knowing she hadn't been taken in by the same man twice was a balm to her pride.

He lifted one finger to caress her cheek, unnerving her, sending her thoughts in scattering directions. She smiled. "Dane, if you'd admitted who you were when I first contacted you, I'd have taken off."

He frowned at that possibility.

"I was so afraid of you," she explained, "of all the Carter family, but especially you." His eyes darkened to golden amber, and her stomach muscles constricted in reaction. She had to force herself back on track.

"Derek had told me so many horrible stories of how ruthless and unforgiving you could be."

He pulled her close, pressing her head to his shoulder and rocking her. She had the feeling he was comforting himself as much as her. "Derek and I had major disagreements on the family, and on the company. He felt challenged by all the games, while I was sickened by them. I suppose he didn't like it much that I walked away." He hesitated, then whispered, "And now he's gone."

Needing to reassure him, Angel pushed back and smiled up at him. "He always spoke of you with admiration, making you out to be bigger than life, and twice as frightening. I didn't trust anyone in your family, and there was only a marginal amount of trust for Derek. But deep down, despite everything, I thought he'd do the right thing for his son."

Dane pulled her close again. "So you're saying it's actually a good thing I didn't introduce myself up front?" He kissed her chin, featherlight, then her temple. "If I had, you'd have taken off and who knows what might have happened to you?"

He shuddered roughly with the thought, and then he kissed her. All her turbulent emotions of the day seemed to swell and heat into one overwhelming need. She wasn't used to the sexual demands of her body and didn't know how to temper them. All that they'd done the night before, all the ways he'd touched her and pleasured her, came swamping back. Heat pounded beneath her skin and her legs suddenly felt weak and shaky. She wanted to lie down beneath him, she wanted him inside her again, making her shudder with nearly painful

pleasure. She wanted him to help her forget—at least for
a little while.

"Let me make love to you, Angel."

The quiet plea was whispered into her ear, his warm
breath a caress on its own. She wanted him, and that
single focus drowned out everything else.

He'd asked her to marry him so he could protect
Grayson. He was noble enough to go to any lengths to
make sure the baby was taken care of. And now he
needed her, if only in a physical way.

It was such a huge risk, letting her heart get involved
when he'd made his motivations crystal clear. But she
found she had no choice. She'd used up all her energy
for the day, and for now, nothing seemed more right than
making love with Dane. "Yes."

DANE WANTED TO SHOUT like a conqueror when Angel
went soft and willing against him. God knew, after the
turmoil of the day, he needed a distraction and he
couldn't think of a nicer one than sinking himself into
her warm body.

He did nearly shout when her small hand suddenly
snaked down his chest and cupped over his fly. He
choked and got an erection at the same time.

"Angel?" Her name was a harsh groan, but he
couldn't help that. Too many emotions were slamming
into him. He'd planned on wearing her down slowly,
using the advantages he had: her love of Grayson and
her need for protection, combined with their com-
patibility in bed. Loving Grayson wouldn't be a
hardship; the baby was adorable and had owned Dane's
heart from the first moment he'd met him. And even
before he'd known Angel had no part in Derek's death,

he'd felt compelled to protect her. He'd die before he let her suffer the same fate as his brother.

No woman had ever affected him so strongly.

He didn't understand her sudden submission to his lust, not when she'd been outraged only an hour or so before, but he wasn't fool enough to question her on it. He covered her small, soft hand with his own and pressed hard, catching his breath at the exquisite feel of her holding him. He watched her bright green eyes widen, saw her lips part on a deeply indrawn breath, and he kissed her again. He wasn't gentle. He possessed her mouth with his own, giving her his tongue and groaning when she sucked on it. Her fingers curled around his erection, stroking, proving what a deft learner she could be.

His revelations of the day, the fear he felt for her, his frustration in being unable to solve the mystery of his brother's death, all clamored inside him. He needed her, her comfort. Being with her overrode everything else.

He lifted his fingers to her breast and teased. Already her nipples were peaked, thrusting against the worn material of the sweatshirt she wore. Dane moved his mouth down to her throat, over the sensitive, ultra-soft skin beneath her chin, then to her ear. When he took a breath, he noticed the smoke smell still clinging to her and wanted to pull her into himself, to make her a part of him and forever keep her safe. She and Mick had claimed the fire to be a mere threat, without the intent of burning her out, but he wasn't so sure and the idea that someone could have gotten to her so easily filled him with an ice-cold rage. He *would* protect her.

Ruthlessly, hoping to banish the disturbing thoughts,

he backstepped her up to the brick wall beside the fire-place and pinned her there with his hips. His hands jerked up her sweatshirt and he covered both plump, tender breasts with his rough palms. "You're mine now, Angel."

She moved against him, inciting him, encouraging him, and he reacted to her on a primitive level. He jerked back, lowered his head and carefully closed his teeth over one erect nipple. Angel cried out. He knew her breasts were sensitive; he'd found that out last night, taking extra care with her then. But now, he wanted to dominate her, to make her beg, to make her admit that she needed him, and not just for convenience and the safety he afforded. It was disquieting to feel such depth of emotion with this one particular woman. He hadn't wanted to ever again care so much, not like this. But now he had to admit, especially to himself, that what he felt for Angel had no comparison. It was crazy, given the short amount of time he'd known her, but he couldn't fight it—didn't even want to try. He wouldn't feel guilty about it, either. Derek had thrown away his chance to have her. Dane felt guilty for a lot of things, but not for this.

"Dane," she cried, digging her fingers into his back, and he relished the small pain for bringing him a measure of control.

"Say my name again," he told her as he began unfastening her jeans.

"I want you, Dane."

"Now, Angel, right here."

Her eyes widened, but he tugged her jeans down to her knees and turned her. "Brace your hands on the wall."

"Dane?" Eyes wide with confusion, she looked at him over her shoulder.

"Do it, honey." Not waiting for her to comply, he took her wrists in his hands and flattened her palms on the wall, wide on either side of her head. "Now don't move."

He could hear her frantic breaths, her small whimpers, a mixture of excitement and uncertain anxiety. Grimly he smiled as he released himself from his slacks. He was rock hard and throbbing and more than ready to explode. When his arms came around her to ply her breasts, his fingertips plucking at her nipples, his erection just naturally nestled in the cleft of her rounded bottom. Angel gasped, pressing her head back, and at the same time, pushing her hips more closely to him.

He moved his pelvis, stroking her, teasing. He felt blind with lust, but also determined to accomplish his goals. "I want to get married tomorrow, no later than Wednesday."

"Yes."

A startled squeak escaped her when his arms squeezed her tight, but his relief was a living thing and there was no way to get close enough. He hated rushing her into marriage after everything else she'd been through. She deserved a proper courtship, with moonlight dates and flowers and gentle promises, all the things she hadn't had, all the things women wanted. But he had to do what he thought was best for both of them, and right now, tying her to him was his first priority.

Slowly, making himself as crazy as she, he dragged his palm down her ribs to her belly, and when she held her breath he bit her shoulder, a soft, wet love bite—then cupped her fully, taking her by surprise, loving the sound of her startled pleasure as she jerked and moaned.

His fingers gently pressed and found her ready for him, her feminine flesh swollen, the soft petals slick and hot. His middle finger glided over her, barely touching until her hips began moving in a counterpoint. He kept the pressure light and easy, teasing. She tried to hurry him, to encourage him to give her what she now needed, what she desperately wanted, but he resisted. Once, she started to drop her hands but he quickly repositioned her as he wanted her, vulnerable to him, submissive. Judging by the sounds of her panting breaths and raw moans, she loved it as much as he did.

"Dane, please..."

Just as he'd plucked at her nipples, he used his fingertips now to torment her again, but this flesh was so much more sensitive, the feelings so acute, she cried out and almost jerked away from him. His free arm locked around her, holding her in place for his sensual torment.

"You're mine, Angel. Mine." His words were harsh, commanding, breathed against her temple as he thrust against her, his fingers unrelenting.

To his satisfaction and deep pleasure, she came.

Her arms stiffened, her head dropped forward and her body jerked and bucked as her hips pressed hard against him. Dane groaned with her, encouraging her, continuing the gentle abrasion of her most sensitive flesh. As she quieted, he praised her, telling her how crazy she made him, how special she was. He had no idea if she heard him, and she gave no reply other than her gratified groans.

He'd never before resented the use of protection, but

now, as he fumbled in a rush to get the condom in place, he cursed the use of them.

Angel was barely staying upright, her body now slumped fully against the wall, her arms no longer stiff and straight. Her cheek pressed to the warm brick and he feared the abrasion against her soft skin, so he pulled her away and lowered her to the carpet, entering her at the same time.

Her tight jeans restricted his movements, but it didn't matter. He simply needed to be inside her, like he needed his next breath and the occasional sunshine and a few hours' sleep. *He needed her.*

Riding her hard, pushing errant thoughts of the danger from his brain, he concentrated on the pleasure. Angel didn't join him again, but chose to watch him instead, her eyes soft in the firelight, her body pliant to his urgent thrusts. One hand lifted and she smoothed his shoulder, smiling gently.

Knowing she watched his every move, that she witnessed every emotion to pass over his face, knowing she could see his explosive pleasure as he came, made it all that much more powerful. He didn't disappoint her, and let himself go completely. He ground his teeth together to keep from shouting and strained against her, knowing she had just taken his heart. His body went rigid and he took his own orgasm with a low, endless growl of blinding pleasure.

He loved Angel Morris, he thought as he slumped against her. He loved her more than he'd ever thought to love anyone or anything. He loved her enough to give his life for her, to do anything to keep her bound to him.

Well damn, he thought, the effort almost painful to

his muddled brain. That sure shot a hole in his altruistic plans of merely offering protection. It was also enough to scare ten years off his life.

CHAPTER NINE

"WELL, THAT DIDN'T go quite as I had planned it."

The words, so softly spoken, drifted around Dane, but it took considerable effort on his part to lift his head. He felt not only physically appeased, but emotionally full, and he didn't want to move, not yet, maybe not ever. He didn't want to lose the feeling, the closeness, and he didn't want reality, with all the present problems, to intrude. But he finally managed to struggle up onto his elbows.

Angel, tender and warm and womanly beneath him, looked at him with gentle, shining eyes, a tiny satisfied smile on her mouth.

God, he loved her. The profound acknowledgment shook him. He'd been careless with her, and just as he'd lost his brother, he could have lost her, too.

He tenderly tucked a pale curl behind her ear. "What didn't go as you planned? Did I disappoint you, sweetheart?" He asked the outrageous question to give his brain a chance for mental recovery. Looking at her now, with the realization of how easily she could crush him, was going to take some getting used to. He wasn't accustomed to feeling fear, but what he felt for Angel scared him down deep in his bones, clear to his masculine core. It also made him feel near to bursting and kept his male flesh, still buried tight inside her, semihard. Nothing would ever be enough with her.

Feeling the way he did, realizing just how special she was, made him doubt what he knew about Derek. His brother couldn't have used Angel as vindictively as everyone thought. No man could possibly spend time with her and not appreciate how special, how unique she was.

Her smooth brow puckered as she frowned at him. He had to laugh, and luckily that lightened the moment for him, at least to the point he could talk coherently without fear of professing undying love. Angel had been badly misused by his family, and he hadn't done much better by her, though that would quickly change. He fully intended to rush her headlong into marriage. Burdening her now with his excess of emotion before she'd had a chance to get used to the rest would be grossly unfair.

And besides all that, he was suddenly a horrible coward. He simply didn't want to lay his heart on the line, not when the odds were she'd disdain his love. She wanted him on a physical level, there was no denying that, not with the heated scent of their lovemaking still thick in the air. And they had the mutual love of Grayson, a binding responsibility for them both. He'd have to build on those things, and hope it would suffice.

Touching his fingertips over one tightly drawn eyebrow, he grinned. "How can you look so embarrassed after what we just did? Your pants are around your knees, I can feel your nipples hard against my chest, and you're still holding me inside you." He leaned down and brushed his mouth over hers. "So tight, Angel, like you never want to let me go."

"Dane." Unconsciously, she lifted her hips into his and he groaned.

"What didn't go as you planned?"

She looked shyly away, charming him anew. That she could be so wild one minute, and yet timid the next, kept his lust on a keen edge, and sharpened the emotional needs he felt to tie her to him, to keep her safe.

"I wanted this time to be different."

He laughed again. She never ceased to surprise him. "More different than making love against a brick wall with your—"

"Dane, hush!" She pressed her hand against his mouth and he kissed her palm, silently laughing.

"I'm sorry," he said, the words muffled until she drew her hand away. "You're too easy to tease."

"This time, I wanted to do stuff…to you. It doesn't seem fair the way you always give so much and I just take."

Those overwhelming emotions washed over him again in a wave of heat, stealing his thoughts and turning his body iron hard. He crushed her against him, burying his face against her throat. He was reminded of the near-fire at her apartment by her smoky scent, and the fact that someone was trying to hurt her, and had likely killed his brother. The events that had brought them together were never far from his mind. Because those same events could tear them apart.

Gently pulling away from her, he sat up. Angel started to do the same, looking at him uncertainly, but he stopped her by lifting one of her feet to his lap and removing her shoe. "You need a shower and some sleep. And Alec and Mick should be here soon." He caught her pants and stripped them the rest of the way off.

"I don't need sleep. I need to see the rest of your house."

"And you will." *Later, after she was rested up.* She may be doing a good job of holding herself together, but he was still running on adrenaline, and a compelling need to ensure her safety. Their lovemaking had only served to blunt the edges of his urgency a bit.

Once he had her naked from the waist down he caught her under the arms and lifted her with him as he stood. He pulled the sweatshirt free, surveyed her naked body with a deep satisfaction, then cupped her face in his hands. "You listen to me, Angel Morris." His thumb coasted over her bottom lip and she nodded.

"We have plenty of time to play sexually. The rest of our lives in fact because I intend to keep you. For better or worse, for richer or poorer. Eventually, we'll both get to do some exploring. But don't ever think you've disappointed me. For one thing, it's not possible, not when you go so wild when we're together. Not when I know that wildness is only for me. That's more of a gift than most women ever give, and most men ever deserve. We're being forced into this marriage, but the perks, to my way of thinking, are damn enticing."

His gaze traveled from her mouth to her breasts, then down, lingering on the damp curls over her mound. His tone dropped, rough with renewed arousal. "As far as I'm concerned, I don't have a single complaint. As your husband, I'll have you on hand day and night, and the way I see it, that's a hell of a bargain. All right?"

She nodded, but her eyes had gone dark and soft again and he knew what he'd said had turned her on, that his words of explanation had put visual images in her mind. Seeing her reaction put them in his mind as well.

He hadn't been this horny or insatiable since high school, and he had to wonder just how much of it was based on a desperate need to reaffirm what they had, before it was taken away. "Come on. While you're showering I'll keep an eye on Grayson and get us something to eat." He eyed her pale naked body as he led her into the hall bathroom, unable to keep his hands from patting her rounded behind, smoothing over her waist and belly. He drew a deep breath and chastened himself to behave. "I'll also find you a robe to wear until your other stuff gets here."

"It feels strange, Dane. Being naked with a man, not being the only one to keep an ear trained for Grayson." She drew a breath, watching him closely. "Not having to be so afraid."

He hoped that meant she felt a measure of trust for him. "I'm not going to let anything happen to you, babe. You can rest a little easier now."

She turned to face him as he pulled two thick towels out of the cabinet and set them close to hand.

"It feels strangest of all to be in your house. That's going to really take some getting used to."

"It's our house," he said firmly, wanting her to feel comfortable, determined to get her fully enmeshed in his life, so much so she wouldn't be able to help but love him back. "When I took over Derek's office, my mother wanted me to move into his house as well. But I drew the line at that. The memories there are too sharp, too suffocating. I feel enough like an interloper as it is, usurping his office, his files…his woman."

Angel shook her head. "I was never that, not really. Derek and I had a brief fling, but it ended long before he got possessive. I'm not sure if he intended to use me all along, or if he just jumped on the opportunity when it presented itself. But almost from the first, I felt more for you than I ever did for him." She looked around, then smiled. "I'm glad this is your house, not his."

He, too, looked around. "I paid to have it decorated because I was clueless and didn't have the time to worry about it anyway, not traveling as often as I did. It's a home base of sorts, but it's always felt kind of…cold to me. So if you get in the mood and want to change things, go right ahead. Just don't ever let anyone in unless I'm here with you."

"I'm not an idiot."

He nodded agreement. "Far from it. But right now, I'm not willing to trust a single soul with your safety. The house is secure, but only if you use the security system correctly. There's an intercom for the front and back door. Don't take any chances, okay?"

She gave a grave nod. He didn't want to frighten her again, but they both knew just how much danger she was in. Hopefully living with him would keep her out of harm's way while he continued his investigation of Derek's death. He would probably bring the police into it shortly, once he'd had a chance to go over things with Alec.

The future stretched out before him, and for the first time that he could remember in too many years to count, he saw more than an endless, empty void. He wanted a future with Angel, with Grayson.

And he wouldn't let anything stand in his way. Not even a murderer.

MOTHER NATURE conspired against them.

Looking out the kitchen window, Angel sipped her

coffee and then sighed. Finally the sun was shining again, though she knew the weather wouldn't clear for a while. Record-breaking lows were predicted for the rest of the week.

She also knew Dane was frustrated, that if it had been up to him, they would have been married already. But the most horrendous snowfall of the season, a good twelve inches, had all but canceled Thanksgiving and confined everyone indoors, making a wedding impossible. It had also stalled his investigation, putting personal queries on hold.

Dane had improvised Thanksgiving, forgetting the plan to meet with his family—to Angel's relief and Celia's disappointment. For lack of a turkey, he made a superb pork roast and surprised Angel with his culinary talents.

It had felt right somehow to spend an evening in the kitchen with Dane, bumping hips and sharing chores, working together. Grayson sat in his pumpkin seat watching them, and the setting would have been picture perfect if it hadn't been for the fact that someone evil was still out there, still a threat, keeping them both edgy despite their efforts to the contrary.

The weather provided the ideal excuse for them to linger in bed, forcing away the dark cloud of menace with an overload of sensuality. Just a few hours ago Dane had awakened her from a sound sleep with warm hands and a warmer mouth, gently encouraging her higher and higher until she'd had to muffle her shouts with a pillow. It amazed her that every time with him seemed better, more intense. She wasn't certain how much more she could take, but was anxious to find out.

He'd left her limp and exhausted in the bed. He had

kissed the tip of her nose, told her he'd be home in a few hours, and then lovingly cupped a breast before turning away and hurrying out. Dane often hurried away from her, as if he were afraid if he lingered, he wouldn't go at all.

Angel had never felt so pampered, or so loved. Only he'd never said anything about love.

It worried her, how easily she had adjusted to being with Dane. He was the perfect father to Grayson, the perfect companion to her, even if he was overly autocratic on occasion.

She understood his worry because she shared it. No matter how many times they went over it, they couldn't come up with a single reason for someone to kill Derek and try to kill her. The idea of never knowing, of always having to be on guard, made her angry.

She had just come up from the basement with a large load of laundry when the phone rang. Expecting it to be Celia, who'd made a habit of calling daily, she balanced the laundry basket on one hip and used her shoulder to hold the phone to her ear. "Hello."

There was no reply, and within a heartbeat the fine hairs on the back of her neck stood up and gooseflesh rose on her arms. *No.* She forced a calm tone and said again, this time more firmly, "Hello?" but still received no answer and she quickly hung up the phone.

Frozen, she stood there, trying to convince herself that it was an accident, a coincidence. Not once since she'd moved in with Dane had there been a threatening call. There was no reason to think this was one of them. She drew a deep breath and tried to convince herself she was right.

At that moment Dane came in. Snowflakes glistened

in his hair and his mellow golden eyes were warm with welcome.

When he saw her just standing there, he hurried to take the basket from her. "Angel, are you all right? Have you hurt your leg again?"

She swallowed hard and automatically repeated the words that had become a litany. The man was too over-protective by half. "Quit pampering me, Dane. It's getting annoying."

"I have a cleaning woman for this—"

"Who hired on to do your laundry, not mine and Grayson's. Besides, I'm perfectly capable of taking care of myself. I don't want a stranger muddling through my things. And," she added when she could see he was con-triving more arguments, "the maid hasn't been able to come here in this weather. Grayson has laundry that needs to be done every day."

"Oh." He looked distracted for just a moment, then suddenly drew her into his arms and swung her in a wide circle. "All right, I'll let that go for now, but only because I have a few surprises for you and I don't think you'll be properly appreciative if you're angry."

"You've found out something?" she asked, her entire body tensing in hope.

Dane lightly kissed the bridge of her nose in apology. "No, I'm sorry, babe. There's nothing yet, but we're working on it. I contacted a few personal friends in the police department and they're doing some checking for me, looking things over again. Something will turn up soon, I promise."

Angel bit her lip as disappointment swelled inside her. She didn't think she could take much more waiting. And she knew it was even harder on Dane. He felt compelled to avenge his brother, and to protect her and Grayson. He'd taken on a lot for her sake, and she worried constantly about him. If he got hurt because of her...

"Hey, no long faces now, honey." He kissed her again, this time more lingering. "I want to see you smiling, not frowning."

She considered telling him about the phone call, but at the moment, his expression so expectant and happy... There would be plenty of time to talk about that later—if it was even important, which she was starting to doubt. The last phone call she'd received had been verbal, and this one had been silent. Likely there was no connection at all, just a wrong number.

"Where did you rush off to this morning?" she asked, shaking off her eerie mood.

Backstepping to a kitchen chair, he sat and pulled her into his lap. His heavy coat was damp in places and he struggled out of it, then laid it on the table next to the laundry basket. One rough fingertip touched her cheek. "My sister is dying to get back out here and see Grayson. And you. She's overflowing with questions and curiosity."

Celia called at least once a day, and she was always cordial and inquisitive, but cautiously so, as if she were taking pains not to be pushy. Angel couldn't help but like her. The rest of his family had been ominously silent.

"How would you feel about having her and Raymond to dinner? The roads are much better today, and with no more snow predicted, by Tuesday they should be fine."

Angel wondered at his reasons for the sudden invitation, but said only, "She's your sister, Dane. If you want to have her over, that's fine." She hesitated, then added, "Maybe you should invite your mother, too. It might help to smooth things over with her."

"Not yet." He said it easily, but Angel was aware of his sudden strain.

"Dane, what ever happened between the two of you? I know Derek told me once that you just didn't see eye to eye, but—"

His laugh, a sound bordering on sarcasm, interrupted her. "A difference of opinion, huh? Well, Derek was right about that. But it's past history honey, and I don't want to bore you."

"Shouldn't I know what's going on, since the past probably plays a part in the tension now? What if your mother says something? I don't like to be kept in the dark."

"It doesn't concern you."

And that, she thought, was the crux of the problem. She wanted everything about him to concern her. "I'm sorry." She tried to get off his lap, but he made a rough sound at her movement and hugged her close.

"Dammit, I didn't mean that quite the way it sounded." He gave her a frustrated look, then shrugged. "All right, you want me to bare my soul, I suppose I can live through it."

He was in such a strange mood, teasing one minute, then solemn, then teasing again. "I don't mean to push you."

"Ha! All right, I'm sorry." He tightened his hold on her. "Don't rush off."

Angel gave him an impatient look.

"All right, dammit, but as soon as I finish this stupid tale of woe, we're moving on to your surprise, okay?"

After a brief hesitation, he said, "I was engaged to be married once." His hands looped around her and he looked off to the side, staring at nothing in particular, merely avoiding her gaze.

"Mother didn't approve, of course, but then I'd already started bucking her on almost everything. Derek went to the college of *her* choice, I went to a state college. Looking back, I realize how infantile I acted, opposing her just for the sake of opposition, but she was so damn controlling about everything, it just naturally rubbed me the wrong way."

Angel couldn't begin to imagine anyone attempting to control Dane. The very idea was ludicrous.

"Both Derek and I had gotten our business degree in the same year my father died. He and Mother had always planned for us to take over, but not that soon. His heart attack took everyone by surprise. Mother, never one to grieve for long, wanted us to jump into the company together. I wanted to get my MBA. Derek was born to run a corporation, was anxious to get started, but I resisted her. I was glad to let Derek handle things, and despite all her carping and complaining, I went back to school."

A heavy silence fell and Angel felt him shift slightly, as if he were uncomfortable.

"I met a woman while I was in school, and I wanted to get married. Since that didn't meet with Mother's plans, she did everything she could, including disowning me so I couldn't touch my inheritance money, as a way to discourage me. But the more she did, the more determined I became. When I told her I fully intended to go through with the wedding, she...she bought Anna off."

Angel had no idea what to say to that. She waited, hoping he'd elaborate. And finally he did.

"I don't like to think it was the money that enticed Anna. She wasn't from the same background as me, and my mother intimidated the hell out of her. She spelled out this grandiose life Anna would be expected to live up to and it spooked her. When Mother offered her the money, she took it and walked away."

What a fool, Angel thought. She knew Dane had money, but he didn't flaunt it. His house was very nice, but it wasn't ostentatious. Everything about him was casual and comfortable and understated. Anna must not have known him at all to believe such idiocy. Or maybe it just hadn't mattered to her. "I'm sorry."

Dane shook his head impatiently. "The worst part was, she was pregnant with my baby."

Angel stiffened, seized by a mingling of jealousy and confusion. Where was the child now?

As if he'd read her thoughts, Dane gave her a squeeze. "By the time I'd caught up with Anna, she told me she'd lost the baby."

He looked so troubled, Angel curled down against his chest and hugged herself close to him. She'd never before seen Dane like this, and she didn't like it. Derek's death had filled him with calculating determination, with a purpose. His mother's disdain had only seemed to amuse him. But now he sounded hurt deep inside. She preferred his arrogance any day. And at that moment she'd have given a lot to ease his pain.

His large hand settled against the back of her head and he idly tangled his fingers in her hair. "I've never admitted this to anyone, but to this day, I'm not sure Anna didn't have an abortion. I blamed my mother because it was a hell of a lot easier to blame her than to accept that I might have been wrong about Anna, that I might have made a colossal mistake marrying a woman who didn't care enough about me to believe in me. She told me, rather tearfully in fact, that she'd been afraid and taking my mother's bribe seemed her only choice."

Angel could feel his pounding heartbeat, a little faster now, and she slipped her hand inside his shirt, smoothing her fingers over his warm, hair-rough skin. Dane went still even as his breathing changed, grew a little rougher and quicker. Angel pulled his shirt from his pants and pushed it upward, kissing his chest, his small tight nipples. Dane groaned and quickly yanked the shirt over his head.

Whispering against his chest, Angel said, "She could have come to you, and that's what bothers you most?"

Dane tilted his head back against the chair. "She didn't trust me."

"I trust you. I've been trusting you with not only my life, but Grayson's." He started to speak and she straightened, cupping his jaw with her palms, holding his head still as she attacked his mouth. Dane groaned again and Angel used that as her cue. With their lips still touching she breathed, "I'm not like her, Dane. Your mother can't send me away. Only you could do that now."

Rather than answer, he kissed her again, and there was hunger in the way he held her, the way his mouth moved heavily over hers. He might not love her, but he needed her, and from that, love could grow.

He pulled himself away from her with a harsh sound of impatience. "Damn woman, you distract me."

"I'm glad."

Laughing, he avoided her mouth as she tried to capture his again. "Your surprise, remember?"

"We could do that later?"

"Insatiable wench. Stop that!" He caught her hands and pulled them away from his belt. When she pretended to pout, he grinned. "Show just a modicum of patience, okay? Now, first off, Mick got your apartment rented, so you can stop worrying about that."

That wasn't at all what she'd been expecting. Dane had insisted, against her and Mick's protests, on keeping up the rent until Mick found a new tenant. Angel knew Mick and his mother needed the money, and she'd felt bad leaving as she had, without notice, but Dane wouldn't hear of her paying the rent herself, and Mick hadn't wanted either of them to pay. He was such a proud young man.

"Who is it?" Angel still worried about Mick. She talked with him often, but she missed their daily school lessons together. As soon as the weather permitted, she intended to start them back up again. Dane was all for the idea.

"You'd never guess so I might as well tell you." He took a moment to build the suspense, but when she gave an impatient growl, he grinned and said, "Alec."

At her look of surprise, he nodded. "Yep, I showed him the apartment myself. It's not too far from the office, and Mick is a fantastic manager, especially for a kid."

"And you wanted Alec there to keep an eye on him, to make certain he was okay?"

"Not at all. I knew you would worry, and I figured this would put your mind at ease for the most part. But

Alec really was looking for a new place, and he likes it there."

Angel smiled at him. "It's a wonderful surprise. Thank you."

"That's only part of the surprise. Now don't get angry before you hear me out, okay?"

Like a red flag waved before her face, his words had the effect of putting her instantly on guard. She stiffened. "What have you done?"

"We've agreed that it's best to get married, and that means I want to do what I can to ensure you and Grayson are taken care of. I know how you feel about money, but it's silly. Thanks to my inheritance—"

"I thought your mother took that!"

He shrugged. "She gave it back, sort of another bribe to bring me back into the fold. It's been sitting in a bank gathering interest because I had no use for it until now."

"I don't want you going against your principles for me, Dane Carter!"

He laughed. "It wasn't a principle. It was plain stubbornness and the fact that I like to prick my mother's temper whenever possible. But since we'll be married Tuesday morning—"

"Whoa!" Angel held out her hands, astounded by having so much information thrown at her at one time. She needed a few minutes to assimilate it all. "What do you mean we're getting married Tuesday morning? Since when was this decided?"

He had the grace to look sheepish. "Ah… Actually just today. That was another part of your surprise. I talked with my doctor and the lab will do the blood tests tomorrow. As soon as we do that, we'll head downtown and pick up the license. A pastor from my sister's church has agreed to do the deed on Tuesday."

There was a brief struggle as Angel tried to remove herself from his lap and he was just as determined to keep her in place.

Dane won.

"You agreed to marry me, honey." He held her securely, his eyes never leaving hers. There was a look of challenge on his face, and something else, something not so easily defined. "We've made the deal, you and I. Grayson needs me, and I'm not about to turn my back on him, not now, not ever. If you're thinking about changing your mind, it's too late."

Realization hit, knocking the breath from her. He wanted things confirmed, he wanted a guarantee, and he was afraid to leave it up to her because he thought she might back out. Knowing he felt such an obligation for Grayson, and that he was afraid of losing the baby, was a revelation. But she couldn't merely condone his autocratic behavior. He'd become a tyrant in no time if she let him.

She scowled darkly, and grumbled, "Next time, check with me first before you set things up."

His eyes widened and the arrogance was immediately back in his gaze, along with a healthy dose of relief. "There won't be a next time, honey. I told you, regardless of why we're getting married, it's still forever."

As he said it, he leaned forward, then kissed her long and slow and deep. When he pulled away, he whispered, "I suppose I should get the rest of it over with."

"There's more?"

"I'm afraid so." He drew a deep breath, then blurted, "I paid off your and Grayson's medical bills."

She should have expected it. But with all that had happened the last few days, her accumulated bills had been the last thing on her mind. In a way, it was almost a relief to be rid of that particular burden, except that she didn't want their relationship to be about what material things he could give her. She wanted more than that.

When she only narrowed her eyes at him, he continued, evidently encouraged by her silence. "I also opened an account in your name. You can add your own money to it if you like, but there's a hefty sum already deposited. Only your name is on the account, so you can do whatever you want with it. Understand, Angel, this isn't for household stuff. If you want to redecorate the house—which by the way, I was thinking Grayson's room could really use some color…"

"Dane."

"Come on, honey, don't get all prickly on me." He ran a hand over his head and his frustration was almost palpable, forcing her to hide a grin. "As far as I'm concerned, what I have is already yours, only you're being too pigheaded about it to let me take care of you."

"Pigheaded? Gee, you smooth-tongued dog, you. You sure do know how to win a gal over."

"Dammit, Angel, I am not my damn brother! You don't have to worry about any hidden motivations on my part."

"And I'm not Anna," she said, just as firmly. "I won't be bought off. You're trying to make sure I have money so if or when your mother offers it, I won't be tempted."

He looked away, his entire body drawn tight, his

shoulders rigid, which to Angel was as good as an admission of guilt. When he turned to face her again his eyes were diamond hard and probing. "Would you be tempted?"

"No!" Trying to calm herself, and at the same time, sort through the words that needed to be said, she took a deep breath, and then another. It didn't help. "Dane, we need to talk. There's something I really need to tell you."

He stiffened, as if bracing himself. "I'm listening," he said, but his expression remained fierce.

Grayson chose that unfavorable moment to give his patented, *I'm awake and I expect some attention* yell, effectively diverting them both. Angel gave Dane one long last look before hurrying out of the kitchen. She heard his soft curse behind her.

It was almost a relief to get sidetracked. She loved him, and he deserved to know that. But he already had so much on his mind, it might be easier for him to not be burdened with her love. He wasn't marrying her for that reason, so he might not even welcome her affections.

She needed to give it more thought before she made any grand declarations. After the threats were resolved would have been ideal, but with him pushing for marriage so soon, that was no longer an option.

She changed Grayson's diaper as the baby cooed at her, impatiently waiting to be fed, then pulled up the rocking chair in his room. She had just settled the baby against her breast when Dane spoke.

"He's such a little glutton."

Dane stood propped in the doorway, more handsome and appealing than any man had a right to be, especially now, with that boyish look of wonder on his face as he watched the baby greedily suckle. He'd put his shirt back on and had it all buttoned up, the sleeves rolled to his elbows.

At her silence, he walked the rest of the way into the room and knelt on the floor beside her chair. "I feel so much guilt, Angel, when I think about what Derek will miss."

Angel silently watched him as he smoothed one finger over Grayson's cheek. "Aside from the way he treated you, which I really don't understand, he was a good man, and he was a damn good brother. He never gave up on me, never sided with the family against me. Most of the time when we were growing up, we were inseparable, best friends as well as brothers. I loved him a lot, but I can't help but be damn glad that I'm the one here with you and Grayson now."

"Oh, Dane." Angel felt tears gather in her throat. She could just imagine the hell he was putting himself through, and there was no way for her to help him.

He squeezed his eyes shut, his jaw tight. "I have to find out what happened to him. It's the very least I owe him, for having my life when his is gone, for taking over where he left off."

"Derek chose his own paths, Dane. You can't blame yourself."

He looked away, his face grim. "If I'd have come back instead of being so stubborn, I might have been able to help him. He might still be alive."

And we wouldn't have found each other. Angel shivered with the thought, then felt her own measure of gripping guilt.

The baby, recognizing Dane's voice, released Angel's

nipple to turn his head. He stared at Dane, his blue eyes alert. Dane smiled, though his expression was still sad. "I love him, you know."

Angel nodded, a lump of emotion gathering in her throat.

Dane came to his feet and dug into his pocket. "I bought you this today. At least this time you can grant me the traditional rights of the groom to spend my money." He handed her a small black box, then gave his attention back to Grayson. The baby stared at him a moment longer before going back to his feeding. Some things were simply more important than others.

Awkwardly, Angel managed to open the small box. Her hands shook and it was difficult maneuvering with the baby in her lap. Inside the box, nestled in cream velvet, was the most beautiful diamond engagement ring she'd ever seen. It was large, but not *too* large, an oval diamond surrounded by rubies. Breathlessly, she whispered, "It's incredible."

"Then you like it?"

"Dane…" She reached for him with her free arm and somehow he managed to embrace them both, making Grayson squirm in protest.

"Why don't you finish what you were going to tell me before I have to go out again."

Surprised, she asked, "Where are you going now?"

Dane took the ring from her and slipped it on her finger. He seemed pleased by the snug fit. "I'm going to close out your post office box. It's too far from here to do you any good and besides—" his gaze met hers in a challenge "—with the threats against you, I want anything and everything that concerns you to come by me now, at least until things are resolved."

Angel curled her fist tight around the ring. "That's fine. I haven't used that box in ages anyway, not since I left Aeric. Take the key from my key ring. It's hanging by the phone in the kitchen."

Dane couldn't quite hide his satisfaction. She saw no reason to fight him on this, not when she didn't use the post office box anyway. "Now what were you going to tell me?"

She needed more time, she thought. Tonight, over dinner, without interruptions or the distractions of wedding dates or suffocating guilt, she'd tell him she loved him. But not now, not when they both felt confused and he was ready to head back out the door.

"Angel?"

"I don't want Grayson to be an only child."

Dane blinked at her, his gaze sharpening. "What did you say?"

Heat rushed into her cheeks, but at least she was giving him a truth. "I never had any brothers or sisters and it was awful. I…I know we'll be married for practical reasons, but I want another child. I thought you deserved to know that before we marry. Just so you're… prepared."

Dane searched her face in silence for several moments, looking more shocked than dismayed. Slowly, a smile broke over his face. He looked at Grayson and chuckled as the baby made grunting, squeaking noises while he nursed. "Nothing would make me happier, honey. As long as we wait a while so you're not overburdened. I want your leg to heal completely and I don't want Grayson to be cheated out of being a baby. Just as you had no siblings, I had one that got half of all my parents' attention. I'm not complaining, but I think there must be a happy medium. And keep in mind, you run the risk of having twins with me. Three in diapers would be a bit much for even the most determined parent."

He hadn't refuted their reasons for marrying, but she wasn't discouraged. The practical reasons did exist, but there was also the love she felt. And tonight, she'd tell him so.

CHAPTER TEN

DANE STOOD BENEATH the post office overhang while the freezing wind whistled around him, blowing open his coat, pelting his face with a dusting of snowflakes caught in the frigid gusts. Nothing could penetrate the heat of his rage.

With deliberate movements he uncurled his fist and stared again at the name on the large manila envelope. His brother had sent Angel one final message.

The overwhelming urge to tear the envelope open was difficult to resist, but Dane knew in his heart he had to bring the letter to Angel. Not only was it a violation of her privacy to look inside, but she might take it as a measure of distrust as well. It could be a love letter—or it could be the information, the missing link to the threats, that they'd been looking for.

He didn't want her hurt.

He didn't want anything his brother might have put in the letter to cause Angel more heartache. And he didn't want to suffer the sweltering jealousy he now felt that was enough to ward off even the worst winter had to offer. *Damn it.* He didn't want his brother eulogized in Angel's heart with a final farewell.

Conflicting feelings of grief, guilt and possessiveness jumbled his thoughts.

The postmaster had watched with a jaundiced eye as Dane tossed out the majority of the mail unceremoniously stuffed into the large mailbox. Dane had only briefly glimpsed the numerous sale ads and magazines and offers before Derek's letter caught his notice. Now, with stiff steps and an anxious stride, he headed for his car. He couldn't understand his own urgency; he just knew he wanted to be with Angel and Grayson. He needed to know they were okay.

It took him all of five minutes to realize he was being followed. Using his cell phone, he impatiently dialed Alec's number.

"Sharpe."

"I'm being trailed," Dane said, no other explanations needed.

"I'm on it."

Over the past few days Dane had been aware of being followed. He couldn't get close enough to figure out who it was, so he'd alerted Alec to watch his back. Dane had told Angel he didn't want her out in the cold, but in truth, he wasn't willing to take the risk that whoever it was might be able to get to her. He preferred keeping her at home, safely behind locked doors and away from any threats.

This morning, he'd specifically opened the account in her name so she'd be protected financially if something happened to him. She'd accused him of not trusting her, but that was no longer true. He simply wasn't willing to leave her future to chance. Though he'd told her the sum in the account was hefty, he knew she couldn't begin to guess the amount. And he wanted it that way. Angel had a prideful tendency to fight him on every little thing he tried to give her. When she saw the bank records, she'd hit the roof. He smiled in anticipation. In some perverse way, he enjoyed arguing with her as much as he enjoyed loving her. Things would never be sedate between them, that was a certainty.

Alec shouldn't be very far behind, and now with Dane's signal, he'd close the gap and they would trap the driver between them.

"Dammit!" Dane muttered the curse into the open phone line as he saw the car swerve away.

"That him taking the entrance ramp to the highway?"

Dane watched his suspect speed away and knew, whoever the man was, he'd been on to them. "Yeah, that was him. How did he figure us?"

There was a shrug in Alec's tone. "Maybe he didn't. Maybe he was going that way all along."

"Nope. He was following me, I know it."

"Want me to go after him?"

Dane considered it, then shook his head to himself. "No, there's no point. I'm heading home to Angel and staying there. Though I doubt it'll do us any good, run a quick check on the plates, just in case we can get lucky for a change." Dane didn't for a minute doubt Alec had the plates memorized. Not much ever got by him.

"I'll get right back to you."

Less than three minutes later, Alec had his news. Both he and Dane had cultivated contacts in every facet of the police force. The information they received, and how they received it, wasn't always on the up and up. But it was generally beneficial to all, so the cops tended to work with them. "The license plate shows a newly rented car."

"Dammit." Dane thumped his fist against the steering

wheel, his frustration level high. "That means the name it's registered under is likely false."

"Yeah, 'fraid so. You want me to go check into the rental agency where the car came from?"

"There's no point. Whoever it is, he's covering his ass. I doubt he'll make any mistakes this late into the game." With an irritated sigh, Dane suggested, "You might as well take the rest of the day off. I'll let you know if anything comes up."

"All right. I do have a few personal things to take care of."

The line went dead before Dane could question that cryptic comment. It was the first time in the history of their acquaintance that Alec had ever alluded to a personal life. Though Dane was certain he must have one, he'd never mentioned it before.

It only took Dane another fifteen minutes before he pulled into the garage. As per his instructions, Angel kept the alarm on, and all the doors and windows locked. It was a hell of a way to live, constantly being on guard, but maybe with the help of Derek's letter they would be able to put the past, and the threats, to rest.

After turning off the car he used his remote to close the garage door. As he came in through the kitchen by the door that attached to the garage, he heard Angel laughing. Following the sound, the manila envelope still clutched in his hand, he found her sprawled on the family room carpet before the fireplace. Grayson was held over her head, and each time the baby gurgled, she laughed and lowered him for a tickling nip of his pudgy belly.

Without intruding, Dane watched their antics, a small smile on his face. Damn, but he loved her. The feeling was starting to settle in, not so scary now, more like a necessary part of him was finally working as it should. He pictured Angel with a baby girl, as well, his daughter, a child that would look like her mother, have her bright green eyes. He'd missed being a part of her pregnancy with Grayson, but this time, he'd be here. *I'm sorry, Derek. But she'll be my wife.*

"When did you come in?"

Dane hadn't even realized she'd turned to him, he'd been so caught up in the comforting images of baby and home and hearth, images he'd long ago given up on. "Just a minute ago." He strode over and sat cross-legged beside the two of them, reaching out to take Grayson into his own lap.

"What do you have there?"

Angel looked at the envelope, her expression inquiring. "It's for you, honey." He let her know by his tone the seriousness of the envelope. "Derek evidently sent it to you. It's postmarked some time ago, from before his death. Haven't you checked your box at all?"

Angel stared at the envelope like it was poison. "There was no reason. I only used it for the information my supervisor wanted me to work on at home. Files he wanted me to prepare before he made a presentation. He didn't trust very many people, or the regular mail. He figured a locked post office box was the most secure way to go. No one knew the number except the two of us."

"And Derek."

She nodded. "I usually kept those files locked up. But I was…anxious to see Derek one day, so I just stuck them in a desk drawer when he called to say he was coming over. I never considered that he might go through my personal things. He must have taken the box number off the envelope."

Dane hated hearing about her and Derek together. He didn't regret loving Angel, he couldn't, but he sometimes felt as if he'd stolen everything good from Derek. Forging his place in the family had never mattered to him, but it had been everything to Derek. Now Dane had taken Derek's place in the family, and in the office.

He'd gladly give up both those dubious perks, but he'd never give up Angel or Grayson.

He knew the night Derek stole the information from Angel was the same night he'd taken her to bed. For that reason, more than any other, Dane had hesitated to discuss it with her. The thought of Derek with her, how he'd hurt her, was almost too difficult to contemplate.

"I was asleep when Derek went through my desk," she said, her tone flat. "We were never…intimate after that, and a month later, he dropped me."

Several silent moments passed, then Dane tried to hand her the envelope. "Go ahead and open it."

With a shudder, Angel pulled back. "No thanks. I'd rather you did it."

"Are you sure?" Even as he asked it, Dane was laying Grayson aside on the blanket. The baby turned his head and directed an intent gaze at the bright flames in the fireplace. Dane slid a finger under the flap of the envelope and pulled it open.

There were several printouts inside, and Dane scanned them quickly. "These are details outlining industrial espionage at Aeric." His blood surged with the ramifications. He lifted one paper after another, finally coming to a personal note addressed to Angel.

"What?" Angel scooted around to peer over Dane's

shoulder. She picked up the discarded printouts and studied them.

Dane laid the last paper aside and stared at Angel. When she felt his gaze, she looked up.

"I'm sorry, honey."

"What is it, Dane?"

He touched her cheek. "Derek was trying to protect you." Dane lifted the sheaf of papers, holding them out to her. "He sent you these as an explanation of why he'd gone to so much trouble to alienate you, why he specifically did it so publicly. He wanted everyone to think your relationship was over, that you meant nothing to him. He suspected some level of danger after he'd discovered several discrepancies in various Aeric research files, shortly after stealing that information from you. He wasn't certain what was happening, but when he investigated further, small accidents started to happen to him. He was afraid you'd be in danger too, by association." Dane touched her cheek, then forced the words out despite the tightness in his throat. "Derek had no problem doing what needed to be done for the takeover, he saw that only as good business, part of the corporate game. But he hadn't deliberately planned to hurt you in the bargain. He cared for you, honey."

Angel squeezed her eyes shut and swallowed hard, clutching at Dane's hand. Dane knew, without asking, the regret she felt because he felt it, too.

The sound of a gun cocking seemed obscenely loud in the silence of the room. Both Angel and Dane jerked up their gazes, and there stood Raymond. The forty-five in his hand made an incongruous sight with his three-piece suit and immaculate presence. "Well, I commend your investigative skills, Dane. Of course, your damn brother pretty much spelled it out for you, didn't he? I knew he was too thorough not to have something written down. And Ms. Morris was the likely person to have the info."

Dane quickly tried to cover his shock, to act calm and in control. He was very aware of Angel sitting frozen beside him. "So that's the reason you've been harassing her?"

Raymond shrugged. "I lost her for a while there, you know, after she moved. It was tedious finding her phone number again, but I had no idea where she'd gone. Unlike you, I don't have connections in these matters. It was rather frustrating, never knowing when she might resurface, if she'd try to discredit me with that damn information your brother put together.

"I tried to hedge my bets a bit by telling your mother, regretfully of course, what a bitch Angel was, how she'd used Derek, how she was likely to come sniffing around with blackmail in mind. I had half hoped she'd find Angel for me, but your mother is getting old and has no taste for revenge. She only hoped to avoid a scandal. Luckily for me, you're not nearly so derelict in your familial duty." Raymond grinned. "You led me right to her."

"Bastard." Dane came smoothly to his feet and deliberately stepped in front of Angel and Grayson, shielding them both with his body. "You killed Derek."

"Now that," he said with a shrug, "was an honest accident. I knew he'd been playing detective—funny that the two of you were even more alike than you knew. But he proved to be rather proficient at it. I tried a few minor scare tactics, and for a while there I thought they'd worked. But the bastard was just biding his time, letting months go by, waiting for me to make another move. He was careful not to call in the authorities, not wanting to scare me off." Raymond held up two fingers, a millimeter apart. "He came that close to nailing my name to his damn discoveries after I thought the coast was clear again."

"My brother was no idiot. And he would have taken any theft from a company he owned as a personal insult."

Raymond laughed. "He was a wily bastard, I'll give him that."

It almost sounded as though Raymond had respected Derek, had maybe liked him. Dane felt sick with disgust.

"Needless to say I had to up the pressure to get him to back off, but the fool didn't drive quite as well as Ms. Morris."

Dane had to fight the urge to lunge at Raymond. Only the fact that doing so would put Angel in more danger kept him still, but he didn't like it. Every muscle in his body twitched with the almost unbearable need to do physical harm. "How did you get in here?"

"I beat you home. Yes, that was me following you. Of course, as soon as I realized you had sicked your watchdog on me, I veered off. Mr. Sharpe really is a nasty-looking fellow. He gives me the creeps."

"Alec's good at what he does."

"It doesn't matter now, does it?" Raymond smiled his perfect artificial smile. "As I was saying. It was easy enough to swing around and with a heavy foot on the gas pedal, I was able to get here before you. I hid in the bushes. Not very dignified, but then, you gave me little choice. When you started to close the garage door, I slipped a small wedge underneath it, and rather than closing tight, it reopened on its own. I waited just long enough to see if you'd double-check it. But you were in too big a hurry to see your ladylove. Such a hurry in fact, that I believe the two of you will elope." He grinned, his expression taunting.

Dane tried to calm his racing heart and his anger. He needed a cool head to deal with Raymond. He only wished he'd trusted in his instincts earlier and not given Raymond the benefit of the doubt. He should have beat the details out of him when he had the chance.

Determined to keep Raymond talking, he asked, "Was that you in the bar with Derek the night he died?"

Raymond looked briefly surprised. "You are good. And yes, that was me. I offered to take Derek out slumming, just because he'd become so maudlin with all his investigations and his regret over Ms. Morris. That's how I knew it wasn't over between the two of them. Women threw themselves at your brother, and he turned them all down."

Angel made a small sound of distress, but Dane ignored her. He didn't want Raymond's attention to waver to her.

"I had hoped he'd confide in me, but he was keeping his secrets to himself that night, no matter how much booze I poured down him."

Dane suppressed a growl. "Alec was the one who discovered Derek had been to a bar that night. He also dislikes you on instinct. If I disappear, he'll be all over you."

Raymond looked briefly alarmed by the prospect, then he visually shored up his confidence again. "Once I'm married to Celia, he won't dare touch me."

Dane narrowed his gaze, trying to figure ahead. "My sister isn't an idiot. She'll never marry you."

Raymond laughed. "She's anxious to be married." His gaze flicked to Angel and quickly back again. "And your mother, now that you've defected to the enemy camp, is anxious to turn the company over into my capable hands. In fact, I believe your mother would give me control whether Celia married me or not. But I've decided I want Celia. It seems like nice insurance if anyone should ever discover you didn't elope."

"I'll kill you."

Raymond merely laughed at the threat. "Not that your mother will question it, will she, Dane? After all, this won't be the first time you've walked away from your family without a backward glance—both times over a woman. You know, your mother has been trying valiantly to keep her mouth shut, to avoid just such a situation, hoping to make amends. Ah, you didn't know that did you? But I've become something of a confidant for her, and she's told me all about how she regrets the past. Too bad you won't have a chance to forgive her, to put her poor old mind to rest. She'll have to spend the rest of her days with regrets."

Angel staggered to her feet beside Dane and when he would have pushed her behind him again, she forced her way forward. "You've set yourself up a small problem, Raymond."

"What's that?" he asked with a touch of amusement. Obviously he believed he had everything well in control.

"I'd already suspected you. And I told people. The police have it on record that I thought someone was trying to kill me."

"They didn't believe you though, did they?" Raymond's smile was smug. "You didn't have enough proof. And I was careful, even with the smoke-fire, to keep the threats from being too serious, gaining too much attention." He laughed at Angel's comprehension. "Yes, that was a nice touch, wasn't it? Running you out of your apartment and then intercepting your phone call at the office. You reacted just as I planned, showing up at the company like a wild woman, demanding answers. I had hoped once you knew the truth, that Dane was only using you, you'd have enough pride to walk away from him. That would have made you more vulnerable. But no, you decide to marry the bastard."

He looked briefly beyond anger, almost enraged. Dane braced himself, but Raymond shook off his anger, his smirk once again in place. "I have everything planned. And unfortunately for you, both Celia and Mrs. Carter will back up the theory that you ran off together. Thanks to the information I sold at Aeric, and your sister's cut in the family coffers, I should be able to live rather comfortably from here on out."

Dane took a small step forward. "You're an idiot, Raymond. Will anyone believe I abandoned my company? Think about it. I walked away from my family, but I never shirked my own responsibilities."

Raymond shrugged again, totally unconcerned. "So now you're in love. Who's to say what you'd do?"

Grayson made a cooing sound and for the briefest moment drew Raymond's attention. Dane started to move, but the gun was quickly leveled at his head. "Ah, ah. I really don't want the mess of it here in the family room."

Angel shifted beside him and Dane grabbed her arm.

"You're not going to hurt my baby," she said, her voice low and fierce as she pulled away from Dane.

"I really hesitate to. After all, I'm not a monster. And the child seems to have softened Mrs. Carter quite a bit. But I see no way around it."

Angel stiffened. When she spoke, her tone was so mean even Dane blinked. "You can't kill us both at the same time," she taunted. "Try it, and one of us will be on you before you can take a second aim." She slipped farther away from Dane, spreading out, making it more difficult for Raymond to maintain control.

Pushed past his composure by her goading, Raymond lifted his arm, taking point-blank aim. His eyes narrowed and his mouth drew tight. Dane felt Angel tensing beside him and realized in horror what she intended. She would attack Raymond, giving Dane the upper hand. The little idiot would sacrifice herself. Panicked, Dane prepared to beat her to it, ready to leap on Raymond full force. He could only hope Angel would use the moment to grab the baby and run.

In the next instant, a shrill screech filled the air, loud and outraged. Dane instinctively leaped toward Angel, pushing her behind him as he stiffened for the additional threat. But they weren't in danger.

Raymond, wide-eyed and frantic, tried to turn. He wasn't fast enough.

Celia lunged around the corner from the kitchen to the family room, still screaming and viciously swinging a heavy crowbar. Raymond ducked, but the length of iron connected with his elbow with satisfying force. There was a sickening crunch as bone gave way, and the gun fell to the carpet. Raymond screamed in agony, his arm hanging at a grotesque angle by his side.

"You miserable worm!" Celia yelled, the perfect epitome of a woman scorned. She hit Raymond again as he tried to roll away, this time thumping the bar against his thigh and eliciting more screams. Dane had no doubt the man's arm was broken, and he couldn't be all too sure of his leg. Celia would have delivered a final blow to his head, ignoring Dane's curses as he reached for the gun, but Alec came storming in and grabbed her from behind. She struggled, and Alec had a time of it subduing her, but finally she calmed.

Alec still held on, his arms circling her, making soft hushing noises in her ear until the crow bar fell to the carpet by their feet. Celia turned in his arms, weeping.

Dane looked at Angel. He was breathing hard, the adrenaline still rushing. "Are you okay?"

She had Grayson squeezed tight in her arms, gently rocking him, kissing him. Tears rolled down her pale cheeks. The baby and Raymond seemed to be vying for the loudest cries, Raymond out of pain, Grayson out of upset. Angel's watery gaze met Dane's and she nodded. He could see her body shake as she drew in jerky, uneven breaths. "Yes. We're fine."

Dane pulled her close and tried to comfort her as best he could, but he himself was shaking with residual fear. Never in his life had anything ever terrorized him like knowing Angel could be shot and even killed. He kissed her full on her trembling lips, verifying her safety, her vitality and warmth. Then he turned to his friend, Angel still tucked safely to his side. He didn't know if he'd ever let her go again.

"Damn, but I'm glad to see you, Alec." It didn't matter that his voice shook, that his eyes felt glazed and moist. All that mattered was the feel of Angel beside him, safe and sound.

Alec smoothed his big hands up and down Celia's back. "I followed her. I don't know how she knew what was going on, but I could tell she was upset."

Celia pushed back from him. "You followed me?"

Alec looked down at her, pushed her head back to his shoulder, and said, "Yeah."

Dane grinned. In the midst of all the chaos, he found Alec's actions incredibly humorous. "Well, I'll be."

"I already called the cops," Alec said, ignoring Dane's laughter. "They should be here any minute. Dammit, will you shut up?" he said to Raymond, while maintaining his tight hold on Celia. "You're lucky I didn't let her kill you."

Again Celia pushed back. "Why didn't you? He deserves it."

"It would have complicated things, especially for you."

"Oh."

Angel stepped away from Dane, then cautiously around Raymond, who was obediently silent. When she reached Celia, she touched the woman's shoulder. "Thank you. You saved our lives."

Celia sniffed and pulled away from Alec's masculine embrace while still standing very close to him. She wiped away her tears and then frowned at Alec, as if some of the drama was his fault. With an obvious effort she returned her attention to Angel. "I caught Raymond making a phone call today, but he hung up real quick when I came in."

Angel gave a quick peek at Dane and he frowned. Had she gotten a call and not told him? "Angel?"

She shrugged, but he could tell the careless effort cost her. "He didn't say anything, Dane, so I thought it was just a wrong number. I was going to tell you, but we got…distracted."

Dane would have had more to say about that, but Celia sniffed again. "Several times now Raymond's not been in his office when he should be. He was acting funny the last few days. I thought he was cheating on me. I knew he was up to something, but I thought it was just another woman, not…not this!" She indicated the entire mess with a wave of her hand.

Alec grunted. "Why the hell would he be after another woman?"

"How should I know?" she snapped. "He was sneaking around, showing up late. But then I had his letter of recommendation from Derek checked and found out it was forged."

Alec looked livid. "So you just decided to follow him and could have gotten yourself killed as well!" He bent down so he could stand nose to nose with Celia. "What the hell did you ever see in him in the first place?"

Angel grinned at Dane while the other two continued to argue. Dane shook his head and pulled Angel close again. He was almost afraid to stop touching her, reassuring himself she was truly okay. "If this isn't the most bizarre thing that's ever happened, I don't know what is."

As Dane spoke to her, Angel turned her gaze on Raymond. He wouldn't be walking any time soon. Angel shivered, and that made Dane furious all over again.

"I'd like to kill him with my bare hands."

Angel touched his mouth. "Shh. Don't say that,

Dane. It's been awful, and you've lost so much, but I want it to end now. For all our sakes."

Grayson gave a last shuddering sob and snuggled close.

Dane pressed his lips to the baby's forehead. "Me, too. God, I was afraid for you and Grayson."

Angel sighed. "Oh, Dane. I feel awful. Your brother wasn't the villain after all. He was trying to protect me."

He smoothed her hair back from her face. "That'll be a comfort to my mother, I think."

"Your mother!" Angel blinked up at him. "Raymond said she was sorry, that she wasn't ignoring us because she was mad, just being careful not to say anything that might drive you away again. You need to talk to her, Dane. When I think of her suffering…"

Police sirens sounded in the distance. "I'll settle things with my mother, honey, just as soon as we get things taken care of here. And then," he added, cupping her face and holding her close, "you and I are going to talk. I have a few things to say to you, Angel Morris, and no matter how angry you get, you're going to listen."

ANGEL WATCHED DANE pace around the bedroom as Grayson began to doze in his strong arms. Dane wore only his slacks, and those were undone. His bare feet left impressions in the thick carpet and the flexed muscles of his forearms left an impression on her.

Love swelled, making her warm and shivery at the same time.

It had been a long day, filled with police interviews and questions and confrontations. Grayson had a difficult time settling down, too many strangers invading his small world at one time. But he charmed the detectives who'd run the investigation, as well as Dane's mother once she showed up. Angel smiled again. She was actually beginning to like Mrs. Carter. How could she not when the woman obviously adored her son and grandson as much as Angel did? Oh, she tried to hide it, but tonight her defenses had cracked just a bit, and Angel had seen the woman beneath the iron.

"Do you think it's okay to put him in his crib now?" Dane whispered, not halting in his even strides around the room. Grayson nestled close against the warmth of Dane's broad, naked chest, one small fist clutching his chest hair.

Angel smiled and laid her brush aside. She was freshly showered and in her nightgown, exhausted, but at the same time elated. Everything was over, all the fear and bad feelings and hurt put to rest. Her confession had been on the tip of her tongue when Grayson had begun fussing. "Do you want me to take him?"

"No, I can do it." Dane gave her a long, sizzling look. "Why don't you get under the covers? I'll be right back."

Her heartbeat picked up its pace and she slid into bed. When Dane returned, he removed his slacks, laid them over the back of a chair, then faced her with his hands on his naked hips.

Angel smiled. "If you ran a board meeting like that, you'd be sure to have everyone's attention."

He looked chagrined for just a moment, then dropped his arms and started toward her. "Right now, I only want your attention."

Angel eyed his naked body. "You have it."

"*Angel…*" He growled her name as he climbed into bed beside her.

"Your mother is a proud woman, Dane. It hurt me to see her so upset."

He stilled his hands, which had been in the process of removing her nightgown. "I know what you mean. It nearly broke my heart to hear her admit to so much guilt. She said it was so hard losing Derek, and the only solace she could find was that maybe I'd finally forgiven her."

Angel stroked his head, knowing what his mother's confession had done to him. "I'm proud of you for how you handled it."

"I wish I'd known how she felt long ago. Maybe it wouldn't have gone on for so long."

"You're both too proud for your own good. But your mother is making the attempt to accept me."

"Ha!" Dane pulled down the right strap of her nightgown and cuddled her bare breast in his rough palm. "My mother adores you. She hides it well, but that's just how she is. I think she sees you as a link, a way to soften our reassociation even though I told her all was forgiven. And there were tears in her eyes when she finally got to hold Grayson." He kissed the slope of her breast, his mouth warm and gentle. "That's the first I've ever seen her cry. You know, she's going to spoil him rotten."

"Thank you for refusing her and Celia's offer to keep Grayson. I'm not ready to be separated from him yet. Not after being afraid for him for so long."

"Me, either. Maybe when I'm old and gray I'll be ready to let him out of my sight. But for now, they can visit him here, and we'll make a point of visiting them often."

They were both silent for a moment, Dane busy in his minute study of Angel's skin, caressing her, kissing her, Angel trying to formulate the words she knew she needed to say.

"My sister is holding up well."

Diverted, Angel asked, "Did you get a chance to talk alone with her?"

"Yeah. I don't think she ever would have gone through with the marriage to Raymond. She was as suspicious of him as I was." Angel felt him tighten and knew he was reliving the horror of the afternoon. He pulled her close and buried his face in her breasts. "You could have been hurt. I don't think I've ever been so frightened in my life."

Angel kissed his temple. "Thank God for your sister."

"Alec wants her." He lifted his head and there was another grin on his face. "Damn, but I can't get over it. Alec and Celia. Somehow it just doesn't fit."

"You know, Celia does have some say about it. Right now, she told me she's in no hurry to get involved with any man again. Raymond really hurt her."

"Mostly her pride. But she's tough. She'll get over it."

"And Alec wasn't speaking to her when he left."

Dane shrugged. "He's always quiet. It's just his way."

She wasn't convinced. "Don't get your hopes up, Dane. I can tell you'd like to see the two of them together, but all things considered, a romance between them would be difficult."

"That's what I thought about us. But look how much I love you."

Angel would have fallen off the bed if Dane hadn't been sprawled on top of her, anchoring her in place. "What did you say?"

"Don't look so shocked." He tugged the other strap

of her nightgown down, baring her to the waist. "I know I deceived you from the start, that I was pretty ruthless at times to get what I wanted."

"When were you ruthless?" Angel felt both numb and cautiously elated. She couldn't quite believe what he was saying.

"I convinced you we needed to marry because you needed protection. But I could protect you without marriage. I lied to get you where I wanted you."

"You did?" Angel shook her head, trying to clear it. "I mean, you said you wanted to marry me so Grayson would have a solid home."

"I have enough money to insure Grayson would be happy and well cared for without marrying you. That just seemed a convenient way to trap you."

Her heart rapped against her ribs, threatening to break something. "I don't feel trapped."

His eyes darkened, turned warm and probing. "Good, because I still want you to marry me, but with no more secrets between us. I love you."

Angel licked her suddenly dry lips. "You know, you beat me to the punch. I was going to tell you the same thing tonight."

Very slowly, a slight, pleased smile tilted his mouth and Dane leaned down and kissed her. "Is that right?"

"Yes." Her breathing accelerated with the touch of his warm breath. "I knew ages ago that I loved you."

"You didn't know me ages ago, honey. Hell, our entire courtship has taken only a heartbeat."

"Well," Angel said, wrapping her arms around him and hugging him tight, "it was long enough to make me irrevocably and madly in love with you."

Dane grinned as he began tugging up the hem of her

nightgown, groaning at the feel of her soft naked belly against his abdomen. "It's a damn good thing, because I have no intention of letting you go."

"Your mother did mention to me what an intelligent businessman you are."

His hand slid over her ribs, then lower, his fingers probing, and he closed his eyes when he found her warm and ready. "I know a good deal when I find it. You, Angel Morris—soon to be Carter—are a very good find."

EPILOGUE

"MICK, MICK!" Grayson came barreling around the corner of the house, chubby arms pumping the air, and threw himself around Mick's long legs. Mick was always greeted with the same amount of verve when he came over after school. He was one of Grayson's favorite people, a surrogate big brother.

Mick swung the seventeen-month-old toddler up into his arms. "Hey, buddy."

"Mick, Mick!"

Angel came in on the heels of her son and dropped onto the couch. "Thank God you're here. He's been screeching your name all day. I can't tell you how glad I am that school's almost over."

Mick, devastatingly gorgeous at eighteen, topping a few inches over six feet, grinned his killer grin at Angel while he tossed Grayson into the air, encouraging the screeches of berserk joy. "You look exhausted, Angel. Is this little monkey wearing you out?"

With a serene smile, Angel said, "I think it's his little brother or sister that's actually doing the trick."

Dazed by her news, Mick tucked Grayson under one leanly muscled arm and staggered into a chair. "You're pregnant?"

She smiled happily, pleased with his reaction. Now

to get Dane's reaction. She heard the front door opening and leaned toward Mick. "I was hoping to have a few minutes alone with Dane, if you—"

"I'll take short-breeches here out to the swing."

"Mick, Mick!"

But as Dane stepped into the house and called out, "I'm home," Grayson launched himself from Mick's arms. Angel gasped, but Mick, quick on the draw, managed to juggle the toddler until he could get both feet on solid ground. And like a shot, Grayson was off again.

"Daddy! Daddy!"

Mick laughed. "To think, he used to be such a peaceful baby."

Dane entered with Grayson perched on his shoulders. He went directly to Angel, who dutifully lifted her face for a kiss. "My mother said you had something to tell me."

Angel glared. "She promised!"

"Promised what?"

Mick lifted Grayson from Dane's shoulders. "The squirt and I are going out to the swing."

"Wait a minute, Mick. I have something for you." Dane reached into his pocket and pulled out an envelope.

"What is it?"

As usual, Mick was still hesitant at the sign of a gift. But Dane, who delighted in trying to spoil Mick as much as he did Angel, only laughed. "I know the academic scholarship you got doesn't pay for everything, so this will help pick up some of the tab."

Mick merely frowned until Dane gave an exaggerated sigh of impatience and opened the envelope. He waved the paper under Mick's nose. "It's from the company. We have our own set of tax deductible donations, and this year, my mother decided to expand into scholarships. The two combined ought to take care of most of your schooling expenses. And let me warn you, if you even think of refusing it, you'll have to deal with Mother. Since Celia left the company and Mother's taken over again, she's more autocratic than ever. I believe she actually missed it. And she's taken to singing your praises, so don't even think to fight her on this."

Mick looked ready to faint and with a numb expression, took the paper from Dane and read it. Silently, Angel retrieved her son, who promptly planted a sloppy kiss on her cheek, then laid his head on her shoulder. With everyone else he was a dynamo of constant motion. With Angel, he loved to cuddle.

Very slowly, a grin settled over Mick's face. Then with a loud whoop, he jumped up and slapped the ceiling. Angel felt like crying every time he acted like the young man he was, rather than the old man he'd been forced to be. Since his mother's death, he spent more time than ever with her and Dane, and they were as close as a family could be.

After a gentle hug to Angel, and a bruising bear hug to Dane, Mick swung Grayson up and headed out the door.

"He's something else, isn't he?"

Angel smiled at Dane. "You've been a good influence on him."

He grunted. "If only I could say the same for my sister."

"Oh no, what did she do now?" About six months ago Celia had decided she'd had enough of the corporate world, and following in Dane's footsteps, she was determined to become a P.I. Dane was horrified, but didn't know how to stop her. In an effort to keep an eye on her, he gave her a job at his office, which rankled Alec no end. Just as Angel had predicted, nothing had come of a romance between them, and instead, their constant bickering kept Dane on the brink of insanity.

Dane gave Angel a telling look. "She almost got shot, that's what she did. She was supposed to *locate* that little chump who jumped bail, not try to bring him in. I don't remember the last time I've seen Alec that mad."

"Why was Alec mad?"

"Because he *did* get shot." Dane quickly grabbed her when she paled. "Now, Angel, he's all right, just a flesh wound. The bullet grazed his thigh. But he's been raising high hell for the past two hours, and Celia, that witch, has steered clear, which means I've had to listen to it all."

It was too much, and Angel fell into a fit of giggles. She'd been so worried about Celia, who'd become reclusive after her emotional hurt with Raymond. But now Celia was determined to experience everything life had to offer, and there was no one who could stop her, not even Alec. And heaven knew, he tried hard enough. Grown men might walk a wide path around him, but Celia continually tried to go through him.

"I'm glad you think it's so funny. Between Mother constantly working to reel me back into the company, and Celia's antics, I'm ready to go hide under my covers." He grinned at Angel. "Want to come with me?"

"Maybe. But first I need to talk to you."

Dane groaned. "Tell me this won't be bad news, babe. I can't take any more bad news."

Angel drew a deep breath. "I told your mother I'd need a leave of absence in about six months." Angel had agreed to fill in for vacationing secretaries, which she thought would be a week's worth of work a month, and instead it was turning out to be more like three weeks' every month. Something always seemed to come up so that she was required. Luckily her mother-in-law didn't mind when she did most of that work at home, so she could be with Grayson. On the days she had to be in the office, Dane adjusted his schedule. Or sometimes Mick, or Celia, or even Alec…

"Is my mother wearing on your nerves? I thought the two of you were getting along pretty good?"

"It's not that. Dane, do you remember when we first talked of getting married?"

He sat down and pulled her onto his lap. "If you're thinking of backing out now, it's too late. You signed the marriage certificate ages ago."

Angel playfully punched his shoulder. "I'm pregnant."

He froze for a heartbeat, then a gorgeous smile spread over his face. "Pregnant?"

She nodded. "Almost two months now. I waited to go to the doctor so I could be sure."

His large hand opened over her abdomen, and as usual, she quickened in response. "It's not twins?" he asked, looking at her body.

"The doctor doesn't think so, so you can relax."

He did, then he grinned some more. His hand on her belly turned caressing and he kissed her throat. "This time will be different, babe. I'll take care of you."

"Dane, I don't regret anything about my pregnancy with Grayson. If things hadn't happened as they did, I might never have had Grayson, and I might never have met you."

"Angel." He kissed her, his hand still resting where his baby grew. "I love you, sweetheart."

Angel spoke past a wobbly, heart-filled smile. "The only thing missing the first time around was you."

Dane kissed her again. "And this time you have me."

"Yes. This time I have everything."

WANTON

CHAPTER ONE

CELIA BIT HER LIP. She felt naked in the tight, flesh-toned dress, too made-up with the cosmetics that had spent more time in her drawer lately than on her face. She was very aware of her bare thighs, of her exposed arms and cleavage. Though the air-conditioning hummed, she felt warm with embarrassment.

Heads turned appropriately as she sauntered through the dim interior and took a direct path to the bar. She didn't want to look too closely, but she was sure Mr. Jacobs, the slime, was here. She had his description and knew this was his prime picking ground. This was where he chose the women. Hopefully, he'd choose her as well.

Slowly sliding onto a bar stool, she worked to gain his attention. Her heart pattered rapidly. Though she couldn't deny the underlying fear she felt, she also relished the excitement, the anticipation…the end satisfaction. It had been laughably easy to leave her old *proper* life behind, though her relatives were still having a hard time accepting it. They expected her to show up at the company office any day, dressed in a business suit, hair neatly tucked away in a functional, professional style, begging for her old job back. Ha.

It didn't matter that no one thought she could do this.

All she had to do was prove to herself that she was
capable, that she wasn't too pristine or squeamish to see
the job through. That she could make a difference in
some other woman's life. She'd do that tonight.

It was a nice enough bar, she thought, smiling at
the bartender as he took her order. They made idle
small talk, and she slipped in the fact that she was a
woman alone, new to town, without relatives or friends
in the area. He lingered, subtly, politely, asking her
more questions. How long would she be in town, did
she have a job. He cautioned her to be careful, and she
almost laughed. He worked with Jacobs, she was sure
of it.

Sipping at the drink she didn't really want, she
watched him walk away. Cool air from a ceiling fan
brushed her bare thigh where her dress had parted at
the side slit. Ever since they'd locked her fiancé away
for crimes too horrific to think about, she'd done all
she could to forget her carnal appetites, to deny an
overly sensual nature. Yet here she was, prepared to do
her damnedest to get a man's attention by using her
body.

Surreptitiously, she glanced down the length of the
bar to the small round table located there, situated in the
far shadows. The man occupying the table, blond and
very good-looking, perfectly matched the description
she had been given. It was easy to recognize Jacobs; he
had the same classic, refined, golden-boy appearance as
her ex-fiancé, a look she now recognized as slick and
phoney.

It took all her control to keep from reacting as he
surveyed her through narrow, contemplative eyes. His
gaze skimmed over her from her loose tousled hair

down to her high-heeled sandals. Not wanting to be too obvious, to look too anxious, she turned her head away and flipped her hair over her mostly bare shoulder.

Seconds later her pulse jumped, then raced wildly as she sensed the approach of a man. She didn't turn to look but she could feel the tingling awareness of him, could detect his male scent, not in the least subtle. Yes! He was going to take the bait. Her palms began to sweat in nervousness but she ignored it. She felt him brush against her while taking his own stool, and that brief touch felt electric, making her jump in surprise. She struggled to moderate her accelerated breathing. He was looking at her; she felt the burning heat of his gaze as strongly as a firm stroke of flesh on flesh.

Mentally rehearsing the speech she'd prepared, she turned to face him, her smile planted as she leaned slightly forward to display as much cleavage as possible, given her small size. Her gaze slowly lifted, met his, and she froze in horror. "Oh no."

"Hello, Celia." The low, barely audible words were said in a familiar growl through clenched, white teeth.

"Oh no."

His smile wasn't a nice thing and sent gooseflesh racing up and down her spine. His eyes locked onto hers, refusing to let her look away, and his lips barely moved when he spoke. "Close your mouth, honey, or you're going to blow your own cover. And I don't feel like fighting my way out of here tonight. But then again, seeing you in that dress, a fight might be just what I need."

She snapped her mouth shut, but it wasn't easy. The eyes looking at her weren't blue, weren't admiring, and didn't belong to the man she was investigating, the man still sitting a good distance away, now watching curiously. These eyes were too familiar, a cold, hard black, and at that moment they reflected undiluted masculine fury.

Her heart raced even faster, urged on by new emotions, new sensations. She felt nearly faint, and collected her thoughts with an effort.

Forcing a shaky smile that actually hurt, Celia whispered, "Just what are you doing here, Alec?" She tried to make it look as if they were merely conversing, getting to know each other. She needed to maintain her camouflage, damn him, and Alec knew it.

Rather than offer an answer, he tossed back a handful of peanuts from the bar and watched her. His black hair—taken to curling toward the ends—hung loose tonight to touch his wide shoulders and reflected the glimmer of colored bar lights. Those same lights shone brightly in his narrowed eyes, eyes that made many a man back up in nervousness without a single word being spoken. His sharply cut, ruthless features seemed etched in stone, accurately reflecting his mood. He even smelled of danger, a hot, spicy, masculine scent that appealed to the senses, even as it amplified her nervousness.

Everyone in the bar seemed to be looking at them, waiting, but then Alec often got that reaction. He exuded menace, and people picked up on the silent threat quickly. He was a man who wore his tiny gold hoop earring and tattoo without artifice; the small decorations merely seemed a part of the overall man. His requisite jeans, scuffed boots and black T-shirt weren't exactly appropriate dress for the upscale bar, but Celia doubted anyone would be brave enough to ask him to leave.

She was brave enough. "Look, Alec—"

His dark, devilish gaze did a slow burn down the length of her body, effectively stifling her protest. He paused on her small breasts as they rose above the neckline of the dress, thanks to the wonders of the push-up bra. She shifted uneasily.

He smiled, not a reassuring sight, and his attention snagged again on her tummy. She felt that look inside herself, then more so as his intense scrutiny lingered on her exposed thigh.

She wanted to smack him for rattling her so, but then she always wanted to smack Alec. He confounded her and angered her more than any man she'd ever met. But worst of all, he made her feel the undeniable reactions of a woman just by his mere presence, and she resented it. She didn't want to want him, not when something inside her was a little afraid of him. He wasn't an easy man, wasn't domestic in the sense of the average male in today's society. When he looked at her, when his black eyes met her own, she sensed a certain degree of savage wildness, of primal masculinity that couldn't be tamed. She always hesitated to push him too far, and that angered her more than anything.

"Answer me, Alec."

His smile was again more taunting than comforting. "I suppose I'm here to save your stubborn little behind, though to tell you the truth, that's not my first inclination. At least, not where your posterior is concerned."

She sucked in a startled breath as heat flooded through her. What in the world did he mean by that? She couldn't quite tell if it was a threat of physical punishment, which she could easily ignore, or a sensual promise, which would be impossible to ignore. Alec did that all the time, made those suspicious little comments that stirred feelings she didn't want to acknowledge. Her one liaison of a romantic nature had ended in tragedy, and made her determined to ignore her baser instincts. They had overruled her common sense once, but never again would she put the people she loved in danger. Now she wanted to help protect women from bastards like her ex-fiancé. But her experiences with him, while making her wiser, hadn't in any way prepared her for a man like Alec Sharpe.

When they'd first met, he'd made his interest in an affair, and his disinterest in marriage, well known. Celia wasn't inclined to indulge either one, so she'd done her best to disregard his attentions—not at all an easy feat considering Alec was an impossible man to disregard on any level. But then she'd left her family's company and joined her brother's private investigations firm where Alec worked. He'd had a fit, appointing himself as her bodyguard, dogging her every step. Nothing had been the same since. Especially not after she'd gotten him shot a couple of weeks ago.

Celia winced, her guilt still keen. "Uh, should you be out and about on your leg already?"

His eyes narrowed, the obsidian depths almost hidden by long, sooty lashes that she envied every time she looked at him. "That's right, this is the first time I've gotten to see you face to face since that bullet hit my leg. Were you worried about me, sweetheart?"

That purring undertone had her defenses rising. Alec ruthlessly used every available opportunity to wear her down, to point out her shortcomings. She shook her head and feigned a casual interest in the bar. "Not at all. Your hide is as tough as nails and Dane said it was only a flesh wound."

"Yet you've still been avoiding me."

"Don't be ridiculous. I've just been…busy."

Alec reached out and caught her chin, bringing her face around so she had no choice but to witness the seriousness of his gaze. Her heart tripped, her senses coming alive with the simple touch. "That bullet was meant for you," he said, his tone low and rough, rubbing along her raw nerve endings. "If I hadn't been there, you would have been shot. I thought you might have learned your lesson then, but obviously you're not as bright as I first figured, considering you're here now."

That was an insult she couldn't let pass. She started to jerk away, then remembered her audience. She desperately wanted this case, wanted to prove she could handle herself while helping others, and if she got into an argument with Alec now, her cover would be blown. Dane had taught her that was the most important thing, the strongest safety measure. She had to remember to stay in character or she put not only herself at risk, but also the client and the other agents—in this case, Alec.

So she leaned toward him instead, seeing his nostrils flare and hearing his indrawn breath as her lips came within a millimeter of his own. Her heart thumped heavily with her daring, but she was getting sick and tired of him playing caretaker, constantly checking up on her. She still thought it was mostly his own fault for getting shot. He'd distracted her by his unexpected presence, otherwise she would have seen the threat before it became a reality.

She felt his incredible heat, smelled his musky, male scent, and felt his breath brush her parted lips. She stared into his dark eyes point-blank and a sense of sheer feminine daring filled her, almost obliterating her nervousness. It was like facing down a wild beast, exhilarating but also terrifying, making mush of her insides.

Against his mouth, she whispered, "I'm smart enough to know you have no say over what I do or don't do, Alec Sharpe. So why don't you just pretend you're not interested in me tonight, and head on back wherever you came from so I can get on with my business?"

Rather than backing off in anger as she expected, his long hard fingers slid from her chin to the back of her head where they tangled with her hair and wrapped around her skull, locking her firmly in place. She saw his small, satisfied smile before his lashes lowered, hiding his eyes. In response, Celia's own eyes opened wide in alarm as she belatedly realized his intent. Too late.

His mouth, hot and deliciously firm, closed over hers.

Slow, softly biting, inexorably consuming, the kiss obliterated all thought. The world seemed to come to a shuddering standstill as his mouth devoured hers, hot and easy. She didn't hear the quiet droning of the bar, no longer felt the bar stool beneath her or the cool air-conditioning on her skin. She lost awareness of the man she was here to investigate. Nothing penetrated her fogged mind but Alec and what he did to her, how he made her feel.

Good grief, the man could kiss.

His teeth teasingly nipped her bottom lip, and when she gasped for breath, his tongue licked inside, then plunged. She moaned in sheer surprise and excitement. He tilted his head, fitting their mouths more surely together and she thought she might have helped him with that, reaching blindly for him. The kiss seemed to go on and on before he finally pulled back, releasing her by slow degrees with soft, tiny kisses meant to appease. She was so stunned, he had to pry her clutching hands from his shoulders and put them in her lap. Her first reaction was regret that he'd stopped—but it was quickly followed by the hot lash of shame.

It had been a long time since she'd been kissed, forever since she'd been kissed like *that,* and she'd responded as if starved. She squeezed her eyes shut and tried to deny the truth about herself, but she couldn't. She had hoped the awful ordeal with her fiancé had cured her of her overly passionate nature. But Alec, a man who didn't care for her, who relished insulting her and tried to bully her at every turn, had gotten an even stronger response from her. How could she have kissed him back like that, losing all sense of time and place and purpose? Where in the world was her pride?

It took her precious minutes to get her bearings again, to hide the embarrassment that threatened to bring her low. And when she did, Alec was helping her off the stool. He had her purse in one fist, had paid her bill, and was leading her out. He walked behind her, automatically protecting her back, she knew, constantly nudging her forward.

Oh no. She hadn't accomplished a thing yet! She stiffened, but Alec's hand came around her waist and curved over her belly. The thin material of her dress was no barrier against the hot hardness of his large palm. His long fingers spread, spanning her from hipbone to hipbone. She sucked in a startled breath in response and retreated backward, attempting to pull away. But that only brought her up flush against the front of Alec and she felt his tall, hard body all along the length of her back. His erection, so blatantly obvious, pushed against her bottom. She felt a new, wilder rush of heat and she locked her knees against the tightening curl of desire.

Alec bent and his lips brushed her ear. To the onlookers, it appeared to be foreplay. To Celia, it was a sizzling threat. "Don't look back or you'll give yourself away. Every man here, including the ones who count, figure I just made arrangements with you for the night. That was your objective, and for the moment, keeps you safe." He pressed his mouth to her temple in a strangely tender kiss, then added, "From them."

From them. Meaning she still had to deal with him and that was much more alarming than what she'd faced in the bar. But she knew he was right. For now, there was no salvaging the night. She could come back tomorrow and hopefully her ruse would be validated by Alec's actions. Mr. Jacobs, the blond, blue-eyed villain she'd been trying to meet, would see her as a desperate woman alone, an easy pick-up.

Celia forcefully snuffed out the small voice in her mind that claimed the ruse a reality. The kiss with Alec was a mistake; she wouldn't let it happen again. She wasn't desperate, or easy—not anymore. She was only determined to see the job done. One way or another, she'd keep her overheated sexuality under control, and she'd nail the man who was ruthlessly ruining young women's lives.

Mr. Jacobs picked up women who seemed to be alone, telling them he wanted them to model for him. Some of their photos might even make it into a small-circulation magazine or two. But that wasn't what he really wanted. And Celia intended to prove it. She only hoped she'd made an attractive enough picture to draw his notice. Combined with the conversation she'd shared with the bartender, she hoped to have left enough bait.

Forcing Jacobs to show his true colors, exposing him to the authorities, would be an absolute pleasure. But her first priority, for now, was saving one young woman in particular. She couldn't forget that; she couldn't forget Hannah.

As Alec led her to his truck, she thought about what she would say to him. The night air was warm and humid in mid-July and the sensual haze lifted while she felt her skin grown damp beneath the slinky dress. He was still behind her, still pressing her forward, and she wanted to run. Alec Sharpe, her brother's number one agent, had kissed her senseless. He had curved his big hand over her belly and she could still feel the imprint of it there though he'd moved it away when opening the door. She felt like an animal.

"I can get home on my own."

Without explaining how he knew it, Alec said, "You didn't drive, and I'm damn sure not letting you get on a bus or wait for a taxi."

She twisted to face him. "You have no say in what I do."

His eyes flashed down at her, then skimmed her body once again. "Wanna bet?"

They waged a silent battle for all of three seconds, but Celia knew she didn't dare cause a scene so close to the bar. Anyone might see, and then questions would be asked, questions she couldn't afford if she wanted to

handle this case without complications, without embarrassing Hannah further.

Taking her silence for acquiescence, Alec opened
the truck door, lifted her by the waist and plopped her
inside. He dropped her purse on her lap then slammed
the truck door, and without a single care, strode to the
driver's side and slid in.

Damn it, she'd known since the day she met him he
was trouble. It didn't matter that her brother, Dane,
trusted him more than any other man he knew. It didn't
matter that her sister-in-law, Angel, actually let him
baby-sit her sweet, innocent little son. It didn't matter
that he always got the job done, that he had never hurt
her, that he had in fact taken a bullet meant for her on
the last assignment she'd botched.

What mattered was that he was lethal to her senses.
He had kissed her, and she'd liked it. But his kiss had
been meant to remove her from the bar without fuss.
He'd used that kiss against her, just as her fiancé had
used her sexuality against her. And it had worked.

She couldn't, wouldn't, let herself get involved with
him. For the past year-and-a-half, she'd effectively put
her sensual, prurient nature under wraps, and she
wanted to keep it that way. As soon as she got home,
she'd call Dane and make him intervene. She hadn't
wanted to do that because it felt too much like tattling,
like using her relationship with the boss to get special
favors. But this was crucial.

She had sworn off relationships after her last disastrous attempt at finding romance. Lust had blinded her
to reality then, and the shame was still a part of her. But
she was now older and wiser and determined to forge a

new life for herself while making amends for past mistakes. *Without sexual involvement.*

Dane was going to have to make Alec leave her alone. That was all there was to it.

CHAPTER TWO

"Put on your seat belt."

Alec was aware of her unease, but he wasn't ready to comfort her yet. He hadn't been kidding when he'd issued his less-than-subtle threat to her posterior. When he'd found her in that bar, playing at being a damn tramp and looking ripe for the part, he'd wanted more than anything to turn her over his knee. But he figured if he ever did have Celia Carter in such an interesting position, punishment would likely be the last thought on his mind. He knew he could never hurt her; hell, he'd taken a bullet rather than let her be hurt. But all other possibilities were still wide open. The things he did want to do to her were numerous, and driving him nuts.

Especially since she seemed to make a career of telling him no—about everything. As a result, he was learning to live with constant frustration.

He could almost feel her gathering her courage. She did that a lot with him and it amused him. Grown men had been steering a wide path around him since his late teens, but not Celia. Right from the start, she'd tried her best to stand up to him, but always there was a touch of fear in her mellow hazel eyes. She'd rail against him, give him hell, but with obvious nervousness. To him, the fact that she stood up to him despite her fear indicated a hell of a lot of guts and he admired that in a woman. In fact, he'd admired a hell of a lot about Celia Carter since first setting eyes on her.

What he didn't admire was her impetuous race for adventure that had kept her on the edge of danger ever since she'd left her family's secure company and joined up with Dane. He still couldn't figure that one out. So her fiancé had turned out to be a grade A bastard? There were plenty of them in the world to go around, and it certainly wasn't Celia's fault that she'd been too inno-cent to see through Raymond's scam. Alec had already been working with Dane to nail Raymond for numerous crimes, not the least of which was the murder of Dane and Celia's brother. At the time, they hadn't known for certain that Raymond was the culprit, but they'd had their suspicions. In the end, Celia was the one who'd saved the day, sneaking up on Raymond and clobber-ing him with a crowbar while he'd held Dane and Angel at gunpoint. Celia had more than vindicated herself in everyone's eyes.

Everyone's but her own.

Alec knew Raymond had hurt her tender feelings, trying to use Celia as a pawn in his schemes. It was the worst emotional insult a man could deal a woman, using her that way. She obviously felt horrible for having ever believed in him. In truth, Alec wondered what the hell she'd seen in Raymond. He'd disliked the man on instinct the moment he'd met him. But then he was good at what he did, and he'd been doing it a long time. The same wasn't true of Celia. For the most part, and despite her loud claims to the contrary, she was still a wide-eyed innocent.

So why the hell did she want to risk her damn neck

day in and day out trying to prove something? The anger washed over him again, fresh and raw, and he growled, "You're not going back there, so you can stop your scheming right now."

Her head snapped around toward him and she glared. "I'm going to talk to Dane. You're not my boss and I want you to quit acting like you are."

Primal satisfaction settled deep into his bones. With this one woman, he wanted every advantage he could get. "Now there's where you're wrong."

He felt a return of her wariness. He was so painfully attuned to her and her feelings, he always seemed to know what she was thinking and feeling. It unnerved him, even as it turned him on and made him more determined to have her. There was a link between them that she did her damnedest to deny. He wouldn't let her do that much longer. When she was lying naked beneath him, he'd see to it that her thoughts were centered solely on accepting him and the incredible pleasure he'd give them both. There'd be no room for doubt or denial.

"What are you talking about?"

He tightened his hands on the wheel, pressed his foot to the accelerator and relished this moment of proper balance between them. He hadn't liked it worth a damn that Dane was her ultimate boss, leaving him no say-so in what Celia did or which job she chose. That had finally changed, and not a moment too soon, given where he'd found her.

Luckily, the darkness hid his smile, but the satisfaction came through in his tone. "With Angel pregnant again, Dane's decided she needs an extended vacation. He's rented a house in the Carribean and he's taking the family there for a month. While he's gone, I'm in charge." He slanted her a look, saw her shock and decided to clarify just to make sure there were no misunderstandings. "So you see, Miss Carter, I am your boss."

"No."

He took great pleasure in nodding. "Afraid so."

"I won't have it!"

"You, Celia, have no choice." Her hands fisted, her entire small body going taut in automatic rebellion. He wanted to pull her close, to cuddle her and reassure her; they were soft urges he hadn't experienced with a woman in fifteen years and he didn't welcome them now. He firmed his resolve, blocking out all the weakening, tender emotions. Protecting Celia was for her own good, so he'd do it whether she liked it or not.

"Listen close, honey. If I find you even thinking about that particular case again, I'll fire you in a heartbeat. As a matter of fact, from here on out, I'll personally give you which assignments I want you to have. And you can bet they won't include dressing like a hussy and putting your sweet little ass on the line."

He finished that grand statement with a flourish, pleased with himself and his implacable stance. But when he slowed the truck for a turn in the road, Celia unsnapped her seat belt and opened the door.

Cursing, Alec slammed on the brakes and tried to steady the wheel. The truck shuddered to an immediate, bone-jarring halt. Alec saw red and reached for her, the idea of getting her over his lap more appealing by the moment. But she was already leaping out, her own anger giving her the advantage of speed. She landed awkwardly on her high heels, fell to her butt, then jerked quickly to her feet again. If his reflexes hadn't been so

good, and he hadn't stopped the truck so quickly, she
might have broken her neck. Waiting for the truck to
actually stop hadn't seemed like a concern to her.

A middle-aged couple who'd been walking by on the
dark night stopped to stare. Alec saw Celia dust herself
off, nod at the people, then start briskly on her way,
limping slightly.

He quickly maneuvered the truck to the curb, jerked
out his keys and trotted after her. *Damned irritant.* Her
brother was sharp as a tack, reasonable, calculating.
There wasn't an impulsive or careless bone in his body.
Dane always knew what he was doing, and how he was
going to go about doing it. He and Alec worked perfectly together, both of them practical, methodical,
sensible. So where the hell had Celia gotten her fool-
hardy, damn-the-consequences attitude?

Alec grabbed her arm and held on while she tried to
jerk away. She swung her purse at him and he dodged
it. "Just settle down, damn it, before you hurt yourself."

"You bullying behemoth, get your hands off me!"

The names she called him usually made him grin.
But not this time, not when he had an important point
to make and already knew how resistant she was going
to be. He clasped both her arms, effectively immobiliz-
ing her. Through clenched teeth, he growled, "Just this
once, Celia, will you please use your head?"

"I am using it," she insisted, her eyes and cheeks hot
with temper. "I'm going to go to the corner and hail a
cab, and from here on out, I want nothing to do with you.
You think you're going to fire me? Ha! I quit."

The pedestrians, still enthralled by the drama taking
place in front of them, moved on quickly enough when
Alec's darkest, most threatening glare shot their way. He

pushed Celia into a small storefront doorway, out of the path and view of anyone else out wandering the streets on this blacker-than-pitch night. The corner streetlamp didn't quite reach them, and they were isolated by the darkness.

He forced himself to take three deep, calming breaths. Her statement that she wanted nothing to do with him had cut like a knife and left him bleeding. Damn her, she would not shut him out. Not anymore.

"You're being unreasonable," he finally said, doing his best to keep his tone calm, to hide his own anger. No one, man or woman, had ever set him off like this, but then it had always been that way with Celia. She elicited more emotion from him, in all forms, than anyone he'd ever known. She could make him furious with a word, amuse him with a burst of temper, or arouse him to the point of pain with a simple shy look. He didn't like it, but more than that, he wasn't quite sure how to deal with it, and feeling helpless was something he hated above all things. The only way he could see to get over it was to finally have her, to sate himself on the scent and feel and taste of her. He could easily spend a week doing just that, and he eventually would. But first he had to insure her safety.

"Do you want to get hurt?" He shook her slightly, both hands now holding her bare shoulders. He was careful not to bruise her, but he wanted her attention, needed her to know he was dead serious. "Do you realize what could have happened to you last time if I hadn't gotten in the way of that bullet?"

She lowered her gaze and stared at his shirtfront. He had the almost overpowering urge to press his lips against the part in her fair hair. She was so damn baby soft all over. Soft hair, soft skin…*soft smell.* His chest suddenly felt tight, his muscles rigid, and he fought against it, against the effect she had on him. The need to kiss her, to eat her alive, was strong. He wanted to make her a part of him so she'd quit fighting so hard.

He gave her another quick, careful shake. "Celia?" he demanded in a growl.

"That was an accident," she muttered, her voice quavering slightly. "I thought the guy was just jumping bail and that he'd be easy enough to bring in." She peeked up at him, her hazel eyes wide and vulnerable, swallowing him whole and making his hands shake. "I didn't mean for you to get hurt."

His fingers flexed on her shoulders, stroking, relishing the tender feel of her warm flesh. A slow burn started in his gut. "Celia…damn it, that's exactly what I'm talking about. You don't know enough yet to get involved in cases like that. They'd grabbed that guy on petty theft, and he was small-time, but he knew bigger, more dangerous guys and you bumbled right into their dealings by following him without backup. You didn't wait for a partner the way you're supposed to and you didn't call the cops when you should have."

She swallowed. "Does…does your leg still hurt?"

It wasn't his leg bothering him. He thought about lying, pondering whether his injury would have any effect on swaying her to stay away from danger. But he doubted it. She was so damn headstrong and unreasonable. "No. It's fine."

"Nothing keeps you down for long, does it?" She peeked up at him again. "You're so invincible."

Hardly. His hands tightened again, because around

her he felt like a naked baby in the woods, but damned if he'd admit it.

"I just wanted to prove I could do it," she whispered, reacting to his anger.

Her words made him want to explode. *"Why?"*

She drew a shuddering breath, and his attention was diverted to her breasts. He wasn't sure how it was done, since understanding the working of women's underwear wasn't high on his list of accomplishments, but her small breasts were fairly bursting out of that damn dress. They taunted him, when usually it was her pert behind that grabbed his undivided attention. That and her unwavering stubbornness, which he admired even as he resented it.

"You wouldn't understand, Alec."

Probably not, since he'd forgotten what the hell they were talking about. He wanted to pull the plunging neckline of the dress two inches lower so he could see her nipples. Would they be pale pink, or a dark dusky rose? He could almost taste her in his mouth, her sweet flesh puckering tight. His erection strained against his jeans. Lord, if just thinking about kissing her breasts made him shake with lust, he wasn't sure he'd actually be able to survive being inside her. He closed his eyes in self-defense and swallowed hard. But shutting out the reality of having her in his grasp only allowed him to dwell on the fantasy of getting her beneath him, warm and soft and ready.

He groaned.

"Alec?"

He forced his eyes open, saw her worried gaze, and frowned. With one fingertip, he tipped up her chin. "What wouldn't I understand, babe? Explain it to me."

She licked her lips, leaving them wet and shiny. "I need to make a difference. I've screwed up a lot in my life, hurt a lot of people."

Her self-recrimination did a lot to dispel his lust and clear his brain, so that her words held all his attention. He started to correct her, to tell her how wrong she was, but decided to let her talk it out instead. Later, he could set her straight.

"I almost lost Dane, and I did lose Derek because I was too dumb to see Raymond for what he was. My entire family was hurt, the company was hurt. Innocent people were victimized. The only way I can live with myself now is if I help someone else."

Alec smoothed his fingers over her cheek, tucking a blond strand behind her small ear. Her hair was soft and fine, with natural curl. "Hooking up with Raymond was a mistake, but we all make them. You can't expect yourself to be exempt. And you can't undo the past."

"I can try to make amends."

"To who? Dane knew what he was getting into, and you couldn't have helped Derek even if you'd known. You didn't even meet Raymond until after Derek had died."

It was an awful situation, one Alec knew she still hadn't come to terms with. She'd only been a stepping stone in Raymond's plot against her family, but of the survivors, she'd been emotionally hurt the worst. Raymond had started with industrial espionage, and quickly advanced into more deadly crimes. It had taken all Alec's fortitude to allow the law to have him, rather than utilizing his own sense of justice. He could have taken care of Raymond without an ounce of remorse.

Celia turned her face away. "I feel like I betrayed them all."

His heart twisted, and the pain was so unfamiliar, he jerked. Slowly, his hands flexed on her smooth shoulders, pulling her closer, which made the pain less noticeable. "Celia," he whispered, the word a reprimand breathed into her ear, "you know that's nonsense. Dane loves you, so of course he doesn't blame you. And Angel adores you. You've become her best friend, a godmother to little Grayson."

Her small hands lifted to his chest and lightly rested there. Her forehead touched his sternum. "I can't believe she's forgiven me. It's because of me that Raymond was able to threaten her." She tilted back to stare up into his face, and her belly pressed against him. "She could have been hurt—"

"Hush." He laid a finger over her lips, fighting the urge to taste her again. That first kiss, meant as a showdown, had made him hard, and being near her had kept him that way. She'd tasted sweet, like cherries, but now her lip gloss was gone and he found her naked mouth even more appealing. "You're not responsible for Raymond's actions, Celia. And the truth is, you saved Angel by showing up when you did and wielding that crowbar like a pro."

He smiled and she managed a skimpy smile in return. "Regardless of what you say, Alec, I know I hold part of the responsibility. And it…it disgusts me so much, knowing I was engaged to that animal, that I might have married him, that I *did* sleep with him."

Alec froze, not wanting that image to invade his mind, but it was never far from there anyway. The thought of Celia having sex with Raymond sickened him and filled him with a killing rage. He dropped his hands and took a step back, trying to distance himself both physically and mentally. He didn't want to care who she'd slept with, as long as she slept with him, too. But it wasn't that simple and he knew it.

He loomed over her, ready to intimidate once again. "You won't change anything by getting yourself killed. Do you think Dane deserves that right now, after he's finally found happiness with Angel and the baby?"

She wrapped her arms around herself, holding tight. "I've learned my lesson. I'll be extra careful from now on. But when I saw this case, I knew I had to do something."

"Damn it, Celia!" His frustration exploded, but he recognized her stubborn look and knew there'd be little chance of changing her mind.

She glared at him, her chin jutting out at an obstinate angle. "Well you just refused it without even giving Mrs. Barrington a reason why!"

In her pique, Celia no longer looked so vulnerable or so small. She stood barely five-foot-six in her heels, a good ten inches shorter than him. But when she gave her anger free rein, she reminded him of an Amazon.

She clutched at the front of his shirt. "Do you know she thinks her daughter is involved in *prostitution?* That she's been forcibly coerced into it? Hannah thought she was joining a modelling agency, but now—"

"Spare me, Celia," he said in disgust, his anger rising once again. "I read the case and I interviewed Mrs. Barrington myself. Her daughter was a spoiled brat who left a very loving family behind to chase the limelight. I've heard it before. Hannah wants to be famous, and she'll likely do whatever it takes to see it come true. Mrs.

Barrington just can't believe her precious daughter would willingly stoop so low. But it happens. There's no one to save this time, and Hannah likely wouldn't appreciate your intrusion into her cozy little life-style, anyway."

Celia thumped her fist, still tangled in his shirt, against his chest. She looked outraged and appalled. "You're not even willing to check it out?"

"I just told you, I already have." He covered her hand with his own, holding it tight against him. "Trust me on this. I know more about it than you ever will and I have eons more experience."

"What does that mean?"

Damn it. He swiped his hand through his hair, unwilling to tell her just how much experience he had with a situation such as this. Even thinking that far into the past made his head hurt. He narrowed his eyes and made his tone deliberately cold. "You've wasted your time coming here. Now let's go. We'll stop at the room you rented so you can pick up your stuff, and then head home. No reason to spend another night here."

He had her halfway to his truck before she dug in her dainty heels. "I'm not going with you, Alec."

His patience was at an end. He turned to her, then bent down until his nose was almost touching hers. "Yes you are. If I have to haul your stubborn hide over my shoulder and tie you in the damn truck, so be it. But one way or another I'm taking you home. Now."

Her small body practically vibrated with anger, her eyes hot with it, and then her eyebrows lowered ferociously. "All right. I'll come with you. But I'm not giving up this case."

"Then you're still fired."

"I still quit," she qualified, and slid into her seat. She didn't look at him, but stared stonily ahead.

Alec braced one hand on the dash and the other on the roof of the truck. He leaned in close, using every intimidation tactic he knew. "When I inform Mrs. Barrington you're no longer with the agency, do you think she'll still be willing to pay your expenses?"

Celia curled her lip, for the moment too angry to be cowed by his excellent routine. One long manicured finger poked him in the chest with stinging force. "Fine. You do that and I'll just work gratis. But one way or another I'm going to find out what's going on with Hannah Barrington. I'm going to find out if her mother's suspicions are correct. *I'm going to help that girl.* And you, Alec Sharpe, can't do a single thing to stop me."

Alec got out of the truck and slammed the door, afraid he'd strangle the little witch if he stayed that close to her a second longer. She knew how to push all his buttons. No one, male or female, had ever seemed to take so much delight in provoking him. Hell, most people were afraid to try! It wasn't what he was used to, what he was accustomed to dealing with. Damn it, he wanted to see this at an end. He wanted Celia Carter kept safe.

He wanted her—period.

What a horrible situation to find himself in. He couldn't do it, no matter how hard he tried, but he knew it would be best if he just stayed the hell away from her. From the day he'd met her, he'd seen all the signs. Miss Celia Carter was trouble with a capital *T,* and he had the bullet wound to prove it.

CHAPTER THREE

THE RIDE TO HER MOTEL was made in absolute silence before Celia decided she couldn't take it anymore. Alec was being so boring, she was about to fall asleep. The quiet, along with the dark night and the breeze from the open windows were proving to be very hypnotic. She wasn't even all that mad anymore. Alec couldn't help being the way he was. His bossy arrogance seemed an innate part of his nature. And overall, she accepted that it was concern which prompted his temper. *Concern for her.* He was one of those incredible men who thought everyone smaller or weaker warranted his protection, and nearly everyone was smaller and weaker than Alec. Not that she would allow him to boss her, but at least she could understand why he wanted to try.

What had really kept her quiet for so long was the way he'd pulled away from her when she'd mentioned sleeping with Raymond. Evidently the awful truth of what she'd done, of what she'd allowed Raymond to do, disturbed him as well. But she couldn't fault him for that, either. No one could disparage her horrid judgement any more than she did.

The quiet had given her plenty of time to think, though, and she'd come to several conclusions. She didn't like it, but she was forced to face the truth. She needed Alec's help.

Staring at his hard profile, she sighed. "So are you going to brood all night?"

"Yes."

She almost laughed at that, her mood lifting slightly. He was such a big, dark, awesome man to admit to actual brooding. But she could see he was more relaxed now, too. That ever-present aura of danger that loomed around him like a thick black cloud had softened. His hands were no longer gripping the steering wheel as if he might snap it in two, and his jaw wasn't as tightly clenched.

Celia smiled at him, hoping to cajole him into a more agreeable frame of mind. "I have a sort of 'off the topic' question for you."

He gave her a suspicious look, his black gaze cutting over her features before he reluctantly shrugged. "Go ahead."

"How did you know where I was? I made a point not to drive, to take the dumb slow bus instead so people would see my car in the driveway and think I was still at home." She didn't mention that the "people" she'd most wanted to elude was Alec. But as usual, he was one step ahead of her.

As she spoke, he pulled into the motel parking lot where she'd rented a room. Celia shook her head in amazement. "And how did you know I was staying here?"

He made an impatient sound and shut off the truck's motor. "I'm a P.I. This is what I do."

He shifted in his seat to face her, one long arm stretching out along the back of the seat, almost touching her. The darkness of the cab's interior closed around them, relieved only by the lights of sporadic traffic. She could smell his scent, feel the warmth of his big body. His arm with the tattoo was closest to her, and she glanced at it. It was too dark for her to see it clearly, but she'd studied it many times and always wondered at the significance. A man like Alec didn't tattoo his arm with a heart, pierced by an arrow, for no reason. She just didn't have the nerve to ask him what that reason might be.

She shifted restlessly in her seat. "But *how?*" she demanded, going back to her original question. He narrowed his gaze, his look calculating, and she warned, "Don't you dare lie to me, Alec."

One finger touched her hair, twining around a loose curl, unnerving her further and filling her stomach with sensual butterflies. He watched his hand, his dark eyes glinting in the soft moonlight. She saw the moment he decided to tell her the truth. His shoulders lifted in a slight, unconcerned shrug. "I broke into your house and found your travel plans."

Her mouth dropped open and she stared at him in utter disbelief. She took refuge from his overwhelming nearness in the flash of anger that jarred her wits back. *"You did what?"*

Disgruntled, he released her and opened his door. Celia scrambled out her own side before he could circle the truck, then stepped in front of him, hands on hips, chin thrust out, blocking his way. "You broke into my house?" she demanded, injecting as much outrage in the words as she could. He ignored her and she had to quickly backstep since he didn't stop, then was forced to skip to keep up with him.

"I didn't do any damage." He said it as if that would be her only concern, as if the invasion of her privacy was nothing at all. He glanced down at her, then added, "You need an alarm system. I'll take care of it when we get back."

Celia slung her purse strap over her shoulder and clasped both hands around the back waistband of his tight jeans as he started up the outside stairs leading to her second-floor room. She dug in her heels, but only got dragged in his wake. "Damn it, Alec, will you wait up a minute?"

"We can talk in your room, honey, while you pack up."

She stumbled on the concrete steps and he reached back, disengaging her hands and pulling her up alongside him. He kept a solicitous hand at her elbow, offering her support in her high heels. "Did you hurt yourself when you leaped out of my truck?"

"No." Nothing more than a tender ankle, and since he'd blown off the impact of a bullet wound to his thigh, she certainly wasn't going to complain about something so minor.

"Good." He continued dragging her along.

Celia seethed. She had no intention of packing up. In fact, she still had hopes of convincing Alec to stay and help her. Alec and Dane were forever claiming "gut instincts" to account for every hunch they had that couldn't be explained, but proved true nonetheless. Well, she had a wrenching, screaming "gut instinct" right now, and it was telling her that Hannah Barrington was in big trouble and Celia was her only hope. She couldn't, wouldn't turn her back on Hannah now, no matter what. If she did give up on the twenty-year-old girl, she'd never again be able to face herself in the mirror. But she was smart enough to know her chances of actually helping Hannah would be much better if Alec lent his expertise. Getting him to do that would be tricky.

Especially if she killed him first.

When they reached the landing and circled to her room, Alec turned to face her. He reached for her purse and Celia knew a physical struggle would be pointless. He was coming in and since she hoped to convince him to help her, she didn't want to cause a fuss about it. Still, she snatched her purse out of his reach and glared at him. "I'll get the key. Just hold on a second."

He was impatient, looming over her as if he expected her to pull out a gun instead. Ha! If she had one, she would already have hit him over the head with it. Celia thrust the key into his hand and said at the same time, "I can't believe your gall. How would you like it if I broke into your home?"

He swung the door open and reached inside for a light. His voice was pitched low, with a husky drawl. "Anytime you want to visit my place, honey, you just let me know. The invitation is always open."

Celia sputtered, annoyed at what she was sure was another sexual reference. Then the light spilled over them and Alec could suddenly see into her room.

For once his look was comical rather than terrorizing. "What the hell?"

Celia peeked around his shoulder, and flinched. She'd forgotten that she'd left the room in such cluttered disarray. The room's dingy carpeting could barely be seen for the objects covering it. Alec slowly turned to stare down at her, one black brow quirked high. "What the hell have you been up to?"

"Exercising?" Her voice emerged as an embarrassed squeak. The personal goals she'd set for herself were just that—personal. She didn't want anyone, especially Alec, to know about them.

He blinked twice, his look filled with skepticism, then again surveyed her room. He took his time, his gaze going over the padded floor mat, the ankle and wrist weights, the five-pound barbells, a jump rope, and finally landing on the expandable chin-up bar she had wedged open in the bathroom doorway. So far, she'd managed to get her chin over it twice. He shook his head, and his long hair skimmed over his shoulders. "Who the hell do you think you are? That crazy broad from the Terminator movie?"

Celia's face burned and she reluctantly followed him inside, pausing beside the door. "I'm just trying to stay in shape. I was getting too soft."

His gaze caught hers and held. Two heartbeats later, he slowly reached around her and shoved the door shut with the flat of his hand. His other palm landed on the wall next to her head, caging her in. She could feel his thick wrists just touching her bare shoulders as he leaned down toward her, angling his chest so close she inhaled his scent with every rapid breath she took. "Crazy Celia," he muttered, nuzzling close to her. "I like you soft."

She thought about ducking. She thought about running. Her body had other thoughts.

When his mouth touched hers, it was like tasting live electricity. She jerked, gasping at the same time and giving him the opportunity to sink his tongue into her open mouth. Her responding groan told him things she didn't want him to know.

He ate at her mouth, big, soft, slow love bites that made her want more, made her chase his mouth with her own. She loved how he kissed. "Alec…"

"Hush, it's okay, baby." And then he gave her that killer kiss again until her arms were tight around his neck, their bodies fused together, rocking. He was so incredibly hard, so solid. She loved the way his breath was broken, how his hands shook, and the way his hips pushed rhythmically against her where she needed the pressure most…

His mouth moved to her throat, making her toes curl.

"I don't want to do this," she whispered, but where the words came from she had no idea. She hadn't been touched like this in a long time, and she wanted him so badly, her body was with him every step of the way.

Alec growled, "Yes you do."

Yes I do.

He skimmed one narrow shoulder strap down her arm while his mouth left damp, hot kisses over the sensitive skin of her collarbone, the hollow of her shoulder, the slope of her upthrust breast. She felt cool air touch her breast, then the incredible, contrasting heat of his rough palm as he slid his hand inside her bra. They both groaned together at the exquisite feel of it.

His forehead touched hers, his eyes closed as if in pain while he caressed her, gently learning the shape of her, weighing her in his palm. She could feel a subtle trembling in his entire body, could feel the harsh, rapid thumping of his heartbeat, echoing her own.

"Celia?" He continued to caress her, but his tone sounded strained, as if he held his control on a very tight, very fragile leash. He rubbed her belly with his erection, making certain she understood what he asked.

Tears threatened. Her body was screaming for her to say yes, to give in. It wouldn't take much to send her over the top, to make her mindless with release. Just the way he cupped her breast, the rough rasping of his thumb over her tender nipple, had her on the verge of climax. She felt empty and hungry, every nerve ending sizzling and alive.

And that's what upset her most of all.

Why did it have to be this way? Why was she so damn easy? She wanted to be ruled by her mind, by her caring and intelligence and pride. Not by animal lust. Alec had made it plain that he thought her incompetent, that he didn't want a relationship with her, only sex. And her body didn't care.

The sob caught her by surprise, shaming her further. Alec froze, going painfully still against her, and then he pulled his hand free and gathered her close and the emotions swelled inside her until they overflowed. She didn't want to cry on his shoulder, but as usual, he wasn't giving her any choice.

She struggled to get away from him, but his arms locked around her, not allowing so much as an inch between them.

"Shhh, it's all right." One big hand pressed to the back of her head and forced it into the notch of his shoulder. She knew her tears were wetting his bare skin; she could feel the hot, soft skin of his throat against her face. His other hand rubbed up and down the length of her spine, consoling her, comforting her, filling her with immeasurable guilt for letting things get so far out of hand.

After half a minute of fighting the inevitable she clutched him tight. It simply felt too good to be held, to be comforted. Through rough sobs and humiliating sniffles, she managed to choke out, "I don't want to want you, damn it."

He rubbed his cheek against her head and answered softly. "Yeah, I think I figured that out."

She didn't have room for much leverage, but she got a fairly decent thump of her fist against his solid chest. "Not y-y-*you,* dummy. Anyone."

His hand paused in its stroking, then picked up the soothing rhythm again. "Care to tell me why?"

"No."

"Celia." His sigh blew over her damp cheek. He tried to look at her face, but she tucked it close to him and held on tight when he tried to tilt her back. She knew her makeup was ruined and she wasn't done crying, so she had no intention of having him ogle her. "Honey, I have a hard-on that could kill, and it's not going to be going away anytime soon. Don't you think it might be nice if you just explained things to me? I really would like to understand."

She shook her head.

"I know you wanted me." Again he tried to look at her, wanting confirmation, and again she resisted. "I mean, with the way you were kissing me and moving against me. And your nipples were—"

She groaned, and quickly nodded.

"Then why not, honey? We're both adults. I wouldn't hurt you, if that's what you're afraid of."

She thumped him again, indignant. "I'm not afraid of you."

She heard the smile in the way he answered. "Yes, you are."

"Well, only sometimes." She sniffed once more and

wiped her eyes on his T-shirt, keeping her face close so he still couldn't look at her. She wasn't ready to face anyone yet, not herself, certainly not him. "You try to make me afraid."

"No."

"Yes you do. You try to make everyone afraid."

His fingers tangled in her hair and began massaging her scalp. She still felt aroused, but now she felt sleepy, too, utterly drained and strangely protected. She hadn't cried much since finding out her fiancé was a slimeball using her to hurt her family and hoping to get rich in the bargain. She'd refused to allow herself that luxury. But crying now had felt good, sort of cathartic and cleansing. She drew a slow deep breath, and ended up hiccuping.

Alec kissed her temple. "Celia, why don't you want to make love with me?"

The way he said that made her want to throw him on the bed and do unspeakable things to his hard, gorgeous body. She started shaking again and he held her a little closer, lending his quiet support. Finally, unable to figure a way out of it, she shamefully whispered, "I'm not like most women."

That gave him pause and she could feel him thinking, coming up with so many ridiculous, off-base ideas. She shook her head. "I don't mean… I'm not physically different. Well, that is…"

"Just tell me straight out, honey. Whatever it is, we'll deal with it."

A nervous, almost hysterical giggle escaped her tight lips. Oh, she had no doubt he'd love to deal with it. Raymond certainly hadn't objected, though he'd occasionally taunted her with her weakness. After he'd been found out, Raymond had taken great pleasure in telling her how easy she'd been, how she'd offered no real challenge at all. Well, she would never be easy again, though Alec Sharpe surely did wear on her convictions.

Her mind froze up with that ugly, painful thought and she jerked away from Alec's hold, turning her back and making a zigzag, awkward path around the cluttered floor to the bathroom. She paused in the open doorway, keeping her back to him. "I want you to leave now."

Two seconds passed, and he said, "Not until you tell me what's going on."

She straightened her back and lifted her chin. He was right, after the way she'd just behaved with him, he deserved the truth. Her throat felt swollen from her recent crying jag, and her head pounded as she forced out the awful words. "I have a…a sexual problem."

Alec didn't say a word. There was such complete suffocating silence that she couldn't bear it. She darted into the bathroom and slammed the door, then leaned back against it and covered her face with her hands. Now he knew the truth. He'd likely leave in disgust, wanting nothing to do with her, and her chances of helping Hannah would diminish to almost zero. How could she help anyone else when she couldn't even help herself?

A hard pounding rattled the door, making her spring away with a short scream. She whirled, one hand clutching her heart.

"Goddammit, Celia, open this door right now!"

She stared, unable to even blink. He was angry?

The door trembled again, threatening to splinter, as Alec hammered on it. She jumped back another cautious step.

"I'm giving you to the count of two, then I'm opening the door my own way."

Celia gawked.

"One!"

He wasn't going to give her much time to consider her options, she thought. But then, there was really only one option anyway. She reached for the doorknob.

CHAPTER FOUR

ALEC WAS SO MAD he could barely see straight. He opened his mouth to shout "two" and heard the lock click open. He propped his hands on his hips and narrowed his eyes, waiting for Celia to present herself. Ha, what did she think, that she could make a crazy statement like that and then just tell him to get lost? Fat chance.

He figured Raymond Stern had something to do with her little bombshell revelation, and he regretted his noble decision to let the law have him. If he could go back and do things over, he would.

"Get your butt out here, Celia."

Reluctantly she opened the door. Her face was ravaged, blotchy red from her tears and with makeup everywhere. His heart softened, making his entire system go on alert. Damn, but he would rather take a beating than see her cry. His jaw worked for a moment while he fought his natural instincts, to lift her in his arms, toss her on the bed, and prove she had not a single problem in the world. Hell, he wanted her so bad, they'd burn up the mattress in record time. And then he'd start on round two. He figured he could make love to her all night long and not get his fill. But judging by her expression, she wasn't up to a sexual marathon at the moment. Right now, she needed him rational, not ruled by an overactive libido.

He hadn't had urges this strong since he'd been a teenager, and back then, he'd had his pick of girls to handle the problem. This time, though, he didn't want anyone but Celia. And he'd wait—for just a little longer.

He drew a long breath, reaching for a modicum of control, but unwilling to let her know what a strain it was. "I want you to take a shower and change." There. That had sounded calm enough. Despite the fact that that damn dress she wore was keeping his need on a razor's edge.

She nodded her head, suspiciously submissive for the moment.

"When you're done," he said, watching her closely, "we're going to talk."

"I thought you wanted to leave right away."

"Later. Maybe even in the morning. For now, just get yourself comfortable, all right?" A thought struck him and he added, "Have you eaten? Are you hungry?"

"No."

No what? No she hadn't eaten or no she wasn't hungry? He decided to make the decision himself, which was what he should have been doing all along. He'd order up some sandwiches and coffee, feed her, then get a few things settled with her.

He sighed again. "Where are your clothes?"

"In the suitcase in the closet."

She stood docile while he opened the case and yanked out jeans and a T-shirt, then handed them to her.

"I need panties, too." She wiped at her eyes with a shaking hand, removing some of the mascara that was smudged there. His heart thumped again, and that damn tenderness threatened to bring him to his knees. Turning back to the case he grabbed up a pair of pale pink nylon panties and thrust them at her. She sniffed, turned her back, and went into the bathroom without a word.

As soon as the door clicked shut Alec thrust both hands into his hair and pulled. Christ, she was making him crazy. First fighting him tooth and nail, refusing to give so much as an inch, and now acting like an obedient child. He wasn't at all certain which he hated worse. Celia was constantly taking him off guard; he thought she probably did it on purpose just so he'd never know how to react.

He heard the water start, pictured her naked in the shower, and slammed one fist against his thigh.

To keep his mind off bare, wet, feminine skin, he called and ordered room service. Even in such a run-down rat motel, they had an attached bar with a fairly varied menu and he ordered two sub sandwiches, a pot of coffee and pie. While he was waiting for that to be delivered, he called Dane.

The line was answered on the second ring.

"Yeah?"

Alec heard feminine giggling in the background. He should have known, given the time of night, Dane would be preoccupied. He rolled his eyes. Dane's marital bliss was about enough to choke a lesser man, but Alec could take it—barely. "I found your sister."

He heard a shuffling, and the next words were muffled. "Shh, just a minute honey. It's Alec." Then into the receiver, "Good job. I never doubted it, Alec. Now I'm kind of busy—"

"She was dressed like a tramp, hanging out in a bar trying to pick up Jacobs."

Dane uttered one short, crude word.

"Yeah, that's how I figured it. I got her out of there, but she's determined to go back. She has some damned vigilante attitude about saving Hannah Barrington." Alec couldn't quite keep the disgust from his tone, but every time he thought of Celia putting herself on the line for the Barrington girl he wanted to rage against the injustice of it.

Very quietly, Dane said, "I'm glad she's concerned, despite how you feel about it, Alec. But I don't want her involved in that mess."

"I threatened to fire her if she didn't back off."

Dane cursed again.

With a wry twist to his mouth, Alec said, "I see you already guessed how she reacted to that."

"You're slipping, buddy."

"Like hell. I'll drag her home if I have to. But I'm not leaving her here alone to tangle with Jacobs."

"Why are you so worried if you really think there's no problem for Hannah?"

Alec stilled as he realized he'd backed himself into a corner. Even Dane didn't know his complete reasoning for wanting no part of this particular case, but being Dane, he was likely making some pretty damn astute guesses. Alec tried for a bluff. "Hannah's probably having the time of her life. But your damn sister alone is trouble waiting to happen."

"Celia's not as fragile as you think." Alec heard a voice in the background, heard Dane whispering, and then he said, "Angel wants to talk to you."

"No! Damn it, Dane, don't you dare—"

"Hello, Alec."

Alec sighed. When he got Dane alone, he was going to strangle him. "Hi, hon. How're you feeling?" Angel didn't seem to have any problems carrying this baby, but like Dane, Alec would feel a lot better if she took things a little easier. The trauma she'd gone through with her first son, Grayson, was still fresh in everyone's mind—except maybe Angel's.

"I'd be feeling a lot better if you'd quit trying to bully Celia."

"Well—"

"I've gotten rather fond of you, Alec, despite my first impressions. And Grayson adores you. But if you don't stop pushing Celia around, she's going to kill you."

"Well—"

"Not only that, but I'd think you could be a little more understanding. She's trying to start a new life, which means putting the old life behind her. But you won't help her at all! All you keep doing is telling her that she can't possibly do it."

"Well—"

"I've finally gotten Dane to lighten up on her a little, and what do you do? You step in and pretend to be her father and big brother and husband all wrapped into one."

Alec held the phone away from his head and stared at it, appalled. He sure as hell didn't feel like a blood relative where Celia was concerned, and he'd be damned if he'd ever be a husband again. He was a man who learned from life's little lessons, and that one in particular was one he'd never forget.

When he cautiously returned the receiver to his ear,

he caught Angel in mid-tirade, still going strong. The water shut off in the bathroom and Alec quickly interrupted Angel. "I gotta go, sweetie. Tell Dane not to worry. I'll take care of things."

"Wait a minute!"

He sighed again, feeling very put upon. "What?"

Angel wasn't the least put off by his surly tone. "Will you stay there and help Celia or not?"

Tonight appeared to be his night to reason with unreasonable women. "It's dangerous, Angel. She could get hurt."

"Not with you there to watch over things. Dane says you're the very best. I know you can handle this and make sure Celia stays safe."

He felt cornered, damn it, and his tone lowered to a growl. "I don't *want* to stay here and make sure she's safe. It's a wasted trip."

"Celia doesn't think so."

The soft way Angel spoke made him feel guilty. Was he being insensitive to Celia? Was it really so dangerous that he couldn't indulge her, or was it just his own personal prejudice against this case that was deciding him?

It took him less than two seconds to realize it was both.

Angel wasn't done laying on the guilt. Funny how all women seemed to instinctively know the shortest route to manipulating a man, even a man they couldn't claim as their own.

Why the hell didn't Dane step in and provide some distraction?

"Alec, are you listening to me?"

"Yeah."

"If you're not going to stay, then I can't possibly go off on a trip and leave Celia alone. She'll need someone who understands and supports her."

Alec wondered if offering understanding and support would soften Celia a little, help remove that damn "no" from her vocabulary.

Dane's hard tone interrupted his musing, blaring into the phone even though Angel still held it. *"He'll stay."*

Giving in to the inevitable, now that he'd admitted to himself he *could* keep Celia safe, Alec echoed with a sigh, "I'll stay."

"Good." There was a second's pause, just enough to prepare him, before she added, "We love you, Alec."

He heard Dane snicker in the background and felt his entire face heat. He hated it when Angel did that, got all mushy on him, and Dane damn well knew it, which was probably why he encouraged her in that melodramatic crap. He didn't want her to say the words and he sure as hell didn't want her to feel them. Not for him. He could do without love, just as he always had. In fact, he preferred it that way.

Of course, what he preferred never seemed to matter much once Angel had her mind set on something. And she'd made him a part of their family, which meant she was determined that he accept her love. Unaccountable female.

Trying not to sound too surly, or worse, like he was embarrassed by her affection, Alec muttered, "Yeah, well, good night." He hung up quickly, just as Celia opened the bathroom door and stepped out.

She had on faded jeans that fit her slim legs to perfection and a soft, thin T-shirt that draped over the small mounds of her breasts. She looked great dressed up, but he found her just as appealing when she dressed down, maybe even more so.

The first thing that clearly registered in his beleaguered brain was the fact she was braless. Then he took in her bare feet, her scrubbed pink face and slicked-back, still-wet hair, and everything in him tightened. Brother, father, husband hell. He wanted to be her lover.

He stood slowly, unable to pull his gaze away from her. "I ordered up some food. It should be here soon."

She nodded, not quite meeting his eyes. She had that killer dress and the high heels in her arms and she laid them aside on the dresser. As she moved, Alec noticed her limping slightly and he scowled.

"Are you hurt?"

"No."

He stepped closer, just about sick of her playing so timid. On some level, he enjoyed scrapping with her, though he'd never admit it to her. But fighting with Celia was, in many ways, more enjoyable than having sex with other women. It surely heated his blood more. Of course, everything to do with Celia heated his blood.

He caught her chin and lifted it. "Don't ever lie to me, Celia. You're limping. Did you hurt yourself when you jumped out of my truck?"

Her lashes were still spiky from the shower. She blinked slowly, her hazel eyes bright, and a slight flush pinkened her skin. "My feet are sore. I'm not used to wearing high heels anymore."

He moved his thumb, gently brushing it back and

forth over her small rounded chin. Her skin was so soft, he wanted to touch her all over, rub himself naked against her, feel that softness under him, accepting him. He took a steadying breath. "I'll rub your feet for you."

Her eyes widened and she nervously blurted, "I want to make a deal with you."

One brow lifted high. He was about to tell her he'd stay and help her with the damn Barrington case, just so she could relax and stop being so jumpy, but now she had him curious. He led her over to the edge of the bed, urged her to sit, then knelt before her. He lifted one small foot into his hands, and as he started rubbing, pressing his thumbs into her arch, he said, "So? What's the deal?" Her toes curled in his hand, making him smile.

"I need your help if I'm going to be able to do any good with this case."

"Yes, you do." He flexed her foot, heard her small groan and began rubbing each small, pink toe. She had nice feet, as intrinsically female as the rest of her. They were so small, so narrow and smooth and pale, they seemed swallowed up by his large rough hands.

"I'll…I'll do anything you want if you'll help me save Hannah."

His hands stilled. His gaze shot from her foot to her face and narrowed there. He didn't say anything, not trusting himself to speak.

Celia appeared to be holding her breath, her eyes round, the pulse in the hollow of her throat fluttering anxiously. When he only watched her, doing his best to keep his anger under wraps, she burst out in nervous explanation. "I know you think I'm not fit to do this work.

You've done nothing but harp on me about quitting, about going back to the family business." She paused, drew a deep breath. "Well, I'll do it."

"It?" He couldn't get his jaw to work, so the one-word question was whispered through clenched teeth.

She nodded. "I'll…I'll go back. But only if you help me to help Hannah first."

The tension eased out of him by slow degrees. She wasn't bartering her body as he'd first assumed. She'd agree to quit, to return to her old job where she'd be safe. It was what he'd wanted, what he knew would be best for her. Angel's words echoed in his mind, making his muscles tense with guilt. *She'll need someone who understands and supports her.* Very slowly, he released her foot and put both hands on her knees. Still holding her gaze, he gently urged her legs apart. Whatever Celia needed, he wanted to give it to her.

Her eyes widened again, but he was already there, already moving up over her, gently easing her down onto the mattress while wedging himself firmly between her soft, spread thighs. He closed his eyes, relishing the feel of her beneath him, the gentle cradle of her open body. Pressing his hips down and in, he moved against her, torturing himself with the pleasure of it.

"Alec?" Her voice was high and thin.

"What if that's not what I want the most, Celia?" He felt his heart drumming, his stomach twisting with need. "What then?"

She swallowed hard, the sound audible in the quiet room. She blinked twice before squarely meeting his gaze. "I can't give up on Hannah."

His senses ignited, heat rushing over him in waves.

All he could think was that she was giving in to him, she wanted him to make love to her.

He leaned down to kiss her, already breathless with anticipation—and a knock sounded on the door.

His head jerked up and his entire body went rigid as he instinctively prepared for the possible threat.

"Room service!"

Several curses came to mind, but it was Celia scrambling out from beneath him, her panic almost tangible as she leapt from the bed and rushed back into the bathroom, that helped him maintain control. Once again, that door was slammed.

Alec flopped down on the bed and flung one arm over his eyes. Tonight wasn't going at all as planned.

And given what had just almost happened, he had a feeling it was going to get a lot worse before it got better. Typical, whenever he dealt with Celia.

CELIA SLOWLY CHEWED on her sandwich. She didn't really want it, not when nothing had been settled between them. She felt like an idiot for fleeing to the bathroom again. At least this time Alec hadn't abused the door to get her out. He'd merely asked her if she was ready to eat, and she'd calmly walked out as if she hadn't been hiding. Dumb. She had to get a grip if she wanted to talk him into helping her.

The noisy air conditioner in her room barely took the edge off the heat. The air felt heavy, thick. The food tasted bland to her nervous tongue. Alec sat across from her at the small, scarred table wedged into the corner of the room. There was barely space to move between it and the edge of the bed. He'd sat so that he faced the door, a conscious decision on his part because Alec was always alert, always prepared. With him, she had no doubt she could save Hannah.

But Alec kept looking at her with his narrow-eyed gaze, speculating, just waiting to start grilling her and putting her on the spot. She decided to beat him to the punch. The key to dealing with Alec was to stay in control.

She cleared her throat, took a large swallow of the coffee, then looked him dead in the eye.

Sheesh, he was gorgeous.

"Come on, honey, out with it." Alec grinned slightly, one eyebrow lifted. "I can see you have something to say, so say it."

Celia scowled. "How do you do that?"

"Read your mind?" He tugged at his earring absently. "I don't know, except that we've got some kind of chemistry going, whether you want to admit it or not."

She lowered her eyes. "Actually, that's part of my… um, problem."

"Your *sexual* problem?"

Heat rushed into her cheeks. She hated the way he just blurted that out, but she knew he was deliberately rattling her, so she lifted her chin and again forced herself to meet his gaze. "Yes."

Alec took a healthy bite of his own sandwich, taking his time while he chewed and swallowed. "Didn't seem to me like you had a problem." His attention dropped to her breasts and her nipples immediately peaked. His eyes narrowed. "Everything appears to be working just fine."

She had to lock her knees to keep from running away again. She was so ashamed of herself, it was all she could do to sit there and face him. "That's part of the problem."

Now he looked surprised, and a tad annoyed. He swallowed the last of his food and glared. "Come again?"

Fiddling with the spoon for her coffee just to give her fingers something to do, Celia admitted, "I'm not very discriminating. I suppose I'm what's called a loose woman." She felt his gaze like a laser burn and this time she couldn't look up.

"A loose woman?"

Something in his tone sounded lethal and she braced herself. "After the way I let Raymond use me, putting so many people in danger, I decided I would never again get involved with a man who didn't really care about me. I thought I had learned my lesson, that my pride was enough to keep me from being foolish. But..." She swallowed hard, searching for the right words. "You...you look at me, and I forget all my convictions."

"This is all because you *want* me?" He sounded irritated and a little disbelieving.

"I want you. But not for the right reasons."

Alec shot out of his chair and she braced herself, watching him wide-eyed. Rather than come to her, he stalked away, his hands on his hips, his shoulders rigid. Through the tight T-shirt, she could clearly see every muscle of his back.

"Alec, when we first met you made it clear you didn't want a relationship. Every time we're together you make it clear that you don't trust me, that you don't even really like me."

He whipped around to stare at her, incredulous.

She faltered just a bit, but her gut instincts toward Hannah couldn't be ignored. "You just want me for sex, and as much as my body might like the idea, my brain is disgusted and ashamed."

"Your brain?" He started toward her, slowly stalking, his eyes narrowed and intent on her face.

She quickly slid out of her chair and stepped behind it. The crowded room gave her little enough space to navigate. "Stop trying to intimidate me! I hate it when you do that, especially when I'm only trying to give you the truth."

"The truth being that you have some harebrained idea that sex without love everlasting is dirty?"

He stopped in front of her, towering, angry. Celia pushed the chair aside and pointed her finger at him, her own anger taking over. "Sex without some kind of emotional commitment is dirty! It's just sex."

"Which can be damn satisfying!"

"Not for me!" She realized they were both screaming and tried to calm herself. Good grief, she didn't want to run him off, and she certainly didn't want everyone in the motel to know their personal business. She pushed a hand through her wet hair and took several deep breaths. "I'm sorry for sort of leading you on. You kiss me, and I forget what I'm doing and what it is I want to do. I'd appreciate it if you wouldn't touch me anymore."

"Like hell."

Celia ignored that. "I have a lot to make up for, Alec, mostly because I was blinded by Raymond and who he was. And the reason I was so blinded—"

"I don't want to hear this, damn it."

"Is because sex between us was—" She almost choked, then forced the words out. "It was great."

"*Goddammit.*" Alec's hand grabbed her arms and pulled her up on tiptoe. "Celia—"

Whatever he was going to say was cut off by the loud beeping of her pager. They both froze for a moment, and Alec seemed to be vibrating with anger, struggling for control. Celia waited, practically hanging in his grip, though strangely not worried. For whatever reason, this time she didn't fear him. Alec would never hurt her, and she knew it.

He slowly released her until her feet touched flat on the floor. She rushed over to the dresser where her beeper lay. She hadn't taken it with her to the bar, too afraid it would go off and Jacobs would discover something that would give her away. She picked it up and read the number blinking at her with a distinct feeling of dread.

Biting her lip, she turned to face Alec.

"Who is it?" He had himself under control, but it was a tenuous hold. Everything he felt was still there in his glittering black eyes, plain for her to see. From the inside out, she felt the trembling start.

Watching him closely, she said, "It's…Mrs. Barrington."

Alec turned away, but Celia was already rushing to him, personal reservations forgotten in the face of Hannah's need. "Alec?" When he didn't answer she shifted around so she was in front of him and he had no choice but to listen to her. "Please, I need your help with this case. Hannah needs your help." She ignored his snort of disbelief and continued. "I have to call her back. Alec? *Please,* will you stay and help me?"

He stared at the ceiling for a good full minute, not answering. Celia could feel his indecision and she held herself still, allowing him to decide while at the same time hoping against hope that he wouldn't turn her down.

Finally he looked at her, and she'd never seen him harder, more determined. Her heartbeat shuddered, then began a rapid tattoo.

"Yeah, Celia, I'll stay. I'll help you save little Hannah Barrington, whether the girl wants saving or not." He looked her over, his gaze more cold than hot now. "But there's a condition."

Despite his cynical, detached attitude, a warmth spread through her, proof of what she'd already guessed, what she'd always known, exactly what he'd want in return. Her legs felt shaky, but she lifted her chin and returned his direct stare, bravado her only defense. "I'm listening."

His eyelids drooped sensually, his thick lashes almost hiding his gaze as he stared at first her mouth, then her breasts, then lower. His tone was soft, a raw growl that made her every nerve ending tingle with awareness. "I want you. Whenever and wherever I decide. Any way I choose to take you—" His gaze lifted, meeting hers again. "—and I'll choose a hell of a lot of ways. You'll say yes. Until this is over, until Hannah is on her way home, you'll be mine."

Celia rolled her lips in to contain a moan, unable to look away, unable to say a single word. Damn, but she was almost relieved. He was going to take the decision out of her hands, and her belly curled in anticipation even as she feared her own response.

Alec smirked, the gesture sensual and ripe with promise. "Oh no, honey," he whispered, "I'm not going to let you play at being a martyr. I'm going to make damn sure you enjoy every little thing I do to you, with no holding back. Whatever the hell you did with Raymond won't be able to compare. And when I'm done, you'll know damn good and well that nothing between us is dirty."

His hands cupped her hot cheeks and turned her face up to his. "You can call Mrs. Barrington and tell her not to worry, that everything will be taken care of." His thumb brushed her bottom lip, hot and rough. "And then you can strip those jeans off and get into bed."

She gasped.

"Or you can tell me to go to hell." His eyes glittered, bright with intent. "The decision is yours."

Celia licked her dry lips, trying to find words around the wild racing of her heart. He hadn't even really touched her yet and she felt ready to lose control. How would she ever survive? Did she have any choice?

"I'll…I'll call Mrs. Barrington."

His eyes blazed with sudden heat at her acceptance, his nostrils flaring in excitement, like a wild animal sensing victory. For just a heartbeat his hands tightened and she thought her time of reckoning was at hand, that he'd lost control. Then he stepped away. "I have to get a few things out of my truck. I can stay with you tonight, because everyone expected it. But tomorrow I'll have to get my own room just in case anyone has the sense to check up on you."

Celia stood mute, watching him.

"Go ahead and make your call. In the morning, I'll figure how out we're going to handle things."

She watched him leave the room, his body moving with fluid grace and blatant strength. She didn't bother asking what they'd do tonight. She already knew.

She drew in a shuddering breath, tamped down on her

guilt and shame while telling herself she was only doing what was necessary. Then she reached for the phone. She didn't want to be occupied when Alec returned; she didn't want to have to disrobe in front of him.

She'd be in the bed, hiding under the covers.

Everything else was up to him.

CHAPTER FIVE

ALEC LINGERED in the parking lot for several reasons.

First and foremost, he had to get control of himself. Holding out a hand, he stared in disgust at the trembling in his own body, a body usually so cold nothing affected it, certainly not a woman. For years, too many to count, he'd been able to take pleasure in a woman's body, to give pleasure back, without letting it get to him.

He felt damn affected now, and he hadn't even really touched the little witch. Heaven help him when he got himself buried deep inside her, when he felt the hot wet clasp of her body, heard her half-frightened, mostly excited moans...

Cursing, he paced furiously around his truck, trying to outrun the truth of his feelings. She did fear him a little, and for now, nothing would change that. He didn't even want to change it because although he made her nervous, she still wanted him, almost as much as he wanted her. He knew having sex with Celia would blow his mind out, and the knowing was almost worse than the actual effects. Like a drug he knew could destroy him, he wanted her anyway. Being as cold and indifferent as possible was his only defense.

But when she looked up at him with those innocent

hazel eyes, he wanted to protect her, even from himself. And that was another reason he hesitated.

He should have killed Raymond; killing him would make Alec feel a whole lot better now. *She'd said sex between them had been great.* He squeezed his eyes shut and considered howling at the moon. The words, and her tortured look that had accompanied them, filled him with such a killing rage, he knew he'd have to do whatever he could to erase that bastard from her body, from her soul. If she didn't thank him in the beginning, she would by the end. He had to believe that.

Knowing he'd stalled long enough, that Celia could well be trying to sneak out the tiny bathroom window, he grabbed his gear from his truck and headed back in. Every muscle in his body felt tight and strained, his jaw locked, his mind in turmoil. The hard-on he'd learned to associate with any close proximity to Celia throbbed insistently. He hated needing her like this. He hated to need anyone.

Half expecting the door to be locked now, he was taken aback when it swung open easily and he found Celia lying wide-eyed in the narrow bed—very obviously naked beneath all the blankets.

The covers were pulled so high, even her chin was hidden, with her rounded eyes looking almost comical over the hem. Twin sets of slender fingers gripped the blankets on either side of her mouth. A strange feeling, like mingled tenderness and raging lust, rushed through him, making him light-headed, almost dizzy with triumph and hunger. He liked seeing her in a bed, waiting for *him.* Oh yeah, he liked it a lot. Too damn much.

His mouth kicked up in a crooked smile as he

dropped his overnight bag on the floor and put his pistol on the bedside table. Celia's eyes rounded even more at the sight of the weapon.

"You carry a…a gun?"

He gave her a level look, amazed at her naiveté. "All the agents do, Celia."

"I don't… That is…should I?"

Alec shook his head, astounded that a feeling as light as amusement could touch him now when he could feel the furious drumming of his heart. "Hell no. One leg wound is enough for me."

"*I* didn't shoot you!"

He started to sit on the side of the bed, then thought better of it. If he got that close, all his plans would end before they could begin. He wasn't ready yet. He needed at least a few more minutes to shore up his determination.

He stepped back a few paces and leaned on the wall, watching her. "I can think of a dozen times in the last few hours when you might have."

"Well…" She considered that, then shrugged in resignation. "Yeah."

His gaze sharpened and he deliberately used a tone he knew drew attention from hired killers. "You don't need a weapon, sweetheart, because after this, you won't be taking any more dangerous cases."

Her fingers tightened on the blankets and her eyes narrowed. But thankfully, for his peace of mind, she kept silent.

Still holding her gaze, Alec reached down and unbuckled his belt. Celia blinked hard, her gaze skimming down his body then immediately shooting back up again in a visibly desperate bid to stay on his face. With a whistling sound, the leather belt slid out of the jean loops and he draped it over the back of a chair.

"Alec?" Her voice was a squeak, anxious and embarrassed and if he was any judge, turned-on. "What are we going to do about Hannah? Do you have a plan?"

He pulled his shirt over his head and heard her soft groan. "I have several plans, sweetheart. Why don't we talk about my plan for tonight, for right now?" After tossing the shirt aside he scratched his bare chest and saw her fascinated gaze. Very softly, he asked, "You want details?"

"No...yes...*no*."

He grinned. "Indecisive, aren't we? Well, I think I want to tell you anyway."

"Alec, I think—"

"You think sex is dirty, I know."

She squeezed her eyes closed and for a brief cowardly moment pulled the blankets over her head. Seconds later she jerked it down again to stare at him.

Celia was no coward.

"Okay." She drew a deep fortifying breath. "What are you going to do, Alec?"

She had to be smothering under all those blankets. The cheap motel had inadequate air, and though the air conditioner rattled and hummed loudly, it couldn't keep up with the oppressive July heat. Alec had already begun to sweat, but then, that had a lot to do with Celia being so close and naked.

Toeing off his low boots then bending to remove his socks, he said, "I'm going to let you get familiar with my body."

"Oh..."

Hearing the trembling in her tone nearly did him in.

He'd always considered himself a strong man; physically he knew it was true, but mentally, emotionally, she had him concerned. He couldn't think of a single challenge he'd ever backed away from, and he always accepted knowing he'd win, his confidence never wavering. But he didn't know if he was strong enough to do this tonight. He hoped so, because Miss Celia Carter was in desperate need of a few lessons, and damned if he'd let any other man give them to her.

Number one, the most important lesson, that he wasn't Raymond and other than gender, had not a single thing in common with that scum.

But just telling her that wouldn't do it. And neither would having sex with her when she was so skittish and unsure of herself. Oh, she'd take him, all right. He had no doubts on that score. She'd take him and enjoy herself immensely. Used to be, that would have been enough for him. But not now.

He wanted her to openly want him, to admit it was right between them. To accept that sometimes sex was just plain meant to be and this was one of those times. There was no shame in that.

If he took her now, she'd be ashamed.

Damn. Alec cursed to himself, but couldn't find any way around that truth. Celia fought against her natural instincts. He'd never seen a woman so responsive, so easily aroused as his Celia. It was a gift, one he planned to enjoy and wanted her to appreciate.

So he planned to teach her, slowly, to accept him and what they could have together for as long as the chemistry lasted. She'd learn, little by little, and he had no doubt he'd die by small degrees with each lesson.

He unbuttoned his fly and slid down the zipper, carefully because he was so fully erect he ached like never before. The soft, hungry moan Celia gave told him eventually he'd have his reward. The torture would be worth it.

"Don't close your eyes, Celia."

Her hands covered her face.

"Celia, look at me." His command was soft, insistent.

She shook her head. "Alec, I can't. I…" Her voice emerged breathy, so aroused she aroused him just by speaking.

"You have no choice, sweetheart, remember?" He pushed the jeans down, taking his dark briefs with them, and stepped away from his clothing. Celia's naked shoulders were now visible and he wanted to start kissing her there, eating her there, then working his way down until he'd devoured every hidden, hot inch of her. He drew a deep breath.

When he was right next to the bed, so close his naked thigh nearly touched the mattress, he said, "Look at me, Celia."

She jumped, startled by his approach. His silent movements often had that effect on people; even Dane had commented on his stealth, cursing him on occasion for taking him unawares.

With her bottom lip firmly caught between her teeth, she slowly lifted her lashes. Heat rushed into her cheeks and her breasts trembled with small, rapid breaths, making the covers flutter.

Alec studied her, forcing himself to stick to his plan despite the gripping need to take her. "Does my body look dirty to you, Celia?"

Gaze glued to his erection, she shook her head no.

He put one knee on the bed and she rolled slightly toward him, her expression almost panicked.

"Shhh. Don't get jumpy on me." He caught the edge of the blankets and they went through a silent tug-of-war before Celia closed her eyes again and released them.

Very slowly, feeling every punch of his heartbeat as it resounded through his body, Alec bared her. He threw the covers completely off the bed. For now at least, they wouldn't need them.

Stiff, nearly frozen, her only movement that of her choked breaths, she remained obediently quiet while Alec visually explored her. Her small rounded breasts were perfect, flushed a warm pink, softly upright, shimmering with her nervousness and excitement. Her nipples were drawn achingly tight, dark rose, and more than anything he wanted them in his mouth, wanted to suck on her and hear her small cries. He swallowed hard and continued his visual feast.

Her skin, pale and so smooth, would chafe easily beneath his whiskers, and he mentally cautioned himself to be careful. Her navel made a slight, tempting dent in her softly rounded belly, and below that...

His nostrils expanded on a sharp breath. Dark blond curls covered her in a small neat triangle. Without his mind's permission, his hand lifted and he covered her, then he groaned softly. Celia jerked, a shocked, highly erotic sound coming from deep in her throat.

"Look, Celia," he urged her. She shook her head and his fingers tightened. "Look at how my hand covers you completely. I can feel the heat pulsing off you." He leaned down and nuzzled her belly, nearly incoherent with lust. "And I can smell your scent. You're every damn bit as turned on as I am."

Panting, she whispered, "Alec?"

He realized she was close, that in only those few moments with nothing more than a scattering of words and a possessive touch, she was nearing the edge. *She was incredible.* In a voice he barely recognized as his own, Alec murmured, "I like seeing you, honey. There sure as hell isn't anything dirty about you."

The sound she made drew his attention back to her face and the sight of her nearly ecstatic pain helped him regain control. He raised his hand to her cheek, then slowly smoothed her mouth, urging her to release her lip from the grip of her teeth. "Don't hurt yourself, baby. Everything's okay."

Tears leaked from beneath her lashes and with a quavery voice she said, "I'm so...so easy."

Alec lay down beside her, no longer needing an incentive to keep himself under control. Her pain had done that for him. He drew her naked body close and above the lust he felt the overwhelming need to protect, to reassure, to comfort. For now at least, she was his woman, and he'd move heaven and earth to keep her from being hurt, even from herself.

"You're special, Celia, a gift to any man lucky enough to grab your attention." Very deliberately, his hand slid down her belly again. He couldn't let her stay like this, not when he knew damn well he could ease her.

Her hips immediately thrust against his searching fingers and she groaned, gripping him tight. "Alec, *please kiss me...*"

He did, devouring her mouth, searching with his tongue as he searched with his fingers.

Her flesh was so soft, so slick with eagerness. His fingers glided, probed, found the friction and rhythm that made her instantly wild. She wriggled against him, deliberately arousing herself further by moving her nipples over his chest, sucking on his tongue. She was hot and carnal and—oh hell—she was his.

Within two minutes she was coming apart in his arms and Alec cursed even as he fought to hold his own reaction at bay. Losing control, releasing himself on her belly, wouldn't do a damn thing toward convincing her that sex was good and wholesome, not something to hide away from.

She bit him, his mouth, his chin, then his shoulder, and her nails dug deep into the muscles of his back, the small stings helping him keep control. When she slumped, sweaty and hot and limp in his arms, Alec kissed her forehead and smoothed her hair back.

"That was a long time coming."

She didn't answer, apparently too dazed to form words.

"Celia, if you act embarrassed or ashamed, I swear I'll turn you over my knee."

She lightly bit him again, this time on his muscled chest. "Don't forget your gun is still close, Sharpe. I'm not afraid to use it."

Grinning, while doing his best to ignore his own pounding need, Alec reached to the floor and snagged the top sheet. Tucking her up against his side, he said, "You're going to sleep right here, against my body, all night, honey. Don't even think of moving away. You got that?"

Her brows lowered as her eyes opened and she stared up at him. "But…sleep? What about—"

He cupped her cheek and kissed her nose. "We're not finishing this little game until you ask me, very nicely, to do so."

She searched his face and he could detect her mental shrug. "All right, I—"

He laid a finger against her lips. "Not now, Celia. Not when you're still all soft from a nice climax." Her cheeks turned bright pink at his frank talk and he smiled. "You'll know when you're ready, when you want me without all this ridiculous reserve. Then I'll take you until neither of us can walk. I promise. But for tonight, we sleep."

He reached over and switched off the light, then gathered her close again. Her thighs cradled his erection, making him grit his teeth. After several silent moments, she whispered, "I won't make it easy on you, Alec."

He shook his head. "You never have, babe."

CELIA WOKE with her nose pressed to a hard, very warm, somewhat hairy chest. She smiled, snuggling closer and deeply inhaling the delicious scent of warm male flesh, but within the space of a single heartbeat she remembered Alec and what he'd done and what she'd done… Oh no. She opened her eyes slowly and like a zombie, lifted her head to survey him.

Breathing deeply in his sleep, more at peace than she'd ever seen him, he looked sexier than any man she'd known. He had one long, muscled arm beneath her neck and around her back, keeping her pressed to his body. His other arm was bent up behind his head, opening his body to her perusal, making him look somewhat vulnerable. She could see the dark tuft of fine hair beneath his arm, the way his biceps bulged even when relaxed. His long silky hair was tousled, lying over his brow and touching his wide shoulders. The single gold earring shone dully in the morning light.

His jaw and chin were very dark with beard shadow, and she knew when he awakened, he'd look more menacing than ever. But for now, his long sooty lashes rested on his high cheekbones, presenting elongated shadows in the dim room, and he looked entirely too…*cuddly*.

Saying he was beautiful would have been an extreme understatement.

A soft sigh escaped her and she felt her heart lurch. Given a choice, she would have cuddled down next to him and gone blissfully back to sleep. But she knew Alec, knew his way, and understood that she couldn't let her guard down around him for a minute. Being the natural predator, he'd take swift advantage of any opening she gave him.

Not that she hadn't already given him plenty, she thought, feeling her face go hot with the memory of the past night. But she wouldn't let him win. He hoped to intimidate her enough to make her head home, leaving poor Hannah abandoned.

That would explain why he'd toyed with her so deliciously without actually taking her. She shivered, aware of him on every level. But while she physically appreciated his finesse, she didn't like his motives. If he wanted to be a caveman, she couldn't fight him, but neither did she dare give in to him completely.

Raymond had hurt her pride, but Alec could kill it.

He shifted in his sleep and her eyes were drawn to his body. The blankets only covered him as high as his navel, leaving a lot of incredible skin still bare. He was naturally dark, determinedly hard, and as much man as any woman could ever hope for.

She looked back up at the broad expanse of his solid shoulders, then gasped. High on his shoulder was a bruise, a bruise she knew had been caused by her teeth.

Last night, when the pleasure had taken her, she'd bitten him.

Her reaction was swift, the bitter reality cutting her deep and forcing her to stifle an instinctive cry of pain. She started to scramble upward, wanting to escape the proof of her own unrestrained tendencies, but suddenly found herself flat on her back. Alec, the cad, was wide awake.

"Where do you think you're going?" His voice was rough velvet, still heavy with sleep, but his eyes were sharply alert.

"Let me go, Alec."

He searched her face, his dark gaze almost obsidian in the vague morning light. She could see him thinking, calculating, and it enraged her. Pushing against his chest with all her might, she said through her teeth, *"Let—me—go."*

Her struggles had no effect on him. She may as well have been fighting solid granite. "You were looking me over, getting used to my body. Why the sudden panic?"

Celia froze. Had he been awake the whole time? Been aware of her scrutiny? "I did not panic."

"No? What would you call it?" Before she could answer, he added in a low rumble, "Damn woman, but you look hot first thing in the morning." And then he kissed her.

Celia tried to resist him, she really did. But he smelled manly and warm and his mouth had a slightly musky taste to it from sleep. His whiskers rasped her cheek as he deepened the kiss, his hands coming up to roughly cradle her breasts. She arched into him, unable to help herself.

And he lifted away. His lips still touching hers, he said, "Now tell me what's wrong."

Her gaze didn't seem to want to focus and her heart was working way too hard for first thing in the morning. "I...I need coffee."

"As soon as you talk to me."

Damn stubborn man. He wouldn't give up, so she had to. Resolving the problem and getting out of the bed, out from under him, was a major priority. Lowering her lashes because she really couldn't look at him while making such an admission, she said in a small voice, "I bit you."

She could hear his grin, felt the renewed caressing of her breasts, gentle and easy. "Several times."

"No, I mean..." She peeked up at him, trying to gather her wits. *Several times?* Oh good grief, it just kept getting worse and worse. She felt almost sick with dread and tried to order her thoughts, but it was extremely difficult with him lying on her, all hard muscle and hot male.

She drew a slow breath. "You have a...a bruise on your shoulder."

He looked over at his shoulder, then dismissed the small mark with a shrug. "So?"

Her bottom lip trembled and she tightened her mouth to still the small giveaway. "I'm sorry."

"Sorry for being sexy? For having an incredibly healthy sex drive? Hell, woman, I *liked* it, okay? That little nibble says you were feeling everything just as I wanted you to feel it. Just as you're supposed to feel it."

"No." She wouldn't let him make light of it, not when she knew different. "I hurt you, Alec. I behaved no better than a...an animal."

His eyes darkened more, then he nuzzled her neck just below her ear. "You had a really nice orgasm, honey, full-blown, just as I wanted you to. I liked it. If you acted like an animal, then so did I, because that little love nibble all but pushed me over the edge, and knowing the reason for it damn sure made me feel pretty terrific." He kissed her earlobe, and his warm, damp tongue tickled over the rim of her ear, making her breath catch. And then he was looking at her again, waiting for her to accept what he'd said.

Heart racing, she thought about it, and pondered her own naiveté in sexual matters. Despite her limited experience, she asked, "Do you...?"

"What?" His slow smile came again. "Bite?"

The humor and hunger and tenderness in his black eyes made her stomach feel empty and her skin feel hot. But the room was dim and quiet, the day still early. Asking intimate questions seemed as perfectly timed as possible. "Yes."

His lids lowered sensually and he moved his mouth to the place where her shoulder and neck met. Celia shivered, then quickly braced herself when she felt his mouth open, felt the touch of his teeth. He did bite, but it didn't hurt. Just the opposite. The bite was wet and soft and he immediately soothed it with his tongue, making her nerves tingle.

"I would never do anything to hurt you."

Her eyes drifted shut. "Alec..."

He scooted downward in the bed, kicking the sheet away and situating himself comfortably. His mouth stayed on her, taking small delicious nibbles all along the way until he reached the tip of her breast. Her heart thundered so that she wondered why it didn't explode. He prepared her, plumping her breast, smoothing the nipple with his calloused thumb until it stiffened and stood turgid beneath his attention. Every nerve in her body seemed suspended, waiting. Then he nipped her.

Celia jumped, groaning at the same time when Alec held her firmly in place. He did it again and again, sometimes plucking with his lips, sometimes tugging with his teeth. It was an erotic mixture of foreplay: taut expectancy—though no real injury ever came—and sinful teasing. Her toes curled under the sheet, her hands fisted in his soft, cool hair.

The man was cruel, playing with her for long minutes and when she did finally think he was through, he only switched to the other breast. When she moaned out a protest, he mumbled something about breakfast and continued. Celia curled her legs around him and squeezed. That didn't help, so she pushed herself against him and Alec helped by curving one large hand over her derriere and urging her into a slow, hypnotic rhythm against his body.

She'd thought herself fully experienced, even jaded after her time with Raymond, but she'd never done anything like this, or anything like last night. Alec was either the most inventive lover in the world, or her experiences with Raymond hadn't been adequate to prepare her for Alec.

She tended to believe it was a mix of the two. Especially when she felt herself on the verge of a climax.

Alec seemed to sense it, too. He lifted his head, staring at her hard, his jaw working as if he felt undecided.

His eyes narrowed, and very slowly, he pushed her back away from him. Her heart broke and she wanted to cry out in shame and disappointment, but he didn't give her a chance. He grasped her hips and leaned down, then nuzzled his face into her belly.

Celia was genuinely shocked. He wasn't leaving her, he was… *"Alec."*

He held her firmly against the mattress, stilling the automatic surge of her body, and sought her out with his tongue, laving her much like a cat. Nearly mindless in sensation, she fought against him even while struggling to get closer. He controlled her with almost no effort, occasionally turning his face and softly biting the fleshy part of her inner thigh. Each sharp nip added to her pleasure, taking her a little higher, forcing her a little closer to the edge until she was beyond desperate.

"Come." Alec gave his command with supreme confidence, then caught her small bud between his teeth to torment her with his tongue, and Celia screamed, fully obedient, arching her back, digging her fingers into the mattress, so overwhelmed with emotion and sensation she could do nothing more than ride along on the wave of extreme pleasure. Nothing, no past experience, no mature knowledge, had prepared her for this.

When it ended, she couldn't exactly say. Her body buzzed, her mind felt blurry. One minute she'd been insensible, and the next, Alec was leaving the bed. She barely got her eyes open. "Alec?" The word was a breathy whisper.

He turned, kissed her hard right on the mouth, making her eyes widen a little, then growled, "I need an icy shower, babe. Just stay put and give me a minute. Then we'll get breakfast and talk."

He stalked, beautifully, sinfully naked into the bathroom and kicked the door shut. A second later the shower started.

Still staring at the closed door, still seeing that sexy, naked, hard-muscled behind, Celia blew out a slow breath. *Oh wow.* She wasn't prepared for this, didn't know how to handle it. Why did he keep giving her pleasure while taking none for himself? Did he expect her to think he didn't want her? Ha. He'd looked ready to self-destruct when he left the bed, all flushed, hot, ready man. Any other man *wouldn't* have left the damn bed.

Did this have something to do with what he'd told her last night? That ridiculous business about insisting she ask for him? Actually, she thought she had. Several times.

She may have even begged.

She'd also thought she knew about sex, but then, no one had ever told her about Alec Sharpe.

CHAPTER SIX

SHE'D EATEN NEARLY as much as he had. Alec grinned. The little lady had worked up an appetite. Or rather, he'd worked one up for her.

Damn, he could still taste her, and she'd been much tastier than the eggs and ham. Delicious, so sweet she could easily become an addiction. Everything about Celia was unique, so he wasn't at all surprised. His own restraint was the only shocker. How the hell he'd summoned up the willpower to walk away from her was the million dollar question. But he knew. Even now, she wouldn't quite meet his eyes, and she blushed every time he spoke to her.

She was ashamed, embarrassed, and he wanted to drag her back off to bed and keep her there until she got over her absurd hang-ups.

He hadn't realized he'd begun scowling at her until she slapped down her fork and finally looked him square in the eyes. "What are you up to, Alec?"

He choked on a sudden laugh, something he hadn't done in too many years to count. His day-to-day life didn't consist of lighthearted moments. Few people ever used that hostile tone with him, even fewer demanded answers of him. But Celia, though she was pink-cheeked and fidgety, managed to dredge up the spunk. He took a sip of his coffee, letting her stew, then said calmly, "Just waiting for you to accept a few facts."

She actually sneered at him, forcing him to repress another smile. "What facts? That you're a great lover? Ha! I'll never know, will I, when you keep running from the bed."

He would not let her rile him. Her bravado was a front for the real issue—her hurt feelings. And he regretted that. "I'm good enough, but then you make the effort a real pleasure."

She started to stand and he caught her wrist. "Don't cause a scene, honey. Remember, you have a cover around here to protect."

With the meanest look he could have imagined on such a sweet face, she reluctantly resettled herself.

"Now," he said, keeping his hold on her delicate wrist, "I wasn't insulting you. No, just listen. I want you, Celia. Don't doubt that, but like I told you, I'll be damned before I add to your skewed perspective on what's shameful and what isn't."

She toyed with her napkin. "After what you…we did, we might as well have…you know."

Taking another sip of unwanted coffee, he stalled for time. He had to play his hand carefully, had to measure his every word. "Do you feel dirty this morning, honey?"

Judging by her reaction, he should have measured a little more. Her small hands fisted on the table and the color in her face now was from anger, not embarrassment.

"Is that it, Alec?" She spoke in a low whisper, mindful of the one other couple in the café so early in the morning. "Are you out to use my own weaknesses against me? If you're hoping I'll give up on Hannah and go home just because you can make me—"

She gasped when he stood and pulled her up from her chair. "Not another word, lady."

She jerked her arm free and turned to walk out. Alec threw money on the table and followed her. Leaving the restaurant was fine by him; what he planned to say to her would be better said without an audience.

Celia stomped across the motel parking lot and started up the outside stairs to her room without once turning to see if Alec followed. That added to his rage as he wrapped his arm around her waist and steered her toward his truck instead. When she started to fight him, he tightened his grip. "Oh no, you're not getting off that easy. We have plans to make today and regardless of your temper, we'll stay on schedule. You want to save little Hannah, well fine. But we're definitely going to get a few things straightened out first."

The day was already sweltering, and heat rolled off the blacktop parking lot in waves. It was nothing compared to his ignited temper. He opened the truck door then waited while she threw him a malicious look before climbing in.

Alec slammed his own door hard enough to rattle the interior. He jammed the key in the ignition, hit the button to lock both doors, then gripped the steering wheel with all his might. Losing his control wouldn't help anything. Oh, Celia was doing her best to act unconcerned, but he knew her well enough by now to read her every thought, and he had her nervous. Rather than cooling his temper, that put it over the edge and he jerked around to face her, barking, "*Goddammit,* I would never hurt you so stop cowering in the damn corner!"

She bristled up like an angry racoon. Shooting across the seat to face him nose to nose, she yelled, "You don't scare me!"

A red haze clouded his vision. Very slowly, his arms crept around her, keeping her from retreating. "Then tell me what you're thinking, damn it."

She hesitated only a moment, biting her lip before lifting her chin. She didn't try to escape his hold, and that was a blessing, because Alec felt entirely too possessive and territorial to have her inching away. He wanted her close, and he wanted her to admit to liking it, too.

She touched the front of his shirt. "I don't understand you, Alec. I don't know what you're doing or why you suddenly got so mad."

Alec dropped his forehead against hers, and allowed his hands to tighten on her just a bit, bringing her breasts closer, arching her into his body. He took several slow breaths, regaining control. "I'm sorry."

Her eyes widened and her mouth fell open. Obviously she hadn't expected that. And with good reason. He couldn't remember ever apologizing to anyone before, at least, not since he'd been a kid, not since he'd learned his own lessons.

To further surprise them both, he admitted, "I don't like it when you compare me to Raymond."

Celia shook her head, her confusion apparent. "I didn't."

"Oh yeah you did." He released her to face the windshield, staring out at the hazy sunshine and the few clouds in the sky. "You do it all the damn time.

Raymond is the one who used you, not me. Raymond is the one who played games with your body and your feelings. Not me."

She bristled again, her face going hot and her eyes glittering, though this reaction was tempered with confusion. "And you don't think what you did last night or this morning qualifies as a game?"

"No." He turned his head toward her, but his hands gripped the steering wheel so tight his knuckles turned white. "When I'm making love to you, it's strictly for pleasure, mine and yours. It's not to hurt you in any way, or to manipulate you."

She barked out an incredulous laugh. "You never take any pleasure!"

He stared at her. "Just seeing you is a pleasure. If you think I can look at you buck naked, that I can make you scream when you come, and not enjoy the hell out of it, you're not as smart as I thought you were."

Her face flamed again, but her eyes turned softer, more accepting. "That's not what I'm talking about, Alec."

He thumped the steering wheel once with a fist. "I want you to trust me. That's all. I want you to see that what's between us is damn good."

She crossed her arms beneath her breasts. "For as long as it lasts?"

He didn't like the way she said that, as something of a challenge. But he wouldn't let her corner him into making false promises. He turned away and started the truck. "Nothing lasts forever. But in the meantime, we're wasting a hell of an opportunity."

"What if I want more, Sharpe?" Her bravado had her once again facing him down, and this time he resented the hell out of it. "What if I want all the things Dane and Angel have?"

He swallowed, feeling a sudden constriction in his chest. He almost said, *What if I don't have that to give,* but he bit the words back at the last moment. Giving away that much of himself wouldn't do.

He put the truck in gear and pulled into the early-morning traffic, giving himself plenty of time to think.

"Alec?"

Now she sounded uncertain again and he hated it. "I don't know. Until Dane found Angel, I'd have said it wasn't possible. But things seem to be...working out for them." He knew he sounded like an idiot, but this was one topic that made him extremely nervous. And he didn't like the feeling worth a damn.

She laughed, incredulous. "They adore each other!"

Turning a corner in the road, he asked, as nonchalantly as possible, "Do you adore me?"

A thick silence filled the truck and he felt himself beginning to sweat despite the icy air blasting from the truck's air conditioner. "That's what I figured. So why all the questions about happily ever after? Why not just take what we can for right now and enjoy it?"

She avoided that question by asking one of her own. "Where are we going?"

"I have to find a place to stay other than with you. It's possible Jacobs will have you watched. If I bunk down with you on occasion, that's fine. He'll expect it of you and it'll only shore up your image of being the type of woman he can approach. But moving in with you entirely is out of the question. Jacobs doesn't prey on women who have protectors."

"You're finally admitting that I was right? That

Jacobs is scum using women like Hannah? My, my. This is turning into one eventful day."

Alec hid his grin behind a look of reproach. She was so full of herself, taunting him. But he preferred that any day over her insecurities or her damn questions about the future. "I did my research, honey. I know what Jacobs is capable of and I never denied that he's a bastard, only whether or not Hannah appreciated the setup he gave her. If she's really unhappy with him, why doesn't she just call her mother and go home?"

Another of those heavy, uncomfortable silences filled the truck and Alec regretted his words. He didn't want to put her back in a dark mood. But then she turned to face him, and her determination was plain to see.

"You wouldn't know what it's like, Alec. You're strong and independent and able to take care of yourself and any situation. I can't imagine anyone or anything ever really hurting you."

She made it sound like an insult, as if along with his strengths he'd become too empty to care. "I'm not invincible, damn it." Far from it, he thought, briefly focusing on the past and a time that was too painful to remember for long.

"You sure seem invincible to me. You see everything as black and white and you always stick to your convictions. But I remember how ashamed I was after Raymond turned out to be such a user."

"Celia…" He didn't want to talk about Raymond again. If he could, he gladly would have erased the man from both their memories.

She didn't plan to give him any choice. "You can just sit there and listen, Alec Sharpe!" When he remained silent, she continued, though she was obviously ruffled just a bit. "I started wondering about Raymond long before I knew how truly evil he was. But by then, everyone knew I had planned to marry him, and my mother accepted him, and you and Dane never once questioned me about him."

Alec glared at her. "Dane thought you were happy. He didn't want to do anything that would hurt you."

"And what was your excuse?"

Alec narrowed his eyes again and said through his teeth, "I knew if I got too damn close to you, which included poking my nose into your business, I wouldn't be able to keep my hands off you. I wanted to get rid of Raymond just so he wouldn't be in my way."

Celia blinked at him, awed by this outpouring of confessions. "I…I had no idea."

"Bull. From the second we met, you felt the pull as much as I did. Don't lie about it now."

She tightened her mouth, but didn't deny it. "All right, maybe I had a clue or two. But you're not an easy man to figure out and I had my hands full already. I was too embarrassed to admit what an awful mistake I'd made with Raymond, that I didn't love him and didn't want to marry him, that I had been duped so thoroughly."

"You weren't the only one he had fooled."

"He didn't fool you. Right from the start you seemed to despise him, and Raymond never understood it. He'd talk about you sometimes, in this almost fearful, reverent way. But he got really angry if I even mentioned your name."

"You mentioned me to him?"

"Oh, for pity's sake. Don't look so smug." Celia rolled

her eyes and shook her head. "Mostly I talked about what a reprehensible character you seemed to be."

Alec laughed.

Another silence stretched out, and Alec glanced at her.

Celia wrung her hands. Speaking in a soft, nearly inaudible voice, she said, "Whenever I mentioned putting the wedding off, Raymond would…"

"Celia." He wasn't at all sure he needed to hear this.

"He'd take me to bed."

She closed her eyes and Alec wished he could do the same. Thinking of her with Raymond tortured him. But this was obviously something she wanted to get off her chest, and if it would ease her, he'd listen. "Go on."

"Everything he'd taught me was so new and exciting. At first I thought I loved him, and that made it seem okay. But little by little, I resented the way he used my…sexuality against me. He'd taunt me over how easy I was and tell me how shocked my family would be if we didn't marry considering I acted like a…a…" She hesitated, drawing a deep breath.

Alec reached over and clasped both her hands. "Like a what, honey?"

"A bitch in heat."

He squeezed her fingers and offered her a slight smile. "Then what would that make me, since I can't seem to think about anything other than staking a claim on you? Right now, Celia, if you asked me and meant it, I'd pull this truck over and you'd find your jeans around your ankles before you had time to blink."

She stared at him, shocked, then she laughed. "Why, you sweet talker you."

Alec laughed, too, though he wanted and needed her

so bad he didn't know how much longer he could hold out. "I have no finesse where you're concerned, honey. You make me feel raw."

She drew a long slow breath and stared at him. "You really are a sweet talker."

Alec shrugged that off. "I keep telling you, Raymond was an ass. Any man who had you and didn't appreciate it is too stupid to waste breath on."

As he finished that declaration, he pulled into a motel and parked his truck. Turning in his seat, he drew her closer and kissed her, moving so his mouth opened, his tongue immediately stroking deep. Against her lips, he whispered, "After I've had you, you won't have the energy to think of him. That's a promise. The only question now is when."

THE MOTEL ALEC CHOSE based on immediate vacancy was actually fairly close to her own by the way the crow flies. However, using the busy roads, it took a good twenty minutes to reach her. This concerned Alec, but Celia insisted there wasn't anything she'd need him for that couldn't wait that long. She didn't want to add to Alec's pressure, since he was actually working with her under duress.

His motel was even seedier than her own, with a horrid bathroom complete with cracked tiles and she'd be willing to bet a lack of hot water. But Alec never blinked an eye at the utilitarian setting. He stowed his few things, made a couple of quick calls, then bundled Celia back into his truck. They spent most of the morning and afternoon shopping.

By the time they were done, Alec had purchased a cell phone for her and a few other precautionary items, like pepper spray and a "screamer," a small can that literally screamed when the nozzle was compressed. Celia tried it once, and got to see just how fast Alec could move. He had it out of her hand and was glaring at her within a heartbeat. She'd felt compelled to offer a mumbled apology, but in truth, she had to hide her smile.

Alec really didn't frighten her anymore. In fact, he almost made her feel cherished.

The precautions he took with her safety didn't feel like a lack of trust, but rather very deep concern for a woman he cared about.

She was pondering that vague possibility when Alec said, "Tell me again what my number is."

"Alec, I have it memorized. We've been over it a dozen times."

"Tell me anyway. I want to make damn sure that if something goes wrong, you know it by heart. You might not have time to think about it…"

She recited the number.

"Good. Now, I put the number in the memory, so all you have to do is dial 1, but—"

"Alec." She shook her head at him. "If the number is in the memory, why did I have to learn it?"

He touched her cheek. "What if Jacobs catches on to you and takes your phone? Or what if you manage to lose it? You might have to use a pay phone. It's best to cover all the bases, babe."

"Okay." She no longer felt the need to fight him on every issue. Strange how sometime during their drive, her attitude had changed. Oh, she was still wary. And she didn't yet trust herself to give in to him completely. But she also wanted him, and she knew he felt the same.

Only he suffered no guilt, no embarrassment at all. He'd told her that her sex drive was "healthy."

Around him, she was in the peak of health.

"Yoo-hoo. Miss Carter?" Alec waved a hand in front of her face. "You want to join me here so we can make these plans, or do you want to stand there daydreaming?"

"You have my undivided attention, Alec."

The look he gave her was skeptical. "Uh-huh. I could tell you were on full alert." He leaned against the wall of her motel room and crossed his arms over his chest. "Do you have something sexy to wear tonight?"

"Yes, I do."

"Make sure it's not too sexy, all right? I don't want to be forced to diffuse a riot."

She felt her cheeks warm. Alec honestly thought she was sexy enough to turn heads, and his confidence helped shore up her own. "I'll be discreetly sexy."

Another skeptical look, as if he didn't think such a thing was possible. "Show up on time. I'll be there around four o'clock, but you shouldn't show up until seven. I don't want anyone to think we're together in any way."

"What should I say if someone asks me? After all, they all noticed us leaving together yesterday."

Alec shrugged. "Say I was lousy in bed."

Celia choked and had to turn quickly away. She paced the small confines of the room, stepping around her exercise equipment. "Maybe I'll say you bored me."

"Whatever. But remember to pay me no mind, no matter what I do."

That had her whipping around. "What do you plan to do?"

"Flirt. Pick up other women."

Groping for the edge of the bed, Celia sat down. Alec came over to stand directly in front of her, which put her eye level with his zipper. He crossed his arms over his chest and growled, "You already know I don't want anyone but you, Celia. But I have to act like the average bar groupie, and that means I'll have to act drunk, obnoxious, and horny."

Celia gulped. "Will you actually—"

"Sleep with anyone? Hell no. My health means a little more to me than that."

She wanted to crumble in relief, but instead she pushed to her feet and tried to get Alec to back up. He didn't.

"I need to start getting ready, so you should go. I have to shower and do my hair and—"

Alec cupped her face. "I hate this. I hate letting you walk into that place and I hate knowing what all those creeps will be thinking about you." He kissed her, gently, teasingly. "Promise me you'll be extra careful. And don't go anywhere with anyone, no matter what. If Jacobs really does know where Hannah is, we'll find her. But I don't want anything to happen to you in the process."

Tenderness threatened to break her control. She forced a smile and voluntarily kissed him this time, just as teasing as he had been. "I promise to be careful if you do. Don't let some hussy have her way with you."

His gaze turned hot and he stepped away from her. "These days I'm saving myself for you. And if you make me wait much longer, I swear I'm going to explode. Keep that in mind, will you?"

Then he walked out the door, checking it to make

certain it had locked. Celia sank back down on the mattress. Keep it in mind? It was damn near all she could think about.

CHAPTER SEVEN

THE MUSIC WAS LOUD when Celia entered the bar. Smoke hung heavy in the air and she felt the eyes of a dozen men watching her as she made her way to a bar stool.

Then she spotted Alec.

In the middle of the dance floor, moving much too slowly for the fast beat of the music, he held a woman with long pale hair and pretended to dance. One of his large hands was curved on her behind and Celia, taken aback by the scene though he'd warned her, froze to the spot.

She wanted to kill him.

Her heart seemed to leap around in her chest, her vision blurred. Then Alec looked up at her, grinned and winked, before releasing the woman and walking her way. He stopped in front of her, his expression arrogant, his black eyes dilated. He flicked the end of her nose in an insolent manner and bent to her ear.

"It's a game, Celia, and you're about to blow it." He kissed her cheek and walked away.

Slouching in a booth at the back of the bar, he called for another drink, and the waitress he'd just been making love to hurried to fetch it.

Belatedly remembering herself, Celia flipped her hair behind her ear and gave him a "humph" shrug, then sat down and ordered her own beverage. Her mind was in such a turmoil, filled with images of Alec with that *other* woman, she barely heard the bartender when he leaned close and asked her if she was all right.

"Oh, don't be silly." She gave him her most dazzling smile while fluttering a hand in dismissal. "I'm perfectly fine."

The bartender eyed her pensively while polishing a glass. "You ask me, you looked a little poleaxed to see your beau here."

Feigning shock, she said, "My beau?" Then with another twittering laugh: "You mean that ragtag bum? Well, I was surprised to see him here considering I'd hoped not to—ever again." She giggled. "Sometimes loneliness can make us do the dumbest things, and going out with that one marks the top of the list."

"Didn't work out quite as you planned, huh?"

The bartender now grinned, too, and Celia leaned closer still, pretending to share a confidence. She whispered, "He's not real bright, and he's entirely too... well...*rough*."

"He does look like a mean hombre, at that. He didn't hurt you, did he?"

"No, of course not. I didn't mean that. It's just that I couldn't get rid of him. He wanted to move in on me! I had to be almost cruel to get rid of him. I felt a little bad about it, but I can barely afford to take care of myself right now, much less someone else."

The bartender patted her hand. "You did the right thing."

Suddenly a new voice intruded and Celia felt every hair on her body tingle. "If you have any more problems with him, you can let me know."

Slowly she turned, and sure enough, Mr. Jacobs had taken the seat beside her. The bartender was quick with the introductions, beaming all the while.

"Miss, this is Marc Jacobs. He owns this bar, among other things, and tends to take the safety of the female clientele real personal."

"That I do, Wally. Especially when the lady is so lovely." His pale blue eyes glittered at Celia, and her blush wasn't in the least feigned. The man was sizing her up, and she'd never felt so exposed, or so disgraced, in her life. She swallowed hard and thought of Alec, sitting only a short distance away.

Looking at Jacobs through her lashes, she whispered in acknowledgment, "Mr. Jacobs."

"Marc. I insist. And you are?" He slowly took her hand from her lap and squeezed her fingers in a familiar way. Repulsed, Celia wanted to jerk back, but more than that, she wanted to find Hannah. And somehow she knew Alec was watching, that he was aware of every little movement she or Jacobs made. She wanted to prove to him that she could do this, and his nearness gave her courage and determination.

"All right, Marc." Her smile was complimenting, teasing. "I'm Celia. Celia…" She hesitated. She didn't want to give him her actual last name in case he had her investigated. But the only other last name that came to mind was Alec's. Wincing inside at her own audacity, she said, "Celia Sharpe."

"Celia. It's a lovely name. Would you like to join me at my table?"

Flirting, she said, "I'd dearly love to join you at your table. Thank you."

He held her hand as she slid off the stool. Her dress,

a cream-colored, silky summer shift cut low in front and back, and held up by tiny cap sleeves, smoothed over her legs as she walked. It fell narrow and straight to just below her knees and was accented by the dreaded, uncomfortable push-up bra, minimal jewelry, and strappy sandals. She caught Jacobs staring at her breasts as they made their way across the crowded floor. When she went to sit, Jacobs's hand strayed over her waist and her hip.

Celia's stomach roiled.

Seconds later a waitress delivered her drink and a fresh one for Jacobs.

"So," he said, smiling at her with impeccable, perfect white teeth, "you're new around here, aren't you? What are you in town for?"

Trying for a look of coy bashfulness, Celia bit her lip and stared down at her hands. "Well, I suppose I wanted excitement most of all. I got really tired of hanging around my small hometown. I used to live close to my grandmother, but she passed away, and then there was really no reason for me to stay there."

Looking falsely sympathetic, Jacobs asked, "No other relatives?"

She shook her head, then sipped at her drink. "No. I'm on my own, and that's sort of a good thing, don't you think? No responsibilities, I mean."

"You could look at it that way." He touched the back of her hand with one finger, a gesture meant to be sympathetic, but felt totally smarmy to Celia considering the look in his eyes. "No husband, or at least a fiancé? I would think a woman as beautiful as you would have been captured by now by some lucky man."

Again she bit her lip. She could just imagine what his

idea of *capture* entailed. "I had a few boyfriends. But they were all yokels. They had these plans of settling down and starting a family." She was every day of twenty-six years old, but for as long as she could remember, folks had told her she looked younger. She hoped it was true, or she was about to make an awful fool of herself.

She cleared her throat and said, "I'm too young to do all that. I have tons of time to settle down after I've done all the things I'd like to do."

Jacobs studied her, making her squirm, then he asked, "You're definitely too young. About twenty or so, right?"

She beamed at him, affecting her ditzy look. "Twenty-one, free and fully legal. Marriage should be when you're, like, thirty or something, right?"

His smile was indulgent. "Absolutely. So Celia, tell me about these things you'd like to do with your life."

She blushed again. A pale complexion had always been the bane of her life, but now she counted herself lucky. She flipped her hair over her shoulders, shrugged and whispered, "You'll think I'm silly."

His fingers drifted over her cheek. "Not at all."

She drew a deep breath, more to steady her stomach than to draw forth her nerve. "Well, my grandmother used to say I was pretty enough to be a model." She peeked up at him. "I know I'm not, but it's something I've always dreamed about. Seeing myself in a magazine. Or maybe being in commercials." She shivered. "It would be so wonderful!"

Jacobs toyed with his glass, swirling the amber liquid around as if in deep thought, while staring at her. His stare was nothing like Alec's. It unnerved her, that much was familiar, but with Alec she felt charged and alive, with this man she felt dread and bone-deep discomfort, something very close to fear.

She sighed. "I know. Fanciful dreams. But I figured I had to at least try or I'd never be able to forgive myself. Only I didn't get much farther than this before I started to run out of money and I have no idea who to contact, or how to go about getting the attention of an agent. Tomorrow I'm going to be practical though. I'm going to find a job somewhere, save up more money, then get started again."

"Where will you work?" he asked with concern.

Shrugging, Celia said, "At a restaurant I suppose. I've seen plenty of signs up for waitresses and they say the tips are good."

"Oh, I've no doubt you'll make plenty in tips, but a job like that would be an insult to a woman as lovely as you." He dragged one long finger around the rim of his glass, as if coming to a decision, then he nodded. "Would you be shocked, Celia, if I told you I was an agent?"

She opened her eyes as wide as she could get them. "You're kidding, right?"

"No." He smiled again. "Celia, would you pose for me?"

She almost swallowed her tongue. Her pulse raced, her heart jumped. "I beg your pardon?"

His look was calculating and predatory. "Along with owning this bar, I have many connections in the fashion world. I'm actually a fairly well-known agent and I work with lots of girls. I want to see if you're comfortable showing yourself to advantage. If you are, why then, I think I may have a proposition for you."

Since she had absolutely no intention of going anywhere alone with this man, she immediately stood and held out her arms. Smiling with false hope, she turned a pirouette and struck several provocative poses. Looking eager, she asked, "Should I stand on a table? I would you know. I desperately want a chance to prove myself."

Jacobs laughed in genuine delight. "That won't be necessary. And besides, I think your boyfriend might object to that. He looks ready to self-destruct."

She resisted the nearly impossible urge to look at Alec. "My boyfriend?"

Jacobs nodded to the other side of the bar. "You caught his attention with your little show and somehow I get the impression he'd like another go at you."

Celia glanced in the direction Jacobs indicated, taking her time before finally focusing on Alec. She saw that damn waitress now perched in his lap, one of her hands under Alec's shirt, stroking his belly. Alec seemed to be giving her mouth-to-mouth.

Celia's disgust was very real. "He's a macho pig. Believe me, he's of no concern at all."

"Excellent. I just thought it prudent to ask."

Celia eagerly reseated herself. "So what is your proposition?"

Again, Jacobs laughed at her enthusiasm. "There's a party tonight. A lot of important people will be there. I'd like you to come."

Her heart nearly exploded at this incredible chance to make headway. Surely Hannah would be there, and if Celia could only talk to her alone for a moment, she might be able to get the girl to go home.

Interrupting her thoughts, Jacobs reached out for her

hand again. "We can leave here in an hour or so. I'll take you myself."

She remembered her precarious position and ducked her face, moaning. "Gosh, I wish I could! This is just awful."

His fingers tightened almost cruelly on her own. "What is it?"

Working up a tear, she said, "I can't go looking like this!" She splayed her hands over her bosom, indicating her attire. "My dress is totally inappropriate. I want to make a grand impression when I do meet someone, not have them thinking I'm a country bumpkin."

He stared at her hands, or rather, her breasts beneath them. He licked his lips. "You're right, of course. But it's not a problem. We'll stop by your room and you can change into something a little…dressier."

Not in this lifetime. Shaking her head, she conjured up the most dejected look she could manage. "You don't understand. I *am* a bumpkin. I don't own anything fancy enough for an important party."

Jacobs checked his watch, letting a little irritation show through. "The boutique owner on Fifth and Main is a friend of mine. I'll call her and tell her you're coming."

Celia was stunned. "But I can't afford…"

Stalling her objection in midsentence, he withdrew his wallet and pulled out a wad of bills. Celia stared wide-eyed, beyond being shocked. Thumbing out a string of twenties, he rolled them and stuffed them into her hand. "Buy yourself something spectacular and sexy—Shirley will help you decide. Leave everything in her capable hands. She works with me often. And then take a cab to the party. Arriving a few minutes late will help you make an entrance. It'll intrigue certain fellows even more."

She stared at the money in her hand. "Are you serious?"

Scribbling an address onto a napkin, Jacobs chuckled. "Absolutely. Believe me, honey, I can afford a new outfit for you, and when you get your first photo shoot, you can pay me back with interest. Agreed?"

"You…you really think there's a possibility?"

"I think it's a done deal." He handed her the napkin. "Just tell the cabbie to deliver you to this address. The doorman will pay him. Be there by ten o'clock, and in the meantime I'll talk you up. You'll make a huge splash tonight."

She felt staggered by how quickly things had progressed, and how incredibly easy it seemed. "This is like a dream." *More like a nightmare. Was this how Hannah had gotten sucked in, so fast she didn't have time to think?*

"Celia?" He tipped up her chin and his eyes were direct, a vague warning shining through the pale blue. "Don't disappoint me now."

A fine trembling had invaded her body. Slowly she stood, moving away from his touch. "I'll be there. And thank you. Thank you so much."

"It's my pleasure."

As she walked away, she thought of how she could warn Alec, how she could let him know what had transpired. But he wasn't even looking at her. He was slumped in the booth, head back, eyes closed, the waitress still on his lap, chewing on his damn neck. Celia hoped she hit an artery. When she saw Alec's hand go to the woman's rump again, she set her teeth and marched on outside, quickly summoning a cab.

It didn't matter that Alec claimed it was a game. She needed him now, and he was playing with another woman. The jealousy was something she'd never experienced before, a devouring evil inside her, making her breath come fast and her heart thump too hard. It staggered her, overriding the euphoria of all she'd accomplished tonight, the headway she'd made.

Rather than planning on how to handle the rest of the evening, she wanted to wreak havoc, to beat on Alec and make him promise her he'd… The thought struck her like a smack to the head, nearly knocking her off her high heels. Dear God.

She was in love with Alec Sharpe.

Slumping back in the cab seat, she groaned and covered her face with her hands. Of all the incredible things to happen. And she had the awful suspicion she'd actually fallen for the tough guy some time ago—like when she'd very first met him. The sight of him excited her. The smell of him excited her. The way he talked and walked and his roughness mixed with his protective instincts…

Well hell. It didn't get much worse than this.

ALEC SAT IN THE DARK, just waiting. Every muscle in his body felt tight, almost quivering, and he thought he might explode at any moment if…

The lock on the door clicked and slowly opened. He didn't move except for the narrowing of his eyes. Every nerve was on alert, ready, almost anxious for any confrontation that would allow him to let off a little steam. And then he recognized her scent; he knew Celia, body and soul, on an elemental level that gripped him gutdeep. He could have picked her out of a hundred women just by the touch of her skin or her arousing fragrance, not store-bought but a part of the woman. *His woman.*

The fact that it was Celia entering, rather than an intruder, was almost better. It certainly allowed some of his panic to recede, making the way clear for his rage. He waited for the door to close so no one would hear the argument about to erupt. When she flipped on a light switch and turned to see him, she gasped, then immediately went on the defensive.

Clutching the front of her dress over her heart with a fist, she said, "Alec! You scared me half to death! What are you doing sneaking in here?"

He came slowly, angrily to his feet. Gaze pinning her, he stalked forward. There was very little talking he planned to do until a few of his questions were answered. "Where the hell have you been?"

He didn't recognize his own voice, but he'd been through twenty kinds of hell in the past hour and he didn't like feeling that much, not when he'd spent a good part of life freezing out deeper emotions and feelings. Yet she consistently, repeatedly, *deliberately* made him feel things.

He didn't touch her, merely loomed over her, feeling every bit as much a demon as he'd often been accused of being.

She glared at him. "If you hadn't been playing sucky-face with that scrawny waitress, I'd have been able to get your attention when I left."

"I saw you leave, damn it." His teeth ached from clenching them so tightly; did she honestly think he hadn't seen every little move she'd made?

He reached out and slowly crowded her back against the wall. She didn't look intimidated, she just looked mad. Good, misery loved company. "Why the hell didn't you wait outside for me?"

"Because I couldn't." Her little nose went into the air. "I had to buy a dress for a party tonight."

A red haze covered his vision. "Forget it."

She suddenly gasped. "You're drunk!"

"Not even close." Her breasts brushed his chest and his stomach tightened.

"I can smell the alcohol on your breath, Alec."

"One glass of whiskey. And believe me, it'd take more than that, so stop trying to turn the tide. You've got some explaining to do, lady, and I'm about clean out of patience."

She searched his face, then suddenly punched his chest. "You have lipstick on your *ear,* damn it! And you smell like a French whore."

What that had to do with anything he couldn't imagine. "She was all over me, Celia. Until I can change clothes, we'll both have to put up with it."

"Wrong. I don't have to put up with anything." She glanced at the clock beside the bed and muttered, "I've only got a half an hour to get changed and get to the party. Hopefully it's not too far away."

Propping both hands beside her head, imprisoning her with his body, he fought to maintain his control. "You're not going to any damn party, baby."

"Oh yes I am! This is the best opportunity in the world to find Hannah. I have to go."

"No."

She drew herself up. "I don't have time for this, Alec." Then just as quickly she asked with a sneer, "Did you enjoy yourself at the bar?"

He wrapped one large hand around her skull to hold

her still, then leaned forward until their noses touched. "With Jacobs leering at you?" The rage bubbled up again and he squeezed his eyes shut. "You don't have any idea how damn hard that was for me, do you?"

"You looked plenty distracted to me."

"Which was the point, damn it!"

She blinked at his raised tone. "You really didn't enjoy kissing her?"

Shoving himself away from the wall with a burst of energy, he paced, then immediately stalked back. He grabbed her hand and pressed it to his fly. "That's reserved for you, lady." She started to pull away but he wouldn't let her. A small groan escaped him. "A sheik's harem wouldn't do it for me now, not when I'm wanting you."

Her fingers curled, caressing him. In a whisper, she asked, "Do you mean that, Alec?"

Staring at her hard, he said, "I've told you all along it's you. If I only wanted to get laid, I damn sure could have done that long before tonight, and with a hell of a lot less trouble than you give me."

Her breath came a little faster and she nervously licked her lips.

Alec groaned, all his anger transferring into red-hot need. He wanted to brand her, put his mark on her for all the world to see. He wanted her acceptance and understanding.

To block the assault of emotions he didn't want to deal with, he kissed her, long and hard and with so much possession and passion she all but forgot about the damn party.

But of course, she couldn't.

In trembling tones, she said, "I want you, too, Alec, I really do."

He leaned back to look at her, his own body shaking.

"But I have to do this. Please." Her eyes pleaded with him and he turned away, but she caught him by the waistband of his jeans and held on. It was either give in to her, or drag her in his wake. "Alec, *please?*"

He had to think, but there really wasn't time. She'd said she had only a half hour. Still without looking at her, not willing to test his control that far, he said, "Tell me everything. Hurry."

She did, and Alec had to agree that the possibilities were endless. Getting into the mind-set of the chase helped to clear his head of the lust. But not completely.

"He even sent me to this shady little boutique where a woman named Shirley dressed me like a damned Thanksgiving turkey, from my earrings down to the sandals I'll wear. I had the feeling this was some sort of arrangement they had, that a lot of girls are paraded through that boutique and outfitted *appropriately.*" In a lower voice, she confided, "Shirley looks like an Alcatraz escapee. Really gave me the willies."

He chewed the side of his mouth, thinking it all through logically before finally accepting that he had little choice in letting her go.

"All right." He turned to glare at her, wanting no misunderstandings. "My instincts as a man tell me to say no way, to tie you to the damn bed and keep you there if necessary. But," he added when she started to object, "as an agent, I know this could be our only opening."

She looked as though she had mixed feelings about his capitulation. "So you agree?"

"Yeah. But I'm going, too. No, don't panic. I'll be outside, but close. If you need me, just hit the button on your phone. Any call at all and I'm coming in, babe, so be careful."

She threw her arms around his neck and squeezed him tight. "I hate to admit it, but I'm glad to know you'll be there."

Holding her so close was like a tonic, both soothing him and setting his blood to pumping. He pressed his nose to her neck and breathed deeply. "Having second thoughts?" She was on tiptoe and he slipped his hands beneath her skirt to fill his palms with her soft bottom. He needed something to tide him over, and touching her was a small consolation.

She groaned, but shook her head. "No, I'm doing this, Alec, I have to. But I feel better about the whole thing, knowing I won't be alone."

Two seconds more of her willing acceptance and he'd crumble. That would sure as hell shoot the night, at the same time demolishing the progress he'd made. Knowing that helped him do the right thing. He pried her arms loose and gently sent her into the bathroom with a firm swat on her perfect fanny. He had a bad feeling about all this, not a gut instinct, which he wouldn't have dared ignore, but just an unsettled feeling in his chest, like a hard fist squeezed around his heart. He didn't like it. "Go get dressed, Celia, before I change my mind. To keep any onlookers from getting suspicious, I'm going out to wait in my car. After the cab picks you up, I'll follow along, but you won't see me, okay?"

"What if Jacobs has guards?"

"They'll never know I'm there."

"You're that good?"

He smiled and deliberately dropped his voice to a low, seductive tone. "I promise to be the best you ever had." He left before she could get her mouth closed or find a suitable comeback. Hopefully he'd have a chance to prove that taunt, and soon.

Most of the world considered him a mean son of a bitch, dangerously lethal, invulnerable, hard-edged. But Celia had never backed down from him. At first her spunk and cursed doggedness, along with her sweet good looks, had merely intrigued him. But now she'd managed to crawl under his skin and he had a feeling her unsettling effect wasn't going to go away any time soon. For a while there, he'd thought making love to her would help, would wash her out of his system so he could start thinking rationally again, with his brains rather than his libido.

Now, he wasn't so sure.

He hoped she came to reason soon, because he really didn't think he could take much more.

CHAPTER EIGHT

HER FACE HURT from smiling, her brain hurt from concentrating so hard on appearing insipid, and every muscle in her body ached from the need to hide herself away. In a house this size, it should have been easy. But not once since she'd entered had she been given a private moment. She felt like a piece of raw meat displayed in the market window.

The brownstone structure was heavily guarded, surrounded by a tall, black, wrought-iron fence complete with automatic locking driveway gate and intercoms at every entrance. Guards stood at several windows, both inside and out. Even if she'd wanted to leave, it would have been impossible.

The outfit Shirley had insisted was perfect hadn't seemed nearly so skimpy in the shop when she'd hurriedly accepted it, as it did now with a largely male audience ogling her every move. The black pantsuit had a loose, low-cut crop top that exposed her cleavage and barely hung low enough to conceal the bottom curves of her breasts. It was briefer than many bathing suit bras she'd seen, and since it hung free from her shoulders, she had to be very careful about how she moved.

Paired with the low-riding, hip-hugger pants, it left a lot of midriff bare. The material was raw silk and the slightly flared pants made her legs look longer, especially with the impossibly high-heeled sandals that made merely walking a concerted effort. Dangling gold earring hoops nearly touched her shoulders, and matched the gold chain around her waist, hanging over her exposed navel.

When the men at the party spoke to her, they tended to stare at her belly, or her cleavage. Two of them had the audacity to take her hand and force her into a circle so they could gape at her behind. Several had felt free to stroke her stomach with the backs of their knuckles—and Celia, who thought she'd known all about shame—had nearly closed in on herself. The possessive touches made her stomach turn, and she'd gulped down a few too many drinks trying to shore up her courage.

One thought kept going through her mind: Alec never made her feel like this. His touch excited her and made her tingle and she knew without a doubt he could easily make her beg for his body. But he never would, because what he offered he offered freely and without restriction, respecting her and her desires as natural and healthy.

There was nothing natural or healthy about the way these men looked at her.

"Are you enjoying yourself, Celia?"

She did her best to look awed. "Oh yes, Marc. Everyone is so fascinating. See that man over there? He told me he's a film producer and said he'd like to see me again! Isn't that exciting?"

Marc Jacobs smiled benignly. "Wonderful. I knew you'd do well. But I have even better news. A fellow colleague would like to talk to you privately."

Her heart seemed to shudder and die in midbeat. She stared at him stupidly.

"Oh, now don't get nervous. You'll do fine." He replaced her empty wineglass with a full one from the tray of a passing waitress. Celia automatically sipped. "You look unquestionably edible, Celia, so I'm not at all surprised that Blair noticed you. He freelances for several major magazines, and if I don't miss my guess, he's already picturing you in several spreads. As your acting agent, I recommend you do your best to ingratiate yourself with him."

Celia was busy trying to cover her nervousness, hoping to come up with a way to avoid yet another isolated meeting, when she and Jacobs were approached by two young women. They were each beautiful, putting Celia to disgrace. One had caramel-colored skin and wide, slanted cat eyes and a generous mouth. Her hair was ruthlessly short, but the style suited her high cheekbones and bold features.

The other woman had long, sleek, flowing black hair. Her skin was flawless, very pale, and she had green eyes fringed by lush lashes that added startling color to her face. She was tall, topping Celia by several inches, and her body was willowy, bordering on waiflike. Both women were grinning, sipping drinks, and appeared happy.

Jacobs put one arm around each and made introductions. "Celia, I asked Jade and Hannah to show you around. They're familiar with everyone here and can help you get acclimated."

Celia nearly bit her tongue. *Hannah.* And the girl was impeccably dressed in designer clothing, her face radiant, her expression carefree. Had Alec been right? Was she wasting her time?

With a bold squeeze to each woman's derriere, Jacobs excused himself. He told Celia he'd be back shortly to escort her in to the private meeting.

As soon as he was gone, Jade rubbed her bottom. "Damn, I hate when he does that." She grinned at Celia and stuck out her hand. "So you're new? I hope you're not one of those wide-eyed hopefuls, though truth to tell, you look a lot older than most of the girls Marc brings around."

Jade looked about fifteen but was surely older. She shook Celia's hand, then turned pleading eyes on Hannah. "Can you do the show and tell? I want to get off my feet for awhile. My legs are killing me, and with Marc gone, this might be my only chance to rest."

Hannah's smile was genuine. "Sure thing." She looped arms with Celia. "We'll tour around and get acquainted. But find someplace private to crash. If Marc finds you hiding, you know he won't like it."

With a crooked smile that made her look even younger, Jade said, "I was thinking of a broom closet, actually." Flicking them an airy wave, she walked away, leaving Hannah chuckling behind her.

Celia tried to take advantage of her private time with the girl. "I'm Celia Sharpe," she improvised.

Hannah smiled again. "I'm just Hannah, you know, like Cher." She took Celia's glass and put it on a table already littered with an overflowing ashtray and a few crumpled napkins. "You've had enough of that, haven't you? You look a bit tipsy."

"I don't drink much," Celia admitted. "But here, someone is constantly—"

"Giving you a new one, I know. I think the men like to keep us tipsy. You can imagine why."

Celia stared at her, hoping to gain her confidence. "Why?"

But Hannah just laughed and shook her head. Celia would have liked to have Hannah's last name verified, but the girl matched the description she'd gotten from Mrs. Barrington, so that was good enough for her.

"What are we supposed to be doing, Hannah?"

"Well, for now, just mingling. If you see anyone looking at you, smile, flirt, encourage him with a look, that sort of thing."

Carefully, Celia asked, "And that'll help us get modeling jobs?"

Hannah groaned. "You *are* a hopeful, aren't you? Honey, get realistic. Do you really expect to make it big through this crowd?"

Feeling like a child needing instruction, especially with Hannah's worldly air, Celia said, "Marc told me—"

"Whatever he had to to get you here. Marc appreciates a beautiful woman. And he'll take care of you, so don't worry about that. He'll dress you nice and set you up in a place to live."

"How, if we're not working?"

Hannah gave her a pitying shake of her head. "You know what?" She took Celia's arm and dragged her around a corner of the main room, behind a large planter. "I shouldn't do this, and if you squeal on me— well, let's just say you really shouldn't, okay? But Celia, if you had any sense at all, you'd get out of here right now."

Celia had to look up to meet the girl's eyes. Measuring her words, she said, "I can't. Marc has a meeting set up for me with someone named Blair."

Hannah's face paled and she closed her eyes. "Well. He's not wasting any time with you, is he? It must be because you are a bit older, and he figures you can handle it."

Celia clutched Hannah's arm. "Hannah, what's going on? Tell me, please. I'd like to help you if I can."

Laughing, Hannah looked at her like she was deranged. "How could you help me? You're even more naive than I was." Then she sobered and shook her head. "Oh God. I shouldn't even be talking to you here. If Marc found out... Come on. Let's go back out and mingle. Forget everything I said."

Celia held back, causing Hannah to stop and look at her. "Hannah..." She bit her lip, then decided to take a major chance. She had no idea when she'd get another opportunity to talk to Hannah alone. "What if I told you I could help you? What if I told you I spoke with your mother this morning and she cried? She desperately wants you to come home, and she's worried sick."

Taking a stunned step backward, Hannah stared at her. Her face went utterly white and her eyes dilated. Then, as if terrified, she looked around to guarantee their privacy and spoke quickly. "You're crazy. Forget you even saw me, okay? And get out of here while you can."

She turned to leave, and practically ran into Jacobs.

He clutched her arms so hard Celia saw the girl wince. "What are you doing, Hannah? Why do you look so stricken?" His gaze shifted to Celia, whose face was, of course, bright red. "Celia? Is everything okay?"

Suspicion reeked from his tone and Celia knew neither of them were going anywhere until Jacobs was ready to let them go. Her heart raced and her wine-muddled brain worked frantically for an excuse.

Quickly, unwilling to let Hannah get in trouble for her folly, she said, "I'm…well, I'm embarrassed to say. I really hoped Hannah could help without anyone else knowing."

Hannah sucked in a breath. Jacobs's eyes darkened and his expression shifted, turning hard. His smile was stiff. "Tell me what the problem is."

"I can't. I'll feel like a fool."

His grip tightened on Hannah until she gasped and stared at Celia with pleading green eyes.

"Do so anyway," Jacobs said. "I insist."

With her face on fire and a hasty look around, Celia mumbled, "I just started my monthly. Oh I know, it's rotten timing and the absolutely worst kind of luck. But I was hoping Hannah could show me where the bathroom is and help me, well, you know. Find what I need." She peeked up at Jacobs to see a bemused expression on his face.

His hands stopped squeezing Hannah to caress her arms instead. Celia wanted to kill him, knowing how shaken Hannah was by their near miss, knowing he'd meant to affect her in just that way. His intimate hold on the girl now was far more lethal than the physical strength in his hands.

Then Jacobs laughed. "Celia, we're all adults here and I work with women on a daily basis. Really, it's not a problem. I'm sure Hannah can help you out. But hurry. Blair is waiting in the den." His gaze went back to Hannah and there was a distinct warning there. "You'll see that she comes directly to the den?"

Hannah smiled, and she appeared for all the world

as carefree as when Celia had first met her moments ago. It was as if the heated, nearly disastrous confrontation had never happened. "We ladies will need just a few moments, then we'll be there. I wouldn't want her to miss anything important."

Jacobs rubbed his chin. "Good." Leaning down, he kissed Hannah on the mouth, proving his possession. Hannah smiled and kissed him back.

As they hurried away, Celia thought she might faint from residual fear. She watched Hannah blink, saw her acceptance replaced with pure hatred and disgust.

Celia had to get her away from here, as soon as humanly possible. And if that meant facing Blair and probable degradation, she could do it.

More than ever, she was determined to save Hannah Barrington.

WAITING WASN'T EASY for Alec; he was more a man of action. His tendency was always direct confrontation. Defeat and remove threats. But that wasn't always legal, and he doubted Celia, or Dane for that matter, would tolerate him taking the law into his own hands right now.

The cell phone sat on the truck seat beside him, and he stared at it, daring it to ring, torn between wanting it to so he could rush in and remove Celia from the brownstone, and hoping she was okay and didn't need him at all.

Memories of long ago flooded in on him, making the air inside the truck too thick and hot to breathe. He didn't want to remember that night, or how badly it had ended. Time had proven him to be a better man, more mentally and physically equipped to handle anything that might come along. He wouldn't make the same mistakes—any of them—again.

Harm wouldn't come to Celia, because he wouldn't let it.

Muscles tight despite the pep talk he'd just given himself, Alec rolled down the window and stared through the darkness with his field glasses, forcefully pushing the oppressing memory away. A guard stood by the gate where Celia had been dropped off in that killer outfit that had almost caused his heart to stop. Another guard waited at the front door.

He had no doubt more loomed around every corner. They were all wired, meaning they could communicate easily with each other.

He had not a single doubt he could get past them all if Celia needed him. But if that situation arose, it didn't bode well for the guards, because he'd protect her at any cost and to hell with what was legal.

A sudden yellow glow flared out over the west side of the lawn from a large window, drawing his attention. Someone had turned on a light. With the glasses, Alec could see shadows of people moving about in the room, through the open draperies. But the angle wasn't right for him to see much more.

Silently, driven by instincts, he left the truck and went to crouch in a scraggly stand of trees on the side of the road. Given the distance from the house, his all-black attire, and his undetectable movements, the guards would never notice him. Again he put the glasses to his eyes and surveyed the house.

He saw Jacobs first, leaning against a desk and sipping a drink. He was smiling, his expression lurid. A lump formed in Alec's throat and even before he saw her, he knew Celia was in that room, that she was the object of Jacobs's interest. He adjusted his position, his body going taut.

Laughing and holding her arms in the air to do another graceful, dancing turn, Celia passed through his line of vision. Another man followed. Heavyset, like a bulldog, and with a crooked smile and avid stare, he watched Celia as she performed. Something happened that made the man laugh. He reached out, cuddled Celia close to his thick side, and kissed her.

Alec dropped the glasses. His heart raced so fast he almost blacked out, rapidly sucking in lungfuls of heavy, humid air. Leaning against a tree, he squeezed his eyes shut and concentrated on breathing, on regaining control so he didn't rush in and start murdering people. But his time would come. Before this was over, he'd meet that man—Jacobs, too—face-to-face. Then the law be damned because he would have his retribution.

Knowing she'd been with Raymond was always hard enough. But at least that was a man Celia had chosen for herself, a man she'd gone to willingly. He could deal with that—barely. The savage, nearly overwhelming possession he felt for her tended to shake him up. It wasn't something he was used to, yet the feelings grew stronger every day. He was almost tired of fighting it, but that insidious remorse from long ago lingered in his guts, reminding him to be cautious.

Forcing himself into an almost impossible calm, blanking out the turmoil he suffered over Celia and doing his best to regard her as any other woman, he wiped the sweat from his brow and again picked up the glasses to watch. She giggled and flirted, but somehow she managed to stay out of reach for the next twenty minutes. When she finally tipped her head and made an apologetic face, Alec could read her mind as clearly as if the words were written before him.

Poor thing, she had no reserve left. The game had completely done her in and she looked weary from her soul out. He wanted to remove her from that place, coddle her, protect her. He'd hoped to make love to her tonight, but now he reconsidered. She needed some peace and quiet to recoup. He knew only too well the emotional toll of mingling with the very devils that visited your nightmares.

He'd been there too many times himself not to know.

Celia was making her excuses now, planning her departure. She had to be careful not to give herself away, and she was. Like a pro, she handled herself beautifully and he nearly burst with pride, at the same time swearing to himself that once this was over, he'd never let her get this embroiled in danger again.

He watched the room until everyone had walked out and the light was turned off. Then he crept back to the truck and slid behind the wheel. He wouldn't leave until she did, and it was less than a half hour, that felt like a week, before a cab pulled up to the gate. The guard, using a built-in intercom, made a call to the house and minutes later Jacobs escorted Celia down the walk.

He opened the door of the cab for her, then touched her cheek in a gesture that should have seemed tender but instead seemed predatory. Celia, smiling up at him, said something Alec couldn't hear and climbed into the back of the cab.

Both Alec and Jacobs watched the cab pull away until it was out of sight. With a lift of his hand, Jacobs signalled another man who hurried to a car and immediately tailed her. Alec worked his jaw. Jacobs wasn't taking any chances with his new recruit, which left Alec with two options.

He could either avoid detection by staying away from Celia tonight. Or he could reach her motel room first and already be inside when she got there, so that no one would see him enter.

To him, there was really no choice at all.

CELIA KNEW SHE WAS being followed and she prayed for Alec to be discreet. Would he know about the other car? She had to think he would, considering Dane claimed him to be the very best agent in the business.

Of all the things she'd been through, she couldn't bear it if Alec got hurt. She needed him, but with the tail Jacobs had called on her, it wasn't likely he could get anywhere near her tonight. Her head pounded from stress and too much alcohol, and she felt utterly drained. The cabbie, thankfully, was silent.

Since Jacobs had prepaid, the moment the cab stopped she jumped out and hurried to the stairs leading to her motel room. She didn't want to wait and have a possible confrontation with the thug following her. Her hand shook terribly as she tried to get her key to work, and when the door finally swung open she practically leaped inside and then slammed it behind her. With numb, shaking fingers, she turned all the locks on the door.

"Celia."

She screamed, he startled her so badly. But in the next instant she realized it was Alec. She didn't need the light to recognize his voice, his scent, his nearness.

Blindly, a sob catching in her throat, she reached out for him. Alec gathered her close, crooning, holding her so tight it should have hurt but instead offered all the comfort she craved. "It's all right now, babe."

She sniffled and tried to collect herself. With a choked laugh, she said, "You're going to think I'm a weenie, carrying on like this."

"No." He chuckled and kissed her forehead. "You've impressed the hell out of me. How did you get out of there so early?"

She tucked her face under his chin and her shoulders shook with nearly hysterical giggles. "I told Jacobs I had my period."

Alec smiled against her cheek. "Smart."

Pushing back, she cradled his face in her hands. "How did you get here before me?"

"Drove like hell, ran red lights, ignored sirens." He squeezed her. "It was either that or wait till morning because Jacobs had you followed."

"I know. I was afraid you'd…wait."

With each beat of silence that passed, a throbbing thickness filled the air. She could feel Alec's gaze, as tangible as his heat and scent. Then he whispered, "Not a chance."

"Alec…" Suddenly her legs wanted to crumble and Alec lifted her, holding her close while he seated himself on the edge of the bed, holding her in his lap. But she pushed against him, trying to get loose, sudden disgust filling her. "I have to shower. I have to get these awful clothes off, I have to—"

"Shhh…"

"You don't understand." Struggling for breath, pushing as hard as she could against his unbreakable hold, she said, "I… I *do* feel dirty now."

Another beat of silence. "Then we'll both shower." Alec lifted her and carried her into the bathroom.

Celia wondered how he could see so well without a single light on. He must have cat eyes, she thought, then blinked against the harsh fluorescent glare when he turned on the light over the sink.

She didn't want him to see her and she would have turned her back except he didn't let her. "Don't hide from me, honey. Ever."

"But I feel—"

"I know. I understand."

"You can't."

"I do." He bent and pulled her sandals off her feet, tossing them aside. "You feel foul from being near them, letting them think you're like them when you never could be."

Her heart raced, her blood pumped fiercely. "Yes."

After sliding down the side zipper, he skimmed her pants down her legs. "And you want to somehow wash it all away. Believe me, I've done the same too many times to count." Celia knew he spoke to her only as a distraction, but she gratefully accepted it anyway.

She nodded, and Alec's smile was tender.

"Did you find Hannah?" he asked as he slipped her panties down her legs. But Celia was so caught up in the question, she couldn't react to her undressing.

"Oh Alec. It was so awful. If you'd seen her yourself, you wouldn't have a single doubt that she's there against her will. She just doesn't know what to do or where to go."

Alec stood, this time paying no mind to her nudity. He pulled the miniscule crop top over her head and

Celia, muffled under the silky material, gasped. She wasn't wearing a bra. Good grief. Alec now had her skinned down to her earrings, and the gold chain around her waist.

He smoothed her tousled hair back into place. "I believe you, sweetheart. And you'll help Hannah. Everything will work out." He pecked her on the nose before dropping the crop top with the pants.

"Alec…"

He gripped the gold belt and effortlessly snapped the links apart, letting the broken chain join the pile of her clothes. Celia stared at him, gold earrings dangling onto her naked shoulders. Being with Alec this way didn't feel wrong. In fact, it felt incredibly right, the first *right* thing all evening.

Holding his gaze and her breath, she swallowed hard, then reached up and unhooked each earring. Alec took them from her to add to the pile.

"They touched me." The words, so loud in her head, emerged as a faint whisper.

Starting at her ribs, Alec smoothed his hands over her skin, down her belly and back up again, then around and under her arms to coast over her spine. His large hands spanned so much of her on each wide sweep, up and down from shoulders to hips. He tipped up her chin to gaze into her eyes. "Now I've touched you."

Her lip quivered. He was the most miraculous man she'd ever met. "Oh, Alec…"

"Don't you see, honey?" His touch was so gentle, his words more so. "If you weren't discriminating, if you were as *easy* as you say, their attentions would have turned you on. I know every man in there had to enjoy the sight of you, because you're beautiful and sexy and sweet. But that didn't happen, did it? You weren't at all flattered."

Very quietly, she said, "No."

He wasn't through making his point. "You thought you loved Raymond, so he was safe."

She wanted to ask, *What do you think I feel for you?* but she held the words back.

As if he'd read her mind, he said, "You trust me, and you know I respect you, so feeling desire for me isn't something that should shame you. And Celia?" He smoothed back her hair, cupped her face in his palms. "You feel something for me, don't you."

It wasn't a question, but rather a statement of fact, something he seemed supremely sure of. "If you didn't, you wouldn't be so sexually comfortable with me. And I've proven that you are comfortable, haven't I, sweetheart?"

She nodded, still very confused, but also overwhelmed.

Alec sucked in a triumphant breath, his dark eyes glittering. He whispered, "I'll make it better, babe. I promise."

And she knew he could. His touch, burning hot, seemed to penetrate beneath her skin, chasing away all the bad feelings. She shuddered and closed her eyes. "I feel a bit tipsy."

He smiled. "I know. I think you're drunk."

Celia shook her head. "No, not drunk. I know exactly what I'm doing, Alec."

"Don't worry. I'll take care of you."

Her eyes opened. "Will you? Or do you plan to leave me again?"

"Celia—"

Knowing it was a combination of drink, upset nerves, and relief that for now it was over, she started to hum. Alec's gaze snapped to hers and he stared.

Celia smiled. "I think I have a lot in common with Thelma Houston."

"Who?" Then he shook his head, his gaze suspicious. "Wait, this isn't another muscle-bound wonderwoman you intend to emulate by lifting weights, is it? Because honey, I have to tell you, I like your body exactly as it is."

"You don't know Thelma Houston? Really?" At his blank stare, she said, "No, she's not a wonderwoman. But I do use her music when I exercise. I have all her old disco songs on CD. She keeps me motivated." Celia could hardly believe she was standing naked with Alec Sharpe and explaining such a thing. She grinned.

"You're kidding, right?" His lip curled. *Disco?*

Again she started humming, ignoring his rude attitude, building up, and her body swayed just a bit. Then, out of the blue, she sang softly, *"Ahhhhh, baby!"*

Alec jumped, then took a step back, hands propped on his hips, a bemused expression on his face.

Celia, not about to let him get away this time, swayed a little closer. She felt giddy and daring and horribly in love, though she wouldn't admit that to Alec. He didn't want her love, but he did want *her,* and she was more than ready for him. She needed him, so his teasing was at an end, whether he liked it or not.

Very low, she sang, *"You started this fire down in my soul—"*

"Celia…"

She kept singing.

"Celia!" Laughing, Alec picked her up and swung her in a circle. "You can stop serenading me."

She cupped his cheeks, so pleased to see his rare laughter, so stunned by his masculine beauty. Loving him so much hurt, but it also made her feel whole and safe. And special.

"The song is called, 'Don't Leave Me This Way.'" She kissed him softly. "You're ready to succumb to my feminine wiles now? Because I want you, Alec Sharpe. I really do." She touched his mouth. "Please, don't leave me this way."

Very gently, he stood her back on her feet and his hands left her. Still with a crooked, immeasurably appealing grin, he began stripping away his own clothes.

Alec was totally unselfconscious in his nudity, kicking off his boots, pushing his jeans down without haste or hesitation. Just looking at him, solid and strong and real, made her feel better. When he was completely naked, he turned to the tub and started the shower. Steam billowed out.

He reached a hand toward her and Celia took it. They stepped into the shower together.

CHAPTER NINE

ALEC COULDN'T RECALL ever being so charmed, or so turned on, in his life. No woman had ever sung to him—if you could call Celia's slightly off-key, tipsy crooning a song. He wasn't familiar with the singer or the lyrics, but then music had never played a big part in his life, and he couldn't recall ever singing a note. Especially not disco.

On rare occasions he'd listened to a little jazz. On very rare occasions. Fifteen years ago, he could remember coming home to the swelling sounds of a jazz band while Marissa danced around the floor, entertaining herself. He'd be dog-tired, sweaty from a long day of working in the sun, and she'd greet him with a swirl of her skirts and a huge smile, ready to take him to bed and ease his aches and pains. It had taken little more to make him content back then.

But the smiles and the greetings hadn't lasted for long.

Alec realized later that it hadn't been the music, so much as her happiness, that he had been drawn to. He'd fed off it like a starving man. Since then, he hadn't had much reason, or any burning inclination, to listen to music.

Music sort of went hand in hand with partying and

a carefree attitude, and he'd sure as hell never been the type to enjoy crowds, raucous laughter, or frivolity.

But Celia obviously was. And he had a feeling his recent show of sexual restraint had something to do with her dredging up that specific tune. *Don't leave me this way*? He smiled. It wasn't exactly a subtle hint, but then Celia wasn't exactly a subtle woman, not where he was concerned.

But none of that mattered now. He had Celia naked, all soft and warm and ready, and his waiting was at an end. He hurt with wanting her from the top of his head down to his big feet with highly concentrated places in-between, and now the only thing holding him back was a desire to make it last a nice long time, the whole damn night if possible.

She tried to face him, but he turned her so her back nestled his chest and the spray from the shower could wash over her breasts. Her nipples peaked and her thighs tightened. She was so hot she made him feel like a horny kid again, ready to explode over just a look. "Let me take care of you first, honey, okay?"

She surprised him by whispering, "Anything you want, Alec."

Damn. Words like that could well push him over the edge. Her body trembled and he knew she was already aroused, which had a similar cause and effect on him. Her body was perfect to him, soft and feminine, but lightly muscled. He thought of the exercise equipment strewn around the floor of her room and he hugged her tighter. She never ceased to surprise him.

In a low rumble, he said, "Relax against me so I can suds you up."

She tipped her head back to see him. "Take your hair out of the ponytail first. I want to see it."

Alec surveyed her curious expression. His hair was long out of disinterest, not out of any need to make a fashion statement. When he worked, as he had tonight, he tied it back to keep it from interfering with his vision. Practicality drove him, not fashion.

But from the day he'd met her, Celia had been fascinated by his lack of social conformity. Her brother was polished; hell, her whole family was polished, down to designer shoes and two-hundred-dollar haircuts that made certain not a single curl strayed out of place. Celia's own hair was usually in a sleek, sophisticated pageboy, but since going undercover, she'd worn it various ways, and he admired her new vamp persona.

If she liked his hair, then he was more than willing to oblige her. He reached back and pulled the band loose. His hair, now long enough to hang to his shoulders, fell free, and Celia gave him a dazed, hot look. "I like it. It makes you look savage, especially with the earring."

Alec grinned again. He had her naked in the shower, both of them strung tight on desire, and they were carrying on a conversation about his hair. "I like *you*. Now hold still while I attend to certain things."

With his hands soapy, he began washing her, starting with her shoulders and upper chest, bypassing her sensitive breasts, regardless of how she squirmed and tried to get his hands to slick over there. He had to go carefully or it'd be done with before he even got started. He'd wanted her so long, fantasized about this for what seemed like forever, that his control was precarious at best. He should have been concerned that she might not be thinking clearly; she'd had a rather eventful night and obviously too much to drink.

But strangely, he *knew* this to be the right decision, for both of them. And truth to tell, he simply wanted her too much to be swayed by scruples he couldn't even pretend to possess.

Washing her slender thighs, he whispered, "Open your legs."

She whimpered softly, but complied. Alec slipped his hands over her, brushing his fingers through her soft intimate curls, letting the rough touch of his callused fingertips mingle with the tantalizing spray from the shower. Celia arched a little, pressing back against him. Her sweet breasts, glistening with water, rose and fell as she struggled for composure; her breathing accelerated, her hands dug into his naked thighs. She was already so close, and he pushed her, his fingers finding a rhythm and stroking deep over slick, tender, swollen flesh.

"I want to kiss you, Alec!"

Heat washed over him, he was so pleased with her. She didn't want to reach her peak without him, afraid, he was certain, that he'd leave her again. He turned her, cradling her shoulders, and kissed her deeply. Against her lips, he explained, "I want you to come now for me, honey, because the devil knows once I get inside you, I won't be able to last long."

She groaned and one small hand slid down his chest to his erection.

Alec sucked in a breath. "That's not going to help, babe."

"We have to be fair," she whispered, looking at him through dazed golden eyes. Her makeup was washed away, her fair hair slicked back by the shower, emphasizing the fine, delicate bones of her face. Her lips were swollen, her cheeks flushed with desire. She was by far the most appealing woman he'd ever seen.

She smiled at him. "You're so gorgeous, Alec, so lean and hard and long-limbed. I probably shouldn't tell you this, but I think about touching you all the time."

He laughed, a little taken aback by her compliment. "I'm not exactly handsome, Celia." He knew, if anything, it was his look of menace that drew women, not classic good looks.

She kissed his chest, his throat, all the time holding him in her small palm, not moving, just holding him, making him crazed. He had to fight the instinct to move his hips, to thrust through her fingers.

"You're rough and dangerous and sinfully sexy. No woman could resist you. I used to feel guilty for wanting you so much." She peeked up. "For all the lurid thoughts I had."

Catching her wrist, he pulled her hand away and pinned it behind her back, which pressed her plump breasts to his ribs. He could feel her stiff little nipples, sliding against his slick wet skin, and adding to his sexual frenzy. When she reached for him with her other hand, he captured it as well, twining his fingers with hers. "You sure as hell held off long enough." The words were low, growled. "Do you have any idea how crazy you make me?"

She squirmed against his tight hold. "Alec, I need you now."

Every time she said it, she drove him closer to the edge. Through gritted teeth, he asked, "Do you still feel dirty, Celia?"

"No." Her wet, naked body writhed against him.

"Are you sure you want me? 'Cause, babe, this won't be a one-time deal. It's going to take a hell of a lot for me to get my fill of you."

Nuzzling against his chest, she found his nipple and licked delicately. "You can take all the time you need."

His control snapped. He released her and within two minutes had finished bathing and rinsing himself. Celia watched, touching him, exploring his body each time he moved. He turned the water off and jerked the shower curtain open. Celia, with a smug, very feminine smile, reached for a towel.

"To hell with that." He picked her up, dripping wet, and walked to the bed.

Now she laughed as he stepped over and around exercise equipment. "Alec, we'll ruin the sheets!"

He didn't bother to answer her as he laid her among the tangle of bedclothes, then went back into the bathroom to fetch his wallet from his jeans. He tossed it onto the nightstand, coming down beside her at the same time and immediately catching a soft breast in his palm. His mouth closed over her nipple, sucking strongly, and Celia gasped. One hand tangled in his hair while her other hand gripped his shoulder, her nails stinging. Licking water from her chest he tasted every inch of her upper body, pausing often to sate himself on her luscious little breasts. Her nipples were rosy, tight, and he couldn't get enough. He thought he might be going too fast, but he wanted to devour her, to devastate her as much as he felt devastated.

When he slipped one hand over her soft belly and thrust two fingers in her, she cried out. She was wet and so damn hot he couldn't wait. His hand moved easily, readying her further, preparing her for him. He felt her muscles clamp down on his fingers, at the same time she moaned.

Cursing, he shoved himself to her side and frantically groped around on the nightstand for his wallet. Celia came to her knees, hugging him from behind, making it more difficult than it should have been to find a condom. When he finally had it on, he flipped her to her back, hooked her legs through his elbows and opened her completely.

She didn't object; her head was back, her eyes closed and her breath came fast and uneven.

Alec slowed, leaning forward by small degrees and watching as his erection pushed into her, past her soft, pink folds. He groaned. *"Celia."*

Her eyes opened, the hazel like warm gold, her pupils dilated. Her cheeks and breasts were warmly flushed and her body trembled beneath him.

"Look at me, babe."

She did, panting in tune to Alec's thundering heart. Their gazes locked. "Tell me you want this, that you want me."

Her fingers knotted fretfully in the sheets and she licked her lips. Her entire body was tight, straining. Alec pushed in a little deeper. He tortured them both, but it was the most sensational thing he'd ever felt.

"I want you, Alec," she groaned, her voice raw and filled with need. "I've wanted you for such a long time." Panting, her hands smoothed over her breasts, as if appeasing an ache, and Alec lost it. Seeing her touch herself was like throwing gasoline on a live fire—instant combustion.

With a harsh growl, he buried himself inside her, forcing his way past the slight natural resistance of her body. Stilling, he dropped forward and they both moaned. Celia locked her legs around him and Alec pressed his face to her throat, smelling the sweet scent of her body, her hair, of Celia. *Too good,* he thought, *too damn good.* Making a quick adjustment, he put one hand beneath her hips and lifted her so she could take all of him and at that moment, she came, shocking the hell out of him and pushing him over the edge.

Her body arched so hard she lifted him from the bed. He thrust just as hard, pinning her down again.

He could feel the clenching of her inner muscles, the slight sting of her nails, and again, her sharp little teeth. He shouted, the pleasure was so acute, and with every muscle straining, he buried himself in her again and again, then joined her, coming until he felt too sated, too incredibly weak, to draw another single breath.

He rested there on her, trying to gather his scattered wits and reconcile how incredible it felt to make love to Celia Carter. He'd known it would be good—knowing had kept him awake many nights and reduced him to an animal on the prowl. But he hadn't expected this, something more than mere sex, something beyond the physical. He didn't like it, but didn't quite know what to do about it.

Her rapid breaths still fanned his ear, and her gentle hands coasted up and down the long length of his damp back. He wanted to shout that he didn't need her comfort, her gentleness, not after she'd so physically satisfied him. But the words wouldn't come. He could barely draw breath. He felt her hesitate, then touch his right biceps.

"Alec?" She spoke softly, breathlessly. "Where did you get the tattoo?"

He closed his eyes. Maybe she'd think he was asleep. Maybe she'd even think he'd died, which actually had been a pretty close thing judging by the furious drumming of his heart and the lack of coordination in his limbs. But his luck wasn't that great.

She tightened her hold, giving him a full body hug, then asked, "Alec?"

He sighed, resigned. Well damn. Bliss can't ever last for more than a few minutes.

Alec pushed up to his elbows. Celia looked so sweet with her wet hair tangled, her cheeks still warm. Almost against his will, he kissed her gently, and he never wanted to stop kissing her. That made him frown as he pulled away. "My wife talked me into it. Fifteen years ago."

Her eyes widened and her face went pale. "You have a wife?"

Rolling to his back and propping his arms behind his head, he stared at the ceiling. Light from the bathroom cast long shadows and showed a fading watermark directly over his head.

He'd known, sooner or later he'd have to tell her if he slept with her. Not that she needed an entire account-ing of his life, no one did. But intimacy in the sack brought about other intimacies. And Celia was a curious woman, always digging in where she shouldn't be. If the situation were reversed, if she'd tried to hide aspects of her life rather than presenting herself as an open book, he'd already have gotten into her personal file at Dane's office, or he'd have run a check on her. But Celia wasn't a natural snoop, and the thought never would have occurred to her to invade his privacy.

One reality touched his tired brain: knowing would likely disgust her and put the distance he needed back between them. Not a physical distance, because he planned to keep her right where she was until he got the ache out of his system and could think rationally again. But the emotional distance was something he needed, and knowing a bit about his past ought to accomplish it. That alone was reason enough to tell her.

He sighed again, then said with no emotion, no inflection whatsoever, "Not anymore. She's dead."

Alec had half expected her to leap from the bed, or to curse him. Knowing Celia, he'd definitely expected some sort of volatile reaction. All he got was a heavy silence that felt like an anvil sitting on his windpipe, before she turned and cuddled up at his side. Surprised, he hesitated, then put one arm around her and prayed she wouldn't start crying. He really hated it when she cried.

"Did you love her?"

Alec stilled. Shit, he hated questions like that. He'd rather deal with a tear or two. "Celia…"

"You must have," she whispered, her voice low and reverent, filled with tenderness, "to put something permanent on your body." With one finger, she lightly traced the faded heart on his arm. "Right here, where the color's kind of smudged…did you have her name removed?"

Her name, but the memory had lingered, so overall it'd been a wasted effort. "Yeah."

"Why didn't you have the whole thing taken off?"

He glanced down at her. Her bare body curled against his, one slender thigh over his thicker, hairier one, her belly pressed up against his hip. Her skin was so fair against his darker body. He felt the renewed stirrings of desire and wanted to end the conversation as quickly as it had started.

With a hot look, he told her, "It hurt like hell, having the thing lasered off, so I took off what I had to and figured to hell with the rest." As a warning he added, "No one ever asks me about it."

"Why did you have to have her name taken off?"

He looked away in disgust, his temper starting on a low boil. Celia heeded his warnings with as much caution as the wall might. "Look, Celia, why don't we talk about this some other time?"

"Because I know you won't. Please, Alec?"

Damn, he both hated and loved the way she asked him so nicely whenever she really wanted something. Her softly spoken words had the effect of bringing his body to full attention; there was no way she could miss his blatant erection.

She didn't. Her hand crept down his belly, stroking the line of dark hair there, paused to toy with his navel for an excruciating moment, then continued on until she curled her small fist around him. His stomach muscles felt like iron, he was strung so taut.

Without inhibition, she explored him, softly cupping his testicles, petting his rigid length, letting her thumb stroke over the very tip of him… Alec ground his teeth together. *Talk about torture…*

"All right. I had her name taken off right after she died because I… Well…"

It wasn't like him to stumble over his words and he resented her for making him do so now. He turned, grabbed both her hands and pinned them over her head. Looming over her, his frown fierce, he barked, "So you want all the gory details, do you?" Her eyes widened, and she held her breath. "All right."

Celia bit her bottom lip. "Alec—"

"My wife was the town slut." He stared down at her, refusing to let her look away. She'd pushed for details and now she could just deal with them. "Like most guys ruled by hormones, the first time I got laid, I stupidly mistook lust for love."

He had to laugh at his own idiocy. Telling Celia about it should have made him uncomfortable, but their circumstances—naked in a bed after having just made love—superseded all other emotion. He wanted the telling through so he could have her again. And again and again, until the wanting went away. He didn't like wanting her; anytime he'd wanted someone, it had ended up hurting like hell. His jaw locked with that pathetic thought and self-loathing filled him. He was a grown man now, and he'd long since learned to take life for what it was, without the illusions. Maybe it was time Celia learned, too.

"I'd had a less than sterling home life after my mother died of ovarian cancer. My old man had run off on us when I was just a little kid, so my grandfather ended up with me. The old guy tried, I'll give him that, but we didn't have much in the way of luxury, and I was already mad as hell at the world. I didn't make things easy on him. Whenever I'd push him too hard—and I was always real good at pushing—he'd get out a birch rod. The old coot had a hell of a swinging arm."

Big, horrified tears welled up in Celia's eyes and Alec shook her, saying through his teeth, "Don't you dare cry for me, Celia. I never got a damn thing that I didn't deserve. Except maybe my wife."

Celia started to speak, but he didn't want to hear anything she had to say. Knowing Celia and her soft heart, she'd try pitying him first, then cajoling, then comfort. He didn't want any of it. He wanted to be inside her again so he could forget everything else in the explosive pleasure.

Loosening his hold on her arms, he said, "She had a similar background to mine, but with her, it was a stepfather to contend with, a real mean son of a bitch that I used to dream about punching out. Of course I never did, but the fantasy was sweet. And if he hadn't run off when he did, I might have eventually gone after him. Marissa celebrated with me the day he skipped town. She dragged me down by the river and went wild over me. That was the first night we had sex.

"I rebelled over my life by being a jerk, but Marissa rebelled by taking any kind of *love* she could get, from any guy who'd give it. I felt sorry for her at first, because she was one pathetic kid, then lovestruck after she gave me my first taste of a female's body. She was experienced enough to know exactly what she was doing, and with almost no effort, she turned me inside out. I let her become my whole focus. I thought she'd change, that I could make her life happy again, that she'd be content just being with me."

He laughed, the sound a little too raw for his liking. "Turned out I was just one more guy in a long line of idiots."

Celia turned her head to stare at the tattoo, the tears now clinging to her lashes. She gave a small, delicate sniff as she fought off the tears, but otherwise was quiet. Alec guessed she'd gotten more in the way of a story than she'd bargained for. He hadn't intended to go into so much detail. The words had just sort of come out, against his will.

He brushed her tears away with his thumbs, then continued. "As soon as we graduated high school, I started making plans for us to get married. I got a job working a construction site, saved as much money as I could, and right before we turned nineteen, we eloped. To me, to the young stupid kid I was back then, that marriage was forever."

Celia's eyes searched over his face, intent and filled with sadness. "Because you loved her."

His laugh was genuine this time. "Love? I don't think so, babe. Hell, no nineteen-year-old knows what he's thinking or feeling, especially when he's only thinking with his gonads and not his brains. I thought I could make a difference, thought I could *save* her. But she straightened me out quick enough. Like your little Hannah, she wanted fame and fortune real bad. She was always talking about us moving away, but I could barely keep us afloat, much less consider packing up and heading out.

"One day I came home from a twelve-hour shift to find a note saying she'd gone to visit a friend in Chicago. It wasn't until the next day that I found out she'd emptied out the savings account, not that we had much, but it would have been enough to pay the bills that were due. I had no idea where she'd gone, or where to find her. It took me awhile to track her down and by the time I caught up to her a couple of months later, she was strung out on dope and didn't hesitate to tell me she liked the city life a lot more than anything I could offer her."

He got quiet, remembering despite himself. With the

memory came the feelings of helplessness, of betrayal.
They'd buried themselves deep in his soul and he'd
never been able to shake them off. Celia touched his jaw
and he admitted, "She was living with three people—
two of them men."

Pressed up against him so tightly, Alec felt her
quickly drawn breath, the way she stiffened. "Oh no.
Alec, what did you do?"

He grinned evilly. "I beat the hell out of both the
guys, though I had no idea which one was for her. Hell,
maybe they both were. Knowing how insatiable she
always was, I wouldn't have put it past her. The cops
got called, I got arrested, and she told me she was going
to file for a divorce. I felt so damn sick, I didn't even
care. Right then, at that moment, standing in that
crowded police station knowing all those uniforms felt
sorry for me and that they were thinking what an ass I
was to have ever fallen for her in the first place, I almost
wanted to kill her myself. I did tell her to stay the hell
out of my life."

Celia wrapped her arms tight around him in a near
choke hold. "She was wrong, Alec. But don't you see?
She didn't know any better—"

"Like your Hannah?" He grabbed her arms to pull
her loose, but she was like a damn spider monkey,
clinging tight.

"No!" Celia leaned back to look in his eyes, but
didn't loosen her hold on him. He didn't want to hurt
her, so he had to give up on prying her loose and let her
squeeze on him all she wanted. "Hannah wants help,
Alec. She's not like that. Her circumstances didn't drive
her away, only her bad judgment did."

"Don't worry, sweetheart." He gave her a twisted

smile that he knew damn good and well wouldn't reassure her one bit, but it was the best he could offer at the present. "Just because I couldn't do a damn thing for my wife doesn't mean I'll leave little Hannah behind. You and I made a deal, and I'll hold up my end of the bargain. I just wonder if she'll thank you in the end."

His cold tone must have disturbed her, for she shivered and said, "Alec? What happened to your wife? You told me she died."

"Yeah." He removed every bit of inflection he could from his tone, not wanting to give anything away, not wanting her pity, or even her understanding. "One month after I walked away without even trying to bring her home, she died. Overdosed during a party with her upscale friends. She never did get that divorce, so they called me, and when I went to see her body…"

His voice trailed off and he closed his eyes, but he could still plainly see her, how ravaged she'd looked, how thin and old. *Jesus.* Her life in the big city had taken its toll. And Alec had never quite forgiven himself for not trying harder to bring her around. It had seemed from the time she was born, she hadn't had a snowball's chance in hell of surviving. Like so many other people, he'd just given up on her. No matter what he told Celia, no matter what excuses he had, he'd let her down.

He knew now he'd never loved her, but he had felt sorry for her and he still did. He'd had a responsibility to her, one that he'd conveniently forgotten when his pride got bruised. Some days he felt so guilty he could taste it.

In so many ways, he felt sorry for Hannah, too, for being gullible and naive and vulnerable. But he didn't want to get involved again. He hadn't saved his wife, so why should he save anyone else? If it weren't for Celia insisting… He hadn't realized his arms had tightened on Celia again until she moved.

She kissed him. "Shhh. I'm sorry I made you dredge that all up."

"I was behind on all my bills after the money she'd taken. I was barely able to catch up, and then she died and I couldn't afford a funeral. My grandfather didn't have any money, and her mother couldn't have cared less. She was off with a new man by then." He closed his eyes. "I had to let the state bury her…"

"Alec." Celia kissed him, giving him so much in the touch of her mouth to his.

In near desperation, Alec cupped her face, holding her still while he took over, while he kissed her hungrily. Celia made him feel stronger and weaker than any other person he'd known. She stole his strength, but gave it back to him in spades.

He opened his mouth against her neck, drawing the skin in against his teeth, moving his mouth down to suck voraciously at her nipples. She groaned, surprised at his urgency, but still responsive as ever. He muttered, his tone thick and dark, "Just give me this, Celia. It's all I want. Just this…"

For an answer, she wrapped her soft slender thighs tightly around his waist—and he was a goner.

He didn't believe in love; what he'd felt for his wife hadn't even been real, but more a pathetic effort to save her and himself, an effort he'd failed miserably. There hadn't been another soul alive he'd let get under his skin since then. He saved people as part of his job. They were simple assignments, nothing more, easy to work through, easy to forget. Hannah could have been an assignment for someone else so he wouldn't have had to get involved.

But now there was Celia. And truth was, she scared him half to death.

Making love to her seemed his only option, a physical way to drown out the sentient turmoil she caused. And now that he'd had release, just a bit of the edge was gone and he could take his time.

Alec did all the things to her he'd ever imagined, and she revelled in each and every one. He made love to her tenderly, and then with primitive determination, almost violent in his need. But she was with him every step of the way, reacting just as explosively, totally uninhibited. Finally, in the wee hours of the morning, they both fell asleep.

Unfortunately, Alec dreamed of his wife, her lush body thin and cold, her sexy features ravaged by death, and somehow her face and Celia's were combined.

And just as he'd failed his wife, he failed Celia. Despite her skewed perspective on things, Alec knew she wouldn't give herself so freely to a man unless she cared, unless she…*loved him.* In a deep part of himself he didn't want to recognize, Alec accepted the truth.

The worst that could happen, had.

CHAPTER TEN

No AMOUNT of physical exertion could chase away her demons this morning. Celia had already worked up a sweat, pushed herself harder than she ever had before, and all she could think of was last night. It had been both the most wonderful, and the most distressful, night of her life. Alec had loved her in ways she'd only dreamed of, ways that would have shocked her not so long ago, but had seemed incredibly romantic and intimate and special last night. *With Alec.*

He'd also been brutally honest about his views of the world—and she didn't fit into his equation.

Celia had stirred when Alec crawled out of bed early that morning. But she didn't tell Alec she was awake. She wanted time alone to think. She heard him washing up in the bathroom, heard him quietly dressing. When he walked over to her side of the bed, she kept her eyes tightly closed. Regulating her breathing wasn't easy, but she just couldn't face him yet, not knowing what she did now about his past—and how difficult it would be for him to trust in love again. Strangely, he didn't seem to blame his wife or his grandfather or anyone else who'd let him down. He only blamed himself. Her heart wanted to crumble for the hurts he'd been dealt.

His rough, wonderful fingers touched her cheek,

smoothed her hair, and seconds later she heard the soft click of the door as it closed behind him. She knew he'd hesitated, that he'd peeked out to make sure it was clear to leave. He'd broken his own rule about staying over and taking chances, and that, too, would anger him at himself. He'd see it as a lack of responsibility on his part. He was so protective…

The tears had started then. All night she'd held them off, knowing he hated to suffer through her excesses of emotion. But her heart hurt and she wanted so badly to curl up and hide away. Of course she didn't.

Minutes after Alec was gone, she left the bed and found his note claiming he'd be back in the early afternoon. At first she was so relieved to find out he wasn't gone for good. She hadn't been certain about that, not with the way she'd pushed him. Then Celia realized that she hadn't told him about the appointment she had with Marc Jacobs's crony at two o'clock. If Alec didn't make it back in time, he'd no doubt be livid to find her gone. He was overprotective to a fault, did the best he could to shield her, but he didn't love her.

And he never would.

Celia squeezed her eyes shut as she did another series of crunches, working to distract herself, but with no success. Even Thelma Houston singing loudly from the portable CD player couldn't penetrate her clamoring thoughts.

She loved Alec, but he had forever shut himself off from love. She had to accept the facts. Her brother, Dane, had been telling her for some time what a loner Alec was, how he seemed to thrive on his seclusion. Even Dane's wife, Angel, whom Alec adored, made him nervous if she offered him the slightest affection.

He approached every job with single-minded, cold de-
liberation, and an absolute lack of personal involvement that effectively settled things with the least amount
of fuss. He didn't want to be involved, not with anyone
for any reason.

He'd told her, and his life-style proved it; Alec
wanted her for sexual release, but with no ties.

He hadn't been wrong about the chemistry between
them. No, she didn't feel used for knowing Alec's
touch. She felt cherished, and that hurt more than
anything.

His poor wife. To Celia, she'd sounded so sad and
misguided. And poor Alec. Despite what he'd said, regardless of how he'd thundered and thumped his chest,
he was hurting still, and his guilt had been as plain to
her as his smudged tattoo with the name removed.

Celia, already sweating, strained to lift herself one
more time on the chin-up bar. To boost herself, she
started singing with Thelma, her own rendition of a
blood-rushing war cry.

"I'd have thought I exercised you plenty last night."

Celia yelped at the intrusion of that amused, masculine voice. Dropping almost to her knees, she whirled
to face Alec. His arms were laden with packages, and
there was a wide, taunting smile on his unshaven face.

He looked delicious, she thought, in his rumpled
jeans, dark T-shirt and flannel, like a renegade, lethal
and sexy and more than capable of anything he set his
mind to. Even though her embarrassment was extreme,
she couldn't help admiring him. "Alec, your note said
you'd be gone till the afternoon!"

"It is afternoon."

"No, it's only eleven."

He shrugged. "Close enough. I got everything taken care of faster than I expected."

Still struggling with his smile, Alec put the boxes and bags on the small table, never quite taking his gaze from her. Legs braced apart, arms crossed over his chest, he was the perfect picture of the arrogantly amused male.

Celia nervously tugged her T-shirt lower. Other than her panties, it was all she wore, all she ever wore while working out in the oppressive summer heat. She cleared her throat. "Actually, I'm glad you're here."

"Me, too." Stalking forward, his eyes on the damp T-shirt clinging to her breasts, he added, "I expected to find you still in bed, all drowsy and sweet, but maybe this is even better." He glanced up, his gaze holding hers. "You're already…warmed up."

"Alec." Celia held her arms out, warding him off. She needed to talk to him, to explain about her plans with Jacobs, but he easily dodged her resistance and in a single move she found herself flat on the bed and Alec firmly planted between her thighs.

"You smell good," he muttered, nuzzling her shoulder and throat.

"I'm sweaty!"

"Earthy. You smell like a woman. I like it."

"Alec, please, I have to talk to you."

"I love how you say *please* so prettily." He kissed her breast through the cotton, lightly nibbled on her nipple. "It turns me on."

She couldn't help but laugh even as her body softened with wanting him. "I'm finding out that everything turns you on."

"Everything about you. Believe it or not, I have icy cold iron control everywhere else."

"Really?" She knew it to be true at work, but did he mean with other women also? The idea pleased her. If she couldn't have everything, at least she had something special.

Alec started inching her shirt up, and she knew once he had her naked, it'd be all over. She gripped his ponytail, making him wince, and blurted out, "Jacobs set up another meeting for me today."

Alec stilled. "When?"

"At two o'clock."

He stared at her hard for a moment, then shoved himself into a sitting position. Glaring down at where she still lay sprawled on the mattress, he asked, "And you're just now telling me?"

Celia scrambled into a sitting position as well, pulling the shirt over her knees to maintain a false sense of modesty. "Well, last night you didn't exactly give me a chance, now did you?"

He leaned forward, nose to nose with her. "So why didn't you tell me this morning instead of playing possum?"

Celia tucked in her chin. "You knew I was awake?"

Alec rolled his eyes and stood to pace. "All right. From now on, business comes first." He looked at her, his eyes black with inner fire, pinning her. "There's nothing I'd rather do than spend a week in bed with you, but that's going to have to come second to solving this business with Jacobs—if you're still determined to see this through?"

She lifted her chin. "Of course I'm still determined."

He muttered a curse. "That's what I figured."

"You're the one who distracted me last night!"

"And I'll damn well distract you again tonight, and

the next night. But from now on, tell me what's going on the minute you see me. No more holding back. What if I hadn't gone shopping this morning? Then we'd be in a hell of a mess."

Celia had no idea what his shopping had to do with her plans for Jacobs. She gave him a blank look and he sighed.

"Celia, I don't want you around Jacobs again without a wire. It's too risky. Watching you from outside that house last night took a good ten years off my life. I don't want to go through that again. Seeing you in there, but not knowing what's going on—anything could happen, and the more we deal with that bastard, the less I like it. The only way I can approve any of this—"

"You can approve!"

"—is if you're wired so I can hear what's going on."

Celia jumped to her feet to face him. Alec was back to his old, stubborn, autocratic self and she wouldn't stand for it. "I thought we'd already decided that I'm going to do whatever I choose, Alec Sharpe! You don't own me."

Propping his hands on his hips and acting totally unaffected by her ire, he said, "If I did, I'd have you on a leash."

She almost exploded with fury, and then somehow, some small niggling suspicion crept into her brain. Alec wanted her anger. He'd tried jumping her bones the minute he'd come in, which would have, in effect, put her in the place he wanted to keep her: as a mere bed partner, her importance defined by physical activities.

But then she'd told him about Jacobs and his natural protective instincts kicked in. Alec felt a noble, if detached, responsibility for almost everyone, especially people smaller, older, or weaker than himself. But he seemed to take a personal interest in Celia. He always had, almost from day one. Why hadn't she ever made serious note of that before?

Because she'd always been too busy fighting off her own attraction for him.

Now she no longer wanted to fight, and she was seeing things much more clearly. Watching him warily, she said, "You're being a jerk, Alec."

"Because I don't want to see you raped by that bastard?"

"No." She shook her head, shaken by his words despite her false bravado. "I accept your concern because I believe it's genuine."

He smirked. "Gee, thanks."

"But it's your attitude that needs work." She narrowed her eyes and looked him over, unsure how far she should push. But this was important. She loved him, and even if he never loved her back, she wanted him to accept that love existed, and that he, especially, was a very worthy man to receive it. "Last night you weren't so obnoxious. You were…understanding, when I first came in."

He laughed. "Last night you were all but falling apart. I don't kick anyone when they're down, especially not a lady I want to get intimate with."

Oh God. He was going for the jugular today. Feeling her resolve weaken, Celia lifted her chin. "I thought you were kind and considerate because you cared about me."

Alec stepped closer, his gaze predatory. "Oh, I do care, honey. But don't give me that doe-eyed innocent look, like you think I should be pledging love everlasting just because we rocked the earth in bed."

Very quietly, she whispered, "I never thought that, Alec."

"Good. Because what we have together is too damn hot to start watering down with false expectations."

"Sex?"

"Damn right. Sensational sex, from both our perspectives, and I've got your claw marks all over me to prove it."

She almost hit him. The air left her in a whoosh and she felt herself folding in, closing down. She couldn't banter with him, not when he was intent on forcing an ugly void between them. Turning, she headed for the bathroom, wanting only an escape, but Alec wrapped one steely arm around her waist, drawing her up short. A physical battle would be beyond stupid; the man was hard as granite whereas she was still trying to develop a little muscle tone. She waited to see what he would do, but he merely held her, pulling her tight against his chest.

She felt his indecision like a tangible thing, pulsing over her, and then his mouth touched her temple, her ear. "Where are you going, babe?"

Celia held herself perfectly still, afraid she'd fall apart and start crying if she moved a single muscle. Not only would she refuse him the satisfaction of winning, her pride demanded she hold tough, that she prove herself capable of dealing with anything he dished out. "I need to shower and get ready."

"Not yet."

"Alec…" She squeezed her eyes shut. If he said one

more hurtful thing to her now, she might not be able to forgive him.

But he simply held her. "We have things to talk about, and I brought you something to eat."

"I'm not hungry."

"You'll eat anyway."

Shoving out of his arms, she faced him again and said, "Get it through your thick head, Sharpe! You're not my keeper."

Eyes glinting, he leaned against the wall and folded his arms over his chest. She recognized that now as his arrogant stance, and she braced herself.

"But I am." The words were soft, satisfied. "Don't you remember our little arrangement? I'd stay and help you save Hannah, and you'd give me…" he shrugged "…anything I want. Right now, I want you to stop running away from me."

Her hands fisted at his fickle attitude. "Then stop trying to drive me away. It's not even necessary. Believe me, Alec, I already figured out where I stand. And I'm not so naive that I have illusions of a lasting love." Bitterness, heartache, threatened to choke her, but she added, "Not with you."

That gave him pause. He pushed away from the wall and paced. Hands on hips, his head dropped forward, he stared at the floor for several moments in a pose of indecision and frustration. Celia could almost feel him thinking, an angry, fretful process, before he finally looked at her again. "Fair enough." He searched her face silently, then shook his head. "Now sit. I really do need to talk to you."

Damned pigheaded man. "Alec, that was only marginally nicer than a dog's command."

He smiled. "I'm sorry. Would you please sit down so I can instruct you on the finer points of a wire, since you'll definitely be in possession of one before you go anywhere near Jacobs or his cronies again."

"Is there time?" She glanced at the clock. "I have to be there in just a few hours."

"Be where, exactly?" he asked, as she seated herself at the tiny, scarred table.

Celia winced. "I gather it's a studio of sorts. I'm supposed to do a...a photo shoot."

Alec closed his eyes, a sure indication that he didn't exactly like what she'd just told him. "And you agreed to do this without even discussing it with me first?"

"Oh, right. What was I supposed to do, Alec? Tell Jacobs's friend, 'Oh excuse me, please, but I have to ask my private eye pal if it's okay?' Get real."

"I'm not your damn *pal,* Celia."

"Don't I know it!"

He gave her a look that said she was pushing it, but kept his calm. "Okay, start over. Who is Jacobs's friend, where are you going, and who will be there?"

Well, shoot. This was going to be the tricky part. She hadn't expected Alec to be in such a rotten mood when she told him. "Jacobs has this friend, Blair Giles, who's supposedly a photographer, but Hannah told me while we were in the bathroom that he's a really nasty sort. She said Jacobs uses him to weed out the girls. If anyone balks at working with Giles, Jacobs drops them as being too risky and too much trouble. So you see, I *had* to do this, Alec. If I hadn't agreed, they'd have been on to me and I wouldn't even have the chance to talk to Hannah again."

Alec leaned back and crossed his ankles. He was too

rock steady for nervous movements, but his hands gripped the edge of the table, giving away his anxiety. "Sounds like you and little Hannah had quite a chat. If she wants to be saved, why didn't she just agree to it then?"

Celia measured her words carefully, unsure of how to convince him. "Yes, we did talk some. But she was too afraid to trust me beyond a few warnings." Celia told him all about her close call with Jacobs and how he'd treated Hannah, how pale and afraid the girl had been afterward. "It was awful, Alec. When we got in the bathroom, she was too scared to listen to much I had to say, and definitely too afraid to linger long enough to give me a chance to convince her. All she wanted to do was warn me."

"About Jacobs?"

Nodding, she said, "Yeah, and this Giles fellow. She told me the only way around him is to not act afraid. He… I guess he sort of likes it when he can scare a woman or make her nervous."

Alec's entire countenance tightened until he was suddenly on his feet, standing over Celia. "Don't go."

Her heart swelled. He could pretend what was between them was only sexual, but the heat in his eyes now told a very different story. Like a battered child, he was wary of caring too much for anyone, shying away from tenderness—or love. She didn't fool herself into thinking she could have his love, not when he guarded it so closely. But she still wanted to give him hers. Alec deserved that much, and more.

Touching his jaw with a gentle hand, she said, "I'm not her, Alec."

He backed up, his gaze diamond hard, but also a bit

panicked. "Besides being melodramatic, what the hell is that supposed to mean?"

Celia stood and walked to him until she could wrap her arms around his waist. He was warm and hard and touching him made her feel more alive than she'd thought possible. "I didn't have a tragic childhood. I'm not naive or desperate. And I'm smart. I can take care of myself, Alec, and while I'm there, I'll have you to help me. It'll be okay."

For the longest time Alec was stiff, his arms hanging at his sides. She knew he was struggling, but in the end, he wrapped her close and rocked her in his arms. "I know you're not dumb, Celia. Far from it. But you're out of your element here."

"And that's why you're helping." She leaned back and smiled at him. "For a price, as you so rudely reminded me."

"Celia…"

"Which," she added, interrupting him, "I'll expect to have to pay as soon as I get home tonight."

His gaze softened and he looked down at her breasts in the clinging cotton. She jumped slightly when his warm palms slid to her barely clad fanny, cuddling her closer. "Is that right? Am I to understand that you'll willingly be at my mercy?"

"Very willingly," she whispered.

His gaze shot to her face, suddenly fierce, and very possessive. Celia shivered, and cleared her throat. Teasing Alec was like tugging on the tiger's tail— exciting, but also a little nerve-wracking. "Where is this wire going to be?" she asked, quickly changing the subject and hoping to distract him. "I don't have to hide it anyplace…*risqué,* do I?"

He laughed, as she had known he would, but it was more a concession to her, an effort to lighten the mood, than in any real humor. "No, if we put it anyplace that muffled it too much, I wouldn't be able to hear a damn thing." Then he smacked her bottom. "Not to mention how uncomfortable it might be for you."

His wicked grin had her smiling too. "Well, thank goodness for that."

Alec released her. "It's lucky for you I went shopping today, though I was thinking more about the night to come at the bar than anything going on this afternoon. I hated not being able to hear what Jacobs said to you, especially when you started dancing around him."

"He'd just asked me to pose."

"And of course you jumped to obey."

"Of course." Then she added, "Actually I was afraid he'd ask me into the back room to do it or something, so instead I jumped the gun and did it right there, in front of everyone. It was horribly embarrassing."

"But you're right, it was better than being alone with him."

She shrugged. "I thought so."

Alec shook his head. "Well, along with food, I picked up a small detecting device that no one will notice as long as you don't advertise it. But I won't even put it directly on you. That's too risky. I was thinking maybe your purse, if you think you can keep it with you all the time."

"Of course."

Alec reached for a bag and dumped out the contents. Besides some things she didn't recognize, he had a fresh box of condoms—which made her cheeks bloom with renewed color—and a very ordinary-looking pen. He held it out to her. "Here you go."

Celia blinked. "What am I supposed to do with that?"

"Keep it close. It's your bug."

"You're kidding?" She touched the ballpoint tip and got a speck of ink on her finger. "It's just a regular pen."

"No, it just looks like a regular pen, but it has a hidden transmitter. That little baby will pick up a whisper forty feet away and it transmits up to five hundred meters with respectable quality, which means I won't have to be too damn close, but I sure as hell intend to be close enough to get you out of there if any trouble starts."

Alec took it from her when she started to inspect it too closely. "Let's not break it, okay? They don't come cheap." He shook his head at her, then reached for her small bag. "If you clip it high on the inside like this, and leave your purse open, we shouldn't have any problems."

She was really impressed. "Wherever did you find it?"

He snorted. "In a town this size? There must be at least a hundred commercial outlets, though I got that one from an underground source."

"Just like that?"

"Celia, I couldn't drive down the block without picking up a couple dozen eavesdropping devices on a scanner. The world is not as pretty, or as secure, as you like to think."

She ignored his continued references to her naiveté. "So how do we know Jacobs doesn't have a bug in here somewhere?"

"Because no one's been in here or I'd know about it. Believe it or not, I do pay attention."

Celia shrugged. "Okay, so you're Super Sleuth. Forgive my doubting tendencies."

"Smart-ass."

"Sorry." She grinned, showing she really wasn't the least bit contrite.

"Celia, you do have to be careful what you say around Hannah. I doubt Jacobs spends the money to bug the girls, because he strikes me as the type to be overly confident in his domination. But be careful all the same, all right?"

Celia nodded, a little overwhelmed by the possibility that any conversation she had might be listened to. With a definite edge of sarcasm, she said, "This is just great, Alec. I feel better about the whole thing already."

A slight smile tugged at his sensual mouth. "Yeah, well don't get too cocky on me. I still don't like this setup worth a damn, and from now on, don't even think about accepting any dates without running it past me first." When she started to object again, he shushed her with a finger pressing on her lips. "I mean it, Celia. Make up any damn excuse you want, tell him you'll have to call him after you free up some time, but no more without me approving it first. Got that?"

She nodded grudgingly. Now that she understood him a little better, she didn't mind his autocratic attitude nearly as much.

Not that she'd let him boss her around, but…

"Now," he said, pulling her into his arms once again. "I've held off as long as I can. You prancing around here like that is making me crazy." His voice dropped and he nuzzled her ear. "I need you, Celia."

Already her skin tingled and her stomach did flips. The way he'd said that had sounded like so much more than just sex. She glanced at the clock. It'd be a rush, but…

"I want you, too, Alec. So much."

The words were no sooner out of her mouth than she found herself in his arms, on her way to the bed. Some things were worth making time for.

CHAPTER ELEVEN

HE'D SCREWED UP royally and he knew it.

Alec, crouched around a corner at the back of the warehouse "studio" where Celia was presently posing, chewed on the inside of his jaw and called himself three kinds of a fool. He'd distracted her, ruining her focus, and then sent her to her destination running late, which had made her frazzled. Whether or not she'd absorbed his last few warnings of caution and discretion, he couldn't say. After he'd kept her in bed for an hour, exorcising his own private demons on her very willing body, she'd had to fly through her shower, and fixing her hair and makeup. She'd thought the result majorly disappointing.

Alec knew any man looking at her would go nuts.

With her slightly tousled hair, her glowing eyes and cheeks and her kiss-swollen lips, she looked like sensuality incarnate, like a woman made to take a man, and there wasn't a male alive who wouldn't recognize and appreciate the picture she presented.

It was one more thing to put him on edge. The whole setup stunk to high heaven. The "studio" was definitely a facade, more an abandoned warehouse in a not-so-great area where law-enforcement didn't make the time to visit with any regularity. The building was old, the brick facing a little rough and dirty in places. Alec had circled the whole building before Celia went in, and on the west side there were even some windows that had been boarded up. It looked as though only part of the warehouse was in use—the part Giles and Jacobs needed to lure in young women.

The blacktop parking lot where Alec crouched was sweltering hot with the midday sun burning down on him. Sweat trickled down his temples and down the small of his back, but he ignored the discomforts, all his focus on Celia and what she was about to do.

Small background noises reached Alec through his receiver as Celia was greeted and walked down a long concrete hallway. He heard the cavernous echoing of her high heels, the sounds of opening and closing doors, then stillness. They'd obviously taken her to a back office.

A male voice intruded, making Alec's senses come alive.

"Ms. Sharpe! You're right on time."

Alec's brows rose. *Ms. Sharpe?* She'd used *his* last name? A grin teased at his mouth until he caught himself and frowned. His instinctive reaction unnerved him, but he didn't have time to ponder the ramifications of it, not when Celia and the man were speaking. He didn't want to miss a single word, though so far the conversation was banal enough. This man, then, wasn't Blair Giles. The voice was young and enthusiastic and slightly flirtatious. Alec could well imagine any young man being enamored of Celia in her light-colored blouse and short skirt, her shapely legs posed in the ridiculously high heels. Something about spiked heels like that made a woman seem vulnerable, like she was almost hobbled, awaiting a man's pleasure. Alec shook his head, remembering how carefully and delicately Celia walked in the damn things.

He sure as hell hadn't been immune.

Then the door opened and closed again, voices spoke softly, and the young man was dismissed.

"Celia, it's good to see you again."

"Hello, Mr. Giles."

She sounded nervous, and Alec wanted to kick his own ass for not doing more to reassure her before letting her go. He'd been intent only on his own pleasures, and on keeping reality at bay. It was bad enough when he'd stupidly stayed the whole night with her, leaving their association open to discovery. Luckily, Jacobs felt she was safe and hadn't had her watched through the night. But it had still been pretty dark when Alec had left this morning, and he'd stuck to the shadows, being careful to avoid announcing his presence.

"What do you think of my studio?"

"It's...it's not quite what I expected."

"But it is perfect. The large space, the concrete floor and high ceilings, make setting up for shoots perfect. The reflection is ideal for my lighting equipment. I was thrilled to find it. And believe me, I've done some of my best work here."

"Then I'm really honored that you asked me to pose here."

"My pleasure." There was quiet, some shuffling. "Now, Celia, none of that. No blushes. There are few relationships as close as that between model and photographer, so you're going to have to accustom yourself to me touching you."

Touching her? Alec saw red and wanted to interrupt

them right now. Much more of this stress and his heart would quit. Only Celia's soft, teasing voice calmed him.

"I'm just flustered to be here. I mean, it's so exciting! To think I might actually be in a magazine!"

"Oh, you'll definitely appear in the spread. I can almost guarantee that." There was a smile in the man's tone that set Alec's teeth on edge. "That is, if you allow me to do my job the best that I can—which means you're going to have to relax. Now, why don't we start with a few simple shots, and then you can change."

A small silence. "Change?"

"Of course." Alec heard a sound like a stool being dragged across the bare floor. "Here you go. Sit your pretty self right here in front of the backdrop while I adjust the lights."

"Oh. They're almost blinding. I can barely see."

"Don't worry about it, you'll get used to it. I can see perfectly, and that's what matters. Just put this leg here—that's right."

Celia giggled, making Alec want to punch through the brick wall he leaned against.

"And this leg like so—lovely. No, don't pull your knees together. This is to be a relaxed pose. Now, chin up and smile."

"Like this?"

"Come, Celia. You can do better than that." The sound of a shutter clicking filled the air. "I want a coy, seductive look. Pretend you're waiting naked in bed for your lover."

She laughed, and the sound was strained. "But I don't have a lover."

Another pause. "Very nice—tilt your head." Then:

"No lover? Why, that's an awful pity for a woman as sexy as yourself. Does this mean you're entirely free?"

"My eyes are watering."

"Go ahead and close them a minute." His voice was oily, calculating. "Can you answer me, please?"

"What? Oh, no, I'm totally free. I don't want to tie myself down with some possessive ape. There's too much I want to do still."

"Hmmm. Then perhaps you'd like to join me tonight for another party. You made quite an impression last night and there are a few other people Marc and I would like to introduce you to."

"Another party? My gosh, there's so much going on here!"

"Never a dull moment. So what do you say? Would you like to meet some more important people?"

Even before she spoke, Alec knew what she would say. The little idiot would disregard the order he'd given her.

"That would be wonderful!"

Alec plowed both hands through his hair. *Damn, damn, damn.*

"Excellent."

"Will there be anyone there I already know? Like Hannah and Jade?"

Alec groaned. *Don't push it, babe.* Though she merely sounded excited, he didn't want her taking any chances by trying to move too fast, or associating herself with one particular person.

"Oh, of course! Hannah is one of Marc's favorite girls. He takes her everywhere. I'm not sure about Jade, but I'll mention it to Marc. I'm sure he won't mind obliging you." There was the rustle of papers. "Here's the address. No, don't get up, I'll just stick it in your purse. Be there at six o'clock, dressed in something sexy. Actually, what you wore last night would work."

"Again? But—"

The paper crinkled against the transmitter, for the moment blocking out all other sounds. But luckily Giles didn't pay the pen any mind because Alec clearly heard the next words, telling him the pen hadn't been disturbed.

"You looked lovely in it, and no will notice or care, I promise you. Now, are you ready? Okay, turn the other way. No, like this."

"Oh!"

"You're very soft, Celia."

"Thank…thank you."

Alec's hands bunched into fists. Nothing that was happening could have been any worse than his imagination. He wanted to kill Giles with his bare hands.

"But it is hot under the lights, isn't it? Even the air-conditioning doesn't help. You must be smothering in that outfit."

Alec stiffened. The bastard. He was touching her and talking softly to her and he didn't even have the decency to try for a believable pretense! His line was so obvious, he may as well have said, *I want you naked now.*

Alec could feel Celia's hesitation when she nervously whispered, "It is rather warm."

"Well, lucky for you, the magazine ad calls for a lot of skin to show. Sometimes we're stuck modeling fur coats! That's really miserable, I can tell you. But the ad I have in mind for you is for an all-over body lotion. I have to send them several shots of different models so they can decide who best suits them, but I honestly believe you have the very best chance. All we need to do is convince them of that, and then you're on your way. Here you go, take this."

"What is it?"

A rough male laugh. "Your costume of sorts. You'll strip down and pose on the stool, using the length of velvet to insure your, ah, modesty. With your fair hair and golden eyes, along with the white backdrop, the red velvet will look…delicious, and make a startling contrast. You really do have excellent skin, so we need to show that off."

"I…ah…"

"Celia, you have a lovely body, one you should be proud of. Models are known, judged and selected for their bodies. If you're serious about this, you have to be willing to flaunt your assets. And believe me, your body, slim but with plenty of proper curves, is an asset. *Use it.*"

Say no, Alec thought, his mind rebelling, his muscles drawing tight, his heart crashing against his ribs, *refuse right now and get the hell out of there.*

There was a heavy pause, pregnant with anticipation, and then he heard Celia ask very softly, "Where should I change?"

Even as he was already moving, one plan after another jumping through his brain, Alec cursed and cursed again. When he got her home…

Thinking of a dire enough threat would slow him down, and right now he needed to keep his focus. He could, and would, figure out what to do with Celia later.

For now, he had to save her sweet little butt.

CELIA'S HEART DRUMMED so roughly she thought it might punch right through her chest. She clutched the red velvet in her fists, trying not to crush it, while fighting the urge to run.

This was her test. Giles was testing her, probably at Jacobs's urging, to see if she was genuine. A real model "wanna-be" in her desperate shoes would likely jump at the opportunity to show herself to favor, especially to the prestigious magazine people Giles claimed to know.

A real P.I. intent on saving another woman wouldn't hesitate to pass the damn test.

It didn't take her long to decide she had no choice, none at all. She would see Hannah tonight, and somehow she'd convince her. Maybe Jade, too. She'd like to shut Jacobs's entire operation down. She wanted him behind bars, where he couldn't ever hurt anyone again.

Her face turned red-hot as she thought about Alec listening in. It was even harder than she'd suspected, knowing he heard every word and that he was no doubt furious, cursing her even as she struggled with her decision. *Please understand, Alec. I have to do this, I have to save Hannah.*

Her train of thought stopped cold when Giles put his hand on her bottom, urging her behind a very slightly curtained area—thankfully still close to where her purse sat so that if need be, she could summon Alec.

"Hurry along now. We don't have all day. You can just leave your clothing—all of it—on the hooks on the wall."

Celia drew in a deep breath. The curtain wasn't all that wide or concealing. Giles could see her from the neck up and the knees down. Never had she felt so exposed, knowing he watched as she forced herself through such an uncomfortable, denigrating situation.

And that had to be his plan. She remembered Hannah telling her Giles enjoyed frightening women. She'd had a taste of his methods already while in Marc Jacobs's den, when Giles had pulled her close and kissed her. She'd wanted to throw up then, to claw his face. Holding back her panic had taken a lot of effort. But he'd known how the rapid familiarity had upset her, and he'd enjoyed it.

Remembering made Celia stiffen her spine. She wouldn't give the cretin the satisfaction of knowing how he'd thrown her off balance again.

Smiling at him, watching his face light up with interest and his green eyes darken, she laid the velvet over the curtain rod and began unbuttoning her blouse. "How long do you think it'll be before we hear about the photos?"

Giles rubbed his hands together, making Celia's stomach turn. His dark hair, usually immaculately in place, looked a little disheveled. Combined with the glee in his eyes, it gave him a slightly crazed look. "Not long, not long."

She kicked her shoes off, which safely lowered her breasts another three inches behind the concealment of the curtain. Her blouse was open now and she wondered if Giles could see the frantic racing of her heart, which caused a resultant trembling in her entire body. She shimmied her shoulders to remove the blouse completely, then put it on a hook. She let her bra straps slip down her arms. "I'm really anxious." She smiled again.

Giles stood, licking his lips and taking a step toward her—and suddenly alarms went off throughout the building. A loud, shrill series of horns and whistles blared and echoed everywhere, bouncing off the empty concrete walls.

Celia's eyes widened and she shouted, "What's going on?"

Giles, looking utterly panicked at the thought of an unknown threat, turned a complete, haphazard circle. He was obviously as confused as Celia by the alarm. And then the sprinkler system kicked in and water sprayed down on them both from high ceilings. Celia yelped, grabbing for her blouse and holding it over her head.

Giles cursed foully and leaped from his camera equipment to his elaborate lighting to his desk littered with papers, trying to cover everything at once, trying to shield things with his body. Celia looked around, uncertain what to do.

Giles spared her a frantic, harassed look. "Get the hell out of here before the fire department arrives!"

His shout was mean and within seconds other people were in the room, rushing to obey his barked orders. Celia hesitated only a moment more, then shoved her feet back in her shoes, snatched up her purse, and headed for the door she'd come through.

"Not that way!" Giles grabbed her naked arm, his grip bruising, and practically thrust her out through another exit. "Go down that corridor. There's a door that opens into the back parking lot. And get dressed for God's sake!"

Celia shoved wet hair out of her face and rushed to obey. Icy water continued to spray her. The pandemonium behind her dimmed as she trotted toward a blinking exit sign. But as she stepped outside, now grateful for the heat and blinding sunshine, curiosity got the better of her. This might be her only chance to spy a little. She looked back at the large brick structure, more a warehouse than a studio, and saw there was a row of dark windows on either side of the door she'd just come through.

She located a broken crate by a Dumpster and dragged it closer to the building. Her blouse was still clutched in her hand, her purse slung over her shoulder, her wet hair dripping down her back and making her shiver despite the warmth of the day.

Just as she started to step up on the crate, an iron-hard arm closed around her waist and jerked her down. She started to scream, but the sound was cut off by a callused palm flattening over her mouth. Her body came into contact with a solid chest, and then she heard a familiar whisper in her ear. "Not a sound, damn it. Someone's coming."

She was dragged behind the Dumpster and forced behind Alec's body while two slender male figures ran outside, soaked through to their skin, hauling camera equipment. When they went out of sight around the corner of the building, Alec pulled her up and grabbed her hand. "This way. And hurry."

She tried, she really did, but the shoes made haste nearly impossible. She started to kick them off, but Alec took her arm and kept her moving. Shoving her toward a retaining wall, he said, "Don't say a word. Not a single damn word."

Speaking was well beyond her anyway. She concentrated on discovering a way to scale the wall, when suddenly Alec grabbed her by the waist and practically threw her over it. Within a heartbeat he'd joined her and there was his truck on the side of the road, shielded by a cluster of wild bushes and a few sparse trees. They both jumped inside and Alec pulled away. "Keep your head down in case anyone sees us."

When she didn't react quickly enough, he flattened his large palm on the crown of her wet head and pushed her down in the seat, her cheek to his thigh. "Stay there until I tell you it's clear."

His idea of clear didn't come for some time. Her head rested practically in his lap, her body twisted painfully. It was a good ten minutes before he stopped at a traffic light and looked down at her. He was plainly enraged.

With his foot tight on the brake, he skinned out of his cotton shirt and dropped it on her. "Put that on."

Celia narrowed her eyes. "Is it okay if I sit up now?"

A grudging, sharp nod was her only answer. Celia saw his hands flex on the steering wheel, his knuckles turning white. Cautiously, she slid up into the seat. For comfort's sake, she kicked out of her heels and dropped her sodden blouse onto the floor. Remembering his order to inform him of things up front, she said, "Ah, I have a party to go to tonight…"

"I heard."

He wouldn't look at her, and she felt bereft. Licking her lips, she tentatively asked, "The sprinkler system?"

"Always goes off when someone sets a fire."

"You?" She shouldn't have been so surprised. Alec was a quick thinker, and he obviously understood the predicament Giles had put her in. When he did no more than ignore her, she said, "Thank you."

And those soft, humble words seemed to set him off. *"Goddammit, Celia."* She jumped a good foot, then sat staring at him. He was beyond furious. "Do you have any idea at all what Giles would have done to you once he had you naked? I doubt screaming would have even brought you any aid, considering everyone on his payroll is likely dirty. You could have been—"

"I know."

"You know? *You know!*" He was so angry, she suspected his shouted words could be heard by the cars passing them by. His neck was red and his black eyes glowed like hot coals. "Then why in hell did you agree?"

"Because I had to. Because it was the test."

He put the truck in drive and lurched back into traffic. "And you have this harebrained idea that you owe the world something because of Raymond. You think you can make retribution? Baby, you don't know anything about it."

She drew in a slow breath. "It may have started out that way. At first, I only wanted to make myself feel better by helping other women. I did see it as a debt of sorts I had to pay." She reached across the seat and touched his arm, right where the tattoo decorated his biceps. She felt his muscle flinch. "But now, I *have* to do it. I have to save Hannah and the other girls—"

His head jerked around to stare at her. "*Other* girls?"

She drew a deep steadying breath. "I met Jade, a very young, very lovely girl, and there were others I didn't meet, but I saw them at the party. I don't doubt I'll see them again tonight." Her fingers tightened on his arm. "Alec, I want to shut Jacobs down."

Alec's fist hit the steering wheel. *"Goddammit!"*

She wished he'd quit swearing like that. It made her heart jump every time, and drove home how opposed he was to the entire effort. "He has to be stopped—"

"That's not what you're being paid to do." He tried to sound reasonable, but his voice shook. With anger? "Mrs. Barrington just wants Hannah back. The rest of it…"

"Yes?" She knew Alec's conscience, knew he wouldn't be able to abide the idea of Jacobs walking free any more than she could.

Surprised that the steering wheel didn't crack under his hands, Celia waited until finally Alec sighed. He flexed his jaw several times and she knew he was striving for control. "So do you have some grand plan that'll convict Jacobs without putting all the girls through the scandal, because believe me, the press will have a field day with a story like this. Every young woman involved will end up very well known for things they'd likely rather forget."

Lifting her chin, Celia said, "I'm going to be the one to testify against them. Blair Giles took pictures of me and made false promises—you heard that much."

"And have it on tape." His expression was stony, but resigned. "The receiver to your transmitter was attached to a small tape recorder."

Celia grinned at him, relieved that some of his anger seemed to be dissolving. "You're fantastic, Alec."

"You won't think so after I turn you over my knee for scaring me half to death."

Since Celia wasn't the least bit afraid of him or his ridiculous threat, she was able to keep her smile. "The thing is, I don't think the little bit we've gotten so far would be enough to convict Jacobs or Giles of anything. And I couldn't ask Hannah to testify. She's so afraid, and you're right, it would cause such a scandal and embarrass her so much." She scooted a little closer to Alec on the seat, then put her hand on his arm again. "I'm going to need to...*push,* just a little more tonight."

Alec swung the truck into the parking lot of his motel. Without a word, he got out and came around to her door. "Come on."

"I don't have much time..."

"You have enough time for me to shake some sense into you." Holding her arm in a firm grip, he led her toward his room.

Celia didn't even try to hold back. "Will you stop with the absurd threats, Alec. We both know you won't hurt me."

He gently pushed her inside and turned the dead bolt on the door. Arms crossed over his chest, he stood blocking the door, and gave her his most intimidating stare.

Celia shook her head. "That won't work, Alec. I'm not afraid of you anymore so you can just stop with the intimidation tactics."

He ignored her statement. "How exactly do you plan to push for more information?"

Celia licked her lips. Alec was in a very strange mood, and for the first time, she couldn't read him at all. "Well, of course I'll want to talk to Hannah again first, to see if I can convince her to leave with me. Then I'm going to act overly enthusiastic about Jacobs and Giles. I'm going to tell them I'll have to go home and give up on my dream if something doesn't happen, something that pays money. I'm going to be really desperate, and I'm going to let them know I'd be willing to do just about anything to gain fame."

Alec pushed away from the door. "No."

"Alec…"

"I've thought it over, and you're right. Jacobs and his cronies have to be stopped. But I'll do it, not you."

"You?"

"That's right." Alec paced, hands on hips, his expression thoughtful as he considered all his angles. "With you out of the picture, I won't be distracted. I can go back to Jacobs's, go through some things. Surely there's some incriminating information there, stored in his files or something. The more I've thought about it, the more certain I am that he'd have to keep information around to hold over the girls."

Celia glared at him as if he was insane. "You want to break into Jacobs's house? Alec, that's the dumbest damn thing you've ever said!" She grabbed his arm when he gave her an impatient look and continued to pace. Her hold stopped him. "Everything is already in place! What you're proposing would be far more dangerous and take a whole lot longer. I want Hannah out of there now, tonight if I can manage it."

Alec grabbed her, his hands tight around her upper arms, and he shook her. Shocked, Celia did no more than hang in his grip. He didn't hurt her, but he looked haunted as he leaned close and growled ferociously, "I don't want to see you hurt, damn it!" He shook her again, a revelation to Celia. "I *won't* see you hurt."

Celia slowly braced her hands against him. "Alec, I'm a grown woman, responsible for myself." She searched his gaze, seeing so much for the first time. "If I choose to go there, if I choose to take a risk—a very minor risk, Alec—well, then, that's on me, not you. Do you understand me?"

He carefully lowered her feet back to the floor and

released her. He took two steps back and he was breathing hard. "Of course I understand you. I'm not simple."

Celia watched him struggle for his famous control. She didn't know quite what else to say, but she knew now that if anything happened to her, he'd blame himself.

She couldn't let that happen. Big, strong, tough Alec had been hurt more than enough already. She wouldn't contribute to his wounds.

Rubbing the back of his neck with one hand, not looking at her, he said, "This could easily backfire on you."

"No. I'll be careful." She spoke softly, convincingly. "But either way, you're not responsible for the decisions I make."

He turned his back on her and that was all it took. Celia hugged him tight from behind. "Alec, I know you blame yourself for what happened to Marissa."

She felt his snort, as if in denial, but he said nothing.

"She was the same age as you, Alec, not a child you were supposed to take care of."

"She was my wife."

"And she was a mixed-up young lady who didn't know what she wanted or where to find it. She didn't ask you for help, and would have refused it in any case. You couldn't have done any more for her than you did."

"If I hadn't walked away from her that day—"

Celia interrupted with, "If I hadn't gotten involved with Raymond…?" She let the sentence dangle, showing him how useless it was to try to relive the past. "We're human and we make mistakes. Sometimes we're ruled by emotions, by our pride. Even the almighty Alec

Sharpe has to deal with regret, but you can't let it change you forever."

He sighed, tipped his head back to stare at the ceiling. Celia could feel his frustration and indecision. She tightened her hold on him and kissed his shoulder. "I'm going tonight, Alec. And I know you'll be there, close if I need you. But if the impossible happens and things don't work out as I planned, then I won't have you blaming yourself. Now promise me."

He twisted around to face her, his gaze disturbingly intent, his expression enigmatic. "I'll promise you this. I'll be outside, watching and waiting. And if I hear so much as a peep that alarms me, if I see one shadow that worries me, or I have one mistrustful intuition, I'm ending it."

Celia supposed that was the best she could get from a man like Alec. He'd worry until it was over, and there was nothing she could do about it. She'd just have to be extra careful to survive unscathed, to prove she could and would handle herself with intelligence and discretion.

She stared back at him and nodded. "All right, Alec."

He tipped up her chin. "And lady, when this is over, it's over. Everything. Because I can't take it anymore."

Including their relationship? She didn't want to, but again she agreed with a small nod. Then, before she had a chance to get emotional again, she went to his phone to call a cab. She only had a few hours left before she needed to be at the party. Alec couldn't take the risk of driving her back to her hotel, not when there was the possibility he might be seen.

Evidently he wouldn't take the risk of caring for her either. After tonight, she'd have met her goals of saving

Hannah Barrington. But with her unwavering determination, she'd driven Alec nuts, and lost out on any hope of having his love.

It was hard to feel happy over her success, when she'd just lost everything she'd ever really wanted.

CHAPTER TWELVE

"HANNAH, I'D LIKE to talk to you."

Hannah barely spared her a glance. "No, leave me alone."

Celia caught her arm as the girl started to stride away. It was the very first chance Celia had of speaking with her. Jacobs and Giles had at first loomed at Celia's side continually, introducing her to several gentlemen and only a few ladies. Giles had tried to laugh off the incident at the warehouse, but his tension was plain to see, and the damage was still being assessed. He apologized gallantly to Celia for his rough treatment of her, explaining that his equipment meant the world to him— without it, he couldn't serve lovely women like herself. Celia had almost snorted at that inane apology.

She had no idea how Alec had started the fire, or what he'd burned. But she could tell by the stilted conversation in both Giles and Jacobs, the incident had put them both on edge. They seemed more alert, more cautious.

Then a waiter had come to whisper to Jacobs and he'd gone to take care of some business. Celia didn't care what the business was as long as Giles went with him.

He didn't, but he did dismiss himself a few minutes later with the promise he'd return to her quickly. Hannah had steered clear of them all, hovering around the wet bar set up in a far corner, grinning and laughing, but Celia saw new circles under her eyes, and a wariness that went bone-deep.

"If you avoid me like this, it'll cause suspicion."

Hannah's gaze widened. Then with a furtive look around, she allowed Celia to tug her over to a small settee situated in a corner of the room. Celia could see all the entrances, everyone coming and going, and there was no way anyone could sneak up on her or overhear her conversation with Hannah.

"Talk to me, Hannah. Please."

Hannah closed her eyes and swallowed hard. Chandelier lights glinted in her gold-and-diamond earrings and reflected off the colorful sequins of her skimpy gown. If Celia hadn't been so intent on other matters, she'd have felt like a total frump in the same black pantsuit. In an effort to at least give the illusion of a different outfit, she'd added a colorful red, lemon and black scarf to her hair, and brightly colored earrings that matched. She figured any woman out to attract the attention of producers would make the effort to present her best appearance. Giles had approved.

"There's nothing to talk about, Celia. I can't go home."

"Can't, or won't?"

"Both. Please, understand. You're wasting your time."

"Your mother doesn't think so, Hannah. Your whole family is devastated that they haven't heard from you, that you're avoiding them. Your mother even thinks you've been brainwashed." Celia smiled sadly. "Or that you're being blackmailed."

An almost desperate laugh escaped Hannah. "My mother was always overdramatizing things."

Celia took her hand and held it. The girl's fingers were cold and stiff. Very gently, Celia asked, "Is she dramatizing now, Hannah?"

Hannah bit her lip and large tears gathered in her eyes. She stared at her lap, at first not answering. Then with a tiny shake of her head, she whispered, "No."

"Ah." Celia felt elated over the small concession, elated and frantic to find out all she could while Hannah was willing to talk. "How is Jacobs keeping you here?"

Hannah turned to look at her. "I've been so stupid." Her smile was filled with self-loathing. "At first, Marc seemed so nice. He helped me out, got me a few photo shoots. I never saw the ads, but I did get the money. He advanced it to me for an apartment, for the new clothes I needed to compete for other photo opportunities. But then, all of a sudden I owed him back more than I could make. The apartment is extravagant, but I signed a lease because Jacobs told me I could eventually afford it. It's owned by another friend of his."

Celia could easily see the circle growing, could envision how a woman would be trapped in Jacobs's web of friends.

"He…he offered me new ways to make more money. And I…I thought it was just a paid escort service." She stared at Celia, desperate. "That's what he told me it was."

Hannah covered her mouth and struggled to keep from crying. Celia quickly patted her back, murmuring to her. "It's all right. I understand. Take a few deep breaths. You have to get control, Hannah. If Jacobs or

Giles sees you crying, they'll wonder what we're talking about. Either of them could come back any minute."

"I'm sorry." She groped for the tissue Celia handed to her and dabbed at her eyes. "I almost never cry anymore. There's no point to it. But things just went so wrong so fast—"

"I know." Still trying to soothe Hannah with a gentle pat to her shoulder, Celia asked, "The escort service was a ruse?"

Again Hannah nodded. "I met a man, and we…I thought we hit it off. He was kind and gentle, and he seemed so sincere. I was so lonely then, and scared and everything was confused." She bit her lip and her cheeks warmed. "We slept together that very first night. He told me I was beautiful and that he couldn't stop wanting to touch me. For the first time in months, things felt right."

Keeping a careful watch out for Jacobs or Giles, and at the same time smiling at the milling crowd so no one would suspect them, Celia asked, "But it wasn't?"

Dully, as if she hardly cared anymore, Hannah said, "When I woke up the next morning, he was gone and there was money beside my bed. He'd…he'd paid me. Like a prostitute." She drew a deep breath and continued. "I was embarrassed and hurt, and I wanted to give the money back to him, but I didn't know where he lived or what his phone number was. Marc just laughed at me when I told him about it, saying I didn't have any reason to be upset, that this would be the perfect way for me to offset my costs and to begin paying him back. I wanted to just walk away. I thought my mother would welcome me back, even though I'd been so awful when I left. But that's when he told me about the photos he had." She looked at Celia, her face filled with desperation. "My family would be so embarrassed, and it'd be all my fault."

Celia felt herself shaking from head to toe. Her suspicions had been correct, but still she was shocked. *Prostitution.* And blackmail. A deep rage filled her when she thought of Jacobs ruthlessly plotting against such a sweet young woman. Celia griped Hannah's hand. "He's an animal, a bastard. But we can take care of that now, Hannah."

"No. My mother would die if those pictures were made public. I thought they were for legitimate magazine ads, but Blair knows how to doctor them so they look even worse than they really did. He showed me a couple, and they were so…so ugly. No, I could never do that to my family."

Celia reached into her purse and withdrew a slip of paper. On it, she wrote the number Alec had made her memorize, the one that reached his cell phone. She stuffed it into Hannah's hand. "I'm going to try to end all this tonight, Hannah. With any luck, Jacobs and Giles will both be going to jail, along with anyone else who works with them. But if you get into any trouble, if you need help at all, I want you to call that number. I promise if you do, everything will be all right."

Hannah looked up, and her wide-eyed expression caused Celia to do the same. She saw both Jacobs and Giles headed toward them and she stood to greet them, smiling as she saw Hannah stuff the small slip of paper into the top of her dress, between her breasts.

"I wondered where you'd both gotten to! I wanted to go looking for you, but Hannah told me we should just wait. She's been very nice in keeping me entertained."

Jacobs smiled at Hannah and pulled her close, his hand resting possessively on her hip. "Well, I have a treat for you, Celia."

With a suitably anxious look, Celia asked, "A treat?"

Giles rubbed his hands. "We're going to go meet a producer. I showed him some of your photos and he's very impressed. He wants to meet you tonight."

"Now?" Celia's mind squirreled around for some way to postpone the meeting, knowing Alec would be outraged. She caught a glimpse of Hannah, who looked appalled by the change in plans, which confirmed in Celia's mind that the threat now was real. But then Giles took her hand and started to lead her away.

"Come, I'll tell you all about it. But we have to hurry."

She glanced back at her purse on the settee, where the pen transmitter was. Unfortunately, when she'd stood, the cushion moved and the purse had dumped. "Oh no, my purse."

Jacobs looked down, scooped up several things and stuffed them back inside. "Here you go. Now hurry along."

Celia, still being tugged along by Giles, saw that the pen was missing. "Wait! My pen—"

"I have plenty of pens, Celia. Don't give it another thought."

"But…it has sentimental value to me."

"I'll call Marc later and have him look for it."

"But…"

"Celia, we need to go. Don't worry. Marc and Hannah will be joining us."

She had no idea how to argue beyond that. With one last wistful look at the settee, she gave up and forced a smile for Giles. There really wasn't anything else she could do. Trying to sound enthusiastic, she asked, "A producer, you say?" but in her mind, she was thinking that getting through this new meeting would likely be a piece of cake, compared to how Alec would react when he caught up to her.

"ARE YOU SURE we're at the right place?" No matter how she tried, Celia couldn't begin to look relaxed. The luxurious resort cabin Blair Giles took her to was remote and it didn't appear to have had a single soul in residence for some time. At least, not a permanent resident. The cottage seemed more like a carefully selected site for doing business. The kind of business is what bothered Celia.

While Giles made himself at home, turning on a minimum of lights and mixing drinks at the small bar, she looked around. The cathedral ceiling was tinted glass, allowing the many stars and muted moonlight to shine through. She could just see the edges of a few branches from tall trees brushing over the roof. The air was heavy with silence, broken only by the clink of ice being dropped into glasses.

"Relax, Celia. He'll be here. Later."

She gulped hard, trying to find a drop of spit in her very dry mouth. "Later?"

Giles grinned widely at her and his eyes were lit like green fire. For the first time, she noticed that he had a gold tooth toward the back of his mouth. She crossed her arms over her bare midriff as he approached.

"Here, drink this. It'll help to calm you."

There was no way she was putting a single sip of alcohol into her system. She needed to be totally clear-headed to deal with this new situation. After setting the glass aside—which made Giles frown—she said, "Blair, I thought we were meeting some other people here. I had no idea you were planning this…this…" She gestured with her hand, indicating the intimate and isolated atmosphere of the cottage.

"This romantic setting?" he supplied, one brow raised, his voice smooth and seductive. "I'm sorry, Celia, but I was desperate to get you alone. And I promise you, you'll meet all the producers you could possibly need. I can already see what a success you're going to be."

He stepped closer and Celia stepped back. She was very afraid. "You mean, you made this up?" While she spoke, she looked around, trying to find some avenue of escape. Not a single hope presented itself. The furniture all looked heavy and masculine. A few statuettes were placed in the corners, and there were heavy ceramic ashtrays on the tables, along with tall deco lamps and a few books.

They were on the ground floor, and a loft was overhead, but there didn't appear to be any exits from there, just the bedroom.

She glanced back to see Giles watching her closely, his expression expectant. He wanted her to try something, she realized. He wanted her afraid and running, so he could chase her down. Instead, she looked directly at him, waiting for an answer.

His smile wavered slightly. "No, of course not. But our guests will come later. Much later."

When the back of her knees hit the sofa, her eyes widened. "Later? But it's almost midnight already."

"Did you have other plans?" He slowly, carefully, took her hands in his, as if savoring the moment.

Celia remembered how this particular man reacted to a woman's fear. By backing away from him, she'd added to his enjoyment of the moment. No more; she wouldn't give him what he wanted, either physically or emotionally.

What would Alec do now? How would he react if he were here?

Trying to clear her mind, Celia forced a smile and abruptly sat down, curling close in the corner of the sofa. She stretched her arms out, at her leisure. The fingertips of her left hand touched the edge of the heavy ashtray, but she couldn't get a good grip on it without being obvious.

Trying to look coy and stall for time, she said, "You really went to all this trouble just for me?"

Eyes narrowed, Giles suddenly reached down and jerked her to her feet. As if impassioned, he pulled her close and said against her mouth, "I want you so damn bad, I'd do just about anything to see it happen." She twisted and his mouth landed on her cheek. "Believe me, I don't usually react this way with the models. But you're different, so lovely and innocent…"

"No!"

One of his hands held the back of her neck with painful force, keeping her from turning her face away from his mouth, while the other clutched at her bottom. He wasn't much taller than her and when he yanked her close, her body came into vivid contact with his from knees to breasts. Her stomach jolted sickly, her skin crawled.

Celia cried out. Reacting solely on instinct, her intentions flown with her panic, she fought him. Though he might look soft and ineffectual, he was a man with a man's strength. He laughed, and when his mouth touched hers again, she bit him.

Giles became giddy, delighted with her fight. "Marc told me I should wait, that I shouldn't rush you. But I knew he was wrong, I knew you'd be perfect."

His hand knotted in her hair and pulled her head back so he could stare down at her breasts. Her scalp burned, but worse than that, she felt his mouth, wet and hot, on her flesh and she simply couldn't stand it.

Allowing her knees to buckle, she dropped, giving him all her weight and losing a lot of hair in the process. He stumbled, trying to hold on to her, but they both fell to the carpet. Celia immediately scrambled back, Giles grabbing for her kicking legs, and when she reached for the table and felt the ashtray, she didn't hesitate. She swung it hard at his head. Giles chuckled, ducking, but the idiot wasn't fast enough. Her next swing hit him in the side of the head with a sickening thunk. He stared blankly at her for only a moment, then his eyes rolled back and he slumped to the carpet.

Celia scrambled to her feet. The crop top to her pantsuit was torn, one shoulder seam hanging so low her nipple was barely covered. Trembling from head to toe, she tried to pull it up, but it kept falling back. She heaved, trying to breathe, trying to get her mind to settle so she could think. All she wanted was to run away, but she wouldn't get far on foot and she didn't know if he'd wake soon and come after her.

She thought about hitting him again, but couldn't bring herself to bludgeon him while he was already unconscious. Swallowing back the tears that would do her no good, she flexed her shoulders, trying to think.

Keys. She'd take his keys and drive away. Not wanting to, but seeing no help for it, she dropped to her knees beside Giles and tried to decide which pocket he'd put the keys in. She was just reaching for him when the door opened and she gave a startled scream, her wild gaze flying up to see who had entered.

Jacobs stood there, his long-fingered hand wrapped tight around Hannah's arm. His gaze moved from Celia, her hair tossed, her makeup ruined, her clothes torn, to Giles out cold on the floor, his temple swollen and spotted with blood. He shook his head in disgust. "I told that damn idiot to wait, but he wouldn't listen."

The door slammed behind him and he roughly shoved Hannah into the room. The girl tripped and almost fell but Celia caught her, helping her to regain her balance. Very slowly, she faced Jacobs, stepping in front of Hannah.

"What are you doing here?"

With two fingers, Jacobs help up the piece of paper she'd given to Hannah. "Conspiring against me, weren't you?"

The bottom dropped out of her stomach. "Hannah had nothing to do with that. I just wanted—"

"Sit down and shut up." Jacobs pulled a gun from inside his suitcoat and waved it at the two women. Trying to stay calm, Celia took Hannah's hand and led her to the sofa. The poor girl was trembling all over, her face totally leeched of color.

"I'm sorry," she whispered to Celia, shaking her head. "I knew what was happening and I wanted to help you. I didn't mean for him to find out…"

"Shhh. I know. It's all right."

Jacobs nudged Giles with his foot, and was rewarded

with a moan. "Get up you ass, or I'll shoot you to save myself the bother of dealing with your idiocy."

Giles moaned again and very gingerly pulled himself into a sitting position. His hand touched his head, and then recognition came. "The little bitch hit me!"

"She did better than that. She knocked you out cold." Jacobs smirked. "Doesn't say much for your seductive powers, now does it?"

Giles roared to his feet, his face bright red with both pain and humiliation. As he lurched toward Celia, sure death in his eyes, she pressed herself back on the sofa. But Jacobs brought him up short with a fist knotted in his collar. "No, don't touch her yet. There's something you need to know."

Giles, heaving in his anger, turned to stare at Jacobs. "Well?"

"Your warehouse caught fire again."

"What!"

"I don't know all the details yet. But evidently whoever set that little fire at the studio returned." Jacobs grinned at Giles's horrified expression and then flicked a glance at Celia. "It's lucky for you, Blair, that I keep my own files because you've had a total loss."

Stammering in his grief, Giles asked, "My photos…?"

"Gone. Every one of them." Jacobs waved at Celia with the gun. "I think we should ask our newest guest here about that. It seems a real coincidence that all the trouble started when she got involved. Well, Celia? Do you want to talk to me or should I let Giles go ahead and have his fun with your body first?"

Celia lifted her chin; bravado was all she had left and she'd use it for Hannah's sake as well as her own. "Touch me and you'll regret it. I'm not afraid of you, of either of you. And if you don't let us go right now, I'll testify against you both and you'll spend the rest of your lives in jail."

Jacobs thought her threat was immeasurably funny, judging by his loud laugh. Giles did little more than glare at her. "Did you hear her, Blair? She's going to testify against us."

Giles slanted her an evil look. "Give me a few hours with her before you kill her."

Hannah began to cry softly, but Celia ignored her for the moment. They meant to intimidate her, to break her. But she'd been dealing with Alec for too long to shrivel up and fall apart over a few threatening words. She gave them both a look of contempt, the best she could muster, then said, "You're both too damn stupid to realize it's all over. Do you really think I'd have come here alone? A woman, by myself?"

Jacobs snarled a curse and retaliated against her contempt by backhanding her. Since Jacobs had gone from confident good humor to outright rage in an instant, Celia hadn't been at all prepared for the blow. Even when she saw it coming, she didn't have time to do more than gasp before she was knocked completely off the sofa. Crying out, she landed hard on the floor, bruising her knees and scraping her palms. Her head felt as if it had exploded and she prayed she wasn't wrong about Alec, that he'd somehow, despite the fact she'd lost her wired pen, known where she was going, that he wasn't far behind.

As if she'd summoned him with her desperation, Alec chose that exact moment to burst through the door. He literally kicked it in, causing wood to splinter and glass to crack, and Celia, thankful that he was on her side, wondered how one man could manage so much menace by his mere presence. He looked like an enraged bull, his dark eyes filled with murder. When his gaze quickly took in the entire scene and he saw Celia on her knees, holding her cheek, he gave a shout of rage reminiscent of a berserker that made all the windows rattle.

Hannah crouched down beside Celia, clutching at her and hiding her face in her shoulder. Giles completely froze, his face paper-white with terror and his hands up as if to ward off evil.

That left Jacobs, and he tried to bring the gun up and around in time, but Alec was already on him. His first kick sent the gun clattering across the room to crash against the stone fireplace. His second kick had Jacobs grabbing his ribs, shouting in pain.

Celia was still a little stunned, watching the whole thing in fascinated horror, her heart fluttering, her body frozen. She seemed to see it in slow motion, but in truth, Alec's movements were a blur. From the time he'd burst in to putting Jacobs on the floor had taken little more than a few seconds. She felt awed by seeing Alec in action, though she'd heard enough stories she shouldn't have been surprised.

Despite her fascination, she noticed when Giles suddenly moved, trying to run across the room after the gun, and she reacted quickly. Shoving Hannah aside, she told the girl, "Get back," then leaped after Giles. The man was just about to bend over for the gun when Celia threw herself on his back. Her weight knocked him off balance and the momentum of his reach kept him going headfirst into the stone fireplace. Once again, he slumped down unconscious and Celia gave only a brief thought as to whether or not she'd killed him this time.

Through the broken front door she heard the distant approach of sirens. She grabbed for the fireplace poker to help Alec, but when she turned, she saw that Jacobs wasn't fighting anymore. He merely dangled in Alec's grip, taking the punishment Alec seemed intent on doling out. Marc Jacobs's face was no longer handsome, but grotesquely swollen, and his fair hair was matted with blood.

Celia, filled with a new horror, threw the poker aside and leaped onto Alec's back this time. "Alec, no!"

Neither her weight nor her shout seemed to have any impact on him. He drew back to hit Jacobs again and Celia yelled right into his ear, "I love you, Alec!"

He froze with his fist in midair. Jacobs hung limply in his grip, making mewling sounds, and Alec released him to fall with a loud thump to the floor. Celia scrambled around to face Alec, desperate to reach him. "If you kill him, you'll end up in jail."

Alec didn't say anything, just stared at her. His face was still set, his eyes hard and distant, as if he had trouble bringing himself back under control. His chest moved slowly as he drew deep breaths.

Celia's heart began to beat so hard it hurt. She couldn't believe what she'd told him, but at least it had gotten him to stop. "Do...do you remember when I wanted to kill Raymond, and you told me it would only complicate my life?"

Still Alec stared at her. "I remember."

She dropped her gaze to his chest, touched his collarbone. "I don't want your life complicated because of me, Alec."

His fingers gently brushed her bruised, swollen cheek. His voice was low and full of concern when he asked, "Are you all right?"

"Other than a headache, I'm fine." Then she glanced at Giles. "I imagine his head hurts much worse." She couldn't help herself, she grinned nervously. "I knocked him out twice."

Alec didn't smile. Instead he walked toward the fireplace, continually looking back at Celia with a narrow-eyed gaze, as if afraid to let her out of his sight. He picked up the gun by the end of the barrel and set it out of reach. The sirens grew steadily louder.

Celia turned to find Hannah pressed up to a wall, her eyes wide on Alec. Celia grinned. She remembered having that exact same reaction the first time she'd met Alec Sharpe. No man had ever affected her, frightened her, touched her, the way he had. He could scare the breath out of grown men with a look, but he was the gentlest, most honorable man she knew. "Hannah, this is a good friend of mine, Alec Sharpe. He's been working with me to help get you away from Jacobs."

Alec nodded to the girl, who blinked cautiously.

"Come here, Hannah. He won't bite."

Alec gave her a heated look, reminding her that he did in fact indulge in a nibble every now and again. Celia felt a blush start and wanted to smack him. "Alec, quit intimidating her."

With a wry frown at Celia, Alec removed his cotton shirt and gently slipped it over Hannah's shoulders. "She's in shock. See if you can find her something sweet to drink and a cold rag. I'll take care of these two." Alec started to turn away, then suddenly stopped. "Oh, Hannah? Any evidence they had against you is gone."

Hannah stared from Alec to Celia and back again. She gave a very fainthearted, "Oh?"

Alec nodded. "The inside of the warehouse was gutted; the files all caught on fire."

Celia nearly burst with pride. She just knew Alec was responsible for that. "When did that happen, Alec?"

"While you were getting ready for your damn party."

She grinned again.

With a completely straight face, he added to Hannah, "And I just found out that someone broke into Marc Jacobs's house and emptied out his office. No fire there, just a burglary, it seems. There's enough evidence left to convict him, but nothing that will embarrass you in any way."

Unable to hold back a moment more, Celia released Hannah to throw her arms around Alec's neck. He gathered her close in a breath-depriving bear hug, lifting her completely off her feet and pressing his face hard into her neck.

"You're wonderful, Alec," she managed to squeak when his hold loosened.

To her surprise, he suddenly set her away from him and said, "Go wait in the kitchenette with Hannah. I'll take care of the cops and then we'll talk later." There was so much coldness in him, she flinched.

"Alec?"

His expression darkened and his jaw worked. He bent low, jutting out his chin and looking her in the eye. In guttural tones, he said, "You almost died." Glancing at Hannah, he said, "And her, too. Do you have any idea what would have happened if Hannah hadn't called me? If I hadn't gotten here when I did?"

Celia took a step back, and she too, glanced at

Hannah. The girl gave her a weak, apologetic shrug. "She called you?"

"Thank God you at least had the sense to give her my number before you ran off with a lunatic, *without* the wire."

Celia shifted. "The pen fell into the couch and I couldn't—"

"Save it for later." Alec cut her off, apparently not interested in her excuses. "I'll take care of everything from here on. Hopefully I can manage better than you did."

He turned away to greet several uniformed officers who came cautiously through the door, guns drawn. Celia wanted to grab him, to pull him back, to explain. She felt a chill creeping up on her and realized the night air had cooled considerably, but her chill was more from the inside out. Still, she rubbed her hands up and down her bare arms.

Then she turned to see Hannah standing there shivering, wrapped in Alec's flannel. Her eyes were dilated, her cheeks pale. As he'd said, she easily could have been killed and it would have been her fault. Celia had no idea what Jacobs had done to her after finding the slip of paper on her. They both might have died if it hadn't been for Alec.

Celia looked around as cops stepped through the room. One of them glanced at her torn outfit and, blushing, handed her his jacket. Celia accepted it gratefully, suddenly anxious to cover herself, to hide the evidence of what she'd just gone through.

The house was in a shambles with a shattered door and broken furniture. Two men were unconscious on the floor, blood seeping into the beautiful carpet. She didn't even know who owned the cottage.

For a minute there, she'd been on an adrenaline high, pleased with the fact she'd survived, that Jacobs's madness was at an end. But Alec's censure had cut through all that.

She closed her eyes. Oh God, she'd made a mess of things. Alec had told her, had warned her. And now he was angry. But there was no way he could be more disappointed than she was.

Alec was right. She wasn't cut out for this. And as he'd said, it was all at an end.

She'd been a fool.

ALEC WATCHED CELIA walk numbly through the motel room. It was nearly dawn and he knew she was beat, but as usual, she held herself together without complaining. He wished she'd talk to him, give her usual chatter. She hadn't voluntarily said two words to him since the police had finished their questioning. By the time they were through, Alec figured he'd met damn near every officer in the unit. Jacobs had been transferred to a hospital, though Alec knew the bastard was all right.

Thanks to Celia.

If she hadn't stopped him, he very well might have done serious damage. He didn't want to think he was capable of actually killing so easily, but when he'd seen Jacobs hit her through the door window, when he crashed in and saw Celia down on the floor, her face bruised, he'd lost all reason. Never in his life had he been in such a killing rage. Yet Celia had stopped him with three little words. *I love you.*

Alec cocked a brow. At the moment, she didn't look too fond of him. She looked dejected and hurt and it damn near brought him to his knees. He knew he *would* kill for her. Hell, he'd die for her if it ever came to that. She meant so much to him he was still shaking from the near miss of maybe losing her. His hurtful words, and he knew damn well they had been hurtful, had been more a gut reaction to his own fear than anything else.

Crossing his arms over his chest, he leaned against the wall and watched her open her suitcase onto the bed. She began stuffing clothes inside, moving by rote, with no real thought involved. Alec sighed. "Hannah seemed anxious to get home to her mother."

He got his first smile in hours, and it didn't even rate as a full-fledged sign of cheer, more like weary relief. "Once she knew Jacobs and Giles couldn't embarrass her family with any photos she was agreeable. Especially when I told her all the lengths her mother had gone to just to get her back."

"They really won't be ashamed, will they? Because her involvement will come out in the trial. People will know what happened, they just won't have pictures to go with the story."

Her smile this time was more genuine, if a little sad. "I knew you were responsible for that. All that nonsense about a break-in—"

"Was my way of covering my ass. I figured while you prettied up for your party, I should make good use of my time. I kept my cell phone close so you could reach me if you'd needed to."

"The chances you took going there…"

Alec shrugged. He was never the one at risk, but he

didn't say so just yet. "I didn't destroy the whole warehouse, just the stuff that might embarrass the girls. The same is true of Jacobs's files. I slipped in there easily enough and within minutes found everything I was looking for. It never ceases to amaze me the evidence some people keep around, arrogantly thinking they'll never be caught. There's plenty there to prove what a scum he is, just nothing that will make innocent people pay."

Celia sighed. "You're pretty wonderful, Alec, you know that?"

His heart tripped and his muscles tightened. "Is that why you're trying to run away from me again?"

Her hands full of clothes, Celia looked up in surprise. "I'm not."

He pointed out the obvious. "You're packing."

She looked confused, then finally shook her head. "It's time to go home. We're done here. You said so yourself."

Alec narrowed his eyes and said low, "We had a deal, lady."

She dropped the clothes and stared up at him. "You're kidding, right?"

Very slowly he shook his head, then advanced on her. If he didn't touch her soon he was going to lose it. When he was standing right in front of her, he said, "You promised to do what I want if I helped, and the day isn't over yet. I figure you still owe me till morning."

"Alec…"

"I want you in bed." He scooped up her suitcase and dropped it on the floor. Clothes fluttered out, and he gained Celia's immediate ire. She went on tiptoe to yell at him, making it damn near impossible for him to hold back a smile. He'd take her fire any day over the dejection she'd just been feeling.

With one finger, she pointed at the bed while never looking away from him. "That is the very *worst* place for me. Yes, I made a deal with you, but that was when…" Her voice trailed off. She dropped back flat on her feet and stepped away. She bit her bottom lip.

Alec picked her up and, despite her struggles, got her stretched out on her back on the mattress. "When what, honey?" He kissed her beautiful face, her tipped-up nose, her lush mouth. "Tell me."

Celia turned her face away. "When I thought I could stand it. When I thought I could love you and just walk away."

His heart breaking, Alec touched her chin and brought her gaze back around to his. Celia drew in a deep breath. "But I'm not as strong as you, Alec. And Jacobs's little slap didn't hurt nearly as much as your rejection and lack of respect."

"Celia." He'd held back too long, and kissing her seemed like the most important thing in the world to him, an affirmation that she was truly alive and well.

Celia didn't fight him. Her mouth opened to his, and the kiss was gentle but deep, hungry and giving. Alec cupped her face in his hands, careful not to hurt her bruised cheek, and fed off her, knowing he'd never have enough, that three lifetimes wouldn't be enough with this woman.

When he finally pulled back she gulped down a sob and practically yelled right in his face, "You're a fool, Alec Sharpe! And a damned coward." Her voice cracked and she said in a quavering tones, "Because if you weren't, you wouldn't give up on love."

Alec smiled. "I know."

"You're also—what do you mean, you know?"

It was past time he told her how he felt, how much she meant to him. "I respect you, Celia. More than any man or woman I know. You believe in something, like saving Hannah, then you do whatever it takes to get the job done. Not many people have that much conviction, or are that brave."

"Really?"

She looked so skeptical he wanted to bundle her up close and never let anything hurt her again. "I also trust you, and worry about you." He kissed her, a kiss so giving he had to fight his own tears. "And I love you. More than anything this earth has to offer."

She sucked in a startled breath. "You love me?"

Alec swallowed hard, then scowled, trying to cover his loss of control. "Hell, I must, otherwise I surely would have strangled you by now for always scaring me half to death. Look at what you do to me, honey."

He held out his hand and they both saw that he was still shaking like a wet pup. His voice dropped even lower and he groaned, "I thought I might lose you, and that's something I couldn't bear. You're right when you say I'm a coward. I used to be afraid of what you made me feel, of how you affected me. Now I'm just afraid of having to go on without you."

Big tears slid down her cheeks, but they were happy tears. "Oh, Alec, I was so scared!"

He understood the delayed reaction, of how the adrenaline rush would wear off and you were left depleted and hollow inside. He settled his body more firmly over hers, surrounding her with himself, his heat and his love. He whispered, "The fear is normal, babe.

But the important thing is that you kept your head. You didn't panic and you reacted when you needed to. Everyone gets in over his head every now and then, and you're not immune. But you handled yourself well, and I think you've more than proved you have what it takes to make a great P.I."

His very well-rehearsed speech was met with mute surprise.

Alec cleared his throat. "I'd only ask two things, though. One, that you not endanger yourself like that again. No more undercover stuff because my heart really can't take it. And two—"

Celia laid her palm on his mouth. She was smiling, a wide, happy smile now. "Alec, when I said I was afraid, I wasn't talking about today, though that was pretty scary, too. I meant I was so afraid that you'd never want me, that you'd never love me back."

He kissed her palm and then pulled her hand away. "Not a chance, babe. You're definitely stuck with me."

"Alec." All the love she felt was there for him to see, and now, it filled him up rather than shaking him.

He wanted to get back to business and see things settled. "Number two, would you marry me, Celia?"

She froze for a heartbeat, then squealed in excitement. Alec laughed, aware of how tense he'd been holding himself, not sure of her answer because he'd never been easy with her. But with the choke hold she had on his neck, he figured her answer was yes. He still wanted to hear her say it.

"Answer me, woman."

"Yes!"

"And about the undercover work?"

Celia pulled back just enough to laugh in his face.

"Alec Sharpe, being married to you will likely be all the excitement I need."

As she pulled his head back down, intent on seducing him if he didn't miss his guess, Alec muttered, "Somehow I don't think I'll be able to hold you to that…"

EPILOGUE

"You know everyone's going to think you're pregnant with the way Alec rushed things."

Celia looked down at where Angel, moderately pregnant herself, straightened a ruffle in Celia's elegant wedding gown. Alec had somehow, with her mother's help, gotten everything arranged in just under two months.

"My mother is hopeful." Celia grinned, knowing that didn't quite answer Angel's implied question. But she had no intention of telling anyone until after she'd told the father.

Angel scowled and slowly straightened. Dane, Angel's overly doting husband, came into the room just then and hurried to assist his wife.

"You shouldn't be bending like that," he said, and gently hauled her to her feet. Once there, he pulled her close and kissed her—then didn't want to stop kissing her. Celia just smiled, since Alec now behaved in a similar fashion, always touching her, kissing her, making sinfully naughty, exciting promises in her ear that he knew would make her blush and make everyone else curious.

She blushed now, just thinking of the night to come. *Her wedding night.*

Angel pulled away, then shook her head at both Dane and Celia. "You two are incorrigible. Just look at you both. Dane, behave. And Celia, what in the world are you blushing about? It's not like you shouldn't be used to your brother by now."

Dane chuckled. "She's used to me. It's Alec that has her getting all flustered. You should see him pacing around outside. If I didn't know better, I'd swear he was actually nervous. And he asked me how long he had to hang out at the reception before he and Celia could get away. Good grief, you'd think he could at least wait a few hours." Dane cast a teasing glance at his sister. "I think you've managed to pickle his brain."

Angel sniffed. "If you'll recall, I said all along they were meant for each other."

"Yes, you did. But it still boggles the mind." He cast another swift glance at Celia. "I thought she drove him crazy. And he's such a damn loner—"

Celia sighed. "*Used* to be a loner—not anymore. And for your information, I do drive him crazy. It's one of my more redeeming qualities. He says it keeps him on his toes."

Dane and Angel both grinned. "Is *that* what it does to him?"

Organ music started in the background. Celia had been in the room for over an hour, getting the last-minute primping taken care of, with Angel's help. She should have known her brother wouldn't be able to stay away from his wife that long.

She started to shoo them out the door so they could take their places, when suddenly Alec was there, looming in the doorway, looking incredibly sexy in his black tux. His golden earring glinted, but his hair had been trimmed, still a little long, but there was no need to tie it back. Celia sort of missed that ponytail, but even without it, he was gorgeous enough to bring the heat right back to her face.

He looked vastly annoyed and gave her his patented killer glare, which still made grown men cower but had no real effect on Celia. "It's been hours. What's taking so long?"

Angel squealed and tried to shield Celia behind her body. "You're not supposed to see the bride before the ceremony!"

"The damn ceremony is beginning and everyone is in here."

Dane laughed out loud, shaking his head and taking his wife's hand. "Leave him be, honey. He's got it bad." He tugged Angel away, then out the door. To Alec he muttered, "You really ought to get a grip."

Alec stepped forward and lifted Celia into his arms. "Now that I have a grip on you, maybe we can get this show on the road." Without hesitation, he started out the door.

Celia tucked her face into his throat. "It's pretty unorthodox for the bride to be carried to the altar by the groom. What will people think?"

"That I love you and don't want to wait anymore."

He made that statement in his usual certain, determined way, then followed Dane and Angel into the crowded hall.

Celia kissed his throat. "I suppose it's a little unorthodox also, for the bride to find out on the day of her wedding that she's going to be a mama, but then, we've never done things by the book."

Alec froze. Celia could feel him tremble before she

got such a tight squeeze she had to squeak in protest. As Alec entered the main room, carrying Celia with no effort at all while kissing the breath right out of her, applause broke out. The organ music continued, and the baffled bridesmaids fell into step behind the groom.

Dane, laughing again, said, "What the hell," and went over to grab his wife, pulling her out of line and keeping her at his side. The rest of the procession, confused, merely found a spot to stand around Celia and Alec.

Celia's mother was thoroughly scandalized, but she couldn't quite keep the grin off her face. Little Grayson, Dane and Angel's son, cheered loudly next to his grand-mother.

When the preacher cleared his throat—twice—Alec finally managed to release Celia from the kiss. But against her mouth he whispered, "You just can't help but constantly take me off guard, can you?"

And Celia, laughing and crying and ruining her care-fully applied makeup, kissed him again and said, "It's what I do best, Alec."

He stared at her mouth, ignored the snickering in the audience, the coughing of the preacher, and Dane's outright laughter. He answered, "Oh, I wouldn't exactly say that…."

UNCOVERED

CHAPTER ONE

BECAUSE IT WAS DRIZZLING out, Harris Black pulled on a windbreaker before he headed outside to jog. Street-lamps left long slithery ribbons of light across the wet blacktop drive. After the heat of the mid-August day, the light rain had a sauna effect, making the air downright steamy.

He preferred jogging at night for two reasons: less human and automotive traffic, and Clair Caldwell.

Clair lived in the apartment building across the lot and always joined Harris in his evening run. For a dozen different reasons, Harris liked her a lot.

Unlike most women, Clair enjoyed the same things he enjoyed—televised sports, running, and junk food. Not once had she ever forced him to sit through a romantic comedy, thank God. But once, on a lazy Saturday afternoon, they'd watched the entire *Alien* series, back to back, without budging from the couch.

Clair's job fascinated him. When two well-respected private investigators relocated their offices close to Chester, Ohio, the town they lived in, Clair had jumped at the chance to work for them as a receptionist. She was an adventurous sort and enjoyed the excitement of the job. But her duties went beyond secretarial. She was a computer guru, helping with online investigations, and an all around know-it-all. She always had entertaining stories to share.

By the same token, she liked to hear about his work and his friends. Being a firefighter left him open to a lot of bawdy jokes, and Clair seemed to know them all. She teased him about the fires he put out, the length of his hose, and his specialized gear. But when he was serious, she was too, automatically picking up on his moods in a way no one else ever had. Even with his best friends, Buck, Ethan and Riley, he had to put on the occasional front. No one wanted a morose or moody friend, even if he'd just spent hours fighting a fire that sometimes didn't have the best conclusion. They always wanted to joke him into a better mood.

Not Clair. Once, after a really grueling car fire that resulted in two deaths, Clair had just sat beside him on the couch and held his hand. They'd stared at the television, but Harris knew neither of them was really paying any attention to the movie.

What mattered most about Clair, though, was the no-pressure tone of their relationship. He saw her when he wanted to, yet he never felt he had to call. Oddly enough, because of that, he called and hooked up with her often.

They hung out without any implied intimacy to muddy the waters. She didn't care if he shaved or if he ate Twinkies for lunch or if he stayed out all night with the guys. At first, her disinterest had bugged him, but after Ethan and Riley had up and married, Harris became leery of smiling women—and with good reason. The females had detected a nonexistent pattern of matrimony, and they pushed him constantly, to the point that he'd about given up dating.

Which meant he was celibate and that sucked, but it beat dodging topics of "happily ever after." Nothing messed up good sex like a woman grasping too far into the future.

With Clair, sex was never an issue. It just didn't come up. They were friends, totally at ease with each other, but neither of them ever crossed the line. It was such a relaxing relationship that he spent more time with Clair than with his buddies. Of course, Ethan and Riley now preferred the company of their wives, anyway.

As Harris stepped out from beneath the building's overhang, a fat raindrop landed on his nose. Given the heavy static in the air, he knew it'd be storming before they finished their run. He sprinted across the lot at the same time that Clair's doors opened and she strolled outside. Harris stared toward her with a smile.

Her personality put her somewhere between an egghead and a jock; she loved sports of all kinds, and was almost too smart for her own good. But no matter what the situation, and despite a lack of feminine flair, Clair always looked stylish. Granted, it was her own unique style, but her appearance was always deliberate, not one created out of lack of taste or time.

A few weeks ago she'd cut her glossy, dark brown hair shorter, and now she wore it in a stubby ponytail that looked real cute. She'd attached an elasticized band to her black-framed, oval glasses to hold them on her head while she ran. Somehow, on Clair, the look of an athletic librarian worked.

With her hair pulled back that way, Harris noticed for the first time that she didn't have pierced ears. In fact, he realized he'd never seen Clair with jewelry of any kind. Odd. In this day and age, he thought every grown woman had her ears, if not other body parts, adorned. But then he'd always known Clair was different from other women.

At five feet five inches tall, she would be considered medium height except that she was all legs. Very long, sexy legs that even in clunky running shoes looked great. Tonight she had those gams displayed in comfortably loose, short shorts. Like Harris, she'd made a concession to the rain and wore a nylon pullover.

Harris looked up at the black sky. There was no moon, no stars to be seen through the thick clouds. Branches on the trees bent beneath an angry wind. Debris scuttled across the road. "Looks like we'll get one hell of a storm tonight."

"Backing out on me, sugar? Afraid you'll melt in the rain?" She swatted him on the ass. Hard. Then took off.

Grinning, Harris followed. "Paybacks are hell, sweetheart."

To tease him, she put a little extra sway in her backside for a few steps, then she got serious again. They ran side by side, silent except for the slapping of their sneakers on the damp ground and the soughing of their steady breaths. Within fifteen minutes, the drizzle changed into a light rain. Clair said nothing, so Harris didn't either. He could take it if she could.

After about a mile, Harris glanced toward her. She wore a concentrated expression, and her short ponytail, now darker with rain, bounced in time to her long stride. "Anything interesting happen at work today?" he asked.

She scrunched up her brow. "Dane caught a guy screwing around on his wife." Disgust dripped from her tone. "Dane was pissed when he came in to file it. Said the wife was real sweet and better off without the guy, but that she was bawling her eyes out."

"Shame." Harris didn't want to marry, but if he ever did, he knew he'd be a faithful hound. He thought spouses who cheated were lower than slugs. If you wanted to screw around still—as he did—then you shouldn't say the vows.

Clair pushed a little harder, her feet eating up the ground with a rhythmic slap, slap, slap. "I wouldn't cry." Her hands balled into fists and she picked up her pace even more until they were running instead of jogging.

"What would you do?"

The seconds ticked by and she slowed, gradually going loose and limber once again. With an evil, antici-patory grin, she said, "I'd take a ball bat to him. *Then* I'd leave him."

"Effective." Harris laughed. "But I think that's illegal."

"Yeah. Well, I'd find some way to make him pay—"

A slash of white lightning illuminated the entire area, followed by a crack of thunder that seemed to rip the night. They both pulled to a startled halt.

"Wow." Clair propped her hands on her knees, breathing hard, wide-eyed in awe of Mother Nature's display.

"This is nuts. Come on." Harris grabbed her arm and hauled her toward the main street. "Time to head back." Normally they'd take the long route to extend their jogging time, but now Harris just wanted to have Clair safely out of the storm.

She didn't protest, but then that was another of Clair's assets—sound common sense. He'd found it rare for people to have both book smarts and everyday logic. But Clair had both, which was another reason he liked her so much.

They were within minutes of their apartments when the rain turned into a deluge, soaking them through to the skin in a matter of seconds, making visibility nil. The sewers couldn't handle the flow and the streets filled like creek beds, washing icy water up past their ankles. With the help of the wind, the rain stung like tiny needles, making Harris curse. Trying to protect Clair with his body, he steered them toward a closed clothing shop and into a dark, recessed doorway. The opening was narrow, forcing them close together. Clair didn't seem to notice the intimate proximity.

Her hair was plastered to her skull, her entire body dripping. She shivered, but she didn't complain. "You think it'll let up soon?"

Another fat finger of lightning snaked across the ominous sky. The accompanying thunder shook the ground beneath them. "No. But we'll wait here a few minutes to see."

With a sigh, Clair pulled off her glasses, now beaded with rain. Lifting her pullover, she located a dry patch on her T-shirt beneath, and wiped them off. In the process, Harris got a peek at her belly. Not much of a peek, considering it was dark as Hades and she stood so close her elbows kept prodding him. He narrowed his eyes, straining to see her better.

She noticed him peeking—and flashed him, yanking both her pullover and tee above her breasts for a single split second. Startled, Harris shot his gaze up to her face.

She grinned. "There, did that take care of your curiosity?"

He almost strangled on his tongue. "No." It took his brain a moment to assimilate what he'd seen, and then he asked, "Is that a sports bra?"

Laughing, Clair elbowed him, harder this time so that he grunted in discomfort. He crowded closer still, stealing some of her warmth and hindering her more violent tendencies.

"Yeah, as concealing as a bathing suit top, so put your eyeballs away. You didn't think I'd actually show you anything important, did you?" She tsked. "The rain must have made your brain soggy."

"I saw a flash of white," Harris argued, "and didn't know if it was boobs or cloth. Can't blame a guy for wanting clarification."

"I don't have enough boob to go around showing them off."

In the crowded confines, with icy rain blowing in against his back, there was no way to get comfortable. Harris flattened one hand on the wall behind her and leaned in a bit, inching farther away from the storm— and closer to Clair. With his gaze zeroed in on her chest, he murmured, "You have enough," and he meant it.

"Spoken like a loyal friend. Thanks." And before Harris could say more on that topic, she went on tiptoe to look over his shoulder. "Hey, the rain's letting up a little. Looks like the worst of the storm is moving away from us. Let's get home before we freeze."

The rain *was* cold, and with it, the temperature had dropped by at least ten degrees. Not that Harris was especially chilled. Discussing a woman's upper works with her, even a woman he wasn't intimate with, had a decisive effect on his libido. Given that the woman was also pressed up against him—well, he was having some surprisingly lascivious thoughts. But then, he'd been on a month-long, self-imposed dry spell. Under those circumstances, just about anything could turn him on.

Maybe on his next day off he'd have to break down and take his chances with a little one-on-one comfort of the female kind.

Together, he and Clair continued on their way, not jogging now, but not exactly taking their time either. Since Clair stayed silent, Harris had too much time to think. About her boobs.

He gave her body a surreptitious look without turning his head. The cold had tightened her nipples, and with her clothes wet and clinging, there was no way to miss it. His pulse sped up a bit, doing more to warm him than their jaunt.

The snug sports bra didn't allow for much jiggling, but he judged her to be a B cup. Plenty enough there to fill his hands. Well, not *his* hands, but some other guy's... No, he didn't like that thought either. Not that he had any claim on Clair other than friendship. But the idea of her snuggled up and intimate with some faceless, nameless bozo didn't sit right. Harris shoved the disturbing image away and concentrated on her comment.

Why did women assume men were only drawn to pinup models? A woman was a woman was a woman. Each different, each sweet and soft in her own way.

"Hurry up, slowpoke. I swear, my granny could move faster than you."

Maybe not so sweet, Harris admitted to himself with a grin. But definitely soft. He fell behind another step and took in the sight of Clair's full bottom. No lack of curves there. Yep, even egghead jocks were soft when you looked in the right place.

Clair turned to face him, walking backward. "Want a cup of hot chocolate? I'm going to make me some."

Her glasses were beginning to fog over, her ponytail was more out of its band than in, and water dripped from her ears.

Harris shook his head. "Can't. I'm on first shift this week. I need to get home, shower, and hit the sack." As a firefighter, Harris had a rotating schedule. The good part was that every third week he got extra days off, and the third week was rolling around.

"Okay." They were only feet away from his apartment building. Clair turned back around to head across the street. "I'll see you tomorrow then."

Harris took swift advantage. The moment she presented him with the opportunity, he landed a stinging swat on her behind. Given that her shorts were wet, it had a little more impact than he'd intended.

Her hands slapped over her butt in shock. Before her gasp of outrage had a chance to fade away, Harris darted to his side of the street, barely muffling his chuckles. "Good night, Clair!"

He bounded up the steps to his apartment, but waited at the door, watching as he always did until Clair had time to get inside. She rubbed her bottom as she climbed her own steps, muttering and casting him dirty looks. Moments later, a light came on in her living room, then Clair was at the window, waving to him. Harris waved back.

At first, Clair had objected to his protectiveness. But he'd worn her down until now she did the routine by rote. While he waited, she went in and checked out her place, then waved to let him know she was safely inside. Alone.

One of these days she'd have a boyfriend to look after her. But until then, Harris didn't mind keeping watch. In fact, he insisted on it.

Within half an hour he was showered and stretched out in bed, his hands folded behind his head. He should have been relaxed, but instead his naked body hummed with tension. He listened to the drubbing of rain on the windows, the continual rumble of thunder, and he watched the strobe effect of the lightning on his ceiling.

Storms always made him horny.

Touching women's butts made him horny.

Was Clair making him... No. He scoffed at himself, even laughed out loud in the silence of his dark room. That was just nuts. He wouldn't think about her that way.

Determined to get to sleep, he closed his eyes, metered his breathing—and saw again that flash peek of Clair's belly and sports bra. He groaned, and gave up the fight, allowing himself to ease into a very vivid dream where he stripped Clair naked, kissed her from head to toe, and loved every minute of it. The dream was both disturbing in its intensity and comforting in the rightness of it.

Sometime during the night, the storm knocked out the electricity. His internal clock woke him to a dark house and street, and the continuation of the storm. Without being able to make coffee or catch the morning news, he headed into work early. And good thing, too, because not five minutes after he dashed through the pouring rain into the station, the fire alarm went off.

Lightning had struck the back of an abandoned building and someone saw smoke.

When Harris caught the address of the building, his heart shot into his throat. It was his block—*right next door to Clair.* Not since his first year as a firefighter had he suffered the debilitating effects of fear, but damn it, he felt them now. Even with the drizzling rain, the high wind could spread a fire quickly. Without electricity, Clair might sleep late, unaware of the danger. Worry plagued Harris all the way to the location.

But the moment the fire engine blared onto the street, Harris saw the crowd. Umbrellas formed a large canopy around the area, as if everyone had crawled from their beds and braved the weather for a show. Clair still looked sleep-rumpled under her cheery red umbrella, but she was fully dressed and in charge of things. In typical Clair mode, she urged curious onlookers farther away from possible harm. Harris was so relieved to see her he nearly fell off the truck. But knowing she was safe, he put her from his mind to do the job he'd been trained to do.

The storm was a real bother. Even through his Bunker Gear of fire-retardant jacket and trousers, helmet, and pull-on boots, he got soaked. The fire hadn't done too much damage yet, mostly to the exterior rear wall where the lightning had hit.

The abandoned structure had been up for lease for over six weeks and wasn't in the best of shape anyway. There were already broken windows in back and debris everywhere. In the process of putting out the blaze, a forgotten metal Dumpster in the back alley got knocked over. It was packed full, but luckily, not with the type of trash that got more disgusting with time. Mostly papers, probably from the previous businessman. In less than an hour, they had everything taken care of. The rain had let up and the sun even struggled to shine through the gray clouds.

Harris pulled off his helmet, wiping soot and rain and sweat off his face. He was contemplating all the mess, both from the spilled trash and the damage of the fire, when Ethan, a fellow firefighter and one of his best friends, let out a whistle. Harris turned, saw Ethan riffling through a shoebox from the Dumpster, and raised a brow. Usually that absorbed expression on Ethan's face was reserved for his wife, Rosie. Harris went to investigate.

"Whatcha got?"

Without looking up, Ethan said, "Pictures of a naked woman."

"No shit?" Harris forgot his fatigue for the moment and muscled his way next to Ethan. Yep, sure enough, that was an unclothed female. A very sexy, naked female. "Wow."

Harris picked up one photo of her reclining facedown on a twin bed. Her mussed hair was long enough to hide her face, but who cared when she had a beautifully bare backside on display? Harris tried, but he couldn't look away.

"Check out this one." Ethan handed him another.

The same woman, judging by the shape of her body, was stepping into the tub. Again, she had her face averted as she moved the shower curtain aside, but this shot showed her entire body in profile. Breasts, belly, long sleek thighs. Harris let out a slow breath. "*Hello* sweetheart."

"Wonder if she lives around here," Ethan commented. "Or maybe she was the last one to lease the building."

"The last person here was a guy. I never met him, but I saw him occasionally." Harris peered toward the shoebox Ethan held. "Any more pictures in there?"

"One more—of her pulling on her panties." Ethan laughed. "You still can't see her face, but it's a damn fine rear shot."

Feeling strangely territorial, though he didn't know why, Harris snatched the photo away from Ethan. "Let me have that."

"Hey, I was going to keep it."

"No way. You'd just show it to Buck and Riley."

Ethan raised both brows. "So? How come you get to look and we don't?"

"You must've forgotten, but you and Riley are married now."

"I'm still swimming in marital bliss, so how could I forget?" He grinned as he said that.

"Then think what Rosie will do," Harris murmured while studying the photo with rising heat, "if she catches you ogling some strange naked woman."

Looking much struck, Ethan said, "She'd probably kill me. Here." He shoved the entire shoebox into Harris's arms. "There are notes and such, too. Maybe an address, since you're so interested. And so single."

Wincing, Harris said, "Don't tell me you've taken up the campaign to get me hitched, too?"

"No, I like women too much for that."

"Ha ha."

"But Rosie wants you and Buck both married so I can't be around any of your single female friends." With a lot of satisfaction, Ethan added, "She's a jealous little thing."

"She trusts you."

"Yeah, but she doesn't trust the women you two date." Ethan strode away, giving orders as he went.

Harris didn't bother to reply to that jab. Buck might still be going strong, but Harris hadn't dated *anyone* lately. Rosie could rest easy on that score.

Now the woman in the picture... If he could look her up he just might be interested. Strolling over to lounge against the back wall of the alley, Harris held his helmet under his arm and rummaged through the shoebox. Unfortunately, he didn't find any addresses, but he pulled out one folded sheet of paper. Confusion reigned around him, but he gave all his attention to the feminine script on the note.

I'm sorry for just leaving a note. I know you wanted me to call, but there's no point. You'd just try to convince me to go with you, but it's over. It's not you, so please don't think of this as an insult. You knew how I felt all along.

I'm hung up on Harris.

Harris's eyes widened. Talk about coincidences. How many guys could there be with that name? It wasn't like a Tom, Dick or Harry.

It'd be tough for any other guy to measure up to him. If being a firefighter isn't heroic enough...

Harris nearly dropped the shoebox. Coincidence, hell! She was talking about *him.* Suddenly feeling on display, he glanced around the surrounding area, but no one paid him any attention. The crowd had dispersed.

Those who'd stopped to watch the firefighters work were now scuffling back into their homes. The other firefighters were chatting, bitching about the weather, generally just hanging around.

Harris swallowed hard and went back to reading.

... he's also funny. He makes me laugh all the time. And he's so generous. You don't notice it at first, because Harris likes to clown around, but he's really very sensitive to other people.

No shit? Harris blinked in disbelief. She thought he was sensitive?

He works hard and he's proud and I love him.
Again, I'm sorry.

She loved him. Wow. Harris looked, but there was no signature, damn it. He turned the note over, but no, it was blank. Who had written it? The idea of a secret admirer tantalized him, made him feel warm and full and anxious. He lifted another photo, the one of her stepping into her panties, and smiled. Sweet. Very sweet.

"Slug. Shouldn't you be helping out instead of snooping through the garbage?"

Startled by the verbal intrusion, Harris glanced up and got snared in Clair's disapproving green gaze. Her hair was loose, parted on the side and hanging in blunt lines to just skim the tops of her shoulders. She had her head tipped forward a bit to look at him over the rim of her glasses. Her eyes were twinkling at the pleasure of insulting him. Obviously, *she* didn't consider him sensitive.

"It's not garbage," he grumbled.

"No?" She went on tiptoe to peer over his shoulder.

Harris held the photo out of reach. "You don't want to see this, Clair."

"I do too."

"I doubt that." He grinned, imagining her reaction if he showed her. "They're photos."

"That's private. You shouldn't be looking either."

"Someone threw them away." He shrugged. "Free for the pickings."

Hands on her hips, she demanded, "Let me see, Harris."

Prodded by the devil in him, Harris decided *why not?* With a flourish, he handed her the photo.

Her face went beet-red and she gasped so hard she nearly strangled. "Harris!"

"Hey, I'm not the photographer." He winked. "I just found it."

"That's...that's obscene."

"You really think so?" He took it back from her and stared some more before murmuring with great sincerity, "Nice ass."

"Pig."

Laughing, Harris searched through the box. "Here's another." He handed her the one of the woman getting into the shower. In that pose, she had one shapely leg bent, one arm raised. Gorgeous.

Clair narrowed her eyes and accepted the photo. After several moments scrutinizing it, a small frown pulled down her brows. But at least this time she didn't choke.

"And one more." Harris gave her his favorite, the one of the woman reclined in bed. He thought she might be sleeping, she looked so boneless and relaxed. Her back was smooth and graceful, rising up to a plump rump, then tapering down again to long thighs and shapely calves.

Clair stared so long that Harris cleared his throat. "Anytime you're done with it..."

"Oh, sorry." She looked bothered about something, then glared. "I can dispose of those for you if you want."

"Not on your life." Harris held the photos protectively out of her reach. "I'm keeping them."

Clair's mouth fell open. "Keeping them? But that's... lecherous! You don't even know that woman." And then in a smaller voice: "Do you?"

"Nope. But I know she has a major case for me." He tapped the letter. "Says so right here."

Clair went white. She tried to grab the note. "You just said you don't know her."

"I don't. Yet. But she obviously knows me." Harris opened the paper and pointed out his name. "Harris the firefighter. Gotta be me, right?" He folded it and put it back in the shoebox for safekeeping. "So actually, this pertains to me. I have a right to this stuff."

"You're sick."

"I'm in lust." Harris touched her nose. "But then, you wouldn't know about that, would you, Clair?"

Her back snapped straight. "What the hell is that supposed to mean?"

"I'm just saying that you don't date much. Now if you'll excuse me, I gotta get to work."

Smiling sweetly, Clair said, "Want me to hold that shoebox for you?"

"No." Harris laughed at her fallen expression. "I'm

going to run it over to my place and lock it inside, safe and sound."

The way her jaw worked, Harris thought she might be grinding her teeth. "So you can stare at the photos and fantasize tonight?"

"Don't sneer, Clair. It makes you look like a prude." As he walked away, Harris heard Clair call him a choice name. He glanced around in time to witness her stomping toward her apartment. Too bad Clair didn't understand about lust. If she ever turned all that emotion loose in the sack, she just might be magnificent.

Harris caught his train of thought and growled. He'd better find his mystery lady soon, because lack of nookie was making him crazed.

He needed a woman—his mystery woman. Sexy. Provocative. And she thought he was sensitive. What more could a guy ask for?

CHAPTER TWO

THANKS TO THE DUAL effects of worry and mortification, Clair suffered through an endlessly long, sleepless night and was dragging as she headed into work the next day.

Thank God Harris hadn't recognized her.

Just thinking about his expression as he'd stared at her—Clair shuddered in agonizing horror. This was too unbelievable. If she ever found Kyle, the jerk she'd dated, the jerk who'd taken those pictures without her knowing, she'd strangle him.

During the darkest hours of the night, memories had flooded back on Clair, memories of Kyle begging her to let him photograph her, and the distinct recollection of her saying a firm, unequivocal *no*.

But she also recalled him showing off a teeny tiny camera, one he used to take photos without anyone knowing. At the time, he'd claimed it was to get candid, rather than posed shots of people for his gallery. And he had taken some, but to her knowledge, he'd never shown one without a signed permission slip and financial compensation.

At least he hadn't put hers in the gallery. But to throw them away behind the building...had the idiot never heard of a paper shredder? And to include her notes with them! Clair pulled into the lot where she worked and took a moment to cover her face with her hands. The only saving grace was that she hadn't signed any of the notes. If Harris had seen her signature at the end... Well, she honestly didn't know what he'd do.

It had taken Clair a moment to realize she was the subject of the photos. Her hair had been longer then, and her face hidden. But she had recognized herself. Harris, however, had been utterly oblivious to that fact. He plain and simply didn't see her as a sexual woman, which emphasized how little attention he paid to her femaleness.

That had been really frustrating over the past few months, but now she was more than a little grateful. She only hoped he never showed the photos to anyone. Even if no one ever guessed her identity, she couldn't bear the thought of people seeing her in the raw.

Because moping wasn't something she enjoyed, she shoved her car door open and stepped out into the blistering day. If the humidity had been bad before the storm, it was ten times worse now. Immediately her shirt stuck to her back, and even through her dressy, flat-heeled sandals, she could feel the scorching heat of the blacktop. As a concession to the weather, she wore a sleeveless cotton shirt and loose, flowing skirt. She slung a canvas bag over her arm and started in.

She'd use the day at work as a distraction to get her mind off nude photos, thickheaded men, and her jackass ex-boyfriend. At the moment, there wasn't anything she could do about any of them, so it was best not to dwell on it.

Cool air-conditioning rolled over her the moment she entered the building. Though she was early, Dane and Alec, the P.I.s she worked for, already had a client in the inner office with them. They'd relocated from the city so they'd have more free time for their wives and kids. But it seemed their small town was rife with drama, and they often stayed busy. At least here, though, the cases were seldom all that threatening.

Clair could hear their quiet conversation, see the movement of male bodies through opaque glass. She put her purse away and turned her computer on, then went straight to the coffeepot.

She already had things underway when Dane stuck his head out the door. "Clair, would you mind bringing in some coffee?"

"Not at all. It'll be done in two more minutes."

"Thanks." He ducked back inside.

Making coffee wasn't in her job description, but small requests never offended Clair. It helped that Dane and Alec were consummate gentlemen and didn't take her, or her talents, for granted. As often as not, they carried coffee to her.

A few minutes later, with sugar, powdered creamer and three mugs of steaming coffee on a tray, Clair used her foot to tap at the door. Alec opened it. He looked darker and more intense than usual, but then Alec could be a poster model for tall, dark and dangerous.

He gave her a nod. "Nothing like caffeine to kick off the day."

Clair smiled. "Tough case?"

"Different, that's for sure." He took the tray from her and she started to exit the office.

"Hey, Clair."

At the sound of Harris's voice, Clair froze in midstep. *Oh no. Please, no.* Slowly, wincing with dread, she pivoted stiffly to face him.

He was at Dane's workstation—the cursed photos spread out on the surface.

Oh. Dear. God.

Heat rolled from her chest right up to her hairline, making her dizzy with the shock of it. For a single moment, Clair thought she might faint, especially when Dane picked up the shower shot for a closer look.

Alec rejoined the men, staring at *her* naked body with a frown. "Do you see any distinguishing marks? Moles or scars or anything?"

Clair's knees trembled, threatening to buckle.

"No. No jewelry either."

Did she have time to run out and get her ears pierced?

Dane shook his head. "Just lots of smooth skin. Maybe we should have these photos blown up."

Clair staggered back against the door. Blow them up? *Blow them up!* As in, make them...bigger? Her throat closed and she couldn't draw breath, couldn't say a single word. She tried to get out a denial, to dissuade them from that horrendous plan, but all that emerged was an appalled squeak.

Harris glanced her way, did a double take, then rushed toward her. "Damn, Clair, you okay?" He caught her arms and physically forced her into a chair. Good thing too, because she was about ready to sink to the floor. Maybe *through* the floor if she got lucky.

Over his shoulder, Harris said to Alec, "I think she's been in the heat too long this morning. You got a cold cloth or something?"

Alec was a man of action. Within seconds, he had a pad of paper towels, dripping with icy water from the rest room.

All three big men loomed around her, Harris trying to slap the wet towels against her face, Dane fanning her with a stack of papers, and Alec taking her pulse.

They'd seen her naked.

It wasn't to be borne. Never in her life had she known such bone-deep humiliation, and it numbed her.

Harris reached for the top button of her blouse. "I'm going to loosen her clothes. She still looks too pale."

That brought Clair around. She shot to her feet, staggered, got steadied by six big hands, and shoved away from them all. She waved a fist with credible intent. "Touch my clothes and I'll brain you."

Harris straightened. He still looked concerned. "You're all right now?"

She wanted to die. "I, uh...you were right. It was just the heat. I'm fine."

Dane cocked a brow. "You're not pregnant, are you?"

Clair stared at him, aghast that he'd come to such a conclusion.

Alec nodded. "Celia stayed light-headed when she was pregnant. Especially when she got too warm."

Laughing, Harris said, "Clair's not even dating, so unless you can get pregnant from a toilet seat, I don't think that's the problem." He again tried to reach for her top button.

Clair swatted at him. "I'm not preg—"

"She dates," Dane argued. "Okay, not much, but I know a few months back she was seeing some guy."

Harris scowled. "She was?" He turned to Clair. "When were you dating? Who was he?"

Ohmigod. No way in hell was Clair going to talk about Kyle. Not with his photographic efforts spread out in all their lack of glory on Dane's desk. She swallowed, found her voice, and rasped, "Enough. From all of you."

They stared at her. Three pairs of discriminating, curious eyes. Eyes that had just been looking at her in the most revealing poses.

"My personal business is none of your concern." And before Harris could object, Clair added, "We *jog* together, Harris. In no way does that entitle you to pry." *Even if you have seen me in the nude.*

Harris's eyes narrowed and he crossed his arms over his chest. "Keeping secrets?" His hot stare threatened to bring on a swoon. "I'll find out, you know."

Over her dead body! She tucked in her chin and summoned her most serious, meanest voice. "You'll leave me alone."

Dane cleared his throat. "So you two are good friends? I thought you were just neighbors."

Harris kept his gaze trained on Clair. "I told Dane and Alec that I learned about them through you."

Alec gave her a fierce, speculative glance. "You make me sound fearsome, Clair. I'm not sure if I should thank you or not."

She rolled her eyes. Alec Sharpe lived up to his reputation and he knew it. Marriage and kids hadn't softened him. He was still dark as the devil and so strong and imposing that even in his mid-forties, he intimidated men with a mere glance. Dane wasn't much better. Both men were walking icons of masculinity. Not that Harris seemed intimidated. No, if anything, he'd bonded. But then, in her opinion, Harris fit right in.

Dane put an arm around her. "Harris is right, Clair. You still look a little shaky. You want to take the day off?"

So they could get back to perusing her photos? Not a chance. "Of course not." Inspiration struck and she said, "You want me to take something to the developers for you? You mentioned enlarging some photos."

"I can do it on the scanner," Alec said, ruining her chances to steal the photos. "You just rest up and regain your breath. You sound wheezy."

Dane steered her toward her desk. "If you really want to help, you can do a search and find out who leased the building where the pictures and notes were found."

Alec picked up the photo of her putting on her panties, making her go pale, then red-hot again. "Assuming the last guy who lived there took them, we can hunt him up and ask him about the...model."

All three men grinned, and their humor in light of her disgrace rubbed Clair the wrong way.

"You know damn good and well that woman wasn't modeling."

"Probably not," Dane agreed. "But neither was she objecting."

Ready to blast him for his misassumption, Clair opened her mouth, but snapped it shut again. How could she explain without giving herself away? No, she hadn't objected because she hadn't even known the pervert was looking at her, much less that he had a camera. She'd only slept with Kyle twice, and both times were disastrous.

She hadn't realized how disastrous until she saw the sneaky photos.

Clair closed her eyes. "All right. Sure." She'd hunt from now till the end of time without giving them Kyle's name. If they had a name, Alec and Dane would find Kyle. And then the jig would be up.

In fact, if she forced herself to face reality, she knew they'd eventually find him even without her help. They were good. Better than good, they were the best. They were, as she'd often bragged to Harris, awesome. If enough opportunities arose for her to sabotage their efforts, she maybe had a month. Less, if they did some of the computer work themselves, as they occasionally did.

Harris paced to a window overlooking the back lot. "I hope you can find him. It's driving me nuts not knowing who she is."

If Dane and Alec hadn't been in the room, Clair would have kicked Harris in his sexy backside for that remark.

"We'll find him," Alec assured Harris. "Even if we don't, we'll figure out who she is. She had to be local, someone you come into contact with, maybe on a daily basis. Eventually someone will recognize her."

Spots danced in front of Clair's eyes. She gasped, drawing a lot of male attention. In a raw whisper, she pleaded, "Don't tell me you intend to show those photos to people?"

"No." Dane's statement allowed her heart to slow to a more normal pace, until he added, "At least not yet. We'll try other routes first."

"What other routes?"

He shrugged. "We'll hunt for the owner."

And with any luck, she'd find Kyle before they did and rip his heart out—or at least his tongue, so he couldn't tell them about her.

"We'll talk to photography shops to see if anyone remembers developing any photos like those."

A dead end for sure, since Kyle did his own developing. Not that it mattered, because by then her photos would have made the rounds of the neighborhood.

"But eventually it might come down to going door-to-door and asking about him or her or both."

"That's an invasion of her privacy," Alec explained, "so a last resort. But if all else fails..."

Clair knew that if she didn't get out of there right then, she was going to be sick. She plastered on a very false smile. "Well then, by all means, let me do my best to find him on the computer first." She went to her desk.

Unfortunately, Harris followed on her heels. "You feeling better?"

No, never. "I keep telling you, I'm fine."

"You're sure?"

She stared at him, adjusted her glasses, and said with succinct finality, "I'm. Fine."

Harris held up both hands. "All right, all right. Don't get in a temper. I have to get to work and I wanted to make sure you're up to jogging tonight, that's all. If you're not, then I don't want you to push it."

She didn't want to. She wanted to hide. But any variance in their routine right now might tip him off. She forced another fake smile. "I wouldn't miss it."

He nodded, still watching her curiously. "Great." He started backing toward the door. "I'll see you then."

Once the door closed behind him, Clair started to relax, but Alec didn't give her time. He came out of the office with the pictures in hand.

Straightening in her chair, Clair said, "He left them with you?" Maybe she could swipe them after all. Or spill coffee on them. Or...

"Not a chance. These are copies we ran off when he first got here. Your friend Harris is carrying the originals in his front pocket like a lovesick swain." Alec smiled. "Funny guy."

"He's an idiot."

"He has a secret admirer and he's hooked. It's understandable. Not only is the woman attractive and sexy as hell—"

"Being naked does not necessarily make her sexy."

Alec's slow smile looked positively wicked. "Yeah, it does."

Well, hell. Clair slumped under another wave of embarrassment. So all it took was a little nudity for a guy to find a woman sexy? How stupid was that? What about her personality? What about her interests?

Alec seemed to read her mind. "She said some pretty profound things about him in her notes, too. Any guy would be intrigued."

Profound? She'd only spoken the truth.

"I'm going to enlarge and enhance these," Alec said, tapping the copies against his thigh, "to see if I can pick up any details."

Details—like her identity? He disappeared into the backroom. Heart in her throat, her stomach in knots, Clair kept her eyes on that door for a full five minutes until Alec returned—carrying a stack of 8 x 10 photos.

The one on top was of her right shoulder, boob, and ribs.

Clair gulped. He'd taken each photo and divided it into fours, then enlarged each piece. When put together, her buck-naked body would be poster size.

Worse and worse and worse. But Alec didn't so much as glance at her on his way back to talk to Dane, so he still hadn't recognized her.

It took her a few more minutes of slowly dying inside

before she realized Dane must not have recognized her either. No one budged from the office. There were no outbursts of hilarity, no accusing stares. They were probably too engrossed with ogling the oversize photos.

And here she'd always considered Dane and Alec astute. What was she, invisible? Clair pulled off her tortoiseshell glasses and looked at them. Like Clark Kent's specs, were her glasses an ingenious disguise that instantly afforded her anonymity?

The door opened and Clair hastened to shove her glasses back on, almost poking herself in the eye. Her face burned. Much more blushing and she'd be permanently scalded.

Both men looked at her with expectant expressions. Clair shriveled inside, until Dane prompted, "Make any headway?"

She hadn't even started. "Oh. Um, no. Not yet. I'll keep looking."

"Thanks." Dane and Alec headed for the door.

"Where are you two going?" In a panic, Clair left her seat and rushed after them. Surely, they weren't going to show those pictures around *now.*

Alec barely slowed. "I have to appear in court, remember?"

"Oh yeah."

Dane paused. "I'm working on a missing person." He stopped and faced her with concern. "Are you sure you're okay, Clair?"

Did they have to keep asking her that? "Of course. I just forgot, that's all." Reluctantly, she asked, "What about the photos?"

"Harris is impatient, but we'll spend a week or two exploring alternatives before we show them to anyone."

Thank you, thank you, thank you. "I think that's best." She couldn't help adding, "Can you imagine how embarrassed she'll be if she finds out that you showed them?"

On his way out the door, Dane laughed and pointed at her. "A good reason to never pose nude, huh?"

Or date photographers with sneaky streaks and lack of moral fiber. Clair groaned. With everyone gone, she ran into Dane's office—and stumbled to a horrified halt. She pressed a fist to her mouth. They had the photos up on a pegboard. Pieced together.

Adrenaline carried her to the board in a flash. It took Clair all of thirty seconds to snatch them down and hide them under a stack of files, but she didn't dare destroy them. That'd look too suspicious, and what was the point? They'd only make more.

She dragged herself back to her desk and collapsed in her chair, her face in her hands, her stomach roiling. Sooner or later, they'd know it was her—and then she'd have to quit and move to Outer Mongolia.

Unless... She swallowed hard and tried to think beyond her embarrassment. It wasn't easy, but she tried to take an objective view of the situation.

First, Alec claimed Harris was smitten. And Harris had acted obsessed with the "mystery woman." Heaven knew she'd been obsessed with him forever. But he hadn't shown any sexual interest, and she was too proud to throw herself at him. So they were friends. Clair knew he liked her as a person, but she'd assumed he didn't find her attractive in "that" way.

But judging by his rapt expression when he'd looked at the photos, he definitely liked what he saw.

So, secondly, what did she have to lose now? Not her modesty. After today, she had no modesty to protect.

And as to her pride...well, pride didn't help much when you saw your own behind in an 8 x 10 glossy, held on a presentation board with a thumbtack.

Maybe, just maybe, if she worked this right, she could use her newfound knowledge of Harris's interest to make him fall in love with her—before he found out she was his secret admirer.

It was either that or tell him straight up that he'd seen her naked and that she'd written those notes. He'd know all of her secrets then, leaving her soul as bare as her body. But if he felt the same, it wouldn't be nearly as embarrassing.

She'd probably have to seduce him, and that wouldn't be easy because she couldn't take off her glasses and she definitely couldn't take off her clothes. If she did, he might make the connection too soon. It'd be a tricky bit of business, but she'd figure something out. Maybe she'd just ensure they only got romantic in the dark. That might work.

Given Alec and Dane's expertise, there wouldn't be any time to waste. She'd jump-start Harris on their new relationship tonight. If she was good enough, maybe he'd even give up on the mystery woman and she'd never have to tell him anything at all.

HARRIS WAITED IMPATIENTLY for Clair to present herself. The storms had left the night air fresh and clean. It felt good, but it was warm. Deciding against a shirt, he wore only black jogging shorts with socks and running shoes. The shorts had a single back pocket to hold his apartment key—and the photo of his secret admirer reclining on the bed. He hadn't wanted to leave her behind.

Not that he intended to show it to anyone. He appreciated Dane and Alec's efforts to uncover the woman's identity, but already he felt protective and possessive of her. He didn't want anyone else, especially anyone male, to see her.

Something about her, some vague intangible thing, seemed familiar to Harris. He wished he could pin it down. Maybe she reminded him of someone. But who? While he stretched, preparing to run, his mind churned.

Work had been uneventful, which was a relief after the fire the day before. Unfortunately, that had given Harris too much time to think—about the notes, the sexy photos. And about Clair's old boyfriend.

Neither Dane nor Alec would give him any details on the guy. They claimed not to have any. They said they knew Clair had dated, because she'd gotten a few calls at work. Period. Nothing more. They didn't understand why he cared. Hell, he didn't understand either.

But why hadn't she told him? They were friends. Close friends. Didn't friends share that kind of info?

Harris's internal grumbling got interrupted when the entrance door to Clair's building pushed open and she stepped out. The streetlight reflected off the lenses of her glasses. She, too, had trimmed down to the barest covering. Dressed in snowy white cotton shorts and a tank top, she looked...good. Real good.

She smiled at him, adjusted the white band holding her glasses in place and joined him at the street. "Ready?"

Harris studied her. He figured it was the combined effects of sleeping alone, his mystery woman, and hearing about Clair's boyfriend that had him seeing her with a new perspective. "How come you've never gotten contacts?"

Bending this way and that, stretching her arms high, Clair asked, "Why? You don't like my glasses?"

"I didn't say that." Watching her flex was getting to Harris. She was a supple little thing. Funny how he'd never noticed that before.

Clair straightened, then stared up at him with her big green eyes, magnified behind the lenses of her glasses. "I tried contacts once, but they bugged me. I think my eyes are just too sensitive. Besides, I like wearing different frames."

"I noticed that." Tonight her frames were red, a stark contrast to the white shorts and tank. What she lacked in jewelry she made up for in eyewear.

"I have as many pairs of glasses as I do bras."

Harris did a double take. Bras? Why the hell did she have to mention her unmentionables? His besieged brain launched into a series of visuals: Clair in something white and lacy. Clair in something black and slinky. Clair in something barely there.

Clair in his bed.

She said again, "Ready?"

Oh yeah, he was ready all right. For all kinds of things. His gaze dipped to her breasts, but he didn't see any telltale signs of lace through her tee. "How many bras do you have?"

Laughing, Clair shook her head and started walking at a pre-run clip, leaving him two paces behind her. "What is this? Twenty questions?"

"It just occurs to me that I don't know you that well." He tried, but he couldn't seem to get his gaze off her ass.

Was she sashaying just a bit? Putting a little extra swing in the swing and sway?

Turning to walk backward, depriving him of his preoccupation with her behind, Clair frowned. "You know me better than most people."

"I didn't know you had a boyfriend." Harris took satisfaction in pointing that out.

She turned her back again and started moving a little faster. "What'd you think, Harris? That I was a virgin? A nun? A misanthrope?"

"A misan-what?" Harris trotted to keep up.

"Misanthrope. You know, a hater of men."

"No." He was sure of one thing. "You like me and I'm a man."

Over her shoulder, she smiled at him, a smile unlike any he'd ever seen from Clair before. "That you are."

Harris's eyes widened. Was she flirting? Did Clair even know how to flirt? But her voice was different, too, sort of soft and playful. He caught up to her. "So who was the boyfriend?"

"No one important." They began jogging in earnest, gliding along smoothly. "Just a guy I knew who seemed nice enough and interesting enough to pass the time."

"You weren't serious about him?"

She snorted, giving Harris all the answer he needed—though why he needed an answer, he couldn't say.

They loped on in silence, past the dark, quiet park, along deserted streets where older homes sat back in majestic splendor, along the levy where a concrete path had been poured.

Their movements were fluid, well timed to match. They had a great rhythm together. Harris groaned. He could just imagine setting the pace in bed, and how easily Clair could keep up.

"So how many bras do you have?"

Her laugh got carried away on the evening wind. "At least one for every day of the week."

He thought about that. "A special one for each day?"

"No, just variety. Different colors, different fabrics."

Like French lace or slinky nylon or maybe... "What are you wearing tonight?"

"We're jogging, sweating. So it's plain old comfortable white cotton."

Somehow, when he pictured it on Clair, cotton didn't seem the least plain. He was wondering about her panties, whether they matched the bra or not, when Clair slowed, veered off the pavement to mosey into the grass, then leaned her shoulders against a thick maple tree.

That far from the street, the light of lampposts barely penetrated.

Immediately, Harris was beside her. "Hey, you okay?"

"Mmm-hmm." She tipped her head back and closed her eyes. "Just a little tired today."

She'd been pale earlier, unsteady on her feet, and now she was tired? Clair never got tired. Hell, usually he was the first to get winded when they ran, and he knew he was in extremely good shape. All firefighters were.

Come to that, so was Clair, and he didn't mean healthwise, although that applied too. Her white shirt and shorts reflected the scant moonlight, emphasizing certain swells and hollows, making her body look more feminine than ever.

She bent one knee, stuck the other leg out straight.

The pose showed off the length of her long legs, causing Harris's mouth to go dry. Her dark brown hair, hanging loose tonight, lifted a bit with a gentle breeze. His fingers twitched with the need to smooth it back into place. He resisted.

Still with her eyes closed, Clair smiled.

"Why," Harris asked, full of suspicion now, "are you smiling like that?"

Her eyes opened, her head tilted. "Like what?"

"Like you have a secret."

For a single moment there, Harris thought he saw alarm flicker in her gaze. Then she straightened away from the tree. "Don't be absurd. Can't a woman smile?"

"Sure." He propped his hands on his hips. "When she's got a reason."

"I'm happy," Clair snapped, in a very unhappy tone. "I feel good. The air's fresh, your company, before just now, wasn't too heinous, and so I smiled." She shoved past him. "I won't make that mistake again."

Harris caught her arm and pulled her around. She slammed into his chest, but quickly back-stepped. "You get mad too easy, too fast."

She relented just a bit, tugging free of his hold and folding her arms around her middle. Sounding mulish, she said, "I'm not mad."

"No? Then what?"

She stared up at him, one expression after another crossing her features before she stalked in a circle around him. Harris turned, keeping her in his sights.

"You told me I wouldn't understand about lust."

Oh hell. First bras and now this. Except for the racing of his heart and a twitch of male interest, Harris went very still. "Yeah." *Shut up, Harris. Let it go....* "And?"

"You were wrong."

He shouldn't have pushed for an explanation. "I am, huh?"

She nodded. "I'm...antsy. The guy you were asking about? We broke up two months ago." She peeked up at Harris, all innocent temptation. "I haven't been out with a guy since."

No way could he have this conversation. Not with a platonic girlfriend. Not without a bed around. He took a step back. "Right. Gotcha. Maybe a, uh, run will help."

"No. I need to find a new guy." As if she hadn't just dropped a verbal bombshell, Clair turned away and headed back to the sidewalk. "In the meantime, running just exhausts me so I can sleep at night instead of fantasizing."

Fantasizing! Well, yeah, so all women probably fantasized, same as men. But Clair? Harris stomped after her. "What the hell does that mean, you have to find a new guy? You make it sound like shoe shopping."

She ignored his furious blustering to say, "Come on. Let's finish our run." Rather than wait for him, she took off, forcing Harris to catch up.

Because he was annoyed now, it took him only two long strides to reach her side. "So where do you intend to look for this new guy?"

"I dunno." She glanced at him over her glasses. "You got any suggestions?"

Of all the nerve. "You can't tell me you're horny, then expect me to help you find a guy."

She whipped around so fast he nearly plowed over her. They bumped. Hard. Harris had to catch her arms to keep them both on their feet.

Giving her a small shake, he groused, "What the hell is the matter with you?"

"Me!" She pushed him away, almost landing him on his butt. "I didn't say anything about being *horny*— how crass is that?"

"You think antsy sounds prettier? It means the same thing."

Clair gasped. "It does not."

Disgusted, Harris stared into her sexy green eyes and taunted, "Then I was right. You don't know anything about lust."

Her pupils flared. The seconds passed with the impact of a ticking bomb. He could feel the tension building, stretching almost to the breaking point—and she attacked.

One second Harris was standing there, smirking at her, and then he was flat on his back in the cold dank grass, little rocks prodding his spine, mosquitoes buzzing with delight at the feast thrown to them.

And Clair, well, Clair had an unshakable grip on his skull and her mouth was plastered to his, hot and wet and demanding. Somehow, with the prodding of her tongue, he opened and she plundered, licking and tasting, stealing his objections and melting them with her heat.

Astounded, instantly aroused, Harris cupped her head, felt the silkiness of her hair, the warmth of her skin. He tipped his head for a better angle and let her deepen the kiss more. *Clair,* he thought. This was Clair straddling him, Clair kissing him with so much passion. Her breasts flattened on his chest, her thighs shifted against his, wrenching a deep groan from him.

Then she was gone.

Moon and stars filled Harris's vision. His lungs labored to draw in more cool night air. His body burned. Confused, he pushed up to his elbows. Clair stood over him, hands on her hips, her glasses askew, her white shorts now dirty.

"That," she said, "is lust."

Harris nodded in complete and total agreement. "I'll say."

She offered him a hand, and when he took it, she helped haul him to his feet. Looking down into her earnest face, Harris scrambled for something to say, some way to get back into that full-body contact. But before a single idea could form, Clair touched his chin, his jaw, gently, softly.

Harris went mute with anticipation.

She stepped up against him, cuddling into him, wrapping her arms around him. After a long, meaningful stare into his eyes that scorched him clean through to his bones, she went on tiptoe and kissed him again. This kiss was as different as night and day from the first. It was purposeful, sweet, and it consumed him.

Like a slow burn, she involved his entire body, her small hands touching up and down his bare back, over his shoulders, as if in awe of his muscles and strength. Her feet moved between his, which aligned her soft belly with his groin. She pressed, proving she was aware of his erection.

Her breasts brushed against him, teasing, taunting, until he felt her stiffened nipples and growled.

She made small sounds of pleasure and hunger too, her tongue now shy, loving.

Loving?

With a pat to his rear, Clair pulled away. He watched

as she slowly licked her lips. "And that," she whispered, "is antsy."

Breathless, hot, more than a little ready, Harris reached for her. "I don't think I quite understand yet. You better do a little more explaining."

CHAPTER THREE

CLAIR'S QUICK BACK STEP kept her out of reach. "If that explanation didn't suffice, then nothing will. You're hopeless." She turned away.

Did women always have to be so confusing?

Neither of them jogged this time. Hell, just walking was tough for Harris. He had a major Jones and she just didn't seem all that affected. Except for the wobbly way she walked. And the way she breathed too deeply.

He couldn't just let it go, so after half a dozen steps, he cleared his throat and ventured into murky water. "So...that was just a lesson, huh?"

"Think what you will."

She sounded all prickly again. Clair never got prickly with him. He wasn't used to it and didn't have a clue how to deal with her in this mood. "How about you just explain it?"

One shoulder lifted in a halfhearted shrug. "Men get horny and want to get laid. Women get antsy and want to touch and be touched, to cuddle and be affectionate." She cast him a quick look. "And then make love."

He raised his hand. "I'll take either one."

"I wasn't offering."

"Yeah, you were." When she turned to face him, Harris chastised her with a look. "I'm a little slow on the uptake sometimes, but I'm not a complete dolt. You're coming on to me."

She didn't reply to that one way or the other.

He needed verification, damn it. "I'm willing, Clair."

The incredulous look she gave him didn't bode well. "Willing? Oh great, bring out the band. Harris is *willing*." Her laugh reeked with sarcasm. "How did I get so lucky?"

Figuring her out wasn't going to be easy. "Bad word choice? Should I have said happy to oblige? Anxious? Maybe desperate?"

Her eyes narrowed behind the lenses of her glasses. "Are you?"

"After those killer kisses, what do you think?"

She reached around him to pat his ass again—right over the pocket that held the photo and his key. The woman sure had a thing for his rear.

"I think you're desperate to find your stupid mystery woman and I'd just be a way to pass the time." She crossed her arms over her chest, going all stiff and angry.

Uh-oh.

He took too long trying to figure out what to say, because she demanded, "Isn't that right?"

Harris held out his hands. "C'mon, Clair. I can't just forget about her. But hell, I don't even know her."

"You told me you didn't know me that well either."

They were a good mile from home, which ensured no matter what he said she couldn't just stalk off in a temper. That gave Harris small comfort, though, when he didn't know what the hell to say. "Up until a few minutes ago, I didn't know you were interested in...that."

"That?" she asked meanly, curling her lip, being deliberately derisive.

"Sex. Me."

"The two combined?"

"Exactly." He wrapped his fingers around her upper arm, slowing her furious stomp to a more sedate pace. When she didn't object, he decided to just hang on to her. Touching her was nice. At least now it was. Before she'd kissed him, he hadn't really noticed how it felt to touch her. Realizing that, he said, "I need a few minutes to adjust, that's all. Neither of us has thought that much about sleeping together."

"Speak for yourself."

Was that a confession? His interest sharpened to an ache. "You've thought about me?"

"You're not an ogre, Harris. Most of the time, you're not too moronic. I'm not with anyone else. Do the math."

Harris chewed over those critical and questionable compliments, and didn't like the conclusion he came to. "So like your ex-boyfriend, I'd be filler until something better came along?"

She laughed. "Harris, honey, do try to remember your own credos, okay?"

Honey?

"You don't want to be anything more than filler. You don't want a woman getting ideas of forever after. You're totally against marriage." She waited two heartbeats, then prodded him. "Right?"

"Uh, yeah." But somehow that didn't seem to be the point right now. "So you thought about, what? A quick fling?" He could start with that, maybe work up to more....

"You weren't listening to my instructions a minute ago, were you?" Typically Clair, she turned to walk backward so she could see his face. "I thought I was more than clear that men want it quick. I want it slow and easy. I want to—"

He swallowed hard.

"—take my time." She continued pacing backward. "But there's that mystery lady occupying you right now." Her sigh was absurdly long. "So we can just go on being sexless buds. No problem."

No problem? What about his boner? That was a definite problem. And his curiosity, which was so keen he suddenly felt obsessed with knowing Clair intimately. And there was a strange excitement he'd never felt with any other woman, too. Maybe it was the way she insulted him so energetically. "I may never meet that woman, Clair. I mean, I know Alec and Dane are good, but that doesn't guarantee they'll find her."

"And if they did?"

How should he answer that? The mystery alone made him want to approach the woman, to talk to her, to find out how she knew him and why she hadn't ever told him how she felt. There was her sex appeal, and the notes, her sincerity and admiration...

"Yeah, that's what I thought." Clair reached out and clasped his hand, lacing her fingers with his. "Come on. No more lagging. Time to run."

"I don't think I can." He'd never run with a hard-on before. It didn't seem all that comfortable.

"You can," Clair assured him, "or you'll be heading home alone, because I'm not walking. I'm tired and I want to get to bed."

"So you can *fantasize*," Harris accused. Possibly about him. The way her hand tightened shored up that belief.

"Maybe."

He did not need to hear this. She dragged him along, never once releasing her hold on him, and in a few minutes, they were jogging again. At the pace she set, it didn't take them long before they were on their own street. This close to the burned building, the lingering scent of smoke still hung in the air. It reminded Harris of his reaction when he'd feared Clair might be involved in the fire. His reaction had been extreme, and that was before she'd been flirting with him.

He also thought of the shoebox he'd found, and the tantalizing prospects it had presented. Harris was strangely aware of the photo in his back pocket, and Clair's hand in his.

Two women, both of them making him nuts.

What the hell was a guy supposed to do?

CLAIR STOPPED in front of her steps. So far, Harris seemed more than a little interested in sex, but she wanted more than that. She wanted him to want her, in and out of bed. She felt manipulative, teasing him and then pulling back. Making comments that she knew would get him thinking about sex. But she didn't know what else to do.

And already it was working with Harris. He wanted her now—but he still wanted her alter ego, the Naked Lady, too. Somehow, she had to get him to give up the fantasy prompted by those stupid photos.

Feeling awkward, Clair said, "It's early yet."

A light sheen of sweat dampened Harris's bare shoulders and chest. He had his hands on his hips, breathing deeply, watching her. "You pulled our run short."

Clair shrugged, adjusted her glasses nervously. "Want to come up?"

His gaze sharpened. Like a blue laser, his gaze pinned her in place. Slowly his hands dropped from his hips and he took a step closer. "Are you playing with me again?"

Man, he was still primed, ready to jump the gun— apparently ready to jump her. "I've had you up to my place a dozen times, Harris. For drinks, a snack."

His hands came to settle on her waist. "For more?"

Despite her urge to say *yes,* Clair laughed. "We're both sweaty and you have to be up early."

"I'm never too tired for—"

"Will you send me in alone if I say I just want to talk?"

For a brief moment, his hands tightened, then the heat left his eyes and he released her with a sigh. "What the hell. I always enjoy talking to you." His smile didn't quite reach his eyes. "Lead the way."

Her apartment was dark when they first went in. Clair turned on lamps as she headed to the kitchen. "You want something to eat or drink?"

"Just some water." He trailed behind her, far too close, in Clair's opinion.

She filled two glasses with ice, then got the spring water from the fridge. "So tell me what the attraction is."

"To you?"

He looked perplexed enough that Clair wanted to hit him. "No, not to me. Far as I know, you're *not* attracted to me."

He cocked one brow, then looked pointedly at her body. "I'd be more than happy to prove you wrong on that."

Clair groaned. "So then why do you want the woman in the photos so bad? She gets naked and that makes you so interested you can't let it go?

He immediately shook his head. "She does look hot, no way around that. I mean, any woman who's comfortable being naked is okay in my book."

"Really?"

He grinned. "Hell yeah. If it was up to me, all women would stay naked. At least when we were alone together."

That had Clair blushing a bit, especially as Harris let his gaze roam over her, no doubt imagining her in such a state. Not that he had to imagine, if he only realized....

"But the woman in the photo also said some nice things in her notes."

"So?"

Harris rubbed the back of his neck and paced away. He had a gorgeous back, strong and broad, sleek and hard with muscle. His shorts rode low on his hips, hugging a narrow behind and strong thighs. "This is kind of embarrassing."

She knew all about embarrassing. "Why? We're friends."

He nodded, turned to face her. "She said I'm generous." Harris looked uncomfortable. "And funny and heroic."

Men could be such dolts. "Well, of course she did. Because you *are*." Clair handed him his water. "You're one of the greatest guys I know."

The water never made it to his mouth. "You think so?"

"Absolutely."

"But I didn't know...."

"Harris," she said with aggrieved sigh. "Do you think I'd hang out with a guy who was an idiot?"

His mouth tipped in a crooked grin. "You call me an idiot all the time."

Too true. It had always been her way of making sure she kept her feelings to herself. A self-protection mechanism of sorts that reminded her she wasn't to get too romantic with Harris.

Clair moved back to the living room and dropped onto her overstuffed, oversize couch. She stretched out her legs, caught Harris staring at them, and smiled. "Yeah, well, I insult you with affection. I don't mean it." She sent him a quick grin, just to keep her comments from getting too dramatic. "If I didn't like, respect and admire you, I wouldn't want your company."

His brows came down, his expression arrested. Clair stared at him over her glasses. "Now what's wrong?"

With a small shake of his head, Harris muttered, "I need to think. You've sort of thrown a bunch of stuff at me all at once."

"Thinking is good." Clair waited while he, too, plopped onto the sofa. Because of their conversation, sitting so close to him felt different this time. "You should decide what you'll do once you find this woman. I mean, have you considered that?"

He propped his big feet on her coffee table and let his head fall back. "At least a hundred times."

Clair stared at his abdomen. It, too, was hard, lean and ridged with muscle. A dark, silky line of hair led from his navel to beneath the waistband of his shorts.

She held herself in check, when what she wanted to do was attack him again. "So," she said, sounding a little strained, "what if she's a witch? What if she has an ogre's personality? She could be like a fatal attraction or something. A nut. A slasher even."

Harris rolled his head toward her. "You made your point early on, hon. Now you're just stretching it."

Clair shrugged. "But the point is valid."

"Maybe." Harris stared at her, surveying her face as if trying to read her thoughts. "She didn't sound like a slasher in her notes. She sounded like a nice lady."

Here we go again. "You don't *want* a nice lady, Harris, remember? You want someone who's out for kicks. Nice women tend to get serious thoughts when they're having sex with a guy."

His blue eyes filled with speculative interest. Still lounging back lazily, he said, "You're nice."

Nervousness fluttered through her. Was there a point to that? Maybe something she was missing? She took a big gulp of her water, then agreed, "I'm very nice."

Harris warmed to his topic, leaning toward her a bit, resting his arm along the back of the sofa. His fingers just touched her nape, teasing her a bit. "So if we slept together," he asked in a slow drawl, "you'd want to settle down with me?"

Lord yes. She wanted to claim him as her own, and have babies and make love every night.... "I dunno." Her feigned indifference was laudable. "See, even if we did sleep together..."

"Yes?"

"I have an advantage."

"Do tell. I'm on the edge of my seat here."

Smugly, Clair stated, "Unlike other women you know, I have no illusions. I've watched you revel in your bachelor ways."

"I don't revel." His mouth flattened in distaste. "You

make it sound like I go around dancing and singing about it. I just enjoy my life, that's all."

"Thing is," Clair continued, ignoring his protests, "I'm not sure you really know what you want or feel."

"So I can't figure out you or me, huh? What a dope I must be."

"I didn't say that, Harris. Don't put words in my mouth." He grinned at her, seeming far from insulted. "Look at the way you're panting over a photo. That proves you're anxious for a serious relationship."

"You think so? I thought it just meant I was curious."

So curious, he'd hired two very expensive detectives to find the woman. Clair made a face at him. "What if," she said, determined to get her theory out in the open, "what you really want is to be loved?"

For a suspended moment in time, Harris froze. Then he jeered. "Do I look that needy to you?"

"No." Given the perfect opening, Clair spoke from her heart. "You look like a guy who's a great catch. Earnest when you need to be. Reliable. Dedicated." Melancholy got a stranglehold on her. Helplessly, she said, "You're a hero, Harris. A gorgeous, sexy, funny, bona fide hero."

He slowly straightened in his seat. "Don't overdo it, Clair."

"I'm serious." She scooted closer to him on the couch. "You're an incredible guy."

His gaze zeroed in on her mouth. "Clair, you do realize you're turning me on again, right?" His big warm hand came up to cup her cheek. "I hope that's your intent and not part of this new sadistic streak you've developed."

Clair chewed her lower lip. She did want to arouse

him, but she didn't want to push him too far. She wanted them to talk more before they took the plunge.

"Listen. I've told you what I really think of you." She drew a deep breath for courage—and inhaled his scent. After their jog, he was a little sweaty, but he smelled delicious. The way a man should, the way Harris always did. "Now why don't you tell me what you think of me?"

His thumb brushed her jaw. "Sure." The left side of his mouth kicked up. "You're cute, in a funky egghead, jock sort of way."

The romantic haze cleared from around her. "Be still my heart."

The teasing glimmer in his blue eyes clued her in. "Now Clair, what did you want me to say? You keep changing on me, so I don't know your personality anymore."

He knew her better than anyone, including her family. He just didn't realize it yet.

"I can't even tell what you're thinking most of the time because you always hide behind your glasses." The seductive way he caressed her neck mesmerized her. "Do you shower in them? Sleep in them?" His voice dropped. "Make love in them?"

Clair tried to rear back, but Harris kept her in place with the gentle hold on the back of her neck, and his compelling stare. "I'm not telling," she whispered.

"Then I think I'll find out on my own." He reached for her frames.

Clair couldn't let him take her glasses off! He might recognize her. She shoved him hard, but Harris being Harris—a big, sturdy, physically fit firefighter—he didn't budge.

"You want to wrestle?" he said with a laugh, and he caught her flying hands while somehow managing to tickle her. The next thing Clair knew they were rolling off the couch and onto the floor. She landed on Harris with a grunt, but only had a split second to enjoy that position before he flipped her beneath him. The coffee table got shoved away, and Harris settled himself between her thighs.

Uh-oh. "Harris..."

He caught both her hands in one of his, pinning them in place, keeping her still. And then, with her squawking and protesting, he slid her glasses off and placed them gingerly on the table.

Clair went mute in fear, sure that he'd recognize her.

Instead, he leaned down until his mouth just touched hers. "Can I show you my ideas on the differences between horny and antsy?"

He wasn't wearing a shirt, and all that sleek bare skin was against her. He smelled like a man should, like something that could be bottled and sold to make a fortune. And she could feel his hard, hair-roughened thighs on the tender insides of her legs. "Yes." Her heart threatened to punch out of her chest. "You can show me."

"I love a good sport."

Her breath caught at the word *love,* and then Harris murmured, "Here's horny."

His mouth settled over hers, moving hotly, urging her lips to part so his tongue could sink inside. At the same time, he gently rocked his pelvis against hers, teased her nipples with the pressure of his chest. His breath was hot on her cheek, fast and low.

Wow. When he lifted away, Clair had to struggle to

get her eyes open. "Lust," she whispered in complete agreement.

"Right. And here's antsy." He released her hands to cup her face, holding her still as he kissed her deeply again. Clair groaned. Kissing Harris was a revelation. She now realized that among his other accolades, she'd have to add "awesome kisser."

He eased away. "So what do you think?"

Her head was spinning, her heart beating too fast. "They were the same."

"Right, because there isn't a difference." He dropped a kiss on her nose. "It's just preference, Clair. Sometimes I like it hard and fast."

She groaned again.

"But sometimes," he said, drawing it out and searing her with a look, "I like to make it last all night."

Clair wasn't sure she could take an all-nighter. But then he kissed her temple, and when he spoke, his voice was a rough whisper.

"For you, I'd make it last."

Okay, so maybe she could take it. Clair started to wrap her arms around him, but Harris held her off. His smile looked pained, and his muscles were taut with restraint. He kissed her nose again—and sat up.

"But since you're playing some strange game here and I can't quite figure out the rules yet, I think I better call it a night."

She didn't want him to go now, darn it. She wanted...

Harris touched her cheek, smoothed her hair. "When we sleep together, Clair—and we will, so don't deny it—I don't want any miscommunication or regrets. We'll both be in agreement, and we'll both enjoy it. Okay?"

A little numb, Clair nodded.

When Harris pushed to his feet, she sat up and quickly located her glasses. She felt more self-assured with the visual barrier in place. "Harris?"

He smiled down at her, giving her a sense of déjà vu, but with her in the wrong position. In the park, she'd done this to him—led him on, then walked away.

He tipped his head toward her.

"Thank you."

A smile warmed his expression. "For waiting?

"And for understanding. I...I guess I'm not a hundred percent sure what I want yet."

"Between us?"

"Yes." She bit her lip. "I don't think you are either."

"Now there's where you're wrong. I know what I want—and I know I'll get it. That's the only reason I can be so patient now."

Clair blinked hard. Had she finally made some serious progress?

"Good night, Clair," Harris said, and his expression was warm, intimate. "Sweet dreams."

CHAPTER FOUR

EVEN WHILE HE HOVERED next to Dane, waiting to see the results from the information he'd supplied, Harris kept listening for Clair to get to work. He was curious about the mystery woman still, no two ways about that. When he'd seen a dark-haired woman flirting with him, all his senses had gone on alert. He'd made note of her license plates, and now he waited to see if she could be the one. He hoped so. The suspense was killing him.

But even while he waited in tense silence, more than half his attention was on the door, anticipating Clair's arrival. The way that girl kissed... Hell, she was so hot, he probably should stay in uniform when with her. He needed the fireproof protection.

She was the same Clair he enjoyed so much, but she acted different with him now. He liked the changes, the feminine layers to her personality. The teasing. Like refined foreplay, Clair's advance and retreat kept his excitement very close to the surface, ready to explode with little provocation.

"Her name is Melody Miles." Dane, with his hand over the receiver of the phone, glanced up at Harris. "*Miss* Melody Miles—so she's single."

Somehow, that didn't thrill Harris as much as he'd thought it might.

"Alec says up close, she doesn't look the same to him."

"None of the photos show her face."

"He didn't mention her face." Dane shrugged. "He was talking about her body. She's a little heavier than she seemed in the snapshots, but that could be due to a time difference between when the pictures were taken and now."

The door opened and Clair strolled in. She was smiling—until she saw Harris. Then she snapped to a standstill; her back slowly straightened.

Harris barely heard Dane still talking. Today Clair wore narrow, rectangular glasses that added an air of supreme intelligence to her appearance. Her dark glossy hair was a little windblown, proving she'd ridden to work with her car window down. Beneath the short hem of a navy-blue jumper, her long legs were bare. White sandals matched her white T-shirt. She looked adorable.

He was so glad to see her again. "Clair."

Her mouth flattened. "What are you doing here, Harris?"

Dane hung up and stepped out from behind her desk. "He thought he might have found the mystery lady."

Clair crossed her arms and thrust out a hip in an arrogant pose. "Do tell."

Clearing his throat, very unsure of her mood, Harris said, "Yeah, well. She was flirting with me at this coffee shop where I stopped this morning. I realized I stop there a lot, and that could be the connection. You know, where she knew me from and everything."

"Have you ever met her?"

"No." Clair sounded so...accusatory. "But she could have heard my name from someone. I've been in there with the guys a few times too. Occasionally in uniform, so she'd know I was a firefighter."

"Assuming she hangs out there as well."

"Yeah. Assuming that." Harris wished Dane would offer a little help. He'd acted enthusiastic about the possibility of the woman being "the one," yet now he just stood there and grinned, enjoying Harris's plight.

"Ever notice her before?" Clair asked.

Feeling harassed, Harris said, "No. But that doesn't mean she hasn't noticed me."

"Obviously she has if she's flirting with you." Her eyes narrowed in thought. "Did you ask her if she's the one?"

"No, of course not." Sheepishly, Harris admitted, "I followed her so I could get her license plate number."

"Oh gawd." Clair flounced the rest of the way into the room and dropped her purse on the desk. "A stalker, that's what you've become."

Dane laughed. "No one saw him, Clair, and the plates paid off." Then he turned to Harris. "But as I said, Alec doesn't think it's her."

At the moment, with Clair glaring at him, Harris didn't really care. "All right."

Though he hadn't asked, Dane explained. "Body shape isn't the same." He pulled out the larger photos they'd created. He put the one of the woman's derriere on top of the stack.

Clair made a choking sound, but when Harris glanced at her, she didn't seem to be paying them any mind. In fact, she was busily arranging and rearranging things on her desk.

"Your woman—"

"*His* woman?" Clair repeated with mocking disbelief, her desk and its clutter forgotten.

"—has a heart-shaped behind." Dane shrugged. "The woman you saw in the coffee shop is rounder. Or so Alec tells me."

"Then it must not be her," Harris agreed.

"He's not positive," Dane said, "so he's going to check her out a little more. But he said not to get your hopes up."

Clair started laughing. Loudly. When Harris frowned at her, she put her face on the desk and covered her head with her arms. She roared with hilarity until her shoulders were shaking.

"What," he demanded over the awful noise she made, "is so damn funny?"

Gasping, wheezing with her humor, Clair straightened. She had tears of mirth rolling down her cheeks. "You three," she gasped, apparently including Alec, though he wasn't present. "Tracking a woman by...the shape of...*her ass.*" She burst out laughing again.

Dane cocked a brow. "I guess it does sound funny. Not that we have much else to go on." And then louder, to make his point to Clair, he said, "Since *somebody* hasn't found us the address of the previous owner yet."

Her amusement dried up real quick. "Oh." Her frown was fierce. "I'm working on that."

"Work harder," Dane suggested. "Or better yet, I can do it."

"No! I mean, I've got it covered. I'll have something for you in a few hours." Disgruntled, she seemed to sink in her chair. "Will that be good enough?"

"That'd be great." Dane picked up a file and headed

for the door. "I'll be staking out the Westbrook Motel today if anyone needs me."

"A stakeout?" Dane and Alec handled a lot of mundane, annoying cases—like cheating spouses and stolen lawn ornaments. But they also got involved in some really cool situations that Harris loved hearing about.

"Yeah. The owners of a small motel suspect one of their employees of spying on guests in the pool changing rooms. I'm going to hang out back in the bushes and catch him in the act, then we can call in the cops." Dane winked. "You kids be good. I'll see ya later."

Finally. The second Dane was out the door, Harris headed for Clair. Anticipation hummed inside him. He couldn't wait to taste her again.

As he advanced, her eyes widened and she hastily pushed her chair back, but Harris didn't give her time to retreat. He braced his hands on the arms of her chair, caging her in, and leaned down to take her mouth. She made a small sound of surprise—and then the sound got muffled.

Oh hell yeah, he'd missed her mouth.

Clair stayed stiff for about three seconds, then melted with a small moan. He liked that. He liked her. Maybe a lot more than he'd ever realized. When her lips parted, Harris accepted the invitation and slipped his tongue in for a deep, hot, wet kiss that lasted just long enough to get him semihard.

"I missed you," he growled against her mouth.

Speaking must have broken the spell, because she blinked and shoved him back. She was breathing fast and her lips were slightly swollen and very pink. She readjusted her crooked glasses, then scowled. "Yeah right. You missed me so much that you're following strange women around, desperate to meet your secret admirer."

"Not desperate." Harris wasn't all that steady on his feet at the moment. The idea of laying her out on the desk, pushing up her sensible jumper and indulging in a little office sex tempted him. But she didn't look too receptive to that idea. "Just curious. If some guy was in love with you, wouldn't you be curious?"

A myriad of expressions—anger, frustration, hope-lessness—crossed her face before she sighed and flopped back in her seat. "Maybe." Her chin lifted. "But not if I was interested in someone else."

Harris propped his hip on the desk. He needed the support. "I'm more than interested, Clair."

Eyes flaring, she caught her bottom lip in her teeth. "Really?"

Was she in love with him? As to that, was he in love with her? Harris had always figured that when he fell in love, the realization would hit him over the head. He wouldn't have to wonder about it, he'd just know. But Clair was so different, he couldn't figure her out. And that meant he couldn't really figure himself out either.

Choosing his words carefully, Harris hoped to talk her around to his way of thinking, without looking too pushy or, God forbid, desperate. "I like being with you, Clair. Even before all this sexual teasing started between us." That brought another thought, and he asked, "You won't go changing on me if we get involved, will you?"

Clair was as still as a statue. "What do you mean?"

"You tell me what you think and what you feel. But

you don't get hung up on little stuff. You're always honest with me."

She'd closed her eyes and Harris wasn't sure if she was listening. "Clair?"

Leaving her chair to pace, she said, "We're already involved. We just haven't slept together. If you like me how I am now, well, I can't see why sex should change anything."

"Sex changes *some* stuff."

She turned to face him, one brow raised in an attitude of skepticism. "How?"

How? Harris shook his head and rethought his words. "I should say that sex between *us* will change things. If you were a different woman—"

"Your secret admirer?"

"Don't sneer, Clair." He liked her show of jealousy. It sort of tickled him, because he'd never thought of Clair as a jealous woman. "All I'm saying is that with another woman, I might not care. But if *we* do this, I'll expect some rights."

She crossed her arms over her chest. "What rights?"

Somehow, this was backward, Harris thought, almost laughing at himself. Here he was, a man who avoided commitments, now trying to pin her down. But what had seemed so appealing just days before, now felt too open-ended. Clair never pressured him, never wanted to know where he was or when he'd be back or if he'd call. He was a firefighter, yet, to his knowledge, she never worried. And that had been cool—till now.

If she cared, shouldn't she show a little concern every now and then? Shouldn't she want to know if he was with another woman? Damn right, because if she didn't demand that special consideration, how could he demand it of her? And he wanted to. All this talk about her past boyfriend had him feeling his own dose of jealousy. He didn't want her with anyone else.

Harris pushed away from the desk. "I won't want you to ever jog at night without me." He warmed to his topic, moving closer to her. "Hell, I don't want you to do that now. If I can't make it, you'll skip it."

Her mouth fell open, then snapped shut and she declared with feeling, "I will not."

"Now Clair." He closed the space between them, forcing her to back up. "It's dangerous."

"You never cared before."

He was a dumb ass before. "We didn't have that kind of relationship. Now we will."

"Ha. What if you find your mystery lady? Then I'll be put on hold. So until you resolve your feelings for her, I'll just continue to do as I damn well please."

Harris loomed over her. The thought of her alone at night infuriated him. "Then I guess I'll just have to make sure I jog every damn night until we've got this settled."

Her back touched the wall and stopped her retreat. "You do anyway," she grumbled. And then, a little defeated, she added, "Besides, I don't enjoy jogging without you. Odds are, if you couldn't go, I'd skip it too."

Harris cupped her face. Logical, honest Clair. "Thank you." He kissed her again, but kept it light because he was running late. "I'll be over tonight as soon as I get off work."

"Why?" Thanks to the kiss, her eyes looked soft behind her glasses. "We don't run until it's dark."

"We've got a lot to talk about. Me, you, sex." He

grinned at her. "We'll hash it all out, because I don't think I can wait too much longer."

He started to turn away, and she said, "Harris?"

"Yeah?"

"I don't want to wait either."

Oh hell. A statement like that guaranteed he'd be semihard for most of the day. Not a comfortable circumstance while working with a group of men who lived to harass each other. And no doubt Ethan would be the worst, but then Ethan still prodded him about the shoebox. If he found out how much Harris cared about Clair, there'd never be an end to it. Without another word, Harris made his escape.

But just as he'd suspected, Clair stayed on his mind, distracting him, filling his thoughts and making him edgy. That is, until a truck driver swerved off the road, striking a gas line and sparking an apartment fire on the north side of the town.

The collision smashed a natural gas manifold, and intense, gas-fed flames shot up into the building's roof, turning the four-unit apartment into a gigantic blaze. Harris temporarily plugged the gas lines so the fire was no longer fed, but flames were already licking a large portion of the building. Harris's unit was forced to fight the flames on two fronts, one group using a fog stream to keep the fire contained in the rear, while Harris and several other men engaged in fire attack and an internal overhaul.

Not long after that, gas workers arrived to shut off underground pipes, diminishing the danger. It was still another two hours before the fire was completely out and only smoke remained. Cleanup would take awhile, but thank God, other than a few minor injuries, no one was seriously hurt. The renters, including several small children, all made it out safely. One older woman suffered smoke inhalation, but she'd be okay. A young man had some minor burns and the paramedics were already working on him.

Harris was exhausted, dirty, and reeking of smoke. Muscles in his neck and shoulders cramped. His eyes burned. He shoved aside a pile of embers, making sure they were cold before moving on. Ethan stepped up beside him. He looked as bad as Harris felt, but he was smiling.

Harris said, "There has to be about fifty-thou worth of damage. Three of those apartments are no longer habitable, and a bunch of people are going to be hunting for a place to stay." He pulled off his helmet to swipe black soot from his face. "So why the grin?"

Ethan followed suit, removing his helmet and running one gloved hand through his sweat-soaked hair. "Rosie."

"What about her?"

"Whenever there's a fire, she dotes on me." Ethan elbowed him. "And I don't mean she brings me chicken soup, either."

Reminded of the love between Rosie and Ethan, Harris felt a little melancholy. He forced a smile. "I might be too young to hear this."

"You're definitely too young for details. Let's just say that I'm sorry for the damage, I hate it that people will be displaced, but I'm anxious to get home to my loving wife." Ethan winked, replaced his helmet, and sauntered away.

Harris grumbled to himself. It'd be nice to have a loving woman waiting for him...whoa. He stopped in his tracks, his gaze unseeing. A woman waiting? The same women, *every day?* That sounded a lot like...marriage. Was he ready for that? He knew he wanted Clair, definitely more than he'd ever wanted any other woman. And it wasn't just sexual.

Hell, he'd given up sex with other women, but not once had he considered giving up jogging with her. He felt more alive when he was around her.

As he worked, removing the burned remains of an old lawn chair, tearing down the precariously hanging door on one unit, Harris considered all the different things he felt for Clair. He wanted to be with her, damn near all the time. He never tired of her company. Clair seemed to read his moods, sitting quietly with him when that was what he wanted, or teasing him when he felt like clowning around. Her company never felt intrusive. Being with her just felt...good.

He knew her moods, too. But maybe that was because Clair didn't play games like most women did. If he said something that pissed her off, she told him so. Other than the sexual teasing of late, which he knew they both enjoyed, she was open and honest.

For sure, she didn't like his attention veering to the mystery woman. Harris didn't really like it either. Not anymore. Who needed a woman who left secretive notes and naked pictures rather than confronting him face-to-face? He'd much rather concentrate on Clair and all the new ways she bedeviled his libido and his dreams.

His mind made up, Harris decided that he'd thank Dane and Alec for their help, pay them what he owed them, and pull them off the case. Tomorrow.

Because tonight, he wanted Clair.

He shook off his distraction and got to work. The

sooner they had the site cleared, the sooner his shift
would end. And the sooner he could see Clair.

CLAIR HEARD about the fire on the news and she was so
worried, she couldn't stop pacing. Loving a firefighter
had never been easy, but now, as Harris had claimed,
things were different. She didn't have to hide her
feelings behind friendly camaraderie.

The second she saw Harris's car pull up, she grabbed
her keys and dashed out the door. She didn't think about
her shoes, or Harris's reaction, she only thought about
reaching him, making sure he'd escaped once again
without harm.

Harris was already inside the building, but only just
opening his apartment door when Clair arrived. She
stopped when she saw him, catching her breath, ab-
sorbing the sight of him. He looked...wonderful. Exhausted and red-eyed, but still strong and tall, still the
man she adored with all her heart.

Seeing him now, with the evidence of his work
weighing heavy on his shoulders, Clair didn't know
what to say. Emotion closed her throat, love burned her
eyes. She twisted her fingers together. "Harris."

He'd just shoved his door open and he turned to her
with a smile. "Hey. I was going to change and come over
in a few minutes."

Clair swallowed hard, fighting the urge to leap on
him. "Change into what?" Dunce. What did it matter?

He turned his nose against his shoulder, sniffed, and
made a face. "Something that doesn't still reek of
smoke. I showered at the station, but the damn smell
clings to my hair and my—"

Clair gave up. She couldn't stand it, couldn't wait a

second more, couldn't patiently stand there while he went through cordial chitchat. Launching herself at Harris, she grabbed his neck, kissed his mouth, his chin, his throat, then rested her cheek on his chest and squeezed him tight.

Slowly, Harris brought his arms around her. "Hey? What's wrong?"

Almost too overwhelmed to speak, Clair shook her head, then confessed, "I was...worried."

"I'm sorry." He smoothed her back, returned her bear hug, then caught her arm and urged her inside.

He was sorry? Agog, Clair tried to acclimate herself to Harris's new persona, to his easy acceptance. What did it mean?

His voice low and somber, he said, "Let me shower again and change, then we'll talk."

Clair watched him walk away, and he was whistling. The exhaustion remained, in the set of his shoulders, the dark smudges beneath his eyes. But he seemed more lighthearted, as if she'd pleased him in some way.

Clair looked around herself with dawning realization. Harris was in a mellow, receptive mood. His apartment, other than a small kitchen light, was dark. She had the perfect setting and probably wouldn't get another chance like this anytime soon.

Her heart in her throat, her pulse humming in anticipation, she trailed silently after him. She pushed open his bedroom door to see Harris standing in the middle of the floor, his shirt off, his shoes and socks gone, and his hands at the snap of his jeans.

Almost there, she thought.

Harris looked up, their gazes locked for long moments, and his expression heated. "Clair?"

Not giving herself a chance to back out, she flipped the wall switch, stealing the scant light and filling the room with obscure moon shadows.

Harris, now a vague shadowy blur, asked, "What's this?"

Cautiously moving forward, Clair found his chest, firm and sleek and very hot. She moved her hands up to his broad shoulders, then to the back of his neck. She pulled his head down to hers. "I was afraid for you."

His hands looped around her waist. "I'm good at what I do, honey. You don't have to worry."

"You said sex would change things." Clair tunneled her fingers into the cool softness of his thick hair, such a dramatic contrast to his hard, hot body. "Well, get used to me being concerned. I know you don't like it. God knows you bitch enough any time a woman starts to worry, but if we have sex—"

His hands widened, sliding down to her hips. "We are," he murmured. "Right now in fact."

Clair drew in a breath. "Great. Then I have rights."

She could hear the smile in his voice when he asked, "The right to worry?"

"You betcha. And I also—" He kissed her, cutting off her demands in midsentence. "Harris?"

"I'm open to the new rules, honey. But let's talk about them all in the morning."

Morning? The sun would be out, light flooding through the windows. "Do you expect me to stay the night?"

"Damn right. Next to me. In my bed."

"Oh." Maybe by then it wouldn't matter. Maybe by then he'd realize that he wanted her and only her. Or maybe he'd even figure out that she and the mystery woman were one and the same.

"You followed me into my bedroom, Clair. You're claiming the right to worry. That gives me a few rights too. Like the right to make love to you all night long, whenever the mood strikes me." His hands kept moving on her, caressing her back, her hips, her waist, stroking her, learning her in a way that had been forbidden before now. "In case you get antsy or horny," he teased. He turned, took two steps and lowered them both to the bed, half covering her. In a near growl, he added, "Or if you just plain want me."

"I always want you." Clair closed her eyes as his fingers found her inner thighs. Her heart pounded. "Harris?"

"I smell like smoke," he complained. With his mouth open and damp, he kissed her neck, her shoulder, leaving her skin tinging. "No matter how long I shower or how hard I scrub..."

"I don't mind." Clair pressed her nose to his throat and inhaled. She wondered if the fires affected him that way, made him feel like he couldn't get away from the smoke, the damage. She nuzzled against him. "All I smell is you, Harris, and you smell delicious."

"Yeah?" He chuckled, rising up to smooth her hair. With a smile barely perceptible in the dim room, he removed her glasses, stretching to put them on the night-stand. When he leaned back to her, he caught the hem of her shirt and tugged it up and over her head. His hand found her breast, gently shaped her, then he stilled. "Damn, Clair, I need a light."

"No, not yet." If he turned on the light, he might recognize her. She wanted the intimacy between them before she told him the truth. In the morning, she'd confess. But not yet, not before she had that special bond to cushion her admission.

Harris continued to caress her breast, toying with her nipple, making speech impossible. "Why not?"

Why not? Why not? She forced herself to concentrate, then murmured, "I'm shy?"

Slowly, with delicious precision, he tugged at her nipple. "You don't sound certain, Clair."

Oh Lord, how could he expect her to talk while he did that? "I just...I'd rather leave the lights off."

Harris sat up beside her. "*I'd* rather see you. All of you." Clair tried to protest, but before she'd even raised herself up on her elbows, a lamp came on, spilling light across the bed. Clair hurriedly turned her face away, her breath catching in dread.

The seconds ticked by in agonizing silence. Slowly, because she couldn't bear it any longer, she turned back to Harris. He didn't look the least bit exhausted now. His blue eyes were bright, his gaze piercing while he stared at her breasts. His dark hair fell across his brow; his muscles were tight, delineated. He got to his feet beside the mattress, his gaze still unwavering, and began stripping off his jeans. "Can you see me without your glasses?"

Clair bit her lip. "You're a little fuzzy, but yes, I can see you."

Slowly, he nodded. "Good." His jeans got shoved down and off his hips, and he stepped out of them. Her eyes widened. She could see him, but she wished she still had her glasses on so she wouldn't miss a single detail.

She started to sit up, to get closer to him, and he said, "Now you."

Not yet! If he saw her tush, would he recognize her as the woman in the photo?

Clair tried to scuttle away, but that only amused Harris. He caught the hem of her shorts, and since they had a loose elastic waist, they came right off. Unfortunately, he took her panties with them, leaving her naked. "Harris!"

"Clair." His voice was dark, intense. "You're beautiful."

He still didn't recognize her? Clair couldn't believe it. She should have been only relieved, but damn it, she was nettled too. The man had fawned all over those photos, studied them in detail, had them enhanced. But he didn't see her as a sexy mystery woman, so he didn't make the connection.

When Harris stretched out beside her, she flattened both hands against his chest, holding him away. He tried to kiss her, but Clair wasn't having that. Not yet.

With dark menace, she demanded, "What about your mystery lady?"

CHAPTER FIVE

"WHAT MYSTERY LADY?" Harris murmured with deliberate lack of concern. At this particular moment, he didn't care about anyone else, not with Clair in his bed, ready for him, looking sweet and soft and as perfect as a woman could look. Ready to take the next step in binding their relationship, he pulled her hands away, leaned down and licked her tightened nipple.

Her back arched and her breath caught. "You know who I mean," she panted. Her hands clenched on his shoulders, stinging in force. But still she persisted, saying hesitantly, "I, um, found the name of the guy who leased the place."

With a long, exaggerated sigh, Harris dropped his forehead to her chest. "I don't care, Clair." He cupped her breast, thumbed her now wet nipple. "Can't you see that I'm busy here?"

Clair tried to hold him back again. "You don't care?"

She sounded so stunned, Harris grinned. "Honey, if you don't shut up, how the hell can I make love to you?"

"But you said—" He sucked her nipple into his mouth, drawing on her, teasing with the tip of his tongue. *"Harris."*

Her hips pressed up against his, seeking. He could feel the wild rapping of her heart. In a rough growl,

Harris said, "I know I promised slow and easy, but honey, I'm not sure I can manage that this first time."

"No." She panted too, sounding every bit as affected. "I don't want you to."

Clair wasn't a weak woman, and the way she gripped him now told Harris that she meant it, that she was as anxious as he felt. Unwilling to cheat her, to rush her too much, he switched to her other nipple at the same time his hand moved down her body, tickling her skin into a fever, over her ribs, her waist, her hip. She had a lush, full bottom, and her skin was silky soft, warm. He trailed his fingers over her sleek runner's thighs, and smiled at the way she clenched them together.

Knowing how his words would affect her, he said, "Open your thighs for me, Clair. Let me touch you."

Another moan bubbled up from deep in her throat. She squeezed her eyes shut, trembling from the anticipation, and slowly parted her legs.

Teasing her a bit, Harris traced around her pubic curls.

"Harris..."

He loved the way she said his name. Cupping her mound, he carefully stroked, opening her, then slid one finger in deep. She was hot, wet, and immediately her hips lifted, deepening his penetration.

Clair gasped—and opened her legs more.

Such an honest response, so typical of Clair. With his free arm, he pulled her closer to his chest, to his heart, while still stroking her, bringing her closer and closer to the edge.

"You're the one who smells good, Clair," he couldn't help but tell her. "Sweet and soft. I love how you smell." To emphasize that, he pressed his nose into her neck.

He thought about what Ethan had said, about having a woman coddle him when he got home from a hard day fighting a fire. He wanted that woman to be Clair. He wanted her scent to cloak his body, instead of the scent of smoke. He wanted her to hold him, not any other woman. He wanted to come home to her every day and know that she was his, and only his.

The acknowledgment of his emotions pushed him over the edge. He needed to be inside her, soon. She was gasping, moving rhythmically against his hand, her skin radiating heat. But it wasn't enough. Harris wanted her pleasure to be a foregone conclusion, because God knew once he got inside her, he wouldn't last.

"You'll like this," he told her, and kissed her breasts again, sucking hard, nipping a little with his teeth.

She gasped, then gasped again when he kissed her ribs, gently bit her soft belly, and settled between her legs.

"Harris?"

"God, you smell good, Clair." He pressed closer, inhaling the scent of her excitement, her femaleness. Using his thumbs, he parted her, sought her out with his tongue, and then closed his mouth hotly over her.

Her groan was long and satisfying, accompanied by a stiffening of her legs, the spontaneous lifting of her hips, a surge of new warmth. She whimpered, and in a breathless whisper, said, "Oh God."

Harris pressed himself hard against the mattress, trying to curb the ache her pleasure created. He felt her straining, getting closer and closer, and he worked two fingers into her even as he continued to suckle her clitoris, working her with his tongue—and she came.

Her shout took him by surprise, and thrilled him. He

locked one arm around her, holding her still as she shuddered and trembled and cried out. He could feel her squeezing his fingers, feel the surge of wetness and heat. He loved eating Clair, and if he hadn't wanted her for so long, he could have started all over again.

But he had wanted her, whether he realized it or not. His feelings for her had made it easy to give up other women. Celibacy was much simpler when he wanted only Clair. But no more. He needed her. Now.

Harris realized his hands were shaking when he sat up and fumbled with the bedside drawer, seeking a condom. Clair didn't move. But he could hear her uneven, still-labored breathing, and he smiled.

He had the condom on in record time and then he turned, hooked her legs in his elbows, spread her wide— and surged into her.

She arched hard against him, crying out, sinking her nails into his shoulders. "Yeah," Harris panted, blind with the lust and love, shaken with the fury of his feelings for her. "Come for me again, Clair."

She did, almost too soon, because hearing her moan, feeling her inner muscles grip his cock, forced him to the finish line. She was wet and hot, open to him, letting him in deep, and he lost the battle. He closed his eyes and arched his neck and growled out his release, pumping hard, heaving.

Minutes later, when his heart slowed its frantic beat and he could think coherently again, Harris thought to tell her how he felt, to admit he loved her. He pushed back to see her face, smiled at the sight of her sound asleep, and carefully separated from her.

She mumbled, rolled to her side, and snuggled into his pillow. Harris looked her over again, smiling, but his vision still felt blurry and his heart felt too soft. He removed the condom, turned out the light, and spooned Clair. As he'd already known, she fit him perfectly.

His life, with Clair in it, was good. He hoped like hell she wanted to marry him, because no way would he give her up.

HARRIS MADE LOVE to her once again in the middle of the night, when she rolled to face him, and somehow her leg ended up over his waist and her breast was right there, close to his mouth—too tempting to resist. Though he was half-asleep and just going with the moment, he remembered to protect her—just barely. In the future, he'd have to keep a box of condoms on top of the nightstand, for easy access. Having Clair around and accessible would sorely test him, not that he'd complain.

The second time was slower, gentler, and they rocked together for a long time, kissing softly, cuddling, until Clair started to moan. The sound of her pleasure seemed to ignite him, and once again, he lost the battle with control.

After that, Harris didn't wake up again until he felt Clair leaving the bed. He'd seldom slept the whole night with a woman, but having Clair close was comfortable and comforting. As she slipped away, he protested with a groan and tried to pull her back.

She mumbled and swatted at him. "I have to go get ready for work, Harris."

He got one heavy eyelid open and found the clock. "It's early yet." *With plenty of time for some morning hanky-panky.* He glanced up at Clair, and got both eyes opened.

She was naked, with rumpled hair and sleep-soft eyes, but she'd already put on her glasses. She looked like a fetish come to life. His fetish. He wanted her. Again. Always.

But when he tried to reach for her, she laughed and stepped out of reach. "Down boy. I need a long hot shower."

Harris looked at her soft, sweet belly and murmured, "Shower with me."

"Oh no, not on your life. I know where that'd end up."

"Yeah," he agreed, more awake by the moment.

"Harris, I can't."

"Why?"

Her mouth went crooked in a silly grimace. "I'm a little sore."

Harris shoved into a sitting position. He couldn't help it; he smiled like a conquering warrior. "I was too energetic?" He tried to look at her face, but her body held all his attention. Clair naked was a surprise. A wonderful surprise. She was so damned sexy...

"It's just been a long time, that's all."

Harris looked at her hips, and frowned in thought. He'd never seen her nude body before, yet it all seemed somehow familiar. "I'll be more considerate in the future." *In the future.* He liked saying that.

Clair drew a long, steadying breath. "For the record, you can be as energetic as you want." And then, with a small smile, she added, "In the future."

Damn, he loved her. He patted the side of the bed. "We need to talk."

Worry darkened her eyes and she fretted, looking away from him. "I know."

Why did the idea of talking make her so solemn? Harris didn't like it that her smile had disappeared. He much preferred her teasing, so he decided to put off the talk until later. "It'll wait." And because he couldn't be with her and not want her, he agreed to let her head home. "Go get your shower before I forget I'm a gentleman and drag you back into my bed."

"I'll...see you later?"

Did she have doubts about his intentions? Was that why she looked so burdened? He reached for her hand and laced his fingers with hers. "You'd have one hell of a time getting rid of me."

Her grin returned, filling him with warmth. "Soon?"

Sooner than she expected, most likely. He'd head to her office first to remove Dane and Alec from the case. Mystery women no longer interested him.

"Absolutely." But she'd hesitated too long. Harris left the bed to stand in front of her, pulled her close so he could feel her skin against him, and kissed her.

He'd meant it to be a perfunctory goodbye kiss, but her mouth was soft and warm and she smelled so good, he went a little out of control. Only the worry of causing her more discomfort kept him from making love to her again. Against her lips, he whispered, "Damn woman, I can only take so much provocation and you naked is pretty darn provoking. You better go now while I'm still willing to let you."

Laughing, Clair snatched up her shorts and T-shirt and pulled them on. Harris watched, enjoying the easy familiarity. If he had his way—and he would—he'd be able to watch her dress every morning from now on.

Because he was ready to jump in the shower too, Harris didn't bother to dress when he walked her to his front door. "After today, I'll be off for a week. Will you stay with me?"

"For the whole week?"

Forever. But he'd get to that later. For now, he just wanted the immediate future confirmed. "Yeah. With me, in my apartment." And in a lower, suggestive voice, he added, "In my bed."

She went a little breathless on him, nodding in mute agreement. But two seconds later, she frowned. "I will—if you want me to."

"I want you to." But she didn't look quite convinced. Was she afraid he'd get sidetracked with the woman in the photos again? Not a chance. Harris wanted to tell her that he loved her and only her, but it'd be better to show her first. He could wait until he saw her at her work, when she'd witness him tearing up the photos.

Anticipating her reaction, Harris kissed her one last time, then gently urged her out the door. As soon as she left, he went to his window to keep watch. Moments after she entered her building, her lights came on, and right after that, he saw her wave. He smiled and dropped his curtain.

Soon she'd be living with him, and he wouldn't need to watch her go safely into her own place.

In less than an hour Harris had showered and was at her office. He'd pulled into the parking lot in time to see Dane and Alec entering the front doors. They had their wives with them. Both were blondes, both were attractive. *Well hell,* Harris thought. The presence of wives would make it difficult to discuss photos of a naked woman. He could have put it off till the women left, but he wanted everything taken care of before Clair arrived.

They were all in Dane's inner office when Harris got

there. He went in, lighthearted and eager to get things underway. Maybe he'd even ask Clair to marry him after he tore up the pictures. He grinned, envisioning how that'd play out, what she might say.

Harris raised his fist to tap on the door frame, announcing himself. Almost at the same time, one of the women said, "Dane Carter! Why in the world do you have naked pictures of Clair on the wall?"

Naked pictures of *Clair?* Harris raised a brow, confused, mentally scoffing.

Dane choked. "It's not."

And the other woman said, "Well, of course it is." And then with some confusion, "You didn't know?"

Together, Dane and Alec barked, *"No."*

"How could you not know?" one of them asked. "It looks like her."

"It's her shape," the other added. "Her long legs, her posture, her—"

The woman continued, but Harris wasn't listening. He shook his head in denial, even as the pieces began to click painfully into place. His heart pounded and his head throbbed.

The mystery woman wore no jewelry—because Clair didn't wear any. The mystery woman had longer hair— because Clair had recently cut hers.

The mystery woman had a lush derriere—*just like Clair's.*

He remembered Clair's near hysterical reaction to seeing the photos enlarged, how she'd hidden her head on the desk when he and Dane discussed the mystery woman's posterior.

And he remembered those notes, so full of emotion and love, which meant the woman had to know him, and *not* from afar.

The wives had seen what he hadn't. Until now.

Dane's office was eerily silent as Harris stepped inside. Numb, a little unsteady on his feet, he barked, "Get them down. Now."

Alec, not one to take orders, was already doing just that. He moved faster than Harris could have, given his present state of mind.

Harris drew a slow breath, but it didn't help. He was aware of Dane watching him in appalled consternation, Alec grumbling and scowling. Hell, it almost looked as if Alec was blushing. The wives were silent.

And behind them all, Clair strolled in whistling.

Everyone turned to face the doorway in various stages of disbelief and anxiety.

Clair saw them all congregated together, watching her—and her whistling died a quick death. She took in all the expressions of shock, alarm and dismay, and she stalled. "Um...what's going on?"

Dane and Alec began to sputter and cough, and now they were both red-faced. The wives looked worried, casting Clair looks of sympathy. Dane's wife even scooted closer to him. "Dane?"

Dane said, "Shh," then bent to whisper in her ear, most likely explaining the inexplicable. His wife's eyes widened and she darted a fascinated glance between Harris and Clair.

Harris just stared at Clair, trying to take it all in, trying to accept that he'd passed around naked pictures of the woman he loved. Dane and Alec had seen her. Ethan had seen her.

Not once had she let on.

Alec, his hands full of photos, shoved them against Harris's chest, saying, "Here." Then he grabbed his wife and fled the office. Dane quickly followed, stopping to clap Harris on the shoulder in commiseration while avoiding Clair's gaze.

Dane pulled the door shut behind him with a finality that hung in the air like nuclear fallout.

They stared at each other until Clair, her face white, groped for a chair. "You know, don't you?"

The photos got wadded in his fist. His stomach cramped. Through his teeth, Harris snarled, "Why the hell didn't you tell me?"

Without answering, she dropped her head and shrugged.

Feeling savage, Harris paced a circle around her. "Jesus." Then, leaning close to her nose, he said, *"I let Dane, Alec, and Ethan see."*

Her mouth firmed. "And you carried one photo in your pocket. I know." Curling her lip, she added, "You were smitten, Dane said. And Alec claimed you were totally obsessed."

"With *you,* Clair, if you'd only have admitted it before I..." He shuddered with the awfulness of it. "Before I showed them to other men."

Outrage brought Clair to her feet, to her very tiptoes. "How was I supposed to know you'd do that? But once you did, what would be the point in confessing? It was too late to take it back."

He waved a shot of her behind in her face. "It wasn't too late to keep from having them enlarged!"

She slapped the photo aside. "So you're a pervert! I didn't know that either."

Dane tapped on the door before pushing it open. He stared fixedly at Harris. "Um, we can hear you, and in fact, with the way you're both roaring, most of the people in the building probably can. If you want to tone it down just a little, that'd be good." He cleared his throat, dared a flash peek at Clair. "Uh, Clair? You can have the day off." He snapped the door shut again.

Harris strangled on his anger.

Clair didn't seem to even hear Dane. Somehow, she managed to get her nose even with Harris's. Her hot, angry breath pelted his face with each word. "Why didn't you know it was me, Harris? How could you *not* know? We see each other every damn night." Harris backed up—and Clair followed. "We've been friends a long time, close friends, and yet you never once considered it might be me. So tell me, why would I confess to you when you were never interested in me?"

The shock was slowly wearing off, and Harris began to see things clearly again. Clair wasn't embarrassed— at least, not that he could tell. And she wasn't exactly apologizing for duping him, either. No, she was royally pissed off.

And she accused him of not being interested? Now that was just plain wrong. He stopped retreating and leaned into her anger. "Since when am I not interested?"

She slugged him. Her small fist thumped hard against his pec and, damn it, it hurt. "I don't mean to jog, you moron. I mean for more. For *everything*."

Harris narrowed his eyes. "I was interested enough last night. Twice, as I recall. You could have told me then."

Alec's loud whistling could be heard.

"I was going to tell you today." And then, in a smaller voice, she murmured, "After I got those stupid pictures off the wall."

"They're off now." Harris slapped the crumpled

photos onto the desk behind him—facedown so no one could see them. He tried to get himself under control. Most of his reaction was due to jealousy. He couldn't believe he'd studied her naked ass, in detail, with Dane and Alec. "You told me your boyfriend was nobody. If that's so, why'd you let him take naked pictures—"

She slugged him again, aghast and appalled and wide-eyed. "I didn't *let* him." She swallowed and her eyes looked a little glassy, her bottom lip trembling. "Do you know me at all, Harris?"

She sounded so forlorn, it about ripped him apart. "If you didn't let him, then how did he...get..." Fury erupted, black and mean and sharp-edged. His jaw set, his teeth locked. "That son of a bitch."

Clair looked resigned. "He has a tiny little spy camera. I didn't even know he was looking at me, much less that he was photographing me. I never would have allowed that. I was only with him for a little while, because..." She stared up at him, solemn and sad. "He wasn't you."

Harris's eye twitched. His lips felt stiff. "I'll kill him."

Clair held her breath, then said, "Why?"

"Why?" Harris caught her shoulders and brought her eye level. "I love you, damn it. No way in hell am I going to let some bastard—"

"You love me?"

He gave her shoulders a gentle shake. "What the hell did you think?"

"I don't know." Her eyes were round behind her glasses, filled with hope. "You didn't recognize me. Even after last night, you didn't recognize me."

Harris couldn't believe she was hung up on that. "I looked at those pictures with totally detached lust. It was a naked woman, period. How I looked at them is entirely different from how I looked at you."

"How'd you look at me?"

He pulled her closer. Took a deep breath. "With lust, for sure. God knows, Clair, you make me hot. But with so many other feelings, too—love, tenderness." He hesitated and then added, "Need."

"You need me?"

Harris hauled her into his arms. "I love you so damn much I almost can't think straight, so of course I need you. You make me laugh, and you make me feel easy, sort of rested. Like I've found the perfect place to be. With you."

She smiled up at him, laughing a little, weeping a little. "I love you too."

Finally hearing her say it relaxed something inside him, something he hadn't realized was tense until she fully accepted him. "That's a relief." He released her and rubbed his hands together. "Now if we can just figure out where this ex-boyfriend of yours is, I'll go have a talk with him. Then everything will be perfect."

Dane again tapped on the door before opening it. Alec was beside him. "Give us his name, Clair. We'll handle it."

Clair bit her lip. "I don't know...."

"He could have negatives still," Alec pointed out.

"Or more shots," Dane added.

Harris watched her face flush with anger, saw her hands curl into tight fists. "*I'll* go talk to him—"

Harris pulled her around in a bear hug. "Forget that idea. I don't want you anywhere near the creep."

Dane's eyes narrowed. "You shouldn't go near him either, Harris. You just want to take him apart."

"Damn right."

Alec raised a brow. "Hitting him would only get you in trouble. Whereas we can likely prove what an unscrupulous jerk he is."

"How?" Harris demanded.

"If he did this to Clair," Dane explained, "then he's likely done it to other women, too. All we need is the evidence, and hey, gathering evidence is what we do."

"Then we can have criminal charges filed against him—and neither Clair nor her photos will have to be involved."

It didn't feel right to Harris, letting Dane and Alec take care of the matter. Clair was his, and he felt so damn protective. He needed to punch the guy at least once. Hell, he wanted to break his nose. But he definitely didn't want Clair involved.

"Think of it as a wedding present," Alec urged him.

At the mention of a wedding, Clair pushed away from Harris with a gasp. He hauled her right back again. "We are getting married, Clair."

Her brows snapped down and she looked at him over her glasses. "Since when?"

"Since I just told you I love you and you told me you love me too."

Angel Carter, Dane's wife, grinned. "Sounds reasonable to me, Clair."

Celia Sharpe nodded. "Let Alec go get this awful man, and you and Harris just concentrate on wedding plans."

Clair still looked mutinous. "I expected a proper wedding proposal."

"Everyone in this room has seen you in the buff, Clair. Hell, Dane and Alec were looking at your photos with a magnifying glass, trying to spot details. They were—"

"I'll marry you."

Harris grinned at her burning face and the rushed way she'd interrupted him. But now the wives were scowling at their husbands too, and the husbands looked ready to hang him. Harris laughed. "Sorry. All's fair in love and war."

Dane caught his wife's hand. "Let's go before Clair starts shedding blood and gets my office all messy."

Alec threw his arm around Celia. "Wait for us."

They were gone in moments, leaving Clair and Harris alone. With everything in place, Harris relaxed. "Ethan and Riley are going to be damned pleased, but Buck will have a fit."

"Buck is one of your friends, right?"

"Yeah, soon to be my only single close friend. He won't like it that I've jumped ship too."

"So he should get married."

"He claims he's married to his lumberyard."

Clair rolled her eyes. "Some guys just like the bachelor life, I guess."

"No." Harris tipped up her chin. "Some guys just haven't met the right woman yet. Which is why I have to get you tied to me. I may not have recognized you in the photos, but I definitely recognize you as the perfect woman—for me."

"CAN WE ESCAPE, NOW, do you think?"

Clair smiled at Harris. Because they'd both wanted a small, simple wedding with only close friends and family, they'd been able to organize it all in just under three weeks.

Harris had been very impatient the entire time. The rehearsal dinner had lasted hours, filled with good food and a lot of laughter. Her family loved Harris, and vice versa. Ethan and Riley were beyond pleased, and Buck wasn't too disgruntled. In fact, he seemed to be wallowing in the fact that he was the only single one in the bunch.

Dane and Alec were finally able to look at Clair again without turning red, but they were still more hesitant with her. For her part, she doubted she'd ever be able to face them again without blushing.

"I think we can leave now." Clair scooted closer to him. "You have big plans?"

"Yeah." Harris nuzzled her neck. "Plans to have my way with my soon-to-be-bride."

She sighed, now as anxious as he was to be alone. They made an announcement, put up with a few more toasts, and finally headed out the door.

In the parking lot, however, Celia Sharpe and Angel Carter chased them down. Celia carried a large package and Angel had a manila envelope.

"We've been elected to do the honors," Celia explained when they reached them.

"The men are still shy about that whole photograph thing," Angel added with a shrug. "They say you're too valuable to the office to replace you, but no way can they discuss this with you."

Harris put his arm around Clair and smiled. "Discuss what?"

Angel presented the envelope with a flourish. "They located that ex-boyfriend of yours. They found these."

Clair went blank. "Ohmigod."

Beside her, Harris stiffened in anger. "Damn it. I should have—"

"Dane did that for you. Punched him right in the nose." Angel seemed to relish the retelling. "And he did it in such a way that he wasn't the one who started it. If I know Dane, he goaded the guy into taking a swing first."

Celia nodded. "Then *pow,* Dane laid him out." She laughed. "Alec thought it was great."

Clair bit her lip. "If they found more photos..."

"Not to worry," Celia rushed out. "They went over his place with a fine-tooth comb. There wasn't much that pertained to you. Just a few souvenirs, apparently."

Clair closed her eyes in mortification, then felt Harris hug her to his side.

"It's all right now, Clair."

"It really is," Angel assured her. "He'd done the same with two other women, one that he was still dating. Dane and Alec clued them in, and they confronted the jerk, even ransacked his place until they found some of the photos themselves. They both agreed to prosecute, so he'll be taken care of for sure."

Clair pulled herself together. It was over and she had her whole life ahead of her—a life with Harris. "Please, tell Dane and Alec how much I appreciate it."

"You also get this," Celia said with a grin. "It's a paper shredder. Alec said the photos belonged to you, and you could do whatever you wanted with them. But he said he figured you'd want to shred them."

"He figured right!"

Harris snatched the envelope out of her hand. "We'll definitely do that." He leaned toward Angel for a hug, then to Celia for the same. He held the bulky box under one arm, the envelope in his free hand. "Thank you, ladies. Knowing that situation is settled is the very best wedding present."

Celia and Angel left them with smiles. The moment they were gone, Harris opened the envelope and started to peek inside.

Clair snatched it away and held it behind her back. "Oh no you don't."

Trying to look innocent, and failing, Harris said, "I just wanted to see—"

"I know what you wanted to see. But these are getting destroyed the moment we get home. You've seen all the nude photos of me that you're ever going to see."

Harris grinned, and the grin spread into a laugh. "All right, babe," he soothed. "Don't get all bristly on me." He turned her toward the car.

Clair didn't understand his new mood and thought to soften her denial. "I'm sorry, Harris. I hope you can understand how I feel."

"Yeah, I do." After she was seated, he leaned in the door and kissed her. "I was just teasing you. It doesn't matter to me at all."

"You're sure?"

He took her mouth in a long, satisfying kiss. "Positive. After all, what do I need with photos when I've got the real thing?"

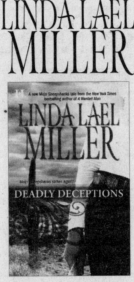

REQUEST YOUR
FREE BOOKS!

2 FREE NOVELS
FROM THE ROMANCE/SUSPENSE
COLLECTION PLUS 2 FREE GIFTS!

YES! Please send me 2 FREE novels from the Romance/Suspense Collection and my 2 FREE gifts (gifts are worth about $10). After receiving them, if I don't wish to receive any more books, I can return the shipping statement marked "cancel." If I don't cancel, I will receive 4 brand-new novels every month and be billed just $5.49 per book in the U.S. or $5.99 per book in Canada, plus 25¢ shipping and handling per book plus applicable taxes, if any*. That's a savings of at least 20% off the cover price! I understand that accepting the 2 free books and gifts places me under no obligation to buy anything. I can always return a shipment and cancel at any time. Even if I never buy another book from the Reader Service, the two free books and gifts are mine to keep forever.

185 MDN EF5Y   385 MDN EF6C

Name	(PLEASE PRINT)	
Address		Apt. #
City	State/Prov.	Zip/Postal Code

Signature (if under 18, a parent or guardian must sign)

Mail to **The Reader Service:**
IN U.S.A.: P.O. Box 1867, Buffalo, NY 14240-1867
IN CANADA: P.O. Box 609, Fort Erie, Ontario L2A 5X3

Not valid to current subscribers to the Romance Collection,
the Suspense Collection or the Romance/Suspense Collection.

Want to try two free books from another line?
Call 1-800-873-8635 or visit www.morefreebooks.com.

* Terms and prices subject to change without notice. N.Y. residents add applicable sales tax. Canadian residents will be charged applicable provinâal taxes and GST. This offer is limited to one order per household. All orders subject to approval. Credit or debit balances in a customer's account(s) may be offset by any other outstanding balance owed by or to the customer. Please allow 4 to 6 weeks for delivery. Offer available while quantities last.

Your Privacy: Harlequin is committed to protecting your privacy. Our Privacy Policy is available online at www.eHarlequin.com or upon request from the Reader Service. From time to time we make our lists of customers available to reputable third parties who may have a product or service of interest to you. If you would prefer we not share your name and address, please check here. ☐

BOB08

HARLEQUIN

More Than Words

"Changing lives stride by stride— I did it my way!"

—**Jeanne Greenberg,** real-life heroine

*Jeanne Greenberg is a Harlequin More Than Words award winner and the founder of **SARI Therapeutic Riding.***

Discover your inner heroine!

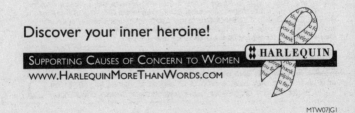

HARLEQUIN
More Than Words

"Jeanne proves that one woman can change the world, with vision, compassion and hard work."

—**Linda Lael Miller,** author

*Linda wrote "Queen of the Rodeo," inspired by Jeanne Greenberg, founder of **SARI Therapeutic Riding.** Since 1978 Jeanne has devoted her life to enriching the lives of disabled children and their families through innovative and exciting therapies on horseback.*

Look for "*Queen of the Rodeo*" in
More Than Words, Vol. 4,
available in April 2008 at eHarlequin.com
or wherever books are sold.

SUPPORTING CAUSES OF CONCERN TO WOMEN   ❝❝ HARLEQUIN
WWW.HARLEQUINMORETHANWORDS.COM

MTW07JG2